THE STATUE OF THREE LIES

THE STATUE OF THREE LIES

David Cargill

Matador
5 Weir Road
Kibworth Beauchamp
Leicester LE8 0LQ, UK
Tel: (+44) 116 279 2299
Fax: (+44) 116 279 2277
Email: books@troubador.co.uk
Web: www.troubador.co.uk/matador

ISBN 978 1848767 515

British Library Cataloguing in Publication Data.
A catalogue record for this book is available from the British Library.

Matador is an imprint of Troubador Publishing Ltd

Printed in Great Britain by the MPG Books Group, Bodmin and King's Lynn ●

*For
Sheila*

DEDICATION

To the memory of JOHN DICKSON CARR (1906-1977) American Author of Distinction and undisputed Master of "Locked Room" Murder Mysteries.

A lifetime of enormous pleasure, collecting and reading his work, was the inspiration that triggered this piece of fiction woven around an incident of fact.

D.C.

ACKNOWLEDGEMENTS

John W. Apperson: President - Society of American Magicians 2004-005 for unearthing Magazines of 1952 Golden Anniversary Convention in Boston, USA

Bill Boles: The Boston Globe

Henry F. Scannell, Reference Librarian, Microtext Department, Boston Public Library for factual information and clipping from Boston Globe June 1, 1952 – page 37

Jennifer Smith, Government Documents Librarian, Boston Public Library for Local Climatological Data reports for November, 1966

Boston Public Library: Telephone Reference Department for description of Library entrance in 1966

Bob Carr, Sales & Marketing, Boston Park Plaza Hotel for history and description of Hotel that, in 1952 was the Statler Hotel and, in 1966, was the Statler Hilton

Pam Carter, PA to Managing Director, St. James's Hotel and Club, for historical information about Simpson's-in-the-Strand

CONTENTS

Chapter 1
DEATH BY MISADVENTURE

Wistful but frowning, Giles Dawson drew reflectively on his second cigar of the day, savoured the flavour, and blew smoke at the lilac-tinted pages in his hand. He stabbed the air with the glowing Havana as if trying to disperse the haze. The riddle in the letter perplexed him. The copperplate writing evoked echoes of happy days – worlds away from the shabby gentility here and now in the Club; of a childhood among friends, endless tales of mystery and magic and the voice of a young girl calling from his adolescence of almost twenty-five years ago. His furrowed brow deepened in academic concentration.

As a member of The Magic Circle he found the clues intriguing, as fragrant as the writing paper, as insubstantial as the wisps of smoke dissipating into his prematurely greying temples. The letter was almost intimate – but cryptic.

Maskelyne Hall   *24 October 1966*

Dear Giles, or should I call you Professor? A voice from the past!
What is the room you leave without entering? What is the room you
enter without leaving? Remember? Remember me? Laura. Jack
Ramsden's little girl – though not so little now.
Remember those ancient riddles we loved to solve?
As we get older, we begin to realise that the biggest riddle of all is
Life. Or is it Death?
But enough of the preliminaries. Now, I need your help.

Remember Daddy – and how he died? Of course you do – though I'm sure you do not know the entire truth. But then neither do we. That's why I need your help.

And remember the story you told me – about Chung Ling Soo, the Magician? How you said his accidental death could have been suicide by proxy – or worse. It has played on my mind for years. People can be so vile to each other. Daddy's death wasn't suicide. It was no accident either. More and more I'm forced to believe that his death was meant to happen. And now the past is closing in on us, and we have to deal with it.

Please come back to Maskelyne Hall! Mother will be seventy on Hallowe'en.

After fourteen years as a widow she doesn't want a party but the rest of us want to celebrate this occasion. And to do that we need to come to terms with…the past.

You must come – as guest of honour and old friend of the family.

You must come. Please! You have to. I desperately need your help. Help me prove that Daddy's 'fatal accident', unlike Chung Ling Soo's, was – Murder! Don't let me down. Call me! The number hasn't changed…help me! For God's sake…

Laura.

The figure in the chair opposite had watched in silence for several minutes as his perturbed friend and associate since RAF days chewed on his cigar and stared unblinkingly at the words in front of him. Freddie Oldsworth was well aware that any interruption in similar circumstances was likely to be unproductive but caution was sacrificed as the brooding and darkening features opposite became more pronounced. He stirred from his sleeping sphinx position.

'What's puzzling you?'

Freddie Oldsworth asked the question, ordered coffee and brandy, then settled back in the leather armchair, in the knowledge that it could well be long enough before he received a reply.

'Puzzling me?' Professor Dawson sounded vaguely distant and the normally enthusiastic glint in his blue eyes was missing. He stabbed the air with his cigar.

'How I wish it could be that easy! What do you make of that?' he said, cryptically, as he passed the letter across.

4

Freddie Oldsworth brushed a hand through his mop of light brown hair, took the letter and fumbled for his spectacles, became aware of the slightly perfumed notepaper and started to read the mysterious contents.

'Laura?' Freddie had an impish look on his face as he tilted his head slightly and posed the question.

Giles frowned, stared across at a Munnings' print of Racehorses on the wall behind Freddie and, in a strangely disembowelled voice, said 'Oh, Laura? Sorry…I was thinking about Lind…So sorry! Laura! Of course…Laura Ramsden!'

'You cunning old fox! You'll go, of course?' Freddie warmed in anticipation.

'Would you?' The Professor took another puff of the cigar, looked Freddie straight in the eye and said, 'Well! Would you? Hmm …yes, I suppose you would!'

'Of course I would…Pretty girl…Well, is she or isn't she?'

The Professor nodded. 'I suppose so!' he said. 'At least she was the last time I saw her.'

'Well there you are then. You've solved most puzzles, conundrums, riddles and illusions in your time! Why not try your hand at *murder?*'

Freddie sat back, clasped both hands behind his neck and continued his questioning.

'Maskelyne Hall! Very, very interesting! Now that's *magic!* Surely that needs an explanation, if I'm not mistaken!'

'Okay, Torquemada, why the Grand Inquisition? Will it be the thumbscrews next?'

'Just curious, that's all. Anyone worth his salt and steeped in the history of magic would be more than curious at the naming of a house after one of the all-time greats!'

'Well Freddie, just remember what curiosity did! One murder, if it was murder, will be more than enough of a problem without trying to solve the death of the cat as well!'

The Prof knocked the ash from his cigar, lifted the glass of brandy that was pushed towards him, savoured the aroma before emptying the glass with one satisfying gulp and said, 'Now…let me see! I have no intention of keeping you in suspense but it all seems so long ago.'

At this point his voice had quietened almost to a whisper; the eyes had glazed over – nostalgia beckoned.

'During the war years I grew up with the Ramsden family in Scotland. Jack Ramsden was almost a second father to me, hence the "old friend of the family" reference in the letter. His tales of Houdini's exploits, without doubt, led to my fascination with stage magic.' The Prof was again using his cigar - now unlit - to pointed effect.

'We were all kids at a time of upheaval. Jack was a cabinetmaker using all of his ingenuity in the production of props for stage illusionists. He'd also started performing, with a young female assistant, at a time when Magic and Illusion, as a form of entertainment, was taking off again after a spell in the doldrums. We all grew up, as kids do, went our separate ways and kept in touch at rather infrequent intervals. Jack's sudden death, in 1952, happened in the library of his home as he was setting things up as part of the preparations for his wife's Birthday celebrations. That was on the 31st October; the exact day that Houdini died twenty-six years earlier in 1926.'

The recollection of that coincidence had a strange effect on Giles. His eyes seemed to stare into the past as if searching for the ghostly figures of a bygone age.

'I never got to know the full details, I was on a lecture-tour of Australia at the time, but it seems that Jack was alone, in what was effectively, a sealed room, when the trick went wrong. He was shot - just as Chung Ling Soo was in 1918 - the difference this time... there was nobody else in the room to fire the gun! Jack died that same night and the subsequent inquest brought in a verdict of...death by misadventure. Suicide had been considered but discounted. Isabella, Jack's wife, was devastated. Her three sons and one daughter tried hard to pick up the pieces. Now, fourteen years later, a doubt is being thrown on the verdict. But murder? Unless...'

The Prof picked up the letter, got up and turned to go.

'Leaving so soon, Giles?'

Giles stopped, absentmindedly stubbed his unlit cigar in the ashtray and said, 'No, I won't be long! I should be back in a wee while. I'm just going to use the phone.' He cleared his throat, with that slightly nervous cough of his and said, 'I'll just let Miss Ramsden know of my intended travel arrangements!'

6

The bright demeanour, non-existent for most of the evening, had returned. 'Oh, Freddie, conjure up another couple of Cognacs! There's a good fellow! You and I have some serious thinking to do!' Then, with a voice charged with quiet menace, he said, 'I've a strange feeling that, before long, I may be face to face with the devil!'

Friday, 28th October 1966 – the 'morning after the night before!'

The London-to-Glasgow express pulled out of Euston Station on time. Only moments before, Professor Giles Dawson had been unceremoniously bundled out of the famous FX4 black cab, officially known as the 'London', after a hair-raising journey from his South-Kensington flat. The affable cabbie, who had skilfully negotiated the 'London Lemmings', pouring out of every Tube Station and across busy streets on their way to work, had been a magician "par excellence" who deserved the generous tip, freely given.

With a cheery, "It's your turn now, guv! So get yer skates on", ringing in his ears, The Prof only had time to purchase a couple of newspapers before clawing himself and his luggage onto an already-moving train.

He sat down to get his second wind and reflect on the events of the previous evening. Gazing out of the compartment window he realised, for the first time that morning, how dull London was looking, as autumn gave way to winter: the thought of a few days in the Scottish countryside lifted spirits and rejuvenated a body that was suddenly in danger of disintegration, after the chariot race from taxi to train with the luggage trolley.

'Luggage!' he called out, turning a few heads in his direction. 'Just talking to myself!' he sheepishly offered as heads returned to morning papers.

The realisation that his two bags, looking like part of an obstacle course, still lay where he had dropped them after clambering aboard had the effect of making The Prof stack them neatly in the proper rack.

'Phew!' he continued, aloud, 'That should do the trick!'

Loosening his tie The Prof caught sight of the newspaper headlines: all week the terrible disaster at Aberfan had shocked a Nation into communal grief and the previous evening, when Freddie and The Prof had the disaster on their minds; it was Freddie who'd introduced the subject of Premonition. It was always Freddie who introduced subjects like Premonition, Telepathy and Precognition. The Prof recognized his friend as a Wizard in the field of Extrasensory Perception and always marvelled at his insight and depth of research.

During last night's conversation, Freddie had predicted that a serious article would be published, in little more than a year, recording the many premonitions about the Aberfan Disaster. His strange tale, of a nine-year-old Welsh girl who, on the 20th October, told her mother she'd had a dream that, when she had gone to school it was not there—something black had come down all over it, was one such premonition. That little girl had died in the disaster. Solid and dependable; Freddie was always providing food for thought.

He lived near Evesham in the Cotswolds with his wife Penny and their two young girls. He'd given up a promising career, as a Teacher of Mathematics, and decided to use his considerable knowledge, allied with his study of a unique system of Racehorse Ratings, in order to "beat the bookies" at The Sport of Kings. In view of the fact they were living in the Sixties The Prof was of the strong opinion that Freddie was less than accurate and should've been talking of The Sport of Queens.

"So what!" was Freddie's usual comment?

He was not so much a gambler as a "seeker of value". Two quotes of his: "If you wanna make money in a casino; own one!" and "It's not gambling that's stupid; it's losing!" always brought a wry smile to The Prof's normally worried face.

Freddie liked to be "ahead of the field" and was a guy who could be readily consulted when facing a crisis that required some logical thought.

From his window seat The Prof watched the dull uniformity of semi-detached London speed by and, eventually, give way to the dream of post-war suburbia. Thoughts turned again to the events of the previous evening after he'd returned from making the phone call.

'Here – get a little of this down you and tell me all about it.' Freddie had said, moving a brandy within easy reach of The Professor whilst cradling the other glass. He looked uneasy as he scanned his friend's furrowed features.

'You look as if you've just seen a ghost!'

'Come to think of it, maybe I have! Laura was relieved to hear from me; she was so afraid I might be too busy to come.'

8

'You're definitely going then?' Freddie's steel-grey eyes winked wickedly.

'Yes, in the morning! Cheers, Freddie,' The Prof took a sip of brandy. 'She sounded…well… so mature and…!'

'Did she say anything that might explain the letter? I mean - good heavens! It's what, fourteen years since her father died – surely, after that time something serious must've happened to start the doubts?'

'I asked her about that and…!'

'And?'

'She said her father didn't commit suicide! If he had wanted to do that *"he would've made a bloody good job of it!"* Her exact words! Something about him being a Yorkshire man. She hinted that, although she couldn't be more specific on the phone, she could now swear, "There was someone else in the room when the shot was fired!" That's not all, Freddie; she sent a shiver down my spine when she suggested…that something else might have been there! Something that wasn't human! Something…*Invisible!* And hell-bent on…*murder!* The problem was…how to prove it!'

The two friends exchanged glances before the silence was broken.

'She sounds a very determined young woman who either knows a lot more than she's saying or she's a bit over the top, clutching at straws and, dare I say it, perhaps looking for a man in her life?' The Prof had looked uncomfortable, as Freddie had added 'Now, are you up for that, my lad? You know…this could be a *racing certainty*, Son!'

The Prof had known Freddie long enough to know there was no such thing as a racing certainty; he also knew that Freddie, forever tongue-in-cheek, had a sincere wish for his ultimate success in the romantic stakes ever since…!

At this point his gaze had returned to the Munnings' print on the lounge wall and the distant memory of a tragic figure, in racing silks, lying on damp grass after a crashing fall in The Ladies' Open at a Warwickshire Point-to Point! It all seemed - so long ago…!

When he and Freddie had, eventually, arrived back at the spacious flat in South Kensington for a nightcap and a final chinwag The Prof had thanked his lucky stars for a friend he could trust implicitly and for their weekly get-together.

Commuting daily from his Cotswold home to the major race meetings around the country Freddie still looked forward to his visit to London each week to meet The Prof for a tête-à-tête that often led to investment opportunity, exchange of ideas on a wide range of topics and the odd difference of opinion.

But that was yesterday and the small hours of today – Friday, 28th October 1966.

Professor Giles Dawson was now travelling back to Scotland to wrestle with, what would be, one of the most complex puzzles he had ever faced? Little did he know that Freddie's statement of last night: "You look as if you've just seen a ghost!" might turn out to be closer to the truth than had been intended?

The Prof, his eyelids beginning to close, had no great desire to fight against the soporific effect of neither the rhythmic noise of the train's wheels nor the added fatigue of a night on the town with Freddie.

He left his fellow travellers to their crosswords and paperback novels and drifted off into oblivion.

Bliss was the next stop.

'...*To waken the dead!*' The Prof surfaced from his deep slumber as a result of those outspoken thoughts of a benign, elderly clergyman who'd been struggling with The Times' crossword until shaken into action.

'Good heavens above!' The clergyman adjusted the spectacles, askew on his florid face; his words almost drowned out by the disembodied voice of a would-be town crier.

'Crewe! Crewe junction! Crewe!'

The voice informed all within a radius of several miles.

'Bless my soul! Will you listen to that? Loud enough – to waken the dead!' The sermon continued from 'florid face'. Doors banged, whistles shrilled and last minute goodbyes were proffered, to the ritual of a flag-waving guard. Seconds later the London-to-Glasgow express juddered a couple of times then gathered speed on the next stage of the journey north.

During the hour or so that followed, as the train stopped at, or sped through, stations between Crewe and Carlisle and across the border into Scotland, The Prof allowed his thoughts to wander into the

10

past and to gaze into the crystal ball of the future. Reminiscences included meeting Freddie at an RAF Station near Liverpool and going together to watch The Grand National at Aintree, in 1947, when 100/1 outsider Caughoo appeared out of the dense fog, to win the race, with the favourite, Prince Regent, in fourth place.

It was, however, the outcome of this next venture into the fog and mist surrounding the death of Illusionist, Jack Ramsden, which was uppermost in his mind.

The verdict "Death by Misadventure" was somehow a phrase he'd never have associated with the master of Maskelyne Hall - but why had it taken so long for Laura to come to the same conclusion? Why was she calling for his help? He was no detective: all his experience of what seemed to be another "locked-room" mystery had been gleaned from reading classic detective fiction. Come to think of it, that might not be detrimental. The historical know-how of hocus-pocus and the jiggery-pokery of Magic might prove to be the essential ingredients required to solve what really happened in this baffling mystery. The commonsense of Freddie might also be invaluable as partner and ally.

As the express slowed, approaching the station at Lockerbie, the sleepy town in Dumfries-shire, Scotland, The Prof removed his bags from the rack, put on his warm Crombie overcoat and prepared to cross swords with his unknown archenemy. *A murderer who, seemingly, could vanish into thin air!*

Chapter 2
THE GENIE OF THE LAMP

The Prof stepped down on to an almost deserted platform – almost, but not quite. About twenty yards away, with her back towards him, a young woman stood and scanned the train. She was dressed in black; pencil slim skirt, jacket, stockings and high-heeled shoes that accentuated legs of eye-catching shape.

He could not help but admire what he saw; she had a figure an archbishop would kick a hole in a stained glass window to look at! She turned to face him with the easy deportment of a professional dancer or of someone well used to theatrical appearances.

He barely had time to feast his eyes on the pristine whiteness of her blouse and her gorgeously symmetrical face framed with auburn hair in which titian highlights danced disturbingly before he capitulated to her magnetic chemistry.

The Prof stared at her as she smiled back at him. Then he turned away as he felt the red flush invade his cheeks. He was looking for someone much older ...and *male!* Surely old George would be there to meet him. George...lodge keeper, groom, gardener and handyman extraordinaire, had always been "old" George since those heady wartime days when Giles and the others were young and carefree. George, despite his prematurely white hair, was in his forties's then and would now be a spry sixty something. Yes – he'd be there all right – Laura had said so on the phone. "George will pick you up with the station wagon," she'd said. Her exact words! Now where the hell was he?

He was startled out of his reverie by the sound of high heels.

'Giles? Can that really be you?'

He turned and looked into the most attractive face he'd gazed at in years. Her hazel eyes twinkled mischievously as she repeated 'Giles? Of course it's you! I'd have known that blush anywhere and you were staring at me. Didn't you recognise me? Little me?'

'I…well…!'

He dropped both bags and fought hard for his composure.

'Your voice hasn't changed much, Laura. But you were only twelve when I last saw you, and you weren't packaged in quite the same way then as you so obviously…! What did you say? I was staring at you! Yes, I was, wasn't I?'

'Yes, my dear Giles! But please don't let that cramp your style. I'm going to enjoy having the attention of a man for a few days. I seem to scare most of them off!'

'I doubt that!'

'Grab your luggage; compliments can wait! Let me drive you home to meet the others. You look exhausted after your journey!'

Laura kissed Giles on the cheek, turned on her heels and led the way out to the car.

Then, and only then, as he picked up his bags, did he become aware that he was standing in an empty station.

The ghost train had somehow, silently and unnoticed left for Glasgow.

The Prof almost ran the short distance out of the station.

The autumn light was already beginning to fade although it was only mid afternoon; the station wagon was nowhere to be seen. In its place was a Jaguar XK150 sports car in bright yellow with red upholstery. The delicious Laura, clad in black, matching the Jaguar's hood, stood at the open boot.

'Pop your luggage in here Giles, and I'll show you how this little number performs! And do me a favour…' Laura giggled infectiously. 'When you've picked up your jaw, before it trips you, there's something you should know! You have a red mark on your cheek and it's fairly obvious you didn't cut it shaving! So let me remove the evidence before you have some explaining to do.'

Giles gazed into the little compact she held in front of his nose.

'How did that get there?' he said as Laura, with the deft movement of a manicured thumb made the mark, shaped like a woman's lips, disappear.

'Strange,' he muttered and put a hand to his cheek. 'Ready when you are, Miss Ramsden!'

Once they were both comfortably settled into the sports car Laura manipulated the Jaguar into exhilarating life and, with a minimum of slick movement, started Giles on a tour of childhood memories.

The car made a sharp left turn at the newsagent where Giles, as a boy, had prepared his paper-round - the town hall, on the right, venue of The Hunt Ball – the library where, during the war, he'd poured over The Illustrated London News and the cinema where he'd spent many times watching the projectionist check, and repair, reels of film with an eager anticipation for small fragments of celluloid.

Up over the railway bridge and climbing above the sleepy town, Laura was soon heading right on the B7068.

'You've been very quiet! What do you think of it, Mister Professor, Sir?'

'I'm still trying to get my breath back, and I'm sure I left my stomach behind when we crossed the bridge!'

'Tut, tut! What do you think of the car, Giles? Do you like it?'

'It beats anything I've experienced. Good job the hood isn't down though as we'd have difficulty holding a conversation over the rush of air.'

'We must try that sometime. I mean drive with the hood down ; we won't need to talk.'

Giles felt the power as the car gathered speed. He glanced at the speedometer then at his companion; she was in total control and enjoying her moment of exhibitionism. Talking was the last thing on The Prof's mind during the next minute or two.

'What are you thinking now, Giles?'

'I'm thinking!' He swallowed hard. 'I'm thinking…this was the stretch of road where I had problems with hill starts, when I was learning to drive, many moons ago!'

Laura eased her foot off the accelerator.

'But the speed, my dear professor! Did you enjoy that?'

'Let me just say this, young woman. I well remember, as a boy, camping with the Scouts, near the river; a lot of us went down *with the*

14

trots after eating tinned rhubarb and, a few moments ago, when you had the foot down, I realised you don't need tinned rhubarb to get the same symptoms.'

She burst into another fit of the giggles as she slowed and turned off to the left, careful to avoid the sheer drop on the right plunging down to some menacing trees.

'We're nearly home!' Laura looked across at Giles and smiled.

Another left turn through an entrance flanked by stone pillars. The iron gates that had hung from the pillars had been removed to help the war effort and never replaced.

They drove slowly past the lodge – home to George and Doreen Gardner. Smoke was spiralling from a chimney but there was no sign of anyone. The Prof imagined "old" George Gardner, Gee-Gee as he was sometimes known, would be somewhere in the grounds clearing leaves or some such task and his wife, Doreen, housekeeper and cook at the big house, would probably be up there preparing afternoon tea. Giles couldn't wait to see buxom Doreen again and sample some of her goodies.

Round the next bend Laura stopped the car. That was where he had his first sight of Maskelyne Hall in over twenty years.

'A sight for sore eyes! That's twice in the last half hour!' he said, turning to Laura.

He looked at the house again. 'It looks smaller than it did; but then everything looked big when we were kids!'

'It's great to have you back, Giles! You don't know how much I need you! I can't understand why we've waited so long!'

Her voice was softer than before.

'Can I ask you something, Laura?' He took her hand and squeezed hard.

'You know you can!'

'I didn't mention it when I phoned you...when was it...last night? God knows, it seems ages ago!'

'Start asking then, my dear Professor.'

'What was the real purpose of the riddle in your letter to me?'

'I had a pretty good idea that, if you were too busy to answer my other distress calls, the riddle might just be the catalyst that would bring you here. You solved the riddle I assume?'

15

'If you mean The Womb and The Tomb, the answer would be…yes! But there's more to it than that. Am I right?'

'You know you are! And that's why you're here! We can talk about that later!'

She put the car into gear and drove towards the house. When they stopped on the gravel outside the main entrance Giles leaned across and whispered in her ear.

'Do you really think you asked the right person to come and help you?'

'No, I don't just think I asked the right person…I know I did! Now, let me look at you! Yes, you'll do! You're quite presentable! Let's go and meet the others!'

The smell of freshly-made scones that pervaded the nostrils as Giles followed Laura into the house made him mindful he'd hardly eaten anything since leaving his South Kensington flat, in a rush, that morning.

Laura took his coat, hung it on the hallstand and, opening the door on the right, said 'Pop in here for a moment, Giles. Make yourself at home and I'll check if Mother is having her afternoon nap! Better still, why don't you visit the kitchen and give cook a surprise! Mrs. Gardner will be delighted to see you again. I'll be with you shortly.'

Laura turned and headed for the lounge on her left. As she crossed the hall, she called back 'If you play your cards right cook might offer you something to whet your appetite and, I promise you, it won't be tinned rhubarb!'

She went into the lounge and closed the door silently behind her.

The Prof walked down the corridor towards the rear of the house passing the library on the way. He put his head round the open doorway of the kitchen.

'Cooee! Anyone at home?'

Mrs. Gardner put a hand up to her ample bosom and turned with a startled expression on her face.

'Bless my soul!' she said. 'You gave me such a fright! Hallowe'en isn't until Monday! Can I help you, young man?'

'I'm just a poor beggar man who is down on his luck!' Giles mimicked with a mock quaver in his voice. 'Do you think I could sample one of your goodies! I haven't eaten one of those for twenty years!'

By this time Giles was on his knees and Mrs. Gardner, with arms akimbo and her whole body shaking with laughter, entered into the spirit of the charade.

'Good heavens! Arise Sir Giles - some beggar man, indeed – a professor of something or other I understand and, a starving professor at that, if I'm not mistaken!' She helped him to his feet. 'Come now, give me a great big hug and you can have one of my buttered scones and some home-made jam.'

'I'll go along with that!' The Prof put his arms around the cuddly cook.

'And so you should!' Laura appeared at the kitchen door. 'Mother's having forty winks at the moment. Grab yourself a quick nibble then I'll take you up to your room.'

He crammed one of cook's warm delights into his eager mouth and followed Laura out of the kitchen.

'Afternoon tea will be ready in half-an-hour!'

Cook's parting words made him smile; it was just like it used to be in the good old days.

Giles collected his bags from Laura's car and found her waiting at the top of the stairs, when he came back in.

'Up here Giles.'

He took the stairs two-at-a-time but Laura was already outside his bedroom, on the right, and had his door open when he caught up with her.

'You'll find everything you need in here. There's a bathrobe in the wardrobe, and plenty of hot water, if you want a bath to freshen up. The bathroom, if you remember, is just along to your right. See you downstairs in half-an-hour.'

The Prof unpacked, undressed, donned the blue bathrobe and padded along, in his bare feet, for the bath that was so inviting.

He started to run the bath and had a good look round the bathroom that was totally unfamiliar to him. It had obviously undergone alterations since he had last used the place.

The bath was luxurious. Longer and wider than before, and somehow appeared to be more sunken than he remembered. A style he had always thought was for him. There was a shower unit in one corner and a large bathroom cabinet had been fixed to the outside wall. The cabinet seemed to contain everything you could want as far as toilet luxury was concerned.

All The Prof wanted, at this moment, was a good soak to ease the tiredness, and that's exactly what he got.

A good soak. A few minutes of tranquility, and time to reflect.

Murder seemed so far away. But that's why he was here!

The Prof knocked on the lounge door and entered. He was dressed in black polo neck and charcoal slacks.

Laura rose and said, 'Come in Giles. You remember Mother?'

'Hello, Mrs. Ramsden. Please don't get up! You know...you haven't changed. It's wonderful to be back!'

'And the boys, of course?'

'Ah, yes – Victor and Conrad – now which is which?'

'Hardly boys, Mother!' Victor held out his hand. 'Victor, at your service.'

'Victor thinks he's a man of the world; now he's single again.' Conrad clasped Giles round the shoulders. 'Allow me to introduce my wife. Mabel, meet Giles, or should I say, Professor Dawson?'

Giles gave Conrad's wife a peck on the cheek. 'My pleasure!' he said.

'Which reminds me,' Victor sneered. 'Congrats Professor...but Professor of what? I'm sure we'd all like to hear how that came about.'

'You'd be bored to tears, I wager!' Giles studied the smirk on Victor's face.

'Blow your trumpet for a change, Giles.' Laura said. 'Even Victor might be impressed.'

'Well I did warn you! So don't blame me!' The Prof took a deep breath.... 'After wangling my demob I went to Oxford and read History. My first love was stage magic; your father had a lot to do with that, and I'd done a bit of entertaining in the services. By then I was a member of The Magic Circle and, at varsity, I delved into the History of the Great Illusionists. Everything seemed to work in parallel. I finished up with my PhD, and was offered the chair. Then, in 1952, I went on a lecture tour of Australia. That made my mind up. I returned home and decided to continue lecturing. The rest is history.' Victor started a slow handclap.

Giles looked him straight in the eyes. 'I have one regret. I was unable to attend your father's funeral. I'm so sorry!' He turned his gaze to Mrs. Ramsden. 'The only consolation I have…! It was your husband that started me on an adventure of mystery. I'll be forever grateful for that!'

'So father was good for something…or someone!' Victor's words were chilling.

'It was Albert Einstein who said, "The most beautiful experience we can have is the mysterious." I do hope you have the good fortune to enjoy it some day!'

'Well said, Giles!' Laura's face was slightly flushed as she added. 'Now I almost forgot the youngest in the family – Edgar. He and his wife Sally are due to arrive on Saturday or Sunday. That's all the introductions over; you've now met everyone at Maskelyne Hall, except "old" George!'

'Laura, please don't be disrespectful.' Mrs Ramsden chided her daughter.

'We've always called him that, Mummy. He really doesn't mind.'

'Will you pour the tea, Laura? Scone, Giles? They're home made!'

Laura, giggling again, looked at Giles and winked.

The door opened and Mrs. Gardner, the cook, came into the lounge.

'Will you be wanting more tea?'

'Another pot wouldn't go wrong, Doreen.'

'I'll have it here in a jiffy.'

Mrs. Gardner left in a swirl of skirts and apron.

Laura got up, closed the curtains and switched on a lamp.

'It's getting quite dark! We'll really be heading for winter when the clocks go back after tomorrow night!'

The lamp Laura had switched on had not only added brightness to the firelight of the burning logs in the grate but had grabbed the attention of The Prof. It was a heavy solid object of beautifully turned wood; rare, with fine graining and of a rich and distinctive colour. The stunning artistry of such a wonderful household object had an immediate impact on Giles.

'Now that's what I call a lamp!'

19

'There's a story attached to that lamp that you might like to hear,' Laura said. 'It has a secret genie and you don't need to rub it! Want to hear about it?'

'Try me!' Giles quipped. 'I love secrets!'

'Not that again!' Victor chipped in. 'You know it's only coincidence!'

'Well I've never heard the secret. You never told me, Conrad.' Mabel said. 'I'd love to hear the story?'

'It's over to you, Conrad!' Laura made a show business gesture with her arms.

'Are you all sitting comfy? Then I'll begin,' Conrad said.

'Let me see…it was early November 1951. I'd been to the Ideal Homes Exhibition in Glasgow. The lamp you see there was on show and I bought it for Mum and Dad's wedding anniversary. There was something about the lamp. The quality of the turned wood or the grain or the colour; something that I couldn't resist.

'Anyway, on the Saturday after I brought it home, we were in this room listening to the radio. The BBC was broadcasting the Manchester November Handicap and father was quite keen to hear the race; Raymond Glendenning was doing the commentary and was talking about the runners down at the start. Father was studying them in the paper and Mother was enthusing about the lamp. "*Good Taste,*" she said at the same time as the commentator said the same two words; it was the name of one of the runners in the race. We all looked at each other in a kind of eerie silence and Mother repeated the words "*Good Taste,*" at the exact same moment as Glendenning spoke the horse's name once again.

"That's going to win!" she said. "I know it is!" Father checked the paper and pooh-poohed the whole idea. He said, "No chance! It isn't even in the betting; 33/1 others. Hasn't a bloody hope!" And that's what we all thought!'

'The race was run in a thick fog. The commentator made the best of a difficult job calling the leading contenders without ever mentioning Good Taste at any time. That is until the last few yards…when the horse appeared out of the mist to win at 28/1. Good Taste was ridden by leading Northern jockey Billy Nevett and trained in Yorkshire. The result was an incredible one to all of us listening. Probably the most dramatic finish to the race ever! Mother was white to the gills, and the rest of us could only stare at her; we couldn't believe it!'

'Pure coincidence! I've said it before and I'll say it again!' Victor was adamant. 'Either that.... or Mother is a witch!'

'Careful, son!' Giles cautioned. 'Don't be too ready to jump to conclusions!'

'I can't listen to any more of this nonsense! I'm going for a walk!' Victor rose and, on the way out, said 'See you at dinner, Giles! Welcome back, by the way!'

'What about a foursome at Bridge you two?' Conrad said, checking his wallet. 'Mabel and I will give you and Giles a run for your money, Laura. That's if you have no objection, mother?'

'Off you go, you lot, but a witches' warning! Giles might be even better at card manipulation than he used to be! So beware! Anyway, let me have a word with him first! And alone, if you please. I'll let him out of my clutches in a few minutes.'

When the others had gone Mrs. Isabella Ramsden folded her hands in her lap and said 'Come and sit closer to me, Giles.'

Giles drew one of the chairs in front of the fire and sat down opposite the matriarch of Maskelyne Hall.

'I know you wish to hear all about that fateful night in 1952 when dear Jack...' She was beginning to stumble over her words. 'I was the first to be at his side after he was shot! I want you to know everything that happened; but not yet!'

Giles nodded, took both her hands in his and waited for her to continue.

'Have you looked into the library yet?'

'No!'

'When you have the time perhaps you'll understand things a little better and maybe understand what Jack was attempting before things went wrong that night.'

'I'd like to think so!'

'Firstly, there is something I want you to do.'

'Anything you say.'

'I want you to open my husband's private safe. Everything is as it was on that terrible night. Nothing has been disturbed! What you find may help to explain events leading to his death; but first you must discover a way to open the safe!'

'More hocus-pocus, Mrs. Ramsden? I'm beginning to understand why you sent for me!'

'I didn't send for you, Laura did!' Mrs. Ramsden's abrupt outburst surprised The Prof. 'That's beside the point! You're here now and I'm coming to the conclusion that Laura made the right decision in getting me to go along with it.'

'I'll do my best! Now what do I have to do to open the safe?'

'Solve a riddle. I believe you're good at that!'

'I have my moments!' Giles said, releasing her hands from his grasp.

'Jack always said, if others were on the same wavelength, they would be able to solve his riddles; a sort of mental telepathy.'

Isabella Ramsden, her coiffured white hair helping to soften her features lit, on one side by the fire and on the other by the magic lamp, picked up her handbag from the floor, reached in, produced two sheets of paper and handed them over.

'One sheet explains the mechanism of the safe and the combination lock; the other is the riddle, which must be solved in order to discover the combination that will open the safe. Once the safe is open you will have the contents that may help you solve a more complex puzzle.'

'Always assuming that nothing has been disturbed, Mrs. Ramsden!'

The old lady smiled. 'Take your time. And remember, Giles, if you should get into any difficulty the Genie of the Lamp is here to help you.'

Giles was about to get up when Mrs. Ramsden caught him by the arm.

'Please read them before you go so that I may have your first impressions.'

Giles looked at the first sheet.

Notes about Safe built into fireplace of Library at Maskelyne Hall – August 1952

The Combination Safe Lock consists of four wheels, or tumblers. With 100 numbers on the dial there are 100 positions for each wheel and a single knob can set all the wheels. Once the combination is known (in this case six digits) there are one million possible combinations.

The knob is turned anticlockwise until the first number of two digits comes opposite the arrow for the fourth time.

The knob is then turned clockwise until the second number of two digits is opposite the arrow for the third time.

Finally the knob is turned counter clockwise to bring the third number of two digits in line with the arrow for the second time. All three slots are then in one line and the handle can be turned to withdraw the bolts.

Being built into the solid fireplace gives additional protection to the entire structure, as the walls floor and ceiling of the safe do not have to be as strong as the door.

On the second sheet was the riddle.

> Beginning or End of Vice?
> With a Wee or With a Wubbleyou?
> To Unlock, Try Beginning at the End
> When This Won't Trouble You!

Giles smiled and was about to speak to Mrs. Ramsden when he noticed her eyes were already closed. He tiptoed quietly out of the room.

Chapter 3
THE MAN WHO COULD WALK THROUGH WALLS

The Prof paused at the door to the library thankful he now had something to take his mind off his dismal performance at the card table. After leaving Isabella Ramsden, asleep by the lounge fire, his brain had been occupied with the imminent opening of the safe and examination of the contents! Winning a rubber at Bridge had been far from his thoughts! It wasn't so much losing to Conrad and Mabel that rankled. It was letting Laura down that hurt the most. Now, at last, he had something to get his teeth into.

The library door opened silently on well-oiled hinges and he stepped into what had been one of his favourite haunts, when he had been privileged to visit the room. He switched on the light and closed the door.

The bookcases, which almost filled the entire wall to his left, were as he remembered them. They contained a treasure trove of biographies, mostly of the great conjurers and magicians, definitive works on the history of magic and priceless volumes on early entertainment in music halls, theatres and circuses around the world, which had been a great passion of the late Jack Ramsden.

The room was floored in solid oak, on the centre of which was a long mahogany table, with an upright chair at each end. Two leather armchairs, one on each side of the large Adam-style fireplace, situated in the middle of the wall opposite the door, served as invitations to potential readers to enjoy a stay in the company of rare books. A standard lamp was conveniently placed beside each armchair and a large, ornate, Japanese screen obscured the fireplace, which contained the safe. To the right of the door were a cocktail cabinet and a writing desk.

The wall opposite the bookcases, had double small-paned sash windows, which overlooked the gardens, set into the left half, nearest to the fireplace, with a long heavy curtain on either side that did not quite reach the floor. The other half of this wall, which backed on to the room next door, was blank except for a large framed poster of Chung Ling Soo, billed as the *Celestial Chinese Conjurer*, who tragically died after performing *The Great Gun Trick* at the Wood Green Empire in North London on 23 March 1918.

Four small-paned sash windows, each fitted with long heavy curtains, were built into the fireplace wall, two on each side of the old fire, and between the two windows to the left facing the door as you entered hung an oil painting.

The painting was a portrait of a female dancer in a Spanish costume of scarlet and vermillion against a sandy background. The pose was theatrically professional and strikingly provocative. In her left hand the dancer carried a fan and, in her right hand, she held *a long thin-bladed stiletto dagger!* It was her face though that really caught his attention. Even though the black hair puzzled him there was no disguising those hazel eyes. The portrait was that of….

'Well, I'm damned! It's you, Laura!' His words sounded like a stage whisper in the silence of the room.

'You're talking to yourself, Giles!' Laura's mildly scolding tone made him jump like a naughty schoolboy found raiding the sweet jar.

'I didn't hear you come in,' he said as he turned to find her standing behind him.

'Of course you didn't! You were much too absorbed with the painting! And you were wrong! It isn't me!'

'But I would've sworn!' Giles' brow creased into a frown as he studied the portrait again.

'Daddy had it commissioned just before he married his young bride. The artist partly worked from a poster of Isabella when she'd been a dancer in Vaudeville in the early 1920's and he was designing and making theatrical sets. Daddy presented it to her as a wedding gift.

'Uncanny, wouldn't you say? You could pass as twins!'

'Well, we're not! Not even modern medical science has been able to produce twins born so long apart!'

'Hang on a minute, Laura! I don't remember seeing the portrait when I was here during the war!'

'Nor did any of us. Daddy had it stored away in a safe place. Anyway, I'm sorry if I upset you. I only came in to see if you'd cracked the safe. I see you haven't!'

'Not yet...' said The Prof, moving the Japanese screen out of the way and getting down on his knees to examine the fireplace and safe: '...but I'm sure I can solve the riddle and the rest should be easy.'

'I'll leave you to get on with it then! See you at dinner!'

He rose and turned to speak only to find the library empty and the door closed. Laura had vanished – as if she'd never been there. The question was...had she really been in the room, or had it all been a figment of his imagination? If she had been there, had she glided silently across the floor and exited via the well-oiled door, in the time it takes to wave a magic wand, or had she, like The Man Who Could Walk Through Walls, done just that and *walked through walls?* He really must get a grip, he thought, and returned to his knees.

Come to think of it, the man who walked through walls brought him back to the job in hand; the opening of the safe. He was pretty sure that the conundrum, which would provide the combination to the safe, referred to the person credited with the ability to walk through walls, Harry Houdini, the Master Escapologist. Firstly, he had to give the safe a thorough going over.

What used to be a large opening in the fireplace was now entirely filled by the solid steel safe. An expert had obviously built the safe into the fireplace; it appeared to be secured by bolts and the top and sides were flush with the top and sides of the opening, which were also made of steel. To remove the safe would've required demolishing the entire granite fireplace. The combination to the locking system was the only means of entry.

The Prof, remembering the conundrum, took no time at all to apply his reasoning to the tumblers, but to no avail. The door to the safe wouldn't budge. It was locked tight! Something was wrong! Was he losing his touch?

As he sat back on his heels, a slight noise to his right made him look towards the windows. It was now very dark outside but he thought he could see something looking in at him. It was a face...and only a face! A face without a body and surrounded by darkness! And it was smiling!

He got up, went over to the windows and looked out. It was difficult to see anything outside but the entire area appeared empty of anyone or anything! Whatever he'd seen, or thought he'd seen, was gone.

Giles closed the curtains and returned to the fireplace. The puzzled frown was back as he thought over his previous actions including the logic behind the interpretation of the conundrum and the solving of the riddle. All the imponderables required consideration. Where had he gone wrong?

He moved across to the door, opened it and was about to switch off the light when he turned to take a last look at the portrait of Isabella. Was it a trick of the light, his imagination, or were his nerves beginning to get the better of him? The painting seemed different! What was it? Did the fan flutter? Was the dagger hand much more threatening? No, it was the face! The face was *smiling*! Had it been smiling when he first looked at it? He wasn't sure! He couldn't remember! One thing he could remember though...the smile was the one he'd seen at the window!!

Something was now rattling the combination tumblers in his brain. The frown was disappearing from his tortured forehead.

He closed the library door, nodded at the dancer with the dagger and the blood-red dress and muttered, 'Let's try again, shall we!' Then, as he knelt down in front of the safe, he could imagine Laura saying, "Giles, you're talking to yourself again."

The Prof, rubbing the tips of his fingers against the material of his black polo neck, as he'd seen the safe crackers do in the old movies, was convinced that The Man Who Could Walk Through Walls, Harry Houdini, was about to open the safe, almost forty years after his death.

The first part of the riddle, referring to *Vice? With a Wee or Wubbleyou* surely meant WEISS. Ehrich Weiss, pronounced vice, was the name that Harry Houdini, the son of a Hungarian rabbi, was given when he was born in 1874. The reference to *beginning at the end* in the riddle must surely refer to the date of Houdini's death. The Prof had used the date 31/10/26 as the three sets of numbers to be introduced to the wheels of the combination locking system. He'd done that, but they hadn't worked the magic! *Why?* Of course - the smile at the window! Someone had been trying to tell him something. He had it the wrong way round and *that someone* had been watching to see when the penny would drop. It was dropping now.

Ehrich Weiss, Hungarian born, had gone to America and changed his name to Harry Houdini - and he became an American citizen! He was an American. An American who died on Hallowe'en in 1926 and, in America, the date of his death would be 10/31/26 and not 31/10/26. The Prof had failed to think the problem through and the smile had triggered the action and reaction necessary for the solving of the puzzle.

His euphoria was complete when the numbers were fed into the wheels and he was able to turn the handle and open the safe.

Dinner, on his first evening back at Maskelyne Hall after an absence of many years, was a convivial affair for Giles. He was in the company of friends; for the time being!

Friends? I suppose so; he thought looking round the table at his companions. Companions who'd welcomed him with open arms and made him feel as if he'd never been away. Nevertheless, if the reason for his visit was as had been suggested by mother and daughter, one of those friends could be - a murderer. It would be his task to discover which one. Which one was playing a part? Perhaps more than one! There was always that possibility!

The Prof allowed his eyes to wander round the animated group at the dinner table. Mrs. Isabella Ramsden, the matriarch of Maskelyne Hall...demure and benign...who wouldn't hurt a fly! Why did the words, from Act 3 Scene 8 of William Congreve's play *The Mourning Bride* leap into his head? *Heaven has no rage, like love to hatred turned, Nor Hell a fury, like a woman scorned.*

Demure and benign! Was she? She sat and listened to an agitated conversation between her two sons, Victor and Conrad.

Victor, aged thirty nine, born same year as Giles, tall, dark hair, dark complexion and brown eyes, he'd always had a chip on his shoulder, even in boyhood, belligerent, uneasy ...but capable of murder? Hardly!

Conrad, slightly shorter than his brother and two years younger at thirty seven, dark brown bushy hair, brown eyes, intelligent, sporting but competitive. The killer type? Very doubtful! Neither seemed likely! But then, neither did Crippen, Ruxton or Haigh.

Mabel, Conrad's wife, fair-hair, blue eyes, pale skin with rosy cheeks, fun loving, supportive and poetic, was giggling as she and Laura enjoyed something amusing. Laura, early thirties, attractive and lively, a mysterious enigmatic adventuress, would try most things. But murder? Unthinkable! He had almost dismissed Mabel as a possible suspect and he wondered why?

'You were miles away, Giles!' Laura's voice brought him out of his coma.

'Penny for them!' said a smiling Mabel.

'Not much profit in that, I'm afraid.' The Prof advised. 'I'm so sorry, I was dreaming.'

'Oh, how …er…interesting!' Mabel's eyes were on Laura as she spoke.

'Victor was trying to get through to you.' Laura informed him gently. 'I think he wanted to ask you a question.'

'I do apologise,' said The Prof, looking across towards Victor. 'I'll do my best to give you an answer. Fire away!' He regretted the use of those last two words as he watched the elder son's eyes giving him a chilly stare under raised brows.

'Conrad and I were having an argument about that story he told this afternoon. You know! The one about the November Handicap and the lamp, and all that! I just cannot go along with the idea that some people can predict the future and I said so! Pure coincidence. Nothing more! Anyway that's what I think. I was trying to ask what you really believe…about prediction or premonition. You know, that sort of thing. You seemed to be in some kind of hypnotic trance!'

'No disrespect intended.' The Prof's tone was subdued. 'Anyway, whether I believe in Prediction or Premonition isn't relevant, I'll leave that to you. Let me just say you're quite correct Victor, about coincidence, I mean.'

'I'm not sure I get your drift.'

'Firstly, we have to decide what are meant by coincidences and whether they have a hidden meaning for us, and what unknown force, if any, they represent.'

Warming to his subject, he continued: 'I have a very close friend…Freddie, Freddie Oldsworth, who lives near Evesham with his wife and two little girls! Anyway, Freddie has been studying this subject for some time now. We're both members of The Society of Psychical Research and The Ghost Club, as well as The Magic Circle. A mathematician by profession, Freddie devotes his expertise these days to the world of horse racing and the science of probability.'

'Daddy would've been more than a little interested in someone like that. Next time you come back to see us bring him with you. He'd be very welcome,' said Laura.

'That's very generous of you. Now where was I? Oh, yes ...coincidences! Freddie and I have tended to accept the wisdom of the Philosopher, Arthur Schopenhauer. He defined Coincidence as the simultaneous occurrence of casually unconnected events.'

'Oh, come on Giles, cut the gobbledegook!' The heckler was Mabel.

'No, no! Please continue,' Isabella Ramsden said, showing interest for the first time. 'I'd like to hear more!'

'Thank you, ma'am! I bow to your superior judgement!' Giles acknowledged with a smile and was about to resume when Laura intervened.

'What say we pour The Prof another glass of wine, Conrad. to help lubricate the throat.' she said with a wink.

'And when you're on your feet, I think we could all do with a refill.' Victor said, looking round for approval.

As glasses were being replenished Mabel banged on the table and, in as deep a voice as she could muster, announced 'Pray silence for his professorship!'

Giles cleared his throat amidst a spontaneous burst of mock clapping. 'Now where was I?' he said. 'Ah, yes... coincidences!' 'Philosopher Arthur What's-his-name,' (a whoop of delight from Mabel stopped him in full flow). 'He, er, divided coincidences into two categories; trivial and significant. The trivial kind has to do with spinning of coins, runs of numbers as in a Casino and, of course, hands of cards!' (More whoops of delight from Mabel along with husband Conrad, the winners at Bridge). The Prof gave the two revellers a stony stare before continuing his lecture.

'Researchers are more concerned with significant coincidences. Those that shuffle together people, events, time and space...your incredible story of the race and the lamp comes into this category.'

'Spoo-oo-ky!'

All eyes turned to look at the source of this comment ...Mabel.

'There are recognisable types of coincidences such as literary ones and warning ones but even you, Victor, must surely agree that the mathematical odds against the commentator, in the November Handicap, and your mother uttering the words "Good Taste" at exactly the same time, miles apart and without being in communication would have to be astronomical! And for that coincidence to be repeated shortly afterwards and then for the horse in question to go on and win the race in dramatic circumstances takes the incident into the realm of something far beyond comprehension. Whatever it is, it has to be something much more than mere coincidence, and certainly bears investigation! Wouldn't you agree?'

'O.K., I take your point,' said Victor 'but it was still coincidence!' With his arrogance more diffused than earlier Victor added: 'I do admit that the way you state the mathematical implications puts a different light on things.'

'Am I right, Giles? Did you say there were literary coincidences and warning coincidences?' It was Laura who spoke.

'ESP!' boomed out from the lips of Isabella and produced a shocked silence from everyone until this was broken by an intermittent gurgle from Conrad that eventually materialized into laughter. 'Ha, ha, ha, he, he, of course, Mother, ESB...I thought you were asleep. ESB, a classic example of what The Prof was talking about! Won the Grand National in '56, I think, when *Devon Loch* collapsed and did the splits, just yards from the winning post when he looked home and dry, as they say. There hasn't been a satisfactory explanation for that either. You really *are* a clever old girl?'

'No!' Isabella explained, slowly and deliberately, 'I said ESP! Not that other horse!'

'Extrasensory Perception!' said The Prof. 'The faculty of receiving and transmitting information through means other than the known senses: Clairvoyance and Clairaudience are the ESP of objects or events, Precognition is the ESP of the future and Telepathy is the ESP of one mind in direct contact with another. Freddie would have a field day if he were here. Experiences such as just knowing something was going to happen before it does or being alerted to danger or disaster are forms of Extrasensory Perception.'

'Very much like someone humming a tune then hearing the same tune when they switch on the radio!' Laura said. 'Or thinking about someone then bumping into them round the next corner!'

'That's just coincidence!' insisted Victor.

'Yes, but it doesn't happen to everyone!' Isabella said as she rose from the table. 'Please excuse me; I'm going to bed. I'll see you all in the morning! I've enjoyed the chat!'

A chorus of "good night" and "sleep well" accompanied her departure.

'Why don't we all head for the lounge,' Laura said when her mother had closed the door, 'Mabel can help me rustle up some coffee and the lads can get the liqueurs and glasses ready. We might be in the mood for a ghost story as the midnight hour approaches!'

'Sp-oo-oo-ooky!'

Mabel's words produced giggles of laughter as the two young women went off to the kitchen.

Victor stoked the lounge fire; Giles arranged sofa and chairs into a cosy semi-circle and Conrad prepared a coffee table with assorted glasses and liqueurs.

The girls arrived with tray complete with pot of coffee, sugar and cream and coffee-cups.

'Cook left everything ready!' said Laura. 'Another example of coincidence, I suppose!'

'Sp-oo-oo-ooky!' Mabel was beginning to enjoy herself.

'Before I get The Prof to elaborate on what he was telling us would you all agree that we should keep the lights off and sit by the glow of the fire? The atmosphere might be more conducive to the subject of mystery and imagination. A bit of the Edgar Allan Poe's!'

Victor's words were met with nods of approval and everyone settled down as if preparing for a séance!

'The coincidences you talk about! I accept that, in some cases, they can't be explained but the majority of them are pretty ordinary. I'd be less sceptical if you could provide evidence of situations involving major happenings! You know; world events!'

'Wasn't there something strange connected with the D-day landings towards the end of the war?' Conrad asked. 'I seem to recall reading something about it. Not sure where though! Didn't you mention something in the dining room about literary and warning coincidences? Could the D-day thing be one of those? I wish I could remember! Now what was it?'

'You're absolutely right!' said The Prof. 'Literary coincidence, the researchers call it; the D-day affair is one of the classic examples!'

'Go on then, Giles; don't keep it to yourself! Laura said, pouring the coffee. 'Black or white, Giles?'

'What?' The Prof looked puzzled.

'*The coffee*, Giles! Black or white?'

'Oh, black please!' He lapsed into silence.

'This is like trying to get blood out of a stone!' Mabel said in comic irritation.

'I think you've just lost him, Mabel!' Conrad said to his wife. 'I do believe you were going to tell us something mysterious about D-day; weren't you, Giles?'

'Was I? Yes I was, wasn't I?'

'Literary coincidence, I think you said it was!' prompted Victor as he poured a drink.

'Quite right!' The Prof gathered his thoughts. 'Just before the Allied Invasion of Europe, in 1944, the campaign to try and end the Second World War was Top Secret and referred to only by code words. The entire operation was known as OVERLORD, the Naval Spearhead disguised as NEPTUNE, the two French beaches, where the landings were to be made, were coded UTAH and OMAHA and the artificial harbours, to be used by the troops at the beachhead, were known as MULBERRY. Incredibly, in the thirty-three days before D-day, which was June 6, each of those secret coded words appeared in the answer to a clue in the *London Daily Telegraph* crossword!'

'Another unlikely mathematical and difficult-to-explain coincidence,' said Conrad, 'unless…'

'Unless what?' Victor probed his younger brother.

'Spies! You know! Secret agents using the Newspapers, to convey information to the enemy, instead of wireless!'

'A possibility, certainly! Ingenious, if true! However, the fact that the enemy was taken by surprise seems to rule out such a theory. Never mind; definitely an explanation well worth consideration! Well done, Conrad!' said The Prof. 'But that's not all,' Giles continued, 'The Key word OVERLORD appeared only four days before the landing! Now that's a classic example of a literary coincidence!'

'You mentioned another kind, Giles. What was that?' Victor asked.

'Yes, as well as the literary coincidence, there is the warning coincidence. History seems to offer many examples. One of the strangest, and this is a combination of the literary and the warning kind, was when a United States' writer, Morgan Robertson, published a novel, back in 1898, about a giant ocean liner called *THE TITAN,* which sank one freezing April night, in the Atlantic, after hitting an iceberg, on her maiden voyage!'

'Don't tell me!' said Laura, 'Let me guess! The prediction came true when the *TITANIC* sank on a freezing April night in 1912 after hitting an iceberg…on her maiden voyage!'

'Spot on! But not the whole story! It is believed that a copy of the novel was in the library of the Titanic on that fateful night. Also the two liners, the one in the story and the one in real life, were around the same tonnage, the disasters occurred in the same stretch of ocean, both were regarded as unsinkable and neither carried enough lifeboats! Fact and fiction…inextricably linked!'

The noise of the fire was the only thing to be heard in the room.

'S-s-spooky!'

It required no guesswork, by the others, to know where that remark came from.

'There is a footnote to my little tale,' Giles was now speaking in a voice reminiscent of The Man in Black, from the BBC radio series, *Appointment With Fear,* broadcast during the War Years. 'A further coincidence happened twenty three years later, in 1935, when the *TITANIAN,* note the similarity of name, that was carrying coal from the Tyne to Canada, was sailing in those same Atlantic waters. A member of the crew began to feel a terrible foreboding and, by the time the Titanian reached the spot where the other ships went down, the feeling was overpowering. He wondered if he should try and stop the ship simply because of a premonition? One thing made his mind up for him. A further coincidence; if you like. 'As he yelled *"Danger Ahead!"* at the top of his voice he was only just in time to alert the helmsman on the bridge and avoid the enormous iceberg in the path of the ship.'

'What was that other, er…coincidence?' Mabel could hardly get the words out.

'The crewman, who screamed the warning, *was born on the night of the Titanic disaster*!'

The crash, following those final words, came from the coffee cup dropping from Mabel's trembling fingers on to the hard surface of the fireplace. It had an electrifying effect!

'I'm so sorry; it just slipped out of my hand!'

Conrad put an arm round his wife's shoulders. 'My God, Mabel, you're as cold as ice! Can I get you anything? What about a brandy?'

'No, I'll be all right. I'll be going to bed shortly! I was a bit carried away by The Prof's story and my imagination! Well it reminded me of a poem by Henry Wadsworth Longfellow! I was thinking of *Haunted Houses*!' Mabel, her composure returned, started to recite.

'All houses wherein men have lived and died
Are haunted houses. Through the open doors
The harmless phantoms on their errands glide,
With feet that make no sound upon the floors.'

As Mabel began to shiver Conrad, with his arm still around her shoulders, escorted his wife from the room.

'I won't be long.' he whispered. 'I'll just put her to bed!'

The door closed behind them.

'I think I'll get the head down as well…' said The Prof '…it's been a long day!'

'Take my advice and have a long lie,' Victor suggested. 'The baby of the family won't arrive until late tomorrow afternoon!'

'You mean…today,' Laura corrected her brother. 'It's already after the witching hour! Goodnight, Giles! See you in the morning.'

Giles, stifling a yawn, slipped out of the lounge and headed upstairs.

As he drifted towards sleep, at the end of that, first, long and exhausting, day at Maskelyne Hall, Giles thought of Jack Ramsden and his strange death. What had really happened in the library on that fateful Hallowe'en? Was this one of those Haunted Houses? He thought of Laura; thought of their meeting in the library; that library again and how she had, secretly, and silently left the room, like one of Longfellow's harmless phantoms that *made no sound upon the floor*. Was she a…?

He turned over and, purring gently, was soon fast asleep.

Chapter 4
"DID YOU SEE DR. HYDE?"

The Prof rubbed the sleep from his eyes and tried to sit up in bed. He struggled to check the time on his watch but his eyes wouldn't focus. The light from his bedroom window was hurting his eyes. Only it wasn't *his* bedroom window! Where the hell was he? He swung his feet on to the floor, almost stood upright, staggered to the window and looked out on to a gravel path, a manicured lawn looking as if mowing was over for the year, with a pile of leaves on one side, a row of trees and, beyond them, what appeared to be a stable block.

His head felt heavy and was starting to throb. Disbelief at his strange surroundings and a lack of balance forced him to steady himself against the window frame until his brain grasped the situation. 'Not London; that's for sure!' He was talking to himself again. Suddenly the mist cleared. 'Of course, Maskelyne Hall!' Had he taken too much to drink last night or was his glass doctored...? The pain increased as he had another glance at his watch. 'Good lord 9.30!'

He slipped his arms into his dressing gown, grabbed his shaving kit and headed for the bedroom door. Something white lay on the floor. It was a small envelope that had been pushed under the door as he slept. There was a familiar perfume as he picked it up, reminding him of the letter that had brought him here in the first place. Inside he found a card with a message.

Meet me in the lounge at 11 o'clock. I need to talk to you. Alone!

No signature! He tucked the card into the pocket of his dressing gown and moved along the hallway towards the bathroom. He tried the door but it was locked.

'That you, Giles?' It was Conrad's voice. 'Shan't be long, but you could try the one across the hall. It should be free!'

The Prof was transported back in time to those wartime childhood years and the unique experience of playing games with friends in a house that boasted of having two bathrooms! Those were the days, he thought. And what games! *Monopoly* and *Sardines* and what else…? Why, *Murder*, of course!

Back to the present with a bump! Was that what the latest message was about? If it were Murder it would no longer be a game!

Showered and shaved and dressed in dark grey slacks, blue shirt and navy sweater, Giles made his way downstairs to the kitchen.

He knocked, opened the kitchen door and came face to face with Mrs. Doreen Gardner, the cook and housekeeper.

'I just thought it might be you, Giles!'

'Like one of the Bisto Kids I was drawn to the aroma like a wasp to a pot of jam!'

'Flatterer! Have you had any breakfast?'

'No, Mrs. Gardner, I'm not long up, as a matter of fact!'

'In that case I could do you some scrambled eggs and toast!'

'That would be very kind of you!'

'Have you seen my husband since you arrived? He's down at the stables! You could give him a quick visit and I'll have your breakfast ready for you when you get back.'

The Prof moved to the back door and, as he was leaving, turned to speak.

'Er…Mrs. Gardner?'

'Yes!'

'I hope you don't mind me asking but do you really know why I've come back to The Hall?'

'Yes, I think I do! I believe we all do…' Mrs. Gardner paused in mid sentence. '…You see, Mrs. Ramsden has always been suspicious about the verdict at the inquest after her husband's death. She would dearly love to lay-to-rest all the ghosts that seem to obscure the truth of that awful night. She believes that, if anyone can get to the bottom of the whole dreadful business, you will! I understand she wishes to speak with you this morning and everyone has been warned to stay away from the lounge!'

'Thank you for being so frank, Mrs. Gardner! You realise, of course, that I may have to question all who were present that evening. That would include you and your husband. The more information I have the easier it will be to arrive at the truth!'

'Hmm! I do hope you get the co-operation of everyone!'

'We'll just wait and see, won't we? Now I think I'll take my constitutional. If I walk down to the stables and say hello to you-know-who, that should help me work up an appetite for those scrambled eggs!'

The Prof winked and left by the back door.

Crunching his way down the gravel path he passed the trees to his right and came in sight of the Vauxhall Victor Estate, which was parked in the courtyard of the stable block. This had to be the car that should have met him at the railway station yesterday afternoon, with "old" George in attendance and not Laura!

He continued towards the stable boxes. An equine head looked out of the top half of one and, from the next one, which was open, came the sound of someone mucking out.

A small, white-haired man, who was dressed in jodhpurs and grey wool sweater, had his back towards The Prof and was brushing the floor with the energy of someone half his age.

A discreet cough failed to distract George from the job in hand and it took two theatrically loud throat clearances before the little man turned around.

'Giles! Giles Dawson, you haven't changed a bit! A touch more distinguished, I'll grant you that but still the same Giles!'

The Prof pumped the extended hand.

'Nor have you, old friend! But what happened yesterday? I was expecting to see you at the station!'

'I was outvoted! Laura wanted to show off her new sports car and she insisted that she be the first to see you after all those years. You've just missed her. She's out riding with Sam!'

The Prof looked a little taken aback; a tinge of jealousy showing.

'Who is Sam?'

'Sam? Short for *Samson*! You must've met *Delilah* next door! They're our two hunters!'

'Ah, yes! Well that explains, doesn't it!'

'I hope so!' The little man said, with a broad grin.

'So do I!'

'You used to ride a bit, Giles; would you fancy taking *Delilah* out tomorrow? It would be company for *Samson* - and Laura!'

'Why not! I used to ride out with a friend. That is, until her accident! Water under the bridge, I'm afraid!'

'That's settled then!'

'Oh, I nearly forgot. Mrs. Gardner's expecting....'

'What! I hope not!' The little man spluttered an interruption.

'What I was about to say was that your wife is expecting me back for breakfast. Scrambled eggs, no less!'

'You'd better go then; you know how she hates to be kept waiting. We can talk later. I'll get this job finished before Laura gets back.'

The Prof approached the door to the lounge and checked his watch; it was 11 o'clock. He owed cook a big vote of thanks for it was she who had alerted him out of his comfortable lethargy as he'd relaxed in the warmth of her kitchen. With breakfast over, her prophetic words, "Time for your meeting, Giles! You know how the old lady hates to be kept waiting!" reminded him of his immediate engagement. Strange how her words were almost identical to those her husband had used at the stables.

He knocked and went in. It was Laura he saw, not her mother! She was dressed in smart jodhpurs and boots, with black riding jacket and lots of colour in her cheeks either from her outing with Sam or from the fire she was preparing. The Prof wasn't sure which.

'I'm sorry, I thought I'd be meeting....'

'That's quite all right, Giles. Mother won't be long! Well, speak of the devil!'

Isabella Ramsden entered, nodded to her daughter who left, without uttering another word, and closed the door behind her.

'Please sit down, Giles. Did you sleep well?'

The Prof nodded. 'It was a long day yesterday and I needed no rocking!'

'Good! That discussion, at dinner last night, was most illuminating. I hope we might continue the subject again quite soon but, now that we're alone, I wish to give you a first hand account of everything that took place on my birthday fourteen years ago and before you have the opportunity to ask any of the others for their version of events. Isn't that what usually happens in the whodunits?'

He smiled and relaxed as he waited for the matriarch of Maskelyne Hall to continue.

Isabella Ramsden went over to the writing desk, produced a notebook and pencil and brought them over to him.

'I wasn't sure you'd want to take notes this morning. My little message was a trifle on the cryptic side, I'm afraid, but there must be many questions you want answered. The truth is what I want but I am aware that it may not be that simple. Memory fades in the fullness of time. No one knows that better than I do, but what happened that night, fourteen years ago, is as vivid as if it had happened yesterday. Yet, what took place didn't make too much sense; I'm certain we all missed something! Got things in the wrong order and jumped to the wrong conclusions. The longer we wait and the more the years go by, the harder it is to come to terms with it. We need to know the truth and you can help!'

Mrs. Ramsden started to sob quietly.

The Prof was genuinely moved but, as he watched her dab her eyes with her handkerchief, he couldn't help feeling that every mannerism, gesture and look were part of a calculated performance; a performance designed by Magicians, the world over, and known as The Art of Misdirection; the Conjuror's stock-in-trade!

'Why don't we just start at the beginning? Try and tell me everything that led to the tragedy. Leave nothing out, no matter how insignificant. If I need clarification about anything …I will ask.'

Mrs. Ramsden clasped her hands in her lap and took a deep breath.

'Every year, on the 31st October – the night of my birthday and, as you well know, the anniversary of the death of Harry Houdini, my husband Jack entertained the household with his latest version of an old illusion. This annual event started when the Second World War was finally over. It had become a sort of family milestone. Jack worked tirelessly, from one year to the next, to improve ideas of some of the wonderful masters of illusion, past and present, in order to add a new dimension to a classic of magic. He staged the premiere before his captive audience and it was always held in the library, prior to dinner, when the family gathered to celebrate my birthday.'

Isabella Ramsden again dabbed her eyes with her handkerchief.

'Jack was a methodical and meticulous man who left little to chance. He had already performed two variations at previous annual occasions; one, of David Devant's *The Artist's Dream* and the other, an unusual treatment of Le Roy's *Levitation Act*.'

Isabella Ramsden paused as The Prof scribbled some notes. Before she could elaborate any further he decided to intervene.

'Pardon me for interrupting at this stage, Mrs. Ramsden, but you've just mentioned two of your husband's earlier performances and I'd like you to clarify something for me. You see it could be vital!'

'Isabella, if you please, Giles. I think we can drop the formality!'

'If that is what you wish! It might be in both our interests, Mrs...er...Isabella! Now where was I? Ah yes, I wanted to ask you about those previous performances. You mentioned The Artist's Dream and it is another interesting co-incidence that this illusion was credited to Chung Ling Soo when he worked with Herrmann. But to get back to the point, you see if I were not mistaken, Jack would normally have used an assistant for *The Artist's Dream* and the *Levitation Act*. Am I right?'

'Why, of course you are. I should have mentioned that. He always had his assistant for the birthday performance, including several practices beforehand.'

'I have one further question to ask, at this stage. Were you always aware of the identity of your husband's assistant?'

'How very strange that you should ask!'

Mrs. Isabella Ramsden paused for several seconds before continuing her reply.

'Now that I come to think of it, the answer to your question would have to be *no*! Jack was always careful to make sure that his assistant was in some form of disguise. The face would be covered, or she would be kept entirely out of sight during rehearsals! He believed it all added to the mystery. She never stayed for dinner.'

'You refer to his assistant as...she. Was his assistant always female?'

'Yes, as a matter of fact she was.'

'Thank you .That's very helpful. Please go on.'

'For most of 1952 Jack had made no secret of the fact that he was going to try and recreate the Bullet Catching Trick of Chung Ling Soo using a different kind of rifle. He made a trip to America at the end of May and his mood changed entirely when he returned. He told me he was almost ready to perform the most amazing illusion ever shown in this part of the world. It was to be something that closely resembled *The Substitution Trunk* but with the library acting as the Trunk and displaying a transformation scene of earth shattering dimension using Robert Louis Stevenson's characters *Dr. Jekyll and Mr. Hyde*. Those were the words he used to describe his intended treat for my birthday. Before I carry on can I now ask you a question?'

'Please do, Isabella.'

'You opened the safe yesterday, didn't you?'

'Yes I did, but only after a little hiccup with numbers!'

'Whatever you discovered somehow contained the clue to Jack's change of mood. You will decide how best to unravel the puzzle but can you give me a hint about your observations and any possible ideas you may have at this stage?'

'The obvious items that interest me are Jack's diary containing entries for the month of May and June and, in particular the dates May 29, 30, 31 and June 1. I also believe the words *Golden Anniversary Convention, SAM, The Hotel Statler* and the initials *K.A.* are of special importance. There was a map of *Boston, Massachusetts, U.S.A*, notes on new variations of special illusions, a brochure of Hotel Statler and a long thin bladed stiletto dagger!'

'Yes, I thought that might intrigue you.'

'There was one other entry in the diary. *How a bottle opener can open more than bottles!* Now that is a puzzle! "Solve that, my boy", I can hear Jack say, "and you're in business!" I have a hunch, as my American friends might say, that a trip to The States could provide many answers! Now you were telling me about Dr. Jekyll and Mr. Hyde and how Jack was…you said his mood changed. In what way?'

'Jack was forever the eternal schoolboy…especially when it concerned a new treatment of the impossible. He showed a fervour and enthusiasm I'd rarely seen before. The cloak and dagger visits by his assistant became more frequent until one day, in September I think, I overheard Jack having an almighty row with her, in the library, during a rehearsal. I couldn't hear what they were saying but it

42

sounded like...*she was threatening...blackmail*! Anyway the next thing I knew was Jack told me she had gone for good and he was altering his act to suit. *We never saw her again!'*

'Can we get back to the night of your birthday?'

'Jack had spent most of the day, in the library, arranging props and other equipment then, at about 7 o'clock, he called everyone to the library to examine the room.'

'At this stage I want you to be very specific and list everyone who was at Maskelyne Hall when your husband called on them to come to the library.'

'Let's see! There were Doreen and George, our longstanding cook and groom, my eldest son Victor and my daughter Laura, and me, of course. That makes five! Conrad was there with his wife Mabel. That's seven! Finally, my youngest son Edgar and his fiancée Sally make a total of nine!' Isabella declared, as she counted everyone present on her fingers.

'Haven't you forgotten someone?' The Prof was still making notes on his pad as he asked the question.

'I don't think so....'

'What about Jack, your husband?' He looked up from his writing as he spoke. 'A grand total of ten, I'd say! Wouldn't you?'

'I'm sorry, I just didn't think to include Jack, yet you're absolutely correct as you were asking about everyone who was at Maskelyne Hall on that night. Yes, yes, I agree. A grand total of ten!'

'I have to be accurate, Isabella. After all he was a central figure in the whole affair.'

The Prof smiled reassuringly before inviting Isabella to continue.

'Did everyone go into the library?'

'No, I don't think so! Sally stayed well outside; she hadn't yet been introduced to her intended father-in-law. Edgar was going to do that after the birthday performance but I did hear him say that his fiancée might wash her hair before meeting Jack. That was when I overheard Laura telling Edgar to get her to use the bathroom opposite the main one as she was going to take a bath.'

'What about the others?'

'Mrs. Gardner was to carry on with her normal chores. She was to check that the windows were locked and curtains drawn and then retire to her kitchen and lock the back door. Her husband, George, said he would go outside and guard the windows, making sure "there was no jiggery pokery " there. Everyone laughed. All the time Jack was urging us to ensure that the library was entirely empty, except for himself, and that no one was left hiding in the room and that the room was locked with no place for anyone to enter. Conrad and Mabel checked behind the Japanese screen then they announced that they were going for a short walk in the grounds until they were called back for the performance. Victor made sure the safe was locked before hurrying off to the lounge. Edgar was next to leave but said he would wait with me in the hall in case there was any skulduggery!'

'You were left in the room, alone with Jack?'

'Yes I was!'

Isabella Ramsden's eyes misted over at this point and The Prof waited patiently for her composure to return.

'Please continue, but, before you do, can you tell me if the gun was in the library before you left?'

'Yes it was! It was on its stand in front of the Chung Ling Soo poster. I should have mentioned that Victor spent some moments examining the gun just after he'd checked the safe.'

A puzzled frown appeared as The Prof made his next comment.

'And then he went off to the lounge?'

'Yes.'

'What made you think he was going there?'

'Because he said so!'

'Aah...! Did you make a final check of the room before leaving?'

'Yes. Jack asked me to look around, to satisfy myself that nobody was hiding. Then he told me I could go out and lock the door.'

'So you were definitely the last to leave the room and Jack was alone when you went out and closed the door?'

'Yes!'

'You're absolutely positive of that?'

'Yes! No doubts at all!'

'You then locked the door on the outside?'

'Yes.'

'Where did you put the key?'

'I kept it in my hand and Edgar was with me all the time.'

'To make sure there was no skulduggery!' The Prof smiled as he read from his notes.

'So what happened after the door was locked?'

'Nothing! There was silence and then the sound of footsteps on the wood floor. You may have noticed that it isn't easy to be aware of noises coming from the library, what with the walls and door being thick, most noise is muffled!'

'Could you identify any sound that came from the library?'

'The first noise I heard clearly was Jack's voice. I heard him say, *"Leave that alone!"* There was no reply to that. Then Jack said, *"Put your mask on!"* and this was followed by *"No, no...don't touch that...it might be...."* A shot rang out followed by a dull thump.'

The Prof raised a hand to stop Mrs. Ramsden from continuing and hurriedly made notes as he sat on the edge of his seat listening to what was almost a running commentary of events that took place fourteen years ago. He nodded to her to continue.

'Jack's voice could be heard again after a short silence. He said, *"Good God, what have you done, Hyde? We must keep the secret...so go now!"*

Isabella Ramsden was shaking as she recalled the events of that final night of her husband's life. In an agitated voice she continued her story.

'I froze, for a moment, before being pushed from behind. Edgar was steering me towards the door. Prodding me into action. He was yelling, "The key, where's the bloody key?" My hands were trembling and I struggled to get the key in the lock. There seemed to be pandemonium everywhere. Cook was rushing from the kitchen and I could hear the front door opening and closing. Conrad and Mabel were barging into the hallway and "old" George was almost colliding with Victor who seemed to be coming from the lounge. When I finally turned the key and opened the door, I saw...Jack! He was lying, on the floor, to the left and just in front of the bookcases with his head turned to look at my portrait. He was holding his chest and there was blood on his hands. Not very much; but it was the colour! Edgar shouted, "I'll get the girls", and dashed off up the stairs. I was the first person at Jack's side after he was shot. He seemed very composed and was speaking in a whisper.'

'What did he say and please be as accurate as you can? It could be vitally important!'

'He said, *"I didn't mean it to end like this,"* then he started to cough. He coughed a couple of times but didn't seem to be in great pain!'

'Endorphins!' muttered The Prof, under his breath.

'What did you say?'

'Nothing, I was thinking of something a medical professor once told me. Please go on!'

'Jack was trying so hard to speak again but I had to go very close to him to hear what he was saying. And what he said next made no sense at all! He looked up at me and said, *"Did you see Dr. Hyde?"* He closed his eyes and never spoke again!'

'He was in shock, Isabella! He'd be confused and desperate to remain lucid.'

'Yes, I suppose so. As I was saying Jack closed his eyes but he was still breathing. I rose and said I would phone for an ambulance but Victor stopped me and said it had already been done. I looked around at everyone who'd crowded into the room; Laura was there in her bare feet and wearing a bathrobe; Sally, with a towel on her head, was clinging to Edgar and asking if he was dead; Conrad and Mabel were at the door, holding hands, and Mrs Gardner, having crossed over to the windows, announced that the windows were still locked and the curtains still drawn.'

'Where was Mr. Gardner? Were you aware of his presence?'

'Oh, he was talking to Victor. Victor had rushed over to the gun on the stand and, as he was coming back, I heard him suggesting that perhaps I should lie down. Victor had a word with cook and she took me to the lounge and poured me a brandy. Laura and Conrad made Jack comfortable until the ambulance arrived. They took Jack to Dumfries but I was told that he never regained consciousness!'

Isabella Ramsden's words were reduced to a barely audible croak.

'And then what?'

'When the police arrived they searched the room and interviewed everybody. The gun was still fixed on the stand. The windows and safe were checked. They were locked. There was a smudge of blood on the locking device of the safe, which later turned out to be Jack's No explanation was ever given as to how it might have got there.'

Isabella Ramsden sighed deeply at this point and appeared exhausted.

'Can I get you anything, Isabella? Something to drink, perhaps?'

'No, I'll be all right in a moment or two!'

'There are some questions I must ask, at this stage. If you don't know the answers please say so. It really is important that I know exactly what was found in the library immediately after the shot was fired.'

'I'll do my best!'

'Was anything found on the library floor close to where Jack was lying; I mean something that wasn't there when you were searching the room earlier?'

'No, not to my knowledge!'

'No bullet or something resembling a bullet?'

'No, definitely not! You see, when Jack was shot the bullet was apparently still lodged in his body!'

'Hmm! At the post-mortem did the pathologist find a second bullet in the body …say in the stomach or gullet?'

'No! Only one shot was fired! I thought I made that clear!' Mrs Ramsden appeared slightly puzzled at this line of questioning.

'You say the gun was still fixed on the stand after the shot was fired!'

'Yes.'

'Did the police find any fingerprints on the gun other than those of your husband?'

'No! Only Jack's!'

'But didn't you say that Victor examined the gun before he left the room? Surely his prints were on the gun?'

'Victor *did* examine the gun but I'm not sure if he touched it. I can't recall him doing that.'

There was silence in the lounge on that Saturday morning; that is, except for the sound of The Prof's pencil as he made a few more notes.

'Can we go back to what you heard coming from the library before you heard the shot! I mean, from what you said, it seems you only heard Jack speak?'

'That's not strictly true! I was sure I heard two people talking in the room. It's just that I…'

'Well?'

'…It's just that I could only make out what Jack was saying! I still swear I could hear two people talking to each other!'

'He couldn't have been talking like a ventriloquist does, could he? You know - making it sound as if there were two when, in actual fact, he was the only one there!'

'You mean…throwing his voice?'

'Yes, I couldn't put it better myself!'

'I don't think so, but….'

'We'll come back to that. You mentioned that he was very excited about performing a transformation scene with Dr. Jekyll and Mr. Hyde as the theme…do you know more about his plan? I mean …was he going to change from one to the other or have both in the same room at the same time?'

'I rather got the impression that he intended to change from one to the other with such a marked difference in the appearance of the two characters that they couldn't possibly be the same person! Then he planned, I think, to introduce both at the same time before getting Hyde to *vanish into thin air!* We never reached the part of the performance when the two individuals were together, yet I swear…'

'Yes?'

'…Believe me, I swear I could hear the two of them talking to each other. No, that's not quite right. I could hear Jack talking to someone. He sounded angry and irritated that, for whatever reason, his arranged plan was not being properly carried out. Jack was talking but it seemed to be a one-way conversation. The other person didn't answer. I got the strange feeling that the other person didn't want to answer. Either that, or it was so muffled, it didn't register!'

'So you don't know if the other person in the room was male or female – or even if he or she was in the room at all?'

'No, but someone or something fired that gun. And Jack's blood! On the locking mechanism of the safe! That didn't get there by itself, unless…'

'Unless, what?'

'…Unless Jack managed to reach the safe, open it and hide whatever it was and then….'

'And then get back to where you found him slumped on the floor in front of the bookcases! I'm sorry, Isabella but the inside of the safe is too small to hold anything large and anyway, when you heard the shot...' The Prof looked back over his notes before resuming, '...when you heard the shot this was followed by a dull thump, presumably the sound of Jack falling to the floor. You see there just wasn't time for him to move to the safe and back again!'

'I suppose you're right!'

The Prof closed the notebook.

'Thank you, Isabella, that wasn't easy for you! You said, at the beginning, that what happened didn't make too much sense and that you were sure you'd missed something. That it was possible that you might have got things in the wrong order and jumped to the wrong conclusions. Now can you be more specific; can you possibly pinpoint something that leads you to make such statements?'

Mrs. Ramsden was silent for a few seconds.

'Yes, I think I can,' she said. 'Something Jack said that night has puzzled me for almost fourteen years. Despite all the experts saying that Jack would be confused and in shock after being shot I know that he would never have blundered with his final words to me! When he said, *"Did you see Dr. Hyde?"* he really did mean what he said...but why?'

The Prof looked at the matriarch of Maskelyne Hall and his blue eyes took on a steely determination.

'That's what I intend to find out. Now if you'll excuse me, Isabella, I'll begin my investigations!'

Chapter 5
THE IRON MAIDEN

Having eaten a late breakfast The Prof excused himself from lunching with Laura and her mother and retired to his bedroom to look over his notes. The meeting with Isabella had provided much food for thought; the others would have to be consulted and statements taken and compared, but he was rapidly coming to the conclusion that he had more questions than answers.

The items found in the safe had a significant part to play in the whole chain of events. He was sure of that! Time enough for decisions to be made. After all it was almost fourteen years since Jack's mysterious death. Time was on his side! A few days, weeks or even months wouldn't make a lot of difference.

The contents of the safe set an intriguing puzzle. *Golden Anniversary* and *SAM* were easy! Logic told him that *SAM* was likely to be The Society of American Magicians. Strange though that the name Sam should come up again after "old" George had told him about *Sam* the Hunter – Samson by name.

The Hotel Statler was, presumably, where the Golden Anniversary Convention had been held and the *Map of Boston, Massachusetts, U.S.A,* an absolute giveaway! A few phone calls would soon confirm if The Society of American Magicians had indeed held their 1952 Convention in Boston with The Hotel Statler as the venue, but the initials *K.A.*and the cryptic words about a *bottle opener* might not be so easy to solve! Boston seemed to hold the key, but that would have to wait! The key? He produced it from his pocket. It was the key to the cellar of Maskelyne Hall. And the cellar was where Jack had stored all his magical props and where he had lovingly designed and made his furniture of illusion and magic.

Giles had asked for the key when he'd excused himself from having lunch. The cellar was probably where the gun could be found. The gun was one of the items, from that fateful night, that wasn't still in the library!

What else had been missing? The stand, of course, on which the gun had been fixed! He'd like to examine that as well!

Looking over his scribbles he was struck by the fact that, if Isabella had been telling the truth, every one of the others at Maskelyne Hall, apart from Jack, and Edgar who had remained with Isabella had been, singly or in pairs, in a different place at the time of the murder! If it was *murder!* Any one of them could have killed Jack or worked with an accomplice to commit the crime assuming he, she or they could get into the room without being noticed by the others. Unless…! A new thought occurred. Unless Jack had been killed from…*outside the room!*

There was one other possibility! Jack's pre-performance arrangements, the suggestions about Jekyll and Hyde and the voices heard by Isabella Ramsden might all have been part of an elaborate plot to end his own life, but something didn't ring true! He would have to examine that gun and stand.

The door to the cellar was at the rear of the house under the back stairs and not far from the kitchen area. Young Giles Dawson had been allowed to visit the cellar, on one occasion, under the supervision of Jack Ramsden, a long time ago. He remembered the place as an Aladdin's cave of theatrical mystery that had helped to fire his imagination and love of magical presentation.

There had been one other time, one other visit to the cellar grotto. Someone had stolen the key, he couldn't remember whom: they had all used the cellar for one of their games. They had played *Murder* on that occasion and, when their misdemeanour was discovered, all had been reprimanded with the parental warning that such an area was definitely not a playground, but a space abounding with *danger!* A space where an accident could mean *death!*

The Prof turned the key in the lock, opened the cellar door and switched on the lights. Closing the door behind him he descended the stone steps into the cellar that ran the entire length and breadth of Maskelyne Hall. The atmosphere was dry and pleasantly warm as he looked around him. At one end of the cellar, at the front of the house, was the workshop; the inner sanctum where Jack had elegantly fashioned a wealth of furniture used by stage magicians. Works of art, of all shapes and sizes, designed to create doubts in the minds of audiences prepared to suspend their disbelief had been made there. The door to the workshop was locked; it required a separate key and he did not have it.

He really didn't need to gain access though: the windows, the only windows in the place, which allowed someone working on the inside to see the storage area of the cellar, gave him the chance to look inside at the lathes, circular saws, work benches and hand tools of a dead craftsman. There was nothing there for which he was searching.

Picking his way carefully along the lines of magical artifacts he made towards the other end at the rear of the house, passing the brick pillars which supported the ceiling throughout, to where the reason for the dry and pleasantly warm atmosphere became clear.

A wall of concrete blocks enclosed an oil-fired heating system that obviously supplied at least some parts of Maskelyne Hall. He now knew the answer to what had puzzled him since his earlier visit to the library. What had been niggling him was how the library had been so comfortable despite the installation of the safe, which had put the fireplace and chimney out of commission.

With the initial inspection over, he began to wander in and out of the lanes of props and attempt to identify each and every one with the relish of a connoisseur. The main purpose of his task was to find the gun and its stand, but nothing in this treasure-trove was going to be overlooked.

He felt he was with friends! The subdued hum of the heating system disguised the profound silence of the cellar without disturbing his concentration, making him feel that he wasn't alone. It was a feeling he was beginning to enjoy. As he surveyed everything around him the terrifying thought manifested itself that perhaps he wasn't alone; that perhaps someone or something was stalking him! But no such thoughts were entering his head at this stage. Not yet!

His first stop was at a set of wooden shelves on which rested countless boxes containing soft-core ropes, Chinese Linking Rings, chains and hand cuffs, Chinese lanterns, packs of playing cards, dice, Cups and Balls of varying sizes, ribbons, handkerchiefs and larger cloths of coloured silks. Each box was labelled and some even exhibited the names of prominent performers associated with many of the items of close-up magic.

He moved along past plinths, baskets and pedestals then stopped again at a large wardrobe. As he inspected the contents of full-length robes, black cloaks with hoods and gloves, conical hats and all the paraphernalia that created images in the minds of receptive audiences, he became interested in the assortment of masks available. He had just picked out a couple and had them in his hands when he thought he heard the sound of a door closing. He stopped, put the masks back and looked around the vast storeroom. There were no signs of anyone, or anything, just row upon row of boxes, crates, large items of furniture and those brick pillars that, if memory served him correctly, had made excellent hiding places on one occasion during his childhood.

Looking towards the ceiling he noted the pulleys and weights hanging from above. They were secured by ropes and tied to hooks attached to the wall. There was nothing to concern him there except…a feeling of *unease!*

He picked up the masks again; either could've been Mr.Hyde. That, at least, explained one problem. There was something else that had to be there! Now where was it? There had to be one! Every magician, of that era, could produce one, and every magician could produce almost anything, out of one! The top hat!

To have really been authentic Jack, as Dr. Jekyll, would have worn a top hat. Or was he being over influenced by the Hollywood version and Spencer Tracy's portrayal in the 1941 film? It had to be here somewhere! He lifted some fans from a drawer and smiled as he recognised one that might have been used in the portrait that was hanging in the library. The top hat could wait. It would have to wait! Much more important than the hat was the gun; he had to find the gun!

The next port of call brought an even bigger smile. He was stopped in his tracks at the sight of a galvanized iron milk can complete with fixing straps and, beside it, a large metal-lined mahogany tank with a plate-glass front, similar to the one Houdini had used when he broke a bone in his foot!

As he turned away from the replicas of those great escapes, he heard a noise that raised the hair on the back of his neck. It was a whisper, almost inaudible and meaningless yet, at the same time, diabolical and threatening. It came from God-knows-where like a darting movement of furtive feet or the sound of someone who did not wish to be heard. The quickening of his pulse combined with the stop-go action of his lungs brought beads of cold sweat to his brow. Where had the noise come from?

'Who's there?' he called out, but words that came from a parched larynx were met with impending silence.

He looked at his watch and realised he'd been in the cellar for the best part of an hour. He moved more rapidly, glanced at boxes of theatrical posters, the memorabilia of a golden age of magic, mentally noted a bathing hut on wheels, swept past several gigantic playing cards hanging from a rail and closed in on an arsenal of swords and knives. Straight swords, curved scimitars, a miscellaneous collection of knives in a cabinet and, what he'd been looking for since he'd entered the cellar, a stand supporting a rifle.

He felt infinitely safer having the swords within easy reach but it was the rifle that grabbed his attention.

It was a Short Magazine Lee Enfield or SMLE Mk 111, simplified to allow mass production and used during the Second World War. It was a .303 calibre rifle with a turn bolt system using ammunition clips of five yet capable of firing single rounds. Closer inspection revealed slight modifications but examination of the stand convinced The Prof that it would not, realistically, have withstood the recoil from the firing of this type of rifle, without some additional means of support. It interested him that Jack had changed from using a front-loading weapon, which had been used in the Chung Ling Soo act, to this type of rifle that he'd used in training exercises. He knew the capabilities of the gun and, even with refinements, doubted its use as an implement of suicide.

Satisfied that he had achieved what he came for he was about to end his inspection of the dead man's collection of priceless stage props when his peripheral vision instinctively drew him towards a group of devices that seemed to belong to a medieval torture chamber.

The Rack was the first thing he saw. It comprised an open, horizontal wooden frame on which a person would be placed.

Moveable bars at each end allowed wrists and ankles to be tied and levers were used to stretch the victim in opposite directions. This means of torture had been used in olden days to extract confessions of heresy and The Prof was now gazing in awe at a piece of apparatus made to create the equivalent of *Sawing a Woman in Half.*

Alongside, in an upright position, was a hinged box shaped like something that would have contained an Egyptian Mummy. The box was closed and, at the back, he could see the sharp points of metal spikes that poked through holes. He was ready to open the front and check inside when the noise, heard earlier, happened again.

It was closer to him this time and, as he looked upwards, he only had time to grasp that it was too late! Whatever it was that hit him was heavy! It crashed down and caught him a blow to the temple! Not enough to kill him but enough to cause him to have the 'lights' go out and lose consciousness!

When he came to, it was the perfume he recognized first. He could only have been out for seconds, certainly not more than a minute or two, when he saw the face looking down at him! It was the same face he'd seen at the library window when he was examining the safe. It was Laura!

As the inky blackness cleared he wondered why she was looking down at him from a strange angle? And then he knew...*fear!* He was lying on his back...*in a coffin!* Laura was bending over him and the lid of the coffin was high above her head and iron spikes were sprouting from inside the lid.

'Come on, Giles,' a voice was saying, 'let's get you out of there before that thing comes down on you!'

With her help he climbed out of the box.

'Naughty boy!' she said wiping a trickle of blood from his forehead. 'You shouldn't have got involved with *The Iron Maiden*! You never know where she's been! Anyway, Daddy always said it was dangerous to play in here!'

'I thought I heard you come in!' he said and winced as she applied a bit more first aid to his brow.

'I rather doubt that! You were completely "out for the count" by the time I got here! I was coming to tell you there had been a phone call for you when I heard an almighty crash that seemed to come from the direction of the kitchen. By the time I was aware the noise had come from the cellar, and not the kitchen, I'd wasted a few seconds. When I looked in here you were nowhere to be seen; then I spotted the heap of weights and chains beside The Iron Maiden, which was lying on the floor, instead of being upright as she normally is. I heard a groan and hurried down here to find you wedged into the open box. If that lid had closed I shudder to think what might have happened!'

'But how did I get in there?'

'You were hit on the head, Giles, don't you remember? I guess you've had a very lucky escape. That block and tackle, hanging from the ceiling, must have come loose. It probably wasn't securely tied!'

'Yes, but that still doesn't explain how I ended up inside the box, does it! That box was closed when I was hit on the head. I'm sure it was!'

'You were hit on the head, Giles! Your memory may be playing tricks on you!'

'Unless....'

'Unless what, Giles?'

'Oh, nothing! I thought I'd heard someone earlier. Never mind!'

'Let's close the lid on this, Giles, and you can help me get the old girl on her feet again. After that you can hang on to me and we'll get you out of here!'

'Ready when you are!'

She manoeuvred him clear of the prostrate "maiden" and closed the lid. The metallic crash reverberated throughout the cellar making The Prof shudder.

'Did someone just walk over your grave?' she asked as she tightened her hold on his arm.

'You could say that!' he said responding to her touch. 'You might be interested to know that I'm beginning to feel better already!'

A decidedly groggy professor helped Laura get The Iron Maiden into the upright position again before he spoke once more.

'You said you were coming to tell me about a phone call!'

'Yes, it was Freddie, Freddie Oldsworth. He said he was phoning from Stockton racecourse but I told him you were otherwise engaged!'

'Do you know what he wanted?'

'No, he didn't say but mentioned he would ring back later. Now, if you think you're well enough to walk with me perhaps we can go!'

56

'I was almost finished in here anyway!'

Laura noticed the colour, which had drained from The Prof's cheeks, was starting to return. She took a fresh grip on his arm and began to steer him towards the cellar steps.

When they were at the top she switched off the lights, pushed him gently out into the hallway, then closed and locked the door.

'Oh, I forgot to tell you, Edgar and Sally arrived when you were exploring the cellar.

Edgar was very surprised to know you were here, you see we hadn't mentioned you were coming for the weekend. He's looking forward to meeting you again. They've gone to freshen up, so we'll meet them when they come down.'

Laura had another look at The Prof's injured forehead, moistened her fingers by running them inside her lips before touching him tenderly on the area that now showed signs of bruising. 'You'll be as right as rain after a drink,' she claimed, 'and especially after I've practised my first aid on your fevered brow!'

They headed for the lounge, arms entwined.

Laura opened the lounge door, ushered The Prof inside and saw her mother reading by the fire.

'Have we a place for the walking wounded, Mama?'

'Goodness gracious!' Isabella exclaimed with concern, 'Whatever has happened? You look as if you've been in an accident!'

'Yes mother, Giles had a minor disagreement with a maiden!'

'Anyone I know? Or is that a secret?'

'Can I just say that, in her time, she could be very persuasive!' echoed Laura with a mischievous smile.

Chapter 6
DO YOU BELIEVE IN GHOSTS?

The Prof knew that he was only dreaming; what else could it be? The sound of footsteps on the stairs coming ever closer to his bedroom; the quickening of his heart beat that produced deafening echoes deep down inside his ears and kept strict tempo with the throbbing in his temples. Ghostly fingers were turning the door handle to gain access to his…tomb! Was that what it was going to be? What is the room you enter without leaving? Wasn't that part of Laura's riddle? Was that really what it was going to be? His tomb! He had to open his eyes, to identify and confront this being! Was it a being with evil intent? He tried to shout; but no sound came! One final effort and The Prof was sitting bolt upright with beads of perspiration, cold and wet, the product of fear, on his brow…! But there was nothing at the foot of his bed and the door was still closed!

He had been dreaming after all; but that had happened years ago! What was happening to him now was…well… different! Standing in front of him this time was The Grim Reaper; a personification of death. A cloaked figure…a skeleton? It could be a skeleton! It was certainly thin enough, cloaked from head to foot in black and holding…! A scythe? No, not a scythe…! Dear God, not a scythe…but a gun!

It was a rifle: a .303 calibre rifle and one that he had fired at some time or other. He tried to think of the name. It was lethal! It was…?

The Prof could only think he must be in a fairground. The figure holding the rifle was aiming at a target and he was standing in the way. He was standing in the way of The Reaper. And he couldn't move! A kind of Aunt Sally; for a bullet!

He shouted out. He could still do that …but it wasn't his voice! It sounded like Jack! But Jack who? "No, no…don't touch that…it might be…!" A shot rang out! It must have hit the target for the sound of the bell ringing was much too vivid to be just part of a dream. The bell was ringing, again and again and again! Then a hand on his shoulder was gently shaking him awake. The sweat was still there on his brow; the noise of his heart still pulsated in his ears and his temple still throbbed…!

'It's Freddie, Giles! He's phoning from Stockton. Do you feel up to speaking to him?'

Laura was gently coaxing him out of his nightmare.

He rose from the comfort of the armchair. The double brandy, courtesy of Laura, had induced sleep that had continued into that nightmare!

'Hello, Freddie, so sorry I missed you when you called earlier! Was there something you wanted?'

'Well, yes. There was something. Something we talked about on Thursday. Is she or isn't she?'

'Come again, Freddie!'

'Is she or isn't she; pretty I mean?'

The Prof looked across the room at Laura before he answered. Then, lowering his voice and covering the mouthpiece, he said, 'Yes! Very!'

'I'll take your word for it, Giles!'

There was a short pause before Freddie continued.

'Now I know you've no transport, but I wondered if we could somehow meet up somewhere for the evening…say near Lockerbie. You see Penny has taken the girls to their Gran's for the weekend….'

'Hang on a minute, Freddie!' He put a hand over the mouthpiece and turned to Laura.

'Is there any way I can get into town and back again tonight?'

'Well I could drive you there; but I have a better idea! Let me have a word with that man on the other end of the phone!'

He handed the telephone over and left her to have a muted conversation with Freddie Oldsworth whilst he went to speak with Isabella. When he looked up again she had already put the receiver down and was looking quite smug as she came across.

'That's settled then! I've given your friend in Stockton instructions and, if his sense of direction is as good as his racing knowledge, he'll be here for dinner! We'll make arrangements to give him a bed for the night once he gets here. Now then, if my ears don't deceive me, I believe you are about to meet baby brother after more than twenty years!'

Before The Prof had time to express his astonishment the lounge door flew open and, framed in the doorway was Edgar Ramsden, and his wife, Sally!

There was little or no recognition between the two men as The Prof rose to face the comparative stranger standing in the doorway. More than twenty years had passed since they'd last seen each other and Edgar had only been eight or nine years old. He was now in his early thirties with dark brown hair, slightly balding, and a sallow complexion. He wore beige corduroy trousers, white shirt and chocolate brown cardigan with leather patches at the elbows. He appeared slight of stature; but then The Prof remembered him as a rather puny little boy, whilst his brothers, on the other hand, had always been in the "well built" category.

Edgar's wife, Sally was slim, dark haired and appeared an inch or two taller than her husband; probably an illusion, he thought! She wore a high-necked, knee length navy blue dress that accentuated her slimness and exaggerated her height. His initial thoughts were more about her striking resemblance to Laura: height, weight and shape were almost identical and, apart from the hair colouring, they could have passed as sisters. He could almost hear Freddie say, in his racing parlance, "She could be a dead ringer, old son!"

There was an awkward silence before The Prof broke the ice.

'Well how nice to meet you both. Now, in your case, I don't think there's much doubt about which one is Edgar and which is Sally!'

'And you must be Giles. A real live professor! Allow me to introduce my wife!'

'You seem to have been in the wars!' Sally exclaimed as she closely examined the plaster adorning his forehead. 'Dare I ask if that's the handiwork of our very own Florence Nightingale?' she continued, taking a peek at Laura.

Edgar took a closer look at the bruising round the edge of the plaster.

'How did you manage to do that and, more importantly, will you be fit enough to ride out on Delilah tomorrow morning? She's quite a spirited mare, you know!'

The Prof raised an enquiring eyebrow at this remark.

'No I'm not clairvoyant, if that's what you're thinking!' Edgar explained. 'Sis told me you were going riding but that was before your accident!'

'I have a funny feeling that he will make a miraculous recovery before then!' said Laura. 'Now why don't we all sit down and compare notes! I'll see if Mrs. Gardner can offer us afternoon tea!'

As she left the room The Prof sat down opposite Edgar and Sally.

'Sis was telling me you lecture in the history of magic!' Edgar said with enthusiasm. 'That means that, not to put too fine a point on it, we're in the same line of business! More or less, wouldn't you say?'

'That sounds interesting! I'd like to hear more!'

'Don't believe a word he says, Giles! Big brother knows best!' Victor swaggered into the room, smoking a cigarette. 'Has Laura gone for the tea? I'm famished!' He spotted the plaster on Giles' forehead and his manner changed. 'Well you look the worse for wear, I must say! Has the phantom of Maskelyne Hall got to you already?' He produced a silver cigarette case, opened it and passed it across. 'Cigarette? You certainly look as if you could do with a smoke!'

'No, but thanks all the same! I stopped smoking cigarettes after I left the forces!'

The lounge door opened again and Conrad and Mabel came in. Conrad was rubbing his hands.

'We've been for a walk in the grounds and it's damned cold out there. Never mind, I believe Laura's bringing some tea.'

'Edgar was about to tell me he's in the magic business!' The sound of cups and saucers, rattling on the tea trolley, drowned out the final words.

'What was Edgar about to tell you when I made my noisy entrance?' enquired a smiling Laura as she brought the trolley to a halt.

'He was about to let the cat out of the bag or, in his case, about to pull the rabbit out of the hat!

All eyes turned to look in the direction of the unexpected voice.

'I thought you were sound asleep, mother. I hope you weren't disturbed!'

'Don't let that concern you, Laura. I've been listening to everything that's been said. I was just resting my eyes.'

Victor's sonorous words interrupted the quiet conversation between mother and daughter. 'What mother was referring to was the fact that Edgar runs a speciality shop; selling items of magic to budding amateurs in a busy part of Manchester!'

'Yes, that is exactly what I was referring to, in my own mystical way; but also that Edgar's wife runs a theatrical agency for dancers and magician's assistants; something she has always been interested in! You could say that they've both continued the work of my dear Jack, since his abrupt demise!'

'Do you understand, everyone,' said Laura, changing the subject, 'that this is the first time we have all been here in Maskelyne Hall since those war years. Not only do we have Giles back with us but we also have Mabel and Sally as part of the family. Don't you think that's something we should celebrate?'

'As the baby of the family I'll certainly be ready to enjoy any party that celebrates us coming together again in the house where we all had so much fun as kids. And I know how much my wife Sally will join in…'

Edgar paused in mid sentence.

'…But I wonder if Giles can tell me why he's come back to Maskelyne Hall?'

'Giles might be a little embarrassed to do that; but I can do it for him!'

The chilling voice of Victor was now the focus of attention for everyone in the room.

'The Prof has come back, believe it or not, to try and prove that one of us…is a murderer!'

If a pin had dropped it would have been deafening in the silence of that room at Maskelyne Hall as daylight began to fade on that last Saturday of October 1966.

'Unless…!'

'Unless what?' Several voices spoke as one.

Mabel, who was in the process of pouring a cup of tea, stopped as if frozen in time, before finally allowing the lid of the teapot to clatter on to the metal tray of the trolley.

All eyes moved to look at the petrified Mabel then back to Victor as he spoke again.

'Unless....' said Victor staring Giles in the eye, 'unless...! Do you believe in ghosts, professor? Do any of you believe in ghosts? I think Father did! Excuse me for a moment, I've got something stashed away and I think we could all do with a drop!'

With his jaw clamped tight Victor left the room in a stunned silence.

'What was all that about?' said Conrad as he helped Mabel tidy the tea things.

'Big brother indulging in one of his idiosyncrasies; he does that from time to time,' explained Laura. 'It will all be forgotten when he gets back with another of his indulgencies and invites us to share in it!'

Laura laid a comforting hand on The Prof's arm.

'Please forgive him, Giles. Another storm in a teacup!'

As the significance of her final remark became obvious Laura allowed a forced giggle to emerge and looked at Mabel who appeared to be on the verge of bursting into tears at any minute.

'Anyone for tea?' Mabel said, and the lounge became a place of animated conversation once more, dissolving the crisis, at least for the time being.

The return of Victor with a jeroboam of champagne paved the way for glasses to be introduced, filled and "clinked" together as friendships were renewed or, more aptly, as when, in days gone by, sworn enemies crossed swords as a prelude to a deadly duel!

Conviviality camouflaged the undercurrent of deception that The Prof sensed was still there in the room and he secretly looked forward to the arrival of his racing friend later that evening. He would then have at least one ally, perhaps two, if he could count on Laura!

Lights were turned on, the fire stoked and glasses replenished as daylight turned to dusk and then darkness. Whether it was the thought of the imminent arrival of Freddie, who would be well on his way to Maskelyne Hall by now, or the analgesic effect of the champagne, The

Prof really couldn't care less: the pain in his head had gone; it had disappeared like the "thing in the cellar" that afternoon!

Dinner at Maskelyne Hall was a lively affair that evening. There were nine seated at the table, the largest number for some time, the lamb was cooked to perfection and Freddie Oldsworth was greeted with the same enthusiastic appetite.

Having arrived in his five-year-old Triumph Spitfire, just in time to freshen up and come down to join the others in the dining room, Freddie was inundated with a chorus of questions before Isabella Ramsden called on everyone to "Please let Mr. Oldsworth catch his breath!"

'Call me Freddie, if you don't mind! You've already made me feel at home. I'd hate it if you stopped now!'

All through the main course at dinner, The Prof gave each and every one at the table a mental examination. Victor, whose accusation at tea had been blunt but irritatingly accurate, had hit the nail on the head. The Prof *was* here as a guest; but the real purpose of his visit was indeed to try and prove *murder* and, if *murder* were proven; there was a good chance that the murderer was sitting at the dinner table. Unless, of course, he or she was enjoying the same meal, as man and wife, in the quiet cosiness of the kitchen at Maskelyne Hall! He had no option but to include Mr. and Mrs. Gardner amongst his final list of suspects. All of them had been there at Maskelyne Hall on the night that Jack had been fatally shot in mysterious circumstances, and he would have to interview everyone and look at possible motives before he could solve this complex puzzle.

Isabella Ramsden seemed to be toying with her food, at the same time keeping her thoughts very much to herself whilst her only daughter, Laura, was monopolising Freddie in conversation, no doubt comparing notes about their respective sports cars or their mutual love of racing.

'Listen to this, everyone!' Laura banged the table. 'You know how we were all deep into a discussion about coincidence last night...that is except Edgar and Sally as they weren't here. Well I've got another one for you! I've just been asking Freddie about his visit to Stockton racecourse, I was wondering "why Stockton" when there were other meetings on today? I'll let Freddie take up the story!'

'I've had a fascination with Stockton ever since I became interested in The Sport of Kings...' Freddie glanced at the frowning Giles before continuing, '...mainly because of a man who was a genius, a brilliant mathematician and a punters' friend, all rolled into one! He was the brain behind the introduction of a wonderful system of evaluating racehorses and their performances and, in 1944 it was his shrewd judgement about one horse in particular...the name of which I'll omit for the moment...that led him to stake his reputation, as well as a small fortune, on this animal for the following season's classic races. The horse in question started his two-year-old career at Stockton and was never beaten at the course. He went on to win The Derby in 1945 run at Newmarket because of the war. That man, who made a note of the great potential of this horse and who had "put his money where his mouth was", influenced my life and virtually made me what I am today!'

'A racecourse reprobate!' interjected The Prof. 'But do carry on, Freddie!'

'As I also understood that this was to be the last day of racing at Stockton because of a change of name there really was no contest between it and the others; it had to be Stockton! From next March I believe the course will be known as Teesside Park, and they call that progress!'

'And,' said Laura, with a questioning look at Freddie, 'what was the name of that horse? You know, The Derby winner that never lost a race at Stockton, Mr. Oldsworth?'

'Curiously enough, the name of that horse is inextricably linked with magic and illusion! It was...*Dante!* I'll leave, Giles, our historian, to add a footnote.'

'Dante, real name August Harry Jansen, was born in Copenhagen in 1883, I think, and moved to St.Paul, Minnesota, U.S.A with his parents when he was six. The name Dante was suggested to him by one of the leading American Illusionists, Howard Franklin Thurston, with whom he toured before branching out on his own. He specialised in illusions involving transformations, and I believe it was just such an illusion that Jack wished to perform, in the library, when he unfortunately made his final exit!'

'So you see,' said Laura, 'there are several coincidences in all of this to make it more than interesting. But that's not quite the end of the story; for, when Freddie told me the name of the jockey who rode Dante, in 1944 and 1945, I couldn't believe it! It was Billy Nevett; the same person who rode Good Taste in Mother's prediction race in 1951!'

'Decidedly Spooky, as Mabel would say!' Isabella Ramsden was almost purring as she spoke. 'I hope we can continue to explore this subject afterwards over coffee in the lounge, but there's one question I would like Giles to answer. The question is the same one that Victor asked him before going for the champagne at teatime. He didn't give him enough time to answer so perhaps he would give us his answer now. Do you believe in ghosts, professor?'

'Yes, I do! At least...' he paused, put a finger to the area of bruising on his brow and his eyes took on that faraway look. Several seconds passed before he continued speaking. '...*I don't disbelieve in them*! But I'll expand on that at some future time. In the meantime....'

He didn't finish; all the lights in the dining room went out and the place was plunged into darkness.

Chapter 7
A-HAUNTING WE WILL GO

Total darkness is something the human eye can cope with, given time; eyes adjust to the lack of light with reasonable speed, like a camera lens, and in a lifetime a complete blackout can be both necessary and comforting.

Take the womb, prior to birth; in Laura's riddle, "the room we leave without entering". In this, darkness is unquestionably essential and comforting to the unborn child. Darkness was also essential and comforting for the Magic Lantern show of the early years, and the transformation into the cinema and theatre. But different people respond and react to darkness in different ways. And so it was when the lights went out at Maskelyne Hall that night.

Since darkness can be more intense immediately after lights have just gone out, inky blackness can cause disorientation, unease, fear, panic, and fright of horrifying proportions, much of it to do with previous experience, auto suggestion or the vivid workings of the imagination. Freud would have something to say on that subject.

When Conrad struck the match that produced the brief flicker of light in that darkened room The Prof looked around at the mixed expressions on the faces of those present. All appeared either slightly bemused or cheerfully entertained; all, that is, except…!

Darkness returned together with a yelp of pain from Conrad, who had burned his fingers; someone knocked over a chair and that was followed by a muffled curse, giggles of laughter, then silence. That was when everyone heard the knock at the door!

A hushed intake of breath was followed by a second knock. Then, as the door opened, a shimmer of light from a wavering candle illuminated the concerned features of "old" George.

'I'm terribly sorry, Ma'am, but something's gone wrong at the main fuse. I'll get everything sorted out as soon as possible!'

'That's all right, George. Perhaps it's because of the ghosts!'

'Beg your pardon, Ma'am?'

'Just my little joke, George! You see the lights went out just as The Prof was talking about ghosts; his timing was impeccable!'

'Is that so? Ah, well! I'll leave this candle for you until you can find others. Meanwhile I'll have a look at those fuses before the ghosts do any more damage; you see I thought I heard them in the cellar this afternoon when I was checking the heating!'

He lit a second candle and placed it on the table. As he did so The Prof made a mental note of that last remark. The little white-haired man turned to Laura.

'Did I hear you say that you and Giles were thinking of going riding in the morning?'

'Yes, George, that's if I can persuade him to get up in time and I can find some of Daddy's clothes to fit him!'

'That's fine then. I'll have the horses ready at the usual time! Oh! And remember the clocks go back one hour tonight!'

George Gardner turned and was about to leave the room when he said 'I'll let Doreen know that you're almost ready for coffee.'

'Thank you Gee Gee!' Laura's wink was not lost on the Family retainer. 'It looks as if we'll be having the coffee black tonight!'

That remark brought a creased smile, distorted in the upward glow from the candle in the little man's hand. To the watchful Giles the candlelit face was reminiscent of Bela Lugosi, the definitive Hollywood portrayer of Bram Stoker's Dracula. He half expected George to turn into a bat as he left the room and closed the door.

Edgar lifted the upturned chair and placed it back at the table.

The Prof studied him, very closely; looking for the signs that were unmistakable when Conrad struck his match a few moments ago; for it was Edgar who had been reacting to the darkness very differently from the others in the room. Something about the look was familiar: he'd seen it before, but he wasn't sure where!

It was significant! It had to be! And, if he could only remember where…and when, he was certain it would help to answer some questions that were puzzling him. That look on Edgar's face had been *fear!* It was still there but not nearly so marked. He had it under control. Edgar had a fear of the dark and he'd had it long ago when Giles knew him as a boy. But why should he be afraid? Many small boys were afraid of the dark but Edgar was no longer a small boy. It had to do with something in Edgar's past. He was sure of it.

'Why don't we go through to the lounge, light a few more candles and create the atmosphere for some proper ghost stories?'

Victor's suggestion was met with general approval and everyone traipsed, in the semi-darkness, through the connecting door to the lounge and the comfort of the log fire.

'A-haunting we will go, a-haunting we will go….' Mabel sang the words to the strains of "The Farmer's In His Den" and everyone joined in a garbled chorus of "…Ee-o My Daddy-o…! But that soon spluttered into an embarrassing silence as the revellers became conscious of what they were saying in the presence of the widow of Maskelyne Hall.

It was Giles who relieved the tension.

'Now, isn't that a coincidence?' he said. 'The words Mabel was singing, "A-Haunting We Will Go", was the title of the Laurel and Hardy film early in the war but there was someone in that film that we've just been talking about tonight! And that someone was Dante the magician!'

'That *is* interesting; do you think Mabel could be psychic, Giles?'

'I'm not sure, Mrs. Ramsden, but there's no harm in trying to find out.'

Giles acknowledged the reproachful look he received from the lady of the house but tried to signal to her that he had not forgotten to use her Christian name but had rather wanted to keep their pact as a secret.

'One person we haven't heard from on the question of premonitions is our new guest, Mr. Oldsworth. I do believe that racing people are superstitious and it would be interesting to know if you have had any experiences that altered your decision-making on the racecourse.'

'If you mean like the one your daughter told me about at dinner! The incident about Good Taste and the November Handicap! I rather doubt it. I'm afraid I rely almost entirely on mathematical science and the probability factor especially when it means backing my judgement with hard cash. That doesn't mean I would completely ignore gypsies warnings or such predictions. On the contrary, I might be inclined to allow them to strengthen my own calculations. You see I am all too aware that signs and signals, most of which are totally ignored, are constantly bombarding us and on the occasions when a prediction does come true we remember that and only that and choose to forget all the others.'

'So, can we take it that you don't believe in coincidence? And does that also apply to extrasensory perception?' The sneeringly sceptical sound of Victor's words metaphorically prodded Freddie for a reply.

'No, I didn't say that and I hope I didn't imply that either. The difficulty is making the distinction between the mundane coincidences that many of us experience, from time to time, and that extraordinary "bolt from the blue" that can unexpectedly make such an impact as to alter the course of events.'

'I'm not sure that I follow you.' declared Mabel making herself comfortable by squatting on the rug in front of the fire.

Freddie looked at her and nodded in agreement. 'I can't say I blame you,' he said, 'the paranormal practice of spiritualism has, for want of a better word, attracted many prominent people in investigative attempts to substantiate or denounce mediums who conducted séances and the happenings at such meetings. But that can wait. We can explore that subject at some other time.'

He looked across to Mabel for some sign that she accepted what he'd said and her smile seemed to confirm that he should continue.

'In my own field of horseracing I totally ignore racecourse gossip, tipsters and those supposed "good things" spotted by early morning watchers on the training gallops…'

'Why do that?' The interruption came from Conrad. 'Surely someone using binoculars and seeing by how much one animal beats another and the way it's done has already accumulated enough evidence to make a sizeable bet!'

'Sorry to disappoint you but it's not as simple as that. You see the person with the binoculars has missed one important piece of information without which a valid judgement cannot be made.'

'Put me out of my misery! What piece of information is missing?'

'Why, the actual weight each horse carries on its back, of course. Without knowing that the result of the gallop is meaningless. Just think about it!'

Conrad nodded. 'Yes, I suppose you're right. Never thought about it like that!'

'Most people don't. They see something happening, believe what they see without knowing essential facts and jump to the wrong conclusion.'

'Just like the reader of a good murder mystery,' declared Sally, with a hint of frustration. 'I always seem to pick out the wrong character when the detective is about to expose the murderer at the end of the novel!'

'Well you're not alone in that!' agreed her husband. 'But, to get back to what Freddie was telling us, could we hear how he goes about picking a likely winner at the races.'

'Certainly! I rely on past performance, genetics, the "going and distance" requirements plus the mathematics of speed and time to arrive at a potential winner and, when I have narrowed the possibilities down to a small few, I check the odds to find the one that presents the best value. Come to think of it, much the same, as we should do when reading the detective story! And not a bad idea for solving a real life murder either!'

Isabella Ramsden half-turned in her chair and fixed Freddie with a penetrating gaze. 'Have you, at anytime, been tempted to alter your chosen selection for a race because of some unexpected coincidence similar to my Good Taste incident?'

Freddie took a moment or two before answering. 'That's a good question, and the answer would have to be no. I will, however, qualify that by telling you of an incident that I considered as an omen that tempted me to increase my bet on a particular horse. It doesn't rank alongside your tale, Mrs. Ramsden, but I have to admit that for someone, like me, who is never put off a decision once made, I found the experience curiously funny.'

'Would that be funny, peculiar or funny, ha-ha?'

There was a titter of laughter that brought a smile to the narrator's face.

'Both, I think! On the eve of the 1959 Grand National I'd done my homework and, although it wasn't a race that I got heavily involved in financially, I finally settled on a horse named Oxo. Later that evening I walked to a local store. It was dark and, as I approached the place, a neon advertisement suddenly flashed in my face. I had never before seen that sign and learned later that it had only been installed that same day. The flashing sign was, believe it or not, advertising *Oxo,* the extract of beef stock used in cooking and some beverages. I doubled my bet and the horse won at 8/1.'

Freddie paused with a look of self satisfaction on his face before continuing.

'I suppose my subconscious took special notice of this coincidence simply because it supported my own findings. Had I chosen a horse with a different name I would certainly have ignored the sign, at least for betting purposes, though no doubt it would have registered with my subconscious. That's where the doubt creeps into the equation. Whenever you have a strong belief in something be it picking the winner of a race or convincing yourself of the existence of ghosts you search for anything that will substantiate your belief and give no credence to factors that contradict your thoughts, no matter how strong those opposing factors are.'

Victor threw his head back and laughed.

'I can just hear Father say, "What the bloody hell has all this got to do with ghosts?" If his spirit was in this room now he'd be laughing fit to kill himself!'

'And maybe that's what he did do Victor. *Kill himself!*' Isabella Ramsden looked at her eldest son with a pitying stare. 'But I don't think so! We may soon know the truth.'

'Can we hear more, Freddie?' Several voices spoke at the same time.

'That's okay by me then. I've never been one to refuse an audience. Let me just go back and we'll come to the subject of ghosts in a little while.'

Taking a sip of his drink and following that with an appreciative, 'Ahh!' he continued:

'When we are confronted with something insignificant we sometimes label it with a meaning it doesn't deserve simply because that is what we want to believe. It suits our purpose. The professional magician is an entertainer who, by using the power of presentation or the compelling authority of autosuggestion, sows the seed of doubt in the minds of his or her audience and it is then that the logic of the viewer becomes confused and distorted because they cannot believe what they are seeing. In many situations facts are misrepresented or vital pieces of information are left out and those involved are lulled into disbelieving that they could possibly be wrong. There is always an explanation if we can allow ourselves to see it. But we wear blinkers! Unlike racehorses, who wear blinkers to help them concentrate, we become blinkered and fail to notice essential information that is there for us if we choose not to ignore it.'

The speaker, who was warming to his subject, looked around at the faces in the flickering light and liked what he saw.

'There are many theories but few explanations for historical facts such as The Marie Celeste, The Bermuda Triangle and The Indian Rope Trick so, when we cannot offer satisfactory explanations, we introduce *ghosts*. That means we bring in the supernatural which may or may not turn out to be the solution we are looking for. But there is something we might just have overlooked. We might just have accepted the historical fact as being a fact without first questioning its authenticity. We tend to believe what we see, read or hear even though it would appear to be impossible or implausible. It is then we bring in the ghost as the miracle worker. When the truth is eventually revealed the ghost theory is discarded and all ghosts are treated with equal disdain. But we forget that when no logical or acceptable explanation is available we should perhaps give the ghost the benefit of the doubt.'

Sally suddenly jumped to her feet with arm raised like a child in the classroom.

'I'd like to ask a question. Why, when there seems to be no evidence to support their existence, do we still want to believe in ghosts?'

'We hear and see what we want to hear and see and although science has explained many of the so called ghostly incidents there are still too many unexplained happenings for us to completely deny their existence and categorise them as total nonsense.'

73

'I think I hear Doreen coming with the coffee,' said Laura clearing a space for the trolley. 'Shall we have a short intermission?'

'Good idea,' said Mabel, struggling to get to her feet, 'I think I've got pins and needles in both legs. I'd love an intermission; it reminds me of the movies.'

The door opened and Mrs. Gardner, complete with trolley, was silhouetted against the light coming in from the hall.

'Goodness me, are you still using the candles?' she said. 'George managed to fix the fuses some time ago.'

Laura went over to help. 'We've been talking about the spirits, Doreen, and it makes it more fun without the electric lights.'

'We seem to be doing more than talking about them.' Isabella said as she lifted a glass to her lips. 'Why don't you come and join us and get George to come along as well. It would be just like old times.'

'That's very kind of you. As you say, just like old times!'

'And with the clocks going back tonight we all get an extra hour in bed! Isn't that true, Mother?'

'Yes, if you say so, Conrad. I never seem to remember when they go back or forward.'

'Quite easy, Mother,' said Victor placing another log on the fire. 'Spring…forward, and Fall…back! A good way to remember; talking of which, I believe Giles did fall back earlier today. He took a nasty turn. Didn't you, Professor?'

'Yes, I did, Victor. I should have been more careful!'

The two protagonists glared at each other, their eyes smouldering until Giles turned away.

'I'll fetch two more chairs from the dining room,' he said, and gave Doreen Gardner a nod and a smile.

Mrs. Gardner scuttled away with a cheery, 'I'll be back in a jiffy!'

Freddie watched the tableau with interest making mental notes until a cup of coffee was thrust into his hands.

In no time at all, Doreen and George Gardner joined the group gathered around the crackling log fire. Introductions were made before The Prof intervened with his nervous cough.

'Aarrrgh! This reminds me so much of those wartime winter evenings when we sat in this very room and played charades that I would like to try a little experiment, before the evening is through. It

74

is to do with word association; it is very simple and I'd like you all to take part. But before that, if Freddie doesn't mind, perhaps he would give us an example of what he was propounding so eloquently before our intermission.'

'So that Doreen and George are put in the picture,' said Laura 'Let me try and explain what Freddie was talking about before, as Daddy would have said, "The Wurlitzer organ came out of the floor." He loved the "pictures", as he used to refer to them, and thought the world of Laurel and Hardy so Mabel's rendering of *A-Haunting We Will Go* would have met with his full approval tonight. Freddie was making the point that events and happenings that somehow defy scientific explanation are listed amongst potential ghost stories until, that is, some logical explanation comes along and the influence of the ghost disappears. He was suggesting that everything depends on how we look at the "facts" and whether the so-called facts really stand up to close scrutiny or whether some factors have been left out or misconstrued or lost in interpretation or folklore. Jumping to conclusions, before making an attempt to look at all the evidence, leads to the introduction of the ghost. Would you say that's a fair summing up of what you were telling us, Freddie?'

'I raise my cup of coffee to you! You were doing such a good job, Laura that I was considering linking up with you for a mental telepathy act! Now I want to tell you a story. It is a tale of drama on the high seas that could easily have created notions of the supernatural and added to the myths surrounding the illusionist and escapologist. Before that here's a footnote to that Laurel and Hardy film mentioned by Laura that illustrates, in a way, what I was saying about looking at all the evidence.'

Freddie appeared to be thoroughly enjoying his spell in the limelight as he looked around at his audience..

'All my life,' he said in a voice that hinted at adulation, 'I've been fascinated by the Art of Magic. Knowing the secret of how something is done has never detracted from my enjoyment, simply because of the sheer brilliance of the artist's performance. That said, the magician Dante is shown in the film *A-Haunting We Will Go* performing one of the great illusions where he has a lady assistant placed on a table and covered by a sheet. He then makes her rise into the air, shows that she is unsupported by taking a large hoop around her body and ends by pulling on the sheet to show that she has disappeared.'

Freddie looked across at his colleague who smiled and nodded.

'Giles told me he saw the act performed by a stage magician before he became a historian of magic and he researched for years in libraries until he knew the secret. I am not at liberty to divulge that knowledge to those of you unfamiliar with the act but if you ever have the opportunity to watch the film again I urge you to keep your eyes on the stage floor when Dante pulls on the sheet. It is just possible that you might notice something that gives you a clue because he performs the illusion without the use of mirrors or trick photography. You probably won't recognise what you see and even if you do you might not be totally aware of its significance. But the point I'm making is that all the evidence is there, in Dante's act, if we can only put it all in the correct order and not assume things which we think happened but in actual fact didn't. Now to my little story.'

'Before you start…would something a little stronger than coffee be to your liking Freddie?'

Laura took his empty cup and saucer and placed them on the trolley. 'Whisky or brandy?' she asked.

'A brandy wouldn't be out of place in this company. And it is just possible you could all do with one after you've heard my story!'

Freddie took the glass offered to him. 'Thanks!' he said, his steel-grey eyes sparkling with mischief in the candlelight.

At that point Victor intervened. 'Can I interest you in a cigarette? Or are you another non-smoker like Giles?'

'It's one of the vices I'm not guilty of but Giles has been known to smoke the occasional cigar, though only when he has something very serious on his mind.' He looked at The Prof who returned the gaze with a slight nod of the head.

Freddie smiled before continuing.

'My story concerns a deep-sea diver using a commercial diving suit and working from a supply ship. The suit, first invented in early nineteenth century by a German inventor, was in one piece and made of heavy rubberised canvas for flexibility. It had a helmet, with built in windows, that was fixed to the breastplate of the suit by a screw ring and a safety lock and it was completely watertight.'

'The back of the helmet had long flexible tubes attached, supplying air and acting as a communication system. The rate of air going into the helmet was controlled by means of a valve on the side of the breastplate and another valve regulated the air breathed out by the diver.'

'Now it was necessary for the pressure of air in the suit to be kept above that of the pressure on the outside and in the event of a failure of the air supply or an air hose being accidentally cut a special safety valve prevented air leaving the suit and causing the possible death of the diver. The communication system was, at that time, agreed between diver and surface crew and amounted to a certain number of pulls on the diver's lifeline.'

Freddie took a sip from the brandy glass and looked at the sea of faces eagerly awaiting the rest of his story.

'Everything was going according to plan until those working on the supply ship were suddenly alerted by the emergency tugs on the diver's lifeline and the realisation that something was going horribly wrong with the supply of air.'

'Desperation set in when the supply crew understood the gravity of the situation and the frantic tugs from below stopped. They knew the diver was either dead or unconscious. They also knew that if they attempted to bring the stricken diver to the surface too quickly they ran the risk of causing the diver to suffer the dreaded "bends" or decompression sickness due to the accumulation of nitrogen in the blood stream. In either case time was of the essence.'

'They brought the man in the diving suit to the surface as quickly as they could. Only to discover…*the man was no longer in the diving suit! He had disappeared. The suit was empty!*'

Amidst a shower of sparks a half-burned log fell out of the fire. Someone jumped and a female voice said 'It's all right Edgar. It's nothing to get upset about.'

George moved to put the charred wood back on the fire and said, 'Will somebody get the lad something a little stronger to drink.'

Isabella Ramsden looked on and, with concern apparent in her voice, said, 'I'm sure he'll be fine. Just give him a moment or two.'

Edgar took the glass of brandy that was offered. 'I'm sorry about that,' he said. 'It must have been my over active imagination. I was wondering what a tremendous appeal that would have had to one of the great escapologists. Just imagine, after escaping from a sack and tied hand and foot and thrown into the water, what an encore to escape from a diving suit at extreme depth! You have an explanation I assume?'

'Oh, yes! But it illustrates what I was suggesting before. That jumping to conclusions can be very misleading and unproductive!'

'When the diving suit was pulled to the surface and found to be empty it was assumed that the diver had left the suit or that ghosts had spirited him away. The reason for that was that he was simply no longer where he was when the crew had last seen him. He had moved to another spot in that confined space where he temporarily remained hidden.'

'You see, when logic took over, the whole grim reality of what had taken place dawned on the crew. When the air supply had failed the return safety valve that should have prevented the escape of air from the suit also packed up. With no air going into the suit and all the air coming out, the enormous pressure of the water on the rubberised suit had crushed and squeezed the entire body of the diver *into the helmet*! A gruesome reminder of an experiment that can be partially demonstrated in a science laboratory.'

'Well I'm blowed!' said George. 'Does that mean that you don't believe in ghosts, Mr. Oldsworth?'

'Please don't put words in my mouth, George. I can call you George, can I? And you can call me anything you like, but please, not Mr. Oldsworth! I was merely making the point that many incidents that appear to involve the influence of things beyond our control can often be explained naturally if all the evidence is taken into account but, and this is the important thing, that still leaves some that cannot be explained by all reasonable means, and that is when we must consider the possibility of ghosts!'

'Spooky, spooky, spooky!' A familiar voice exclaimed. 'The whole thing is quite spooky!'

'I'd like to ask you something, George.' said The Prof stirring from, what had been for him, a long period of silence. 'You mentioned earlier that you had been in the cellar, this afternoon, checking the heating. I thought I'd heard something. How did you get in without me seeing you?'

'Sorry to disappoint you. No magic trick involved, I'm afraid. You see, when Mr. Ramsden had the system installed he had steps built at the rear of the house leading down to a back entrance. That gave me access without having to enter the house.'

'You haven't disappointed me. I was hoping it might be something like that.'

The Prof got to his feet, went over to Laura and whispered in her ear. As she left him and moved to the writing desk he turned towards Mrs. Gardner.

'You've been very quiet, Doreen. Tired?'

'I usually am at this time of year. I was thinking of dear Jack as I was listening to Freddie's story and I couldn't help wondering if ghosts could be ruled out when he was shot or if an explanation would ever be found to put our minds at rest. I suppose it's natural to think of him as we approach Hallowe'en.'

'I'm sure we're all agreed on that,' he said. 'But before the evening gets any older and some of you decide to leave I wonder if you would indulge me. I wish to try a little game. It's a game about word association.'

Laura passed around the group and handed each a sheet of paper and a pencil.

'I want each of you to put your name at the top. Christian name will do!'

'Like the exams all over again!' exclaimed an excited Mabel.

'Now, let me tell you what I want you to do. I will give you four or five words, one at a time. As I give you each word will you write down the first thing that comes into your head when you hear that word? No matter how ridiculous it may seem please write down your thought even if it makes up a short sentence. If nothing comes to you quickly leave a blank. As an example, if I say Night you might write Day or Club or Dress depending on what you associate with the word I give you. Are we ready? Now make your minds go blank!'

'My mind has been blank for ages.' Edgar's remark brought hoots of laughter.

'Here we go then! The first word is *Black!*'

The Prof gave everyone time to finish writing.

'The second word is *Fire!*'

The crackling of the burning logs and the scribbling noise of pencils were the only sounds in the room.

'The next word is *Shot!*'

Giles noticed several upward glances and raised eyebrows before his audience put pencil to paper.

'The next word is *Thirteen!*'

Giles glanced around the room. All but one seemed genuinely involved in making a contribution.

'I used to sail through exams but this is...!' Victor left his mild outburst unfinished.

'The final word is *Boston!*'

When the writing had finished Giles collected the papers and Laura took the pencils back to the writing desk. Everyone started to chatter in groups like students used to do at the end of exams. Isabella, Doreen and George decided it was time for bed. Conrad and Mabel and Edgar and Sally said they would have a final chat before turning in. Laura offered to show Freddie upstairs and Giles agreed to accompany Victor for a short walk outdoors.

The house gradually became quiet, keeping its secrets...at least for the time being.

Chapter 8
DEAD MAN'S SHOES

The extra hour in bed that marked the ending of summertime on that last Sunday of October was a total waste of time as far as The Prof was concerned. He was glad to arise from his fitful attempts at sleep after a night when slumber never came close to providing relief from the gnawing feeling in his stomach.

Wearing the clothing that Laura had left in his bedroom he slipped out of the still silence of the big house and headed for the stables. The sense of excitement and foreboding, at the prospect of getting back up on a hunter again, was heightened by the surge of adrenalin combined with the chill in the morning air.

He paused as he reached the south-facing windows of the library. The curtains were drawn but these were the windows he'd seen the face peering in at him as he wrestled with the problem of the safe – the windows that "old" George had patrolled on the night of the fatal accident. It was clear that, by staying beyond the southeast corner of the library, the windows on the east side could also be watched for signs of "jiggery-pokery".

Moving on in the direction of the rear of the house the thought occurred to him that Freddie's visit was a chance not to be missed. A tête-à-tête about the various opportunities that each member of the household had to enter the library on that fateful night could be very rewarding and the library would be the ideal place for just such a meeting! He would also be able to gather Freddie's reaction to the interesting results of the word association game he'd conducted the previous evening before unsuccessfully trying to sleep. And he smiled at the thought.

With his attention brought back to the job in hand he turned right by the trees that skirted the lawn, quickened his step towards the stable yard and approached the first of the boxes; the one that housed *Delilah*.

Laura had her back to him as he walked in through the open doorway. She was talking to the mare as she fastened and adjusted the saddle and girth and was obviously unaware of his presence.

He produced one of his discreet but nervous coughs clearing his throat before saying his 'Good morning' and, although it was meant as a gentle introduction, it had entirely the opposite effect!

Brushing her auburn hair from her eyes with the back of one hand she wheeled round to face him, her eyes blazing. The look showed how much she had been caught unprepared and the black chunky polo-necked sweater she wore under her open black leather jacket couldn't disguise the rapid rise and fall of her breasts that revealed just how much her composure had been upset.

'Dammit, Giles, you startled me!' she said, breathing heavily.

'I'm sorry!' He leaned forward, put a hand on each of her shoulders and made a feeble attempt to place a friendly peck on her cheek. 'I didn't mean to...!'

He was given no chance to finish his apology. She shrugged off his grasp, placed both her hands on his chest and pushed him violently backwards. Only the wall of the box brought his movement to an abrupt halt and prevented him falling on to the floor. The ferocity of her attack plus the sudden thump of his back against the wall made him gasp for breath; a breath that was denied him as she attacked him again, this time with her whole body. She pressed him against the wall, closed her lips on his and, for what seemed an eternity, made him forget the need for air as a means of survival.

'Now Mister Professor, Sir! I don't think we should keep the lady waiting any longer!' she said as she pulled herself off him and indicated, with a nod of her head, the quiet mare standing with ears pricked and watching them with interest.

'But,' she continued, her tone becoming more matter-of-fact, 'before we go any further and, by that, I mean getting the mare saddled, let me have a good look at you. Hmm! The clothes I left for you seem to be a reasonable fit. Not Savile Row, I admit, but perfectly adequate, don't you agree? The jodhpurs and jacket belong to Conrad

and the sweater, stockings and shoes were Daddy's. I hope you don't
mind?'

'Not at all! Of course I don't mind! In fact I'm discovering, by
the minute, that most things you do for me take my breath away!'

'Touché!' She returned his smile and paused before adding,
'Come on, let's finish with *Delilah* then we'll get you fixed up with a
hard hat and a whip!'

'So, it's going to be that kind of a party!' he wheezed, still
struggling for breath.

'Cheeky!' She screwed up her eyes and squinted at him. 'You're
looking a bit pique this morning. Are you all right?'

'Yes. Didn't sleep too well, that's all. I'm never really at my best
this early in the morning. Don't worry I'll improve as the day goes
on.'

'Why don't you go and pick a hat for yourself. I'll carry on here.
The tack room's open. Anyway there's been a change of plan. You'll
be riding *Samson* this morning. You wouldn't think so looking at her
standing there but *Delilah* has been a bit fractious and, when she's like
that, she can be quite a handful for a new rider. Go next door and see
George. He's saddling your mount and you should find the horse a big
softie. I'll meet you out in the yard.'

The brusqueness of her voice was in stark contrast to the events
that had just taken place and, as he left the box while she turned back
to the patiently waiting mare, he wondered what, if anything, he had
done to upset her.

'Good morning, George!'

'Morning, Professor!' The little white-haired groom, who was
putting the final touches to the magnificent chestnut gelding, cheerily
returned the greeting as The Prof strode into *Samson's* box. The dark-
blue checked flat cap he was wearing accentuated his white hair.

Whilst fiddling with the chinstrap of his helmet Giles was struck
by the appearance of the animal. The winter coat was becoming
evident, that was true, but the horse's body just rippled with health
making his rider-to-be wish he was in the same glowing state. The
horse was huge and seemed to tower over the little groom.

'I know what you're thinking! He's a big lad, all of seventeen
hands and more and alongside me he looks even bigger!' The little

man removed his cap and scratched the back of his white head. 'If the boss had still been alive he would've classed him as a *"big bugger."* That's for sure!'

'The boss?' queried The Prof, wandering to the other side of the gelding's head as the keen eyes inquisitively followed his every movement.

'Why, Jack, of course! Mister Ramsden! He'd have loved this old fella! But shouldn't you be next door with *Delilah*. Isn't she the one you're taking out this morning?'

'No! There's been a change of plan. Laura has decided to ride her today so I'll be up on this one.'

The little man removed his cap a second time and appeared to be thrown by the news but recovered quickly. 'I've done the stirrup leathers to suit Laura but I suppose you can lengthen them once you're in the saddle. Can't you?'

'Yes, yes, George. No worries there! What concerns me more…!'

'Ask away, my friend.'

'Is there anything special I should know about *Samson* before I go out? I mean, does he have any quirky habits?'

'No, not really! Treat him as you would a member of the opposite sex!' At this point in his lecture little George Gardner glanced across to the wall that separated both horses and smiled knowingly. 'Don't rush! That's the secret!' he said, poking a finger to emphasize the point. 'Ease him from the trot to the canter and take it steadily before asking him to gallop. He'll respond and give you a super ride. Come on, I'll lead him out and give you a leg up.' He took hold of the reins and prepared to move to the open doorway. 'Oh, and don't get too close to the one in front. Her, next door, can be a right madam when she likes!'

'And which one would that be?'

Both men tried hard to subdue their spontaneous laughter.

Out in the yard The Prof had been given a leg up and, settling himself in the saddle, was lengthening his stirrup leathers as Laura led out the mare.

'What was that all about, Gee Gee? The two of you sounded as if you were enjoying something back there in the box! Anything I should know about?'

'I'll let you into a secret, my dear young woman! The same thought had occurred to me earlier when I heard strange noises from your box. And it didn't sound like the horse!'

'Oh, that! It was nothing! We were exchanging an idea, that's all!'

The family retainer studied the expression etched on her face and noted that her fiery temperament almost matched the colour of the wisps of hair protruding from under her black hat. He said nothing as he eased her into the saddle with practiced assistance.

'Let's go!' she said, in the manner of a schoolteacher. 'I'll walk on in front. You follow, but keep your distance!'

'Yes, ma'am!'

He turned round in the saddle to look at George and, as he winked at the little man, he glanced up at the house in the background. A flash of light was coming from an upstairs window. Was it a reflection from the hazy early-morning sun? He turned again and, with a prod of his heels, asked his mount to walk on; then it dawned on him what the flash of light had been! Someone was watching them through binoculars!

He put the thought out of his mind and concentrated on his immediate task.

As he settled into the rhythm of the horse's walk he was conscious of the immense power he had beneath the saddle and the understanding that, if his mount decided to take-off with him, nothing on earth would enable him to control such power. Horse power indeed! Someone had been so right to use that term!

After leaving the yard the hunters took a well-worn path that led towards the lodge of Mr. and Mrs. Gardner which then veered to the left before reaching their home. Still at the walk The Prof had time to reflect on his powerful mount and remember so many of the adages his fiancée had contributed. The last time he'd sat on a horse had been shortly before her accident but much of her equestrian advice was fresh in his memory.

"Begin quietly," she invariably told him. "Quietly and steadily!" were her passwords. "Avoid any pulling!" she would tell him tenderly. "Even big, strong, honest horses can have tender mouths!" she'd tease him. God how he missed her at this moment!

She would continually cajole him. "Sit still and quiet," she'd say. "Learn to walk with a long rein and yet try to keep contact with his mouth. Apply just enough pressure to keep him balanced and under control like a good angler plays a fish!" He was, he thought, just about managing to reproduce everything he'd learned.

The hand signal, from up front, snapped him out of his reverie on good horsemanship. Then, as Laura and the mare broke into a jog trot, he and *Samson* did likewise.

The easy gait of his mount was in direct response to his controlled handling and gave posthumous credit to the teachings of...! Almost simultaneously the two hunters changed to the canter and were soon travelling smoothly over an area that reminded him of his boyhood days when he tried, without much success, to follow the local Hunts on foot.

They were lobbing along almost parallel to a road track and, as the leading horse changed to a gallop with the gelding following suit, his heart began pounding to the beat of the hooves. Hedges were looming in the immediate distance. It was jumping time! Laura was putting him to the test! Was that what her violent kiss had been in the stable? Had it been a farewell gesture? Or was it meant as encouragement? He had no time to decide!

Samson was going well and taking hold of his bit. Giles felt at one with his partner. He could see the mare clear the first fence then it was his turn. Keeping his horse collected and riding in towards the obstacle with hands and heels and trying not to interfere with *Samson's* head his well-balanced mount flew the hedge and landed without any loss of impetus.

'Wow!' The exhilarated rider expressed delight and relief. The horse was a natural!

He gathered himself as Laura and *Delilah* soared over the next hedge. He sensed the ability of his partner to put himself right at each jump and realised that, as a rider, his aim was to concentrate at doing nothing that would jeopardise that ability thus allowing the jumper controlled freedom.

He was rewarded with another superb leap at the second obstacle and was positively relishing the experience as they approached the third and what seemed to be a larger hedge than the first two. He was back in the world of dreams; riding in the Grand National and approaching the biggest fence; *The Chair*. The cold morning air slammed into his face and gave him the same impression of the speed he'd had in Laura's sports car on the journey from the railway station. He focused his vision between the pricked ears of his hunter knowing that this time things were different. This time *he* was in control!

But something was wrong! *Delilah* and Laura were over the fence. That was clear! But as he neared the enormous hedge he had time only to note that the mare was galloping away riderless! Laura had disappeared!

Seconds later he and *Samson* were airborne. The well-balanced animal, clever at his fences, and jumping off his hocks, barely touched a twig as they made a safe excursion to the landing side. The Prof was all too aware of the immense pressure on his stirrup leathers as he let out the reins and made every effort to assist in keeping the balance of horse and rider. His attempts were severely tested as *Samson* sidestepped something lying on the grass as they landed.

Looking ahead he could see the riderless animal clear the next and it took him no time at all to ease *Samson* back into a canter and start pulling up. His fiancée would have been proud, as he didn't rush to pull up for fear of damaging his horse in any way.

Wheeling round at the walk he looked back to the obstacle he had just cleared. Then, as he hacked back towards the inert object lying on the grass, he was overcome by the feeling of dread he'd had when his fiancée, Linda, had lain in a similar position after her severe fall in that Point-to-Point.

He dismounted, led *Samson* to a nearby fence post and tied him up. He walked over to the limp motionless figure, removed his leather jacket and placed it gently over her body.

Bending down he heard a soft moan emanating from her lips, those same lips that, earlier, had…! He put the thought from his mind as she stirred.

'Please, don't move!' he implored, placing a restraining hand on one of her shoulders. At just that moment he was aware of the sound of a car engine on the road and looked up to see the Vauxhall Victor Estate coming to a halt with George at the wheel.

Almost before the car had stopped, Conrad and his wife Mabel raced out and approached the scene of the accident.

Against The Prof's advice Laura was soon sitting up and telling those around her that she was all right. Sore, shaken and probably bruised, but all right!

Conrad and Mabel said they would get Laura back to the house and call a doctor. George offered to collect her horse that they could see grazing about two hundred yards away and Giles said he would trot *Samson* back to the stables and wash him down.

'Stay here and we'll go back together. I'd like to have a word with you!' It was the tone of the little groom's words more than the words themselves that convinced him he should pay special heed to them.

Between them Conrad and Mabel helped a groggy Laura into the back of the Estate. Mabel remained in the back of the car with her and Conrad, with a 'See you back at the house, we'll get her to bed and call the doc,' waved an arm, got behind the wheel and, with a rapid but smooth three-point turn, drove away.

As silence returned The Prof noticed something lying in the grass. He went across and picked it up. It was Laura's whip. He untied *Samson* and, leading him by the head, joined George who was looking very serious.

'I'll take that, if you don't mind! The little man grabbed the whip and began to stride out in the direction of an unconcerned *Delilah* who was enjoying a leisurely early breakfast.

Giles hurried after him. 'Was I glad to see you with the car!' he said, opening the conversation. 'But how on earth did you appear so soon?'

'It was Conrad and Mabel! I suppose you could say it was Mabel really. The two of them came rushing down to the stables with a garbled tale that something terrible had happened. Conrad explained that it was his wife who had a premonition there had been a riding accident. She was sure someone had been seriously hurt. She was also sure that person was you! I didn't stop to ask questions, but got them into the car, came down here and saw you trying to help Laura. The rest you know!'

'Do you think they had been watching us from the house? You see I thought I saw someone using binoculars before we left the yard!'

'No, I asked about that. About how they could know and all I got was that it was simply a feeling that Mabel had. She couldn't explain it but said she felt a cold numbness coming over her and insisted we should check it out!'

'Lucky you did! I don't know what we would have done if you hadn't arrived when you did!'

'Well, that's something you don't have to answer. The fact is we did and Laura appears to have escaped serious injury!'

'Mabel seems to be a most unusual young woman. And someone it might be worth keeping a close eye on. Sensitive, emotional, responsive and impressionable, there's no denying she has those qualities but, as for extrasensory perception, that's an entirely different matter!'

'I won't disagree with you, Professor, but something puzzles me much more than whether Conrad's wife has second sight!'

'And what would that be?'

There was a lengthy pause before the little man in the cloth cap replied. He stopped, halted his companion with an outstretched arm and gave the matter some thought.

'What, exactly, made Laura fall?' He let his question sink in before adding, 'After all, she's taken that hedge hundreds of times before and never had a mishap! I know it can happen to anyone, but why today? It wasn't as if she was in a race and under pressure from other competitors. No, it doesn't add up! Think back, Professor! Weren't you supposed to be riding *Delilah* this morning?'

'Yes, but...! You're not suggesting...!'

'I'm not suggesting anything! Oh, I hope not! I sincerely hope not! But, I'll tell you, lad, I think we're about to find out! Come on!'

They started walking again and the mare looked up from her munching as the two men, with the horse, came towards her. She pricked her ears as her groom caught hold of her reins. He checked the bridle and girths. Everything seemed in good order and the saddle was secure. He moved round to the opposite side and The Prof heard the intake of breath followed by a whistling sound of air expelled through pursed lips.

George appeared and the look on his face gave an indication of things to come. 'The stirrup leather, on that side, has snapped. She really had no chance of staying in the saddle. But that's not all. It looks as if it may have been cut!'

The significance of his news was not lost.

'But that means…!'

'Yes, lad! We both know what that means! Now let's get these animals back to their boxes!'

It took over fifteen minutes to walk the horses back to the stables and during most of that time a mutual silence allowed their thoughts plenty of scope. Occasionally they exchanged reminiscences but the possibility that a vital piece of equipment may have been tampered with remained uppermost in both minds.

As they entered the yard The Prof, assuming that Laura had gone back to the house with his jacket, suddenly began to feel the cold. He was made to feel even chillier by George's next remark.

Totally out of context he said, 'Dead man's shoes!'

'Come again!'

'Forgive the expression but, when I helped you into the saddle, I couldn't help but notice you were wearing Jack Ramsden's shoes. I didn't say anything at the time…it was none of my business! But now, in view of the accident, I think it becomes more relevant!'

'You think so?'

'Don't you? Dead man's shoes! You were wearing them, weren't you? You still are! And you were supposed to ride an animal that could be a bit high-spirited and, we now discover, had a dodgy stirrup leather! Think about that, lad! Would *Alice* not have cried, *"Curiouser and curiouser!"* Do you not think it was an accident waiting to happen? Look, I don't want to sound too melodramatic but, if the plan hadn't been changed and you had been aboard the original mount, you might have had the accident and there's just the chance it could have been fatal. Another corpse wearing a dead man's shoes!'

'You make it sound…! Too close for comfort!'

'Look, Giles, go on up to the house and get out of these clothes. You look as if you're getting cold. Either that or it could be that mild shock is setting in. Doreen should have breakfast ready. I'll get mine after I attend to our two special residents.'

'Thanks! I'll do that!'

'Oh, and Professor, maybe I can have a word with you later?'

As he walked towards the house The Prof looked up and tried to identify the window where he thought he'd seen someone watching through binoculars. It could have been one of the windows above the library, possibly the bathroom or one of the bedrooms next to it. He couldn't be certain.

He removed his shoes at the door and, carrying them, dashed upstairs and went straight to the bathroom where he took off his riding hat, splashed his face and towelled himself dry. He opened the window and looked out; he could clearly see the yard where George was washing down one of the horses. Beyond that he doubted if anyone could see as far as where the accident had happened. That posed another question and suggested...?

He grabbed hat and shoes, went straight to his bedroom and changed into polo neck and slacks. A pair of light shoes completed his attire. He dumped the other shoes, the dead man's shoes, under the bed and left his riding clothes on top of the bed in a neat pile, a relic from his RAF days.

Before going downstairs he looked out of his own window and checked the distant view. It was just possible, he supposed, that the accident might have been seen from there. But that meant...!

He felt it was a moment for smoking a cigar but not before breakfast and certainly not this early! He went down to the dining room instead.

Victor, Conrad, Edgar and Sally were already tucking in to a full cooked breakfast and the smell of sausages, bacon and eggs plus the aroma of coffee and toast was more than he could resist. He was ravenous after the events of the morning and said as much!

As he helped himself from the hot platters he sensed four pairs of eyes boring into him.

'Don't you want to hear how your little Laura is?'

'Yes, Conrad, as a matter of fact I do!' he said with a touch of impatience beginning to show in his tone. 'But, before you tell me, perhaps you can explain to me how you knew there had been an accident?'

'It was Mabel! Didn't George explain? She'll tell you herself when she comes down. She's upstairs with Laura and the doc!'

'Are you sure you didn't watch it happening from an upstairs window?'

'I don't know what the hell you're talking about!'

The door opened and Mabel came in.

'You tell him, Mabel. Tell the Professor how his precious Laura is! You put her to bed. Anyway it's your entire fault,' he said pointing a finger at Giles, 'if it hadn't been for you switching horses at the last min…!' Conrad's voice choked to a hoarse whisper.

His wife, Mabel, came to his rescue.

'Laura is sleeping,' she said. When we got back to the house Conrad phoned Doctor Richardson. He lives a short distance away, this side of town, and said he didn't mind it being Sunday. He was here in no time. Laura was in bed when he arrived. He's just gone but says he'll be back tomorrow morning.'

'What else did he say, Mabel?'

'He was sure there were no fractures. She seems to have been very lucky. She's sore and beginning to stiffen up. He suggested rest, gave her a couple of pills and closed her bedroom curtains. He said to give him a call if things got worse! He sounded very reassuring.'

'Thank God for that!'

The door opened and Freddie Oldsworth breezed in with a 'Morning all!' to everyone.

'Did you sleep well?' asked a subdued Victor.

'I'll say! And it's given me an appetite! But why all the glum faces? Is something wrong?'

'There's been an accident!' said Sally, 'But we don't think it's too serious.'

Looking round the room, Freddie intervened with, 'I'm sorry. Is it Mrs. Ramsden?'

'No!' It was Victor who cleared up the misunderstanding. 'Mother's fine. She's having an extra long lie this morning. No, it's Laura! She's had a nasty fall when out riding with Giles. Mabel's just come from her bedroom where the doctor was attending her and the news is not as bad as we thought.'

Edgar rose from the table. 'Why don't you tuck in to some breakfast, Freddie. We've had ours. I'm going to check if the Sunday papers have arrived.'

'I'll come with you,' said Conrad.

Victor discreetly encouraged Mabel and Sally to follow their husbands and allow Giles and Freddie to finish eating and have a private conversation.

'Are you okay?' Freddie asked when the others had gone.

'Yes, at least I think I am.' The Prof poured himself a cup of coffee. 'I've been here less than two full days, Freddie, and already I've had one accident, in a torture chamber, plus a lucky escape from another, in a steeplechase, wearing a dead man's shoes. I've been watched through a window from outside in the dark and spied on from another window in daylight through binoculars. I've been in a room with a woman who seemed to disappear by leaving without opening doors and I've had to open a safe by solving a conundrum about Harry Houdini. One member of the family has also accused me of coming here for the sole purpose of proving that one of them is a murderer and, to cap it all, one of them has accused me of talking to myself!'

'Hang on, Giles! That's hardly a surprise! You're always doing that!'

'Okay, trust you to point that out! But what I'm trying to say is…! It's been all go since the moment I got here. Never a dull moment!'

'What we need to do is collaborate! Join forces, and talk things over.'

'Good! After breakfast I'll show you the library. That's where the fatal accident took place. I'll go over everything I know about what happened fourteen years ago on Hallowe'en and where everyone was at the time of the shooting. With your help we can try and assess which of this lot had opportunity and perhaps things will become a little clearer. Who knows?'

'Two heads are better than one, as they say!'

The Prof forked the remainder of his sausage, bacon and egg into his mouth and swallowed it down with a gulp of coffee. As he pushed his empty plate to one side the dining room door burst open and, framed in the doorway, stood Laura in a pale nightdress. She was terrified out of her wits, took two steps into the room and, trembling with fear, announced, 'I think I've just seen Daddy! He was in my bedroom, and…and…he's left his shoes there!'

'But he's dead, Laura!' Giles said softly as she collapsed in his arms.

'You really are in it up to here, old son!' muttered a bewildered Freddie putting a hand up to his chin. 'And in *"dead man's shoes"* to boot, if you'll pardon the expression!'

Chapter 9
THE CAT O' NINE *"TALES"*

M rs. Gardner had been at work again, for the library curtains, that had been closed when The Prof had passed the windows on his way to ride one of the hunters, were now open and the pale afternoon sunlight filtered in. Shadows were already beginning to form as Giles rearranged the two leather armchairs and looked forward to the first real opportunity, since their meeting in London, for a one-to-one session with Freddie.

Freddie, who had been wandering about the library studying the layout and spending considerable time looking at the portrait of the Spanish Dancer, the poster of Chung Ling Soo and the Japanese screen, finally scrutinised the fireplace and the safe that was securely built into it.

'Everything in here is not what it seems!' he said, as he settled into one of the chairs. 'The whole place oozes mystery!'

'Is that so? Go on, Freddie. Why stop there?'

'Oh, yes! It has all the trappings of a theatrical set. A set designed to misdirect an audience and lure the unsuspecting onlooker into a false sense of security.'

'Them's my sentiments, old son! But let's have your thoughts. Anything in particular?'

Freddie got to his feet and, making pretence at fingering an imaginary barrister's gown, looked around before addressing a non-existent jury.

'I get a very strong impression,' he said, throwing an outstretched arm at the walls that displayed the artwork of Spanish Dancer and Chinese Magician, 'that what we have here are articles intended, by design, to catch the eye; to capture and hold everyone's attention and so allow other apparently insignificant articles to escape notice. In other words, the Magician's Art of Deception and Misdirection!'

'For instance?' The wicked cunning in The Prof's voice was all Freddie required to cajole him to taking centre stage.

'I repeat. Everything is not what it seems! Take the two pictures! Firstly we have a Chinese magician who wasn't!'

'Come, come, Freddie! You must be careful what you say. Inaccuracies will not be tolerated. After all, he *was* a magician!'

'Yes! But not Chinese!'

'I grant you that! We both know that Robinson was his real name. But you were going to mention the other picture as well! What can you find wrong with that?'

'For the very good reason that it is a painting of a Spanish dancer who looks uncannily like…! But isn't!'

'What can you possibly mean by that?' The tongue-in-cheek tone taunted a frowning Freddie.

'Because, apart from the colour of her hair, she looks like Laura! It's meant to be Laura! Isn't it? Or a dead ringer!'

'A ringer! That's true – but not dead!'

'So she looks like Laura, but isn't! That's what was puzzling me! The painting looks older than the lady in the portrait. Unless…!'

'Unless, what, Freddie? And you're absolutely correct! It isn't Laura! And it isn't meant to be Laura!'

'Damn! Of course! Damn, damn, damn!'

'A mild enough expletive for a Sunday, I'd say,' said a smiling Professor, enjoying his companion's annoyance, 'but I would've expected a little more self-control from you under the circumstances!'

'No, no, Giles! You've got it all wrong! I wasn't swearing! It may have sounded like I was swearing just as the painting looked like Laura. I was convinced the painting had been done many years ago, probably before the war when Laura was a little girl, or even before she was born. I couldn't grasp how any artist could produce such a likeness without prior knowledge of how she would be as an adult when it suddenly became as clear as the nose on your face!'

'Thank you very much!'

'You're welcome! You see I wasn't saying damn, as in swearing, but D-A-M as in the mother of this particular filly! The painting is of

Laura's mother! I was jumping to conclusions. A dangerous thing to do as I explained before. You see, everything is not what it seems!'

'You worked that out all by yourself. What a clever fellow you are, Freddie!'

'Getting back to Laura. Is she all right after her appearance as Lady Macbeth in the dining room, when she all but frightened the living daylights out of us?'

'Yes! I spoke to Mrs. Gardner a short time ago. She put her back to bed after her collapse. It seems she was hallucinating; about the shoes, I mean, and seeing her father. When I got back to my room I checked and found the shoes were still there.'

'There you are then!'

'Could be! The strange thing is…the shoes appear to have been moved!'

'Or maybe, Giles, you don't remember exactly where you left them!'

'Referring to "The absent-minded professor" syndrome are we? But have you ever considered how convenient that can be when dealing with people reluctant to talk frankly in your presence?'

'Like someone pretending to be deaf when, all the time, they can hear what is going on?'

'Or actually being deaf yet, at the same time, being a proficient lip-reader! I know someone like that and she can come up with a wealth of information when those around are lured into that false sense of security you were talking about.'

'Hold on a minute, Giles. Your interesting anecdote is food for thought. It brings me back to Laura, her accident and the sleepwalking act she gave this morning. Could it just be possible that Laura has been luring you into a false sense of security?'

'Surely that's a bit far-fetched? I'm not sure I see what you're driving at.'

'Well! Let's see. She's a very clever horsewoman. She could have contrived to cause her own fall from the horse this morning. After all, she was preparing *Delilah* that you thought you were going to ride until the change of plan. And who changed the plan? Laura! That's who!' Freddie was warming to his theory. 'Laura could have faked injury! Didn't the doctor confirm that she wasn't seriously hurt? She could have faked the sleepwalking. Maybe she didn't swallow the pills the doc gave her! Her story about the shoes could have been a complete fabrication!'

'But why, Freddie, why would she go to such lengths when it was she who brought me out here, in the first place, to solve what she believed was her father's murder?'

'Is it possible that she is not only a clever horsewoman but also a clever murderer? She could have brought you here making you believe that she wanted you to solve a murder then set about creating an atmosphere, for your benefit, that would show her to be the least likely suspect and convince you that it hadn't been murder after all.'

'But why would she do that?' Exasperation was beginning to show in his voice as Giles introduced his nervous cough. 'Face facts, Freddie! If Laura had committed murder why couldn't she just have left things as they were? Bringing me back here could be disturbing a hornet's nest!'

'For the very good reason, Giles, that someone in the house suspects her and she wants it to be known that she is the one who wants the whole thing solved and that might let her off the hook. She brings you here and, after a full investigation, you prove there was no murder and she is left in the clear!'

'Do you honestly believe that?'

'No! Not entirely! But you must admit it is a possibility and something to be considered!'

'Yes! I'll go along with that. It is a possibility and something to be considered. But it is nothing more than that. If Laura brought me here to prove that no murder was committed I fear she is going to be disappointed!'

'Why, Giles? Has the little lady rattled your cage?'

The Prof was on the verge of shouting and Freddie waited for the reply to his verbal baiting.

'Why, you ask! For the simple reason that I cannot,' Giles said, banging a fist on to the table, 'and will not prove that no murder was done, because I believe that murder did take place fourteen years ago in this very place. A murder so evil and so cunningly premeditated that it defies comprehension. And,' his words spoken now with quiet strength, 'by God, I will not rest until I have unmasked whoever is responsible!'

The two men sat for a moment, intently watching each other, as those words seemed to reverberate around the silent walls.

'When you declared that all is not what it seems,' said a now more composed Professor, 'were you referring only to the pictures? Or are there other things in the room that puzzle you?'

'Oh, yes! But before we leave the pictures let us not forget that, in each one, there is an instrument of death! A rifle in one and a dagger in the other! I'm also curious about the Japanese screen, the fireplace and the safe!'

'I'm certain the screen was not just meant to hide the safe from view. It's much too large for that and obscures a perfect fireplace. I would think it has to have been part of the props for Jack's last performance and was intended to be used to hide someone or something between screen and safe!'

'But why the safe? It's in a perfectly obvious position. Screening it off would be an irrelevancy, wouldn't it?'

'We'll be better able to answer that when we know why Jack went to Boston. Or, more likely, what he found when he was there!'

'I'm afraid you're losing me again, Giles! What's all this about Boston? You mentioned the place last night in that word association game. Don't you think you should put all your cards on the table?'

'Yes, I believe it is now time to tell you all that I know of the events of that last night in Mr. Jack Ramsden's life, just as Mrs. Isabella Ramsden confided to me. Boston will then become self evident when I tell you about the contents of the safe. After that we can begin to assess the role each and everyone played in the game of *Murder*. Except that it was no game!'

Dark clouds had gathered and the light, coming through the library windows, had changed from pale sunlight to moody shadows during the time The Prof told Freddie about the contents of the safe and everything Isabella Ramsden had related about what took place on Allhallows' Eve fourteen years ago.

The two men sat, as they usually did once a week in London, but this time it was different. This time, instead of being in a club, hotel lounge or premises of The Magic Circle, they were in the library of a house in Scotland, where one of them had enjoyed many childhood days and was now narrating the story of a magician's "trick" that had gone badly wrong, and possibly ended in murder, less than a month before Agatha Christie's play *The Mousetrap* had opened on stage.

Freddie, silent as a watchful cat throughout the narration, listening to every word, finally clasped both hands and, with index fingers together, touched them to his lips in deep thought.

'Quite a tale!' he said with a sigh. 'Or nine tales if you take into account all who are suspects in this possible crime!'

'Or ten tales if we include the cat in this impossible crime!'

'I like that, Giles. The cat being Jack, of course! The Cat o' Nine Tales! Yes I really like that,' said Freddie with obvious relish at the play on words. 'So where do we start?'

'We'll start with the cat! Mr Jack Ramsden.'

'Okay!'

'And if you put the questions and I give the answers, to the best of my knowledge, we may get as close to the truth as is humanly possible.'

'I'll go along with that!' Freddie nodded in agreement. 'Now what do we know of Jack Ramsden?'

'I'd known him since I was a boy. He was a man of integrity, methodical in most activities and close to being a perfectionist. He was down-to-earth, a true Yorkshire man! He had no time for spongers! He was a craftsman who loved cabinet making and magic as art forms and, you'll appreciate this Freddie, wasn't averse to having a bob or two on the horses.'

'Is it possible he might have been in financial difficulties? You know! A losing run at the races, maybe?'

'I don't honestly think so! I know what you're getting at. You're thinking of suicide! Let's leave that for the moment!'

'Why would he get rid of his assistant just a month or so before his spectacular birthday illusion for his wife? Did she walk out on him or was she told to go?'

'I think she was blackmailing him! She wanted extra money. They argued and she left. That's the way I see it! Reading between the lines he more than likely told her to like it or lump it!'

'But if he did that, and she left, would that not have upset his plans for the illusion?'

'Yes! Unless he decided to change the illusion. You see he was a brilliant improviser. He could take an illusion and adapt it to give it an entirely new slant. On the other hand he might just have decided to…!'

'To what?'

'To…get a new assistant!'

'But he didn't do that, did he?'

'Not that I know of! Unless…?'

'Unless what, Giles? Out with it!'

'Unless Jack persuaded a member of his family to act as his assistant! But which one?'

'There is another possibility I think you should consider.'

'And what is that?'

'If his intention all along had been suicide, might he not have deliberately antagonised his original assistant and forced her to leave, so that his being alone on the night of the illusion would be seen as entirely accidental and not of his doing, thus making suicide an easier possibility without any premeditation being suspected?'

'A good try, Freddie. I'll give you that. But, if suicide was what he intended, why did he not make a proper job of it? After all he was a bit of a perfectionist and I remember Laura's words to me on the phone, that night in London, when I'd decided to accept her cry for help. When I asked her about the possibility of suicide she said, "If he had wanted to do that he would've made *a bloody good job of it*." As it happened he was only wounded, though I grant you he never recovered.'

'Okay, Giles! I take your point! Now, don't laugh at this next theory, but if Jack had decided to commit suicide and make it look like an accident or even murder…! What then?'

'That's something I haven't considered! But why would he do that?'

'If suicide was the only way out for him, and we have yet to establish any motive for such an act, what better for a magician than to leave behind the puzzle of an impossible sequence of circumstances. You know…a locked room murder that wasn't!'

'My knowledge of suicides is rather patchy, Freddie, but I do believe that, when it comes down to the final fateful moment of truth, the victims try to make the end as comfortable as they can. The use of a cushion for the head-in-the-gas-oven method, padding for the rope when hanging is used and the application of make-up in the cases when the female of the species is about to take an overdose! No sign of that in this case and, with rifle and bullet available, not to mention a stiletto dagger, surely Jack could have improvised several methods of a way-out death!'

'So we're fairly confident we can rule out suicide. What about the voices in the room?'

'But there was only Jack's voice! Isabella wasn't convinced she heard more than one voice. She merely said it sounded as if he was speaking to someone.'

'Not like you then, Giles, when you're talking to yourself? Do you think he wanted it to sound like there was more than one person in the room?'

'I'm sure of it! In fact I'll go even further. I believe there *was* more than one in here that night!'

'But why was the other person's voice not heard?'

'Has it occurred to you that the other person may not have wished to be recognised by those outside the room but was either following instructions or disobeying instructions depending on whether the illusion was still the main purpose of the deception or murder was the real intent.'

'There could be another explanation, Giles! Your last answer has just given me an idea! What if the second person in the room not only did not wish to be recognised by those outside the room...but did not wish to be recognised by the magician *inside the room*?'

'You know that's something I mentioned to Mrs. Ramsden as a possibility!'

Both men looked at each other in silence as the possibility of Freddie's idea took shape in their minds.

It was the knock on the door and the clink of teacups that brought both men out of their hypnotic trance.

'Goodness me!' exclaimed Mrs. Doreen Gardner as she shuffled across and set her tray down on the mahogany table. 'You can't possibly see to talk to each other. It's getting quite dark in here!' She switched on the standard lamp before crossing to each set of windows and drawing the curtains. 'I thought you might enjoy a pot of tea so I...!'

'And some of your homemade delights!' interrupted Freddie with boyish enthusiasm.

Cook beamed her appreciation. 'There's seconds, if you want more!' She turned to leave.

'Before you go, Mrs. Gardner!'

'Doreen, please! Like the old days, Giles!'

'I have no problem with that, Doreen! Just like the good old days,' The Prof hesitated before speaking again. 'I realise how distressing it all is but I want to take you back in time. To that night; the night of Mr. Ramsden's...' he hesitated again before completing the sentence, '...Mr. Ramsden's accident.'

'What is it you want to know?' Her manner was a little brusque.

'You were in this room with all the others when he was about to get ready for his birthday entertainment?'

'Yes, that's correct!'

'Did Mr. Ramsden ask you to do anything?'

'Yes, he did! He asked me, as he always did on these occasions, to make sure that curtains were drawn on all the windows.'

'Anything else?'

'Yes, he said I was to make absolutely sure that every window was locked.' She stopped abruptly and appeared to be struggling to recall something. 'Oh, yes and he also said I was to do the same thing after the performance. To make certain nothing had been tampered with.'

'And did you do that?'

'Yes! Except that there was no performance!'

'Hmm! I know and I'm sorry. Did you hear the shot?'

'Yes, but I didn't pay too much attention to it. It was just a bang and I wasn't sure what it was. It was normal to wait until called back to the library.'

'Where were you when the gun was fired?'

'In the kitchen where I was supposed to be!'

'Was the back door locked?'

'Yes, it was!'

'So no one could get into the house that way?'

'That's right!'

'You said it was normal to wait until called back to the library, so how was it you went back there?'

'Well after the shot was fired there was a commotion in the hall and I sensed something was wrong!'

'When you got to the library who was there? Can you remember?'

'Yes, Isa...I mean Isabella was there. She was kneeling beside her husband.'

'Was she the only one?'

'No, not quite! Edgar pushed past me on his way out. He was shouting something about getting the girls and dashed off. I think he went upstairs.'

'What did you do then?'

'I checked the windows!'

'Were they still locked?'

'Yes!'

'And the curtains? Were they still drawn?'

'Yes, they were. I swear to God!'

'No need to do that, Doreen! I won't keep you much longer. Now, after you checked the curtains, what more did you notice?'

'Isabella seemed to be listening to what Jack was trying to say. Her ear was very close to his mouth. Victor came rushing in and went straight over to the gun on the stand. My husband, George, said he'd call for an ambulance but Victor said it had already been done. I could see Conrad and Mabel just inside the doorway. I didn't notice them come in. Laura elbowed her way through the group. She was wearing a white bathrobe and was still in her bare feet. She seemed distraught and was calling "Daddy, Daddy!" Most of the others stood in shocked silence, except for Sally. She was standing at the back with her fiancé, Edgar, and she was asking if Jack was dead!'

Mrs. Gardner, having given a fairly graphic account of what happened shortly after the shot was fired, was now breathing heavily and starting to tremble.

'The ordeal is almost finished, Doreen. There's one final question I must ask. Where did you go after you left the library?'

'I waited with Isabella until she was satisfied she could no longer hear Jack say any more. I took her off to the lounge and gave her a brandy.'

'You have been very observant, Doreen. And of tremendous help. Before you go is there any news of Laura?'

Mrs. Gardner brightened up. 'Why, yes,' she said, 'I've just been up to her bedroom with some tea and she intends coming down for dinner.'

'That's great news, Doreen. And thanks for the refreshments though I may need something a little stronger later on to ease the aches and pains!'

'Are you sore, Professor?'

'Just unaccustomed to riding horses over fences, that's all!'

Mrs. Doreen Gardner left the room without further comment, but with shoulders heaving in a silent chuckle.

Freddie Oldsworth, who had never uttered a word throughout the entire interrogation, stood up and stretched.

'That would appear to eliminate the cook as a murder suspect!' he said. 'Even you must concede that.'

'Yes, possibly, but it doesn't eliminate her in the role of accomplice!'

'How do you figure that out?'

'Well don't you see that Mrs. Gardner, by locking the windows and checking them again after the shooting, was partly ensuring a locked room situation? But only if she carried out her duties as she said. What if she didn't lock them before going to the kitchen? What if she left them unlocked until she returned to the library after the shooting, allowing someone to enter and leave by the windows? What if she then locked them after her accomplice had made an escape making it look as if the windows had remained locked? And who was outside the windows making sure there was no jiggery pokery?'

'George Gardner, her husband and faithful retainer!' Freddie allowed the words to softly leave his lips giving them added emphasis. 'Opportunity, I give you that! A definite possibility if you can conceive of a motive. But, if George entered by a window, surely Jack Ramsden would have been suspicious of his entrance?'

'But not if he'd been chosen, by Jack, to be his new assistant.'

'Okay, Giles! If Jack had asked George to be his assistant Mrs. Gardner would have locked the windows and Jack, the magician, would have been the one to unlock them and allow the assistant access. Agreed?'

'Yes!'

'But if George had used the rifle and shot the magician then made his escape via the unlocked windows, they would still have been unlocked when Mrs. Gardner returned to check them after the shot was fired, for the simple reason that the victim of the shooting fell to the floor and couldn't relock them. Unless Mrs. Gardner...!'

'Exactly, Freddie! It is perfectly conceivable that Mrs. Gardner, finding the windows unlocked, on her return, and quickly putting two and two together, immediately reached the conclusion that her husband was the probable assailant and therefore relocked them in order to protect him from discovery.'

The indefatigable Freddie, who had been leaning forward with elbows on the library table and with chin cupped in both hands, now stretched inactive limbs and pressed his frame back into the leather support of his chair.

'So', he said, clasping his hands behind his neck, 'having established that George Gardner could have entered by the windows if he'd been acting as Jack's new assistant, how would you see his entrance if he hadn't been the assistant? Wouldn't Jack have been suspicious and raised the alarm?'

'Yes, yes! I doubt we could arrive at any other conclusion. Unless...!'

'Yes, Giles?'

'I was going to say unless he was disguised!'

'Oh, come off it, Giles. George would have had to be another Lon Chaney to adopt a disguise capable of fooling Jack! After all, he's small, stocky and white-haired! Anyway he wouldn't have had time to apply the necessary make-up!'

'Ah, yes! I don't doubt your premise, Freddie, but there are methods of disguise other than the use of make-up! And take only seconds to put on!'

'I'm listening, old son!'

'Have you ever seen movie news reels of gatherings of that secret organisation the Ku Klux Klan?' The Prof spoke in a low whisper. 'Members are clad, from head to foot in white robes and hoods and, I'll wager, you'd be hard put to distinguish one from another.'

Freddie unclasped his hands from behind his neck.

'Substitute,' he said, with admiration for his colleague beaming out of his face, 'a magician's black robe and hood for those white ones and you could, just could, present the illusion of…! Was that what you meant, last night, when you mentioned the word "black" in the game?'

'I'll come to that later!'

'You cunning old fox!'

Afternoon lengthened into early evening as both men, apart from the occasional short exercise walk around the library and its contents, sat and pondered over the events of Jack Ramsden's last night as told by Isabella Ramsden and relayed by Giles.

Freddie continued to ask pertinent questions with answers, hypothesis and explanation fed back to him where possible.

He made a strong case against Mrs. Ramsden, as a suspect, citing the facts that she was the first to enter the room after the gun was fired and, although the youngest son, Edgar, had followed her in, there was probably a short interval when she was alone with her husband after Edgar dashed off to alert the girls using the bathrooms.

His theory that Mrs. Ramsden might have used a revolver, fitted with a silencer, to do the killing during that short time she was alone was pooh-poohed and dismissed out of hand. Too bulky to hide and not as silent as you'd expect were convincing arguments but the coup de grâce was the forensic evidence. The bullet that killed Jack Ramsden had been fired from the rifle on the stand. It was then agreed she could also have acted as an accomplice but, in that case, her accomplice could only have been Edgar as he'd been in her company, outside the door, throughout.

Laura, who had gone for a bath and Edgar's fiancée, Sally, now his wife, who had used the alternate bathroom in which to wash her hair seemed, on the face of it, to have reasonable alibis, but only if you believed that they had, in fact, gone to the bathrooms as had been stated. Still, either one or both, for that matter, could have gone upstairs then gained access to the library using a concealed entrance that was yet to be discovered. Far too much about their movements was still cloaked in mystery.

The same applied to eldest son, Victor. He had allegedly gone to the lounge, on his own, but there wasn't a shred of evidence to support this and, although his attitude to his father appeared to be one of animosity, a lot more information was required before an accusation could be laid at his door.

Conrad and his wife, Mabel, were similar enigmas. Their walkabout, that night, outside in the grounds of Maskelyne Hall, in the darkness, provided opportunity, if such were needed, to commit a heinous crime of devilish execution. But why? And, more importantly, how? Answers to those questions would have to wait.

The verbal tennis tournament between the two companions that had volleyed and smashed possibility, probability, conjecture and presumption back and forth for several hours finally broke up when Giles looked at his watch.

'Good God,' he exclaimed, 'we'll be late for dinner, if we don't hurry!'

'Didn't notice it until your clarion call,' said Freddie, getting to his feet, 'but the pangs of hunger are starting to gnaw at the inner man!'

His jocular remark was in direct contrast to that of Giles who grabbed his friend by the arm as they prepared to leave the library.

'I have asked that everyone be at the evening meal tonight,' he said in his sombre warning tone. 'And, assuming that Laura is restored to her normal self, they should all be there. That means that, although there is much to be done to prove the identity of the killer, there is not much doubt, in my mind, that the murderer is one of those who'll be at the dinner table. I therefore ask you. No, I implore you, Freddie. Keep your eyes and ears open! So let's go,' he said, reassuringly clapping Freddie on the back, 'let's go and *dine with the Devil!*'

Chapter 10
DINE WITH THE DEVIL

It was Edgar's wife, Sally, whose turn it was to tease the professor. 'Come on, Giles, where is it?' she said.

'I'm sorry I don't follow you!'

'The black cap, silly! Where have you hidden it? You know, you look exactly like the hanging judge about to proclaim the ultimate sentence to the condemned, and placing the black cap on his head usually preceded that. So where is it?'

'Good question, Sally, my dear!'

Edgar looked directly at Giles as he gave his wife verbal encouragement. 'After all,' he said, 'you and Freddie were a long time in the library this afternoon. Did you, by any chance, come to any conclusion about which one of us is the guilty party? Or is *she* not in the room?' His lips curled into a mocking smile as he turned to his wife for the proverbial pat on the back.

The Prof looked again at the empty chair across the table and was aware of Mabel sniggering. He'd been staring at that empty space since he'd sat down to dinner, conscious of the fact that Laura had yet to appear. All the others were there, including George and Doreen Gardner but despite the assurances given in the library about the wellbeing of Laura there was no sign of her.

He continued to sit in silence and wondered if she was too sore to come down. Judging by his own condition he was sure she felt awful. He ached like blazes and although she was much more accustomed to riding and the consequent falls, this particular accident, caused by a broken stirrup, was probably as dangerous as most falls that occurred in steeplechases.

It was Freddie who came to his rescue. Concluding that everyone seated at the table were waiting for a reply to Edgar's question about the deliberations in the library, he calmly took command.

'Giles and I talked a lot about the problems surrounding Mr. Ramsden's fatal shooting and I think it fair to say that we both had to admit that the whole business is a confusing amalgam of ifs and buts. And yet,' he continued with a self congratulatory smile, 'I am confronted with just such a puzzle every time I try to pick the winner of one of those tightly framed handicaps at Royal Ascot or Glorious Goodwood!'

'That's all very well,' said a sceptical Victor, 'but in this case you're not trying to choose a winner in a horse race, you're attempting to name a loser in the most crucial game of all…Life! And, let me remind you, particularly you, Giles, that the outcome is not the possible profit or loss on a racecourse but the breaking up of a family who played together as kids!'

'So! Answer Sally's question!' Edgar said between mouthfuls of roast pork and apple sauce. 'Are you about to put on the black cap or not? Have you decided that one of us is guilty or are your deliberations much the same as they used to be? Daydreams!'

'I know what you're referring to. My childhood fascination with fingerprints.'

'Yes, Giles, and remember, you were the one who always wanted to be the detective.' Victor pointed his fork across the table. 'So use your powers of detection and your knowledge of fingerprints and, most of all, use your head! The only fingerprints found on the rifle were those of my father. He, and only he, could have fired the gun!'

'But surely that's impossible!' The softly spoken words of Isabella Ramsden were directed at her eldest son. 'How could he shoot himself and, at the same time, prevent the gun from leaving the stand? Surely the recoil of the rifle would bring the whole contraption crashing down? And how did he collapse to the floor at the opposite end of the room from where the shot was fired?'

'How the hell should I know? He was the magician! He was the one who could arrange the seemingly impossible! Why don't you ask the one person, who's not in this room, to tell us how Father did the trick with the gun?'

The stunned silence that followed Victor's words as they tumbled out in a relentless stream was broken by a discreet cough and a splutter from family retainer "old" George Gardner.

'Have you taken leave of your senses, Victor? You don't mean Laura?' he said.

'No, I don't mean Laura. I'm referring to the one person who can positively tell us how it was done…Father himself! So why don't we ask him?'

The stupefying speechlessness of everyone as they fixed his or her attention on Victor was interrupted from the open doorway.

'And what's all this nonsense about asking Daddy to tell us how what was done?'

Laura, who was dressed in a black outfit that seemed to accentuate her pallor, stood silhouetted against the light from the hall.

Mrs. Gardner got up and went over to her. 'Victor was implying that your father shot himself, Laura.' she said putting her arms around Laura's shoulders and leading her over to the empty seat at the table. 'He suggested we should ask him how he performed his magic with the gun, but I fail to see how he intends to do that.'

'Why, that's simple, Mrs Gardner. We hold a séance!'

Victor's announcement produced a squeal of delight from Mabel.

'You're not serious, Victor!' said a tired looking Laura as she sat down rather gingerly. 'After all don't you require someone who is a medium before you can conduct a proper séance and, as there isn't one here…'

Laura wasn't allowed to finish as Conrad banged the table using the saltcellar as a gavel giving a fair imitation of the Chairman at a meeting of the Hunt Committee.

'No problem!' he said. 'Why don't we do what used to happen here when we were kids and guests came for the evening on those dark winter nights and we were all packed off to bed!'

Doreen Gardner offered Laura a bowl of hot soup. 'Yes, and didn't I catch the lot of you young rascals sneaking downstairs and peeping into the lounge on more than one occasion?' she said.

Laura looked up at cook and smiled. 'That's right!' she said. 'We were intrigued as to why the grown-ups wanted a pack of Lexicon Cards and an empty wine glass. You soon told us to mind our own business and sent us back to bed with a flea in our ears. But what do you expect to achieve, Victor? Daddy has been dead for fourteen years! You can't mean you want to contact the dead!'

'And why not, Sister dear? Didn't you tell us, only a few hours ago, that you had done just that?'

The Prof watched Laura's reaction to Victor's words. Her eyes seemed hollow and her cheeks sunken; any artificial colour she had applied to her face had drained away and been replaced by fear. He leaned across the table and, in pretence of helping himself to more sauce, whispered in her ear. 'You're looking rather tired, my dear girl. Perhaps you'd feel better if you ate something.'

She nodded in reply and started to sip a little of the soup.

He watched her intently for some moments noticing the rapid rise and fall of her breathing beneath her black dress and was immediately reminded of that brief but explosive encounter in the stable box before her accident early that morning. Try as he might there was no mistaking the all-pervading feeling that was overwhelming him. Was he falling in love with her? If he was, he certainly couldn't make up his mind about her role in the whole affair. If she was hiding some guilty secret and playing a game with him she had to be a magnificent actress and a leading contender for an Oscar. Or else she was…?

'That's settled then!' Conrad said with boyish enthusiasm. 'We can set things up in the lounge after dinner. That's if we can find those blasted cards with the letters of the alphabet on them. It's our turn to play the game this time, eh, Doreen? Which reminds me, Professor, what was that other game all about? The one you played on us last night. All that mumbo jumbo about word association. Does it mean anything and are you any the wiser?'

'All in good time, Conrad. I'll put everyone in the picture later this evening. But to answer your question; yes, I do believe I am wiser. You see the whole idea was to find the first thing that came into your heads on hearing a specific word. It was an attempt to obtain an expression of the subconscious before any defence mechanism came into play!'

'In other words, a sort of lie detector test without being wired up to a machine?'

'I suppose you could say that, but it would be a rather crude attempt at arriving at the truth. You see the results are very much dependent on the spontaneity of the answers.'

111

'Are you implying that what we answered could incriminate us?' Mabel asked with what sounded like humorous concern. 'Like those posters during the war, you know, Careless Words Cost Lives!'

'You're much too young to remember that, my girl!' said a motherly Mrs. Ramsden. 'Anyway I rather think it was Careless Talk and not Words; but that is neither here nor there.'

'I shouldn't worry too much if I were you, Mabel!' Conrad said, rising to bring another bottle of wine to the table. 'If our fingerprint expert were eventually to point the finger of guilt in your direction you'd have no fears that your pretty neck would end up with the deep impressions left by the gallows' noose; it's been more than ten years since they hanged a woman in this country and, after last year's move by the Government, I believe we've seen the end of hanging in Britain, once and for all. More wine anyone?'

'Well thank you, Conrad, my sweet,' Mabel said, moving her empty wine glass towards her husband for a refill, 'your reassuring words are of immense comfort to all us girls.'

'Which means,' added a jocular Conrad, 'that nice accommodating Mr.Pierrepoint won't be calling on you to check your age and vital statistics before that 8am drop. More than likely he'll be spending his time in his Manchester pub, or writing his memoirs!'

Victor reached for the wine bottle after Sally's glass was filled. 'A sordid business!' he said. 'The entire history of the ritual of being found guilty of murder and taken to a place of execution and hanged by the neck until dead has always had macabre undertones, particularly for the accused.' He started to fill his glass. 'Many stories have been told about the incompetence of so many hangmen in the early days and I believe that in one particular prison, on the night before a hanging, inmates would chorus the words of an 18th-century ditty: "The Hangman's Drop Goes Plop, Plop, Plop!"'

'I'm sorry Victor, I really don't know what the significance of that song was', voiced Mabel, 'though I'm sure you're going to tell me.'

'Well Mabel the blunt facts are that in those good old days it often took at least three attempts before a hanging could be successfully completed...hence the Plop, Plop, Plop!'

Victor cast a satisfied glance around those who were expressing some mild horror at his tale before he continued.

'To be fair,' he said, 'the expertise of the executioner in 20th century Britain has been carried out in silence and secrecy and with speedy efficiency; a situation far removed from 14th century times when the condemned man, wearing a striped coat and white shoes and with a hood on his head, rode through the streets of London pinioned to a horse with the hangman riding behind him with the rope in his hand.'

He drained his glass.

'Some years ago,' he continued, 'I was in conversation with a Professor of Medicine from Glasgow University. He had been a prison doctor in South Africa and one of his duties was to examine the body immediately after each execution whilst it was still on the rope. Before he could sign the death certificate he had to be sure that the victim was dead and he claimed that, in some cases, he had to wait half an hour before he could be absolutely certain, lending some credibility to stories of 18th century relatives tugging at the hanging person's feet so that they should die more quickly and with less suffering! A gruesome end to a human life! But perhaps it was justifiable in some instances. Always assuming, of course, that you hanged the right person. So make sure, professor, that you do a thorough job as you examine the facts surrounding my father's death. Even you would be disgusted if, through your bungling assertions, one of us had to spend the rest of his life rotting in prison!'

Victor's mother glowered at her eldest son, her eyes telling him, in no uncertain language, that enough was enough. She dabbed at her mouth with her napkin and turned to address her daughter.

'You're looking rather subdued Laura, my dear. Are you feeling all right?'

'Please don't fuss, Mummy, I'll be fine. I'll get better as the evening goes on.'

'Well I'm sure you know best. Victor's exposition on hanging was hardly the topic to encourage improvement in someone feeling under the weather. I would much prefer to hear from our guest, Mr Oldsworth. Perhaps he could tell us about his visit to Stockton racecourse yesterday. Mr.Oldsworth?'

Freddie looked up from his plate where his attention was riveted on trying to balance the remainder of his garden peas on his knife.

'I do beg your pardon!' he said rather sheepishly. 'My mind was elsewhere.'

Throaty laughter from The Prof preceded an attempt by him to enlighten his friend of Isabella Ramsden's request.

'Our charming hostess was expressing a desire to hear all about your latest day at the races, Freddie. And you, my friend, were engrossed in a balancing act the equal of Blondin over Niagara Falls.'

'Yes, I think we'd all like to hear more,' Conrad said eagerly. 'I, for one, could do with a little help in augmenting the family income. That's if you can come up with some good advice. I'll wager young Edgar would also welcome the chance to make a killing on the racecourse, wouldn't you, Ed?'

'A killing, did you say? Yes, Conrad, but not literally, you understand. I wouldn't want our budding detective to get the wrong idea. You see I do believe that if Professor Dawson ever got it into his head that one of us caused the death of my late father he would pursue his suspect as relentlessly as the hounds at the local Hunt. And we wouldn't want that! Now, would we?'

'You're quite right, Edgar! I won't deny my dogged determination when it comes to solving an inexplicable problem. And, although we have just such a problem here, I believe *I already know who killed your father*!'

This last statement was a bombshell to Edgar who had been acting a little cockily. He was about to explode at The Prof's confident assertion when Laura pushed her half-finished plate of soup to one side and rose unsteadily to her feet.

'I have a suggestion to make,' she said. 'As we all seem to have finished eating, why don't we retire to the lounge and continue our conversation over coffee and liqueurs? It's more comfortable next door and there are one or two questions I'd like answered before Victor tries to get us involved in his séance.'

The log fire, which George had topped up, hissed and spat and threw animated shadows across the room to where Edgar was arranging the letters of the alphabet around an old well-worn oval table of highly polished mahogany.

Mrs.Gardner, who'd known where the Lexicon pack had been, after all those years, had already drawn the heavy curtains across the lounge windows, muffling the low rumble of faraway thunder, and was about to switch on a lamp when she was interrupted by Victor.

'Let's leave the lamps off Doreen, at least for the time being. Séances should be conducted in the dark but for our purposes that will not be possible. It is essential that we are able to watch the movement of the inverted glass but I'm certain that the light from George's excellent fire will be more than adequate without detracting from the unique atmosphere that our assignation with the dead will surely guarantee!'

Victor, who had uttered the warning as he escorted his mother to her usual chair, had to put a comforting arm around her shoulders when the white-haired lady appeared to shiver as he delivered his closing words.

The housekeeper gave Victor a look that could kill before addressing the lady of the house.

'Before you all get too involved with your game I'll bring in the coffee and, with your permission, perhaps I can be excused for the rest of the evening?' Her tone was frosty.

'Splendid idea, Doreen,' said Isabella, with a slight tremor in her voice, 'but I'd prefer if you and George stayed afterwards for Victor's experiment. I'm sure Giles would agree!'

Giles, assisting a visibly unsteady Laura to a fireside seat, squeezed her hand reassuringly and sat down beside her.

Victor produced glasses and liqueurs.

Isabella Ramsden raised her voice.

'Don't you agree, Giles?'

'What?'

'I was suggesting that Doreen and George should remain for the séance. Don't you agree?'

'Why, yes, of course!' mumbled a vaguely bemused professor. 'I suppose if we are going to try and recall what happened on that night fourteen years ago we should have everybody who was present then.'

Freddie arm-in-arm between Mabel and Sally, who were giggling like schoolgirls, advanced into the room as if dancing a sedate Dashing White Sergeant before breaking up to sit as a threesome on the expansive sofa.

Conrad, who'd been hiding behind the Sunday Express as he lounged in an armchair, looked up from the sports page and focused his attention on Freddie.

'I wasn't aware you were quite such a celebrity, squire! Your name is plastered all over the racing page. I think an explanation might be in order.'

The two girls moved closer to Freddie for an interested peek as Conrad passed the paper across to him.

Freddie looked slightly disappointed but relieved as he returned the article in question.

'You had me worried for a moment. The *Freddie* headlined in the Dick Francis column relates to the Scottish trained steeplechaser and not me, but I suppose you know that? He's been second in the last two Nationals and is about to start preparing for another tilt at the big race, but I suppose you already know that as well?'

'Yes, I do know that, I was joking!'

Conrad buried himself behind the newsprint once more only to reappear seconds later.

'Which reminds me,' he said, 'perhaps your absent-minded professor friend could tell us if *he* was joking when he told us he knew who had killed Father!'

'No, Conrad, I wasn't joking. As a matter of fact I don't consider this a joking matter. But let me correct you. I didn't say I knew who killed your father. At this stage I can't be that certain. What I did say was I believed I knew and that's as far as I'm prepared to go. What I require to find out is why and how and I'm as far from knowing the answers to those two questions as I was when I arrived here two days ago.'

'You really mean you're guessing so why not admit it!' Victor didn't wait for a response but continued to provoke his one-time boyhood companion.

'You're hoping for some kind of coincidence to set you in the direction of a trumped-up solution to add weight to what is only an imagined theory. Isn't that it? All weekend you've done nothing but encourage discussion about coincidence as if it was the be-all and end-all of many of the unique events in our entire history!'

'Nothing of the kind!' Giles countered Victor's lunge like a skilled swordsman changing from parry to riposte. 'What I do anticipate though is that along the way some apparently insignificant incident or chance remark might occur to trigger off a thought that will lead me towards a solution. It's simply a question of keeping eyes and ears open before following up with sound judgement. And let me make one final comment. If you continue with your taunting outbursts, Victor, you may well provide me with exactly what I'm looking for!'

Edgar, who had finished setting up the alphabet and chairs for those participating in the séance, came across and joined in the conversation.

'Everything is ready!' he announced. 'But, before we try to communicate with the dead, can I suggest we try to extract some information from the living; that is if Giles has no strong objections about telling us about his word association game from last night!'

'No, I have no objections but I'm not sure if it would mean much to you. I really haven't had time to study the results nor have I arrived at any conclusions! Please be warned, though, I have no intention of divulging what each of you wrote down. Anyway you could easily consult each other if you so wished. What I will do is mention some of the answers without disclosing any names.'

Giles looked at expressions ranging from mild interest to spontaneous indifference.

'For instance I gave you five words and asked you to write down the first thing that came into your heads when you heard each word. The first word was *black* and some of your ideas included *blackmail, black widow* and *blackout*, which can refer to temporary loss of consciousness or the use of screens in wartime to prevent light escaping from buildings that might be seen by enemy aircraft. The next word was *fire* and two of you gave me *escape* whilst there were a variety of interesting jottings including *fire walking* which, as any self-respecting magician or illusionist knows is a phenomenon ranking alongside *The Indian Rope Trick*. After that came *shot* and replies were predictable ones like *shotgun* and *gunshot* but one intrigued me and that was *shot in the dark* with a question mark against it…a reference to my attempts at solving this puzzle perhaps?'

The Prof took a sip of coffee from the cup handed to him and a wry smile flickered across his lips before continuing.

'The word *thirteen* had a fairly unanimous response. *Unlucky* being the choice of most of you though there was another word used that interested me a lot! The final word *Boston* produced what I would have expected even to show associations that were slightly off the mark as far as accuracy was concerned. It is entirely possible that the real significance of what they reveal will not become clear until after I travel to America.'

'So you're going to the United States? Well, well, well! I assume that will entail a visit to Boston, no doubt!' Victor came forward and removed Giles' empty coffee cup as he spoke.

'Yes!' The Prof said, clearing his throat. 'Although I haven't the slightest idea when that will be!'

Laura, who had remained very quiet throughout The Prof's explanation of the word association game, came to life and fixed him with her stare.

'I have some questions I'd like answers to!'

'I'm listening!'

'I would like to ask you why you haven't made any attempt to find out what each member of this household does in respect of career, social attributes, personality and such like and the opinions and recollections of the events of the night Daddy died. After all it's twenty years or more since we all met and some of this family have no acquaintance with you whatsoever; surely it's reasonable to assume that we have changed considerably in that time and the more information you glean could enhance the whole picture and give you a better understanding of what really took place and set our minds at rest!'

A flush of anger was starting to appear amongst the pallor of Laura's cheeks with her extensive question matching the fieriness of her hair colouring. Giles could feel her eyes boring into him.

'You're quite right Laura. It has been remiss of me,' Giles said, trying to take the sting out of the confrontation. 'I have been preoccupied with other things, I'm afraid, but I intend to correct that. Up until now I've been content to keep my eyes and ears open, to watch and listen and absorb as much information as I can without extraneous knowledge interfering with my train of thought, but with the co-operation of everyone in this room, I'd like to spend some time with each of you individually, say tomorrow morning, when I can get to know you all better and ask a few questions. Unlike my little word game you will now have time to prepare your answers and decide how you perceived the events that happened fourteen years ago to the day!'

'I usually have a late rise on my birthday,' Mrs. Ramsden said. 'So you can use this room for your interrogation, Giles. I'm sure Doreen will have the fire burning soon after breakfast.'

'That's all settled then, Isabella, and I'll speak to each of you in any order you choose. There's just one preference I want adhered to in the order of things; I believe I should meet firstly with Laura and then Sally as I know they both have a long day ahead preparing the library for tomorrow night's birthday illusion.'

'Thanks for being so open, Giles.' Laura said. 'I hope you can be just as open in answer to my next question!'

'I'll try!'

'Your party game of last night and your comments about the words chosen leave me slightly puzzled and I know how much you enjoy a cryptic conundrum, but could you expand a little more about what you expect to gain from our answers?'

As she made her point there was a change of expression on Laura's face that seemed to suggest to him that she suspected what he was up to, because of something in their past, and desperately wished confirmation. It was almost as if she'd changed sides, from being the aggressor in her first question to joining forces with him once again. He hoped the look in his eyes and the imperceptible nod of his head signalled his understanding before giving his reply.

'You may not recognise it but both your questions are, in a way, interlinked. Your first question virtually accused me of being remote and neglecting the purpose of my return to Maskelyne Hall and the answer to your second will, I hope, alleviate your doubts.'

Giles put a hand to his mouth and coughed.

'Funnily enough,' he continued, 'it was your father who made me understand how human nature acts and reacts and just how powerful auto-suggestion can be to the mind; a wonderful tool in the hands of an illusionist. You must remember the game we played in this very room as kids, when someone had to sit on a chair and be blindfolded and told to prepare for a flying trip around the room. Two people would lift the chair off the floor and carry it a short distance until your dad would call out a warning that things were a bit out of control, getting higher and much too close to the ceiling, after which he would tap the victim on the head with a book before the chair was brought to rest on the floor and the blindfold removed, usually accompanied by guffaws of laughter. It was all great fun and to someone young and impressionable it could prove to be quite a sensation.'

'Years later I heard a radio play which concerned a young man who wished to become a member of a secret society but had to undergo an initiation ceremony that involved being bound hand and foot to a chair and warned that, to pass his test, he must endure being branded on the forehead with a red hot iron. Everything was prepared; a branding iron placed in the fire amongst red-hot coals until he could observe the metal glowing to a fiery red then white before a blindfold was tied across his eyes. Despite the fact that no brand marks were visible on any member of the society and logic told him that he was being tested to see how far he was prepared to play their game, some doubt started to creep in. When he heard the branding iron being removed from the fire and was able to feel the searing heat close to his head he was bracing himself to call their bluff when, without warning, a block of ice was placed on his brow forcing screams of shocked horror; a prelude to a heart attack caused by an inability to differentiate between extremes of temperature when the mind had already been programmed to expect a particular result!'

'Spooky!' Mabel's single word was spoken with less than her normal animation and was accompanied by muted hollow laughter.

Giles cleared his throat and looked directly at Laura.

'My own little game of words was because of my belief in the power of auto-suggestion and I was hoping my careful selection of words might give me some hint or clue that I wouldn't otherwise get from direct questioning. As I said before it could be some time before I can reveal the success or failure of my experiment but I'm convinced it was a game worth playing! I'm not sure if that explanation satisfies you, Laura, but I'm afraid it will have to do for the moment. Now was there anything else you wanted to ask before we play Victor's little game?'

'Yes, but I'm afraid it's rather personal!' Laura looked at him and there was a distinct glint of mischief in her eyes.

He raised his eyebrows but didn't make any comment. There was a hush of expectancy in the room, as everyone appeared to be anticipating a question that Giles might be reluctant to answer.

'Why have you never married?'

The silence, in the room, was deafening. That is until Victor drained the remains of his drink and put his empty glass down.

'I'm sure all of us would like to hear the answer to that one,' he said. 'What secret are you hiding from us?'

The crackling of the log fire remained the only sound to be heard. The Prof stroked his chin and seemed to be weighing up the words that would be appropriate when Freddie got to his feet. 'If Giles will allow me,' he said, 'I can answer for him!'

'That will not be necessary! Although it always brings back some painful memories I think I can handle it in this present company.'

'Well bravo for you, Giles.' Victor retorted with what sounded like cynicism. 'Did your beloved desert you? Was that it?'

'Not quite!' Giles paused and his eyes caught Laura's attention. 'It was sometime ago...her name was Linda and we were engaged to be married...' His speech faltered and he was silent for a few seconds.

'She was very much involved with horses and it was she who taught me to ride. It was at a Point-to-Point meeting that she suffered the dreadful fall...she never recovered.' He looked across at Laura and summoned up a smile. 'So I suppose Victor is correct when he suggested that she deserted me.'

'Well I'll be damned!' Victor exclaimed. 'Can you believe it? We've almost had another of The Prof's coincidences. Two girls in his life with names beginning with the letter L and both having serious falls from horses jumping fences; one dying and the other God knows how close to death. You must be lucky at cards, Giles, because you're certainly a loser when it comes to love!'

'Wrong, Victor!' Conrad corrected his elder brother. 'Didn't he and Laura lose at Bridge the other day though, I must admit, his mind seemed to be elsewhere?'

'Stop it, both of you!' Laura interjected. 'You're behaving like petulant schoolboys.' She looked straight at Giles and her expression softened. 'I'm sorry. I was totally out of order to ask such a question...I hope you'll forgive me?'

'There's nothing to forgive. Throughout tomorrow morning it will be my turn to ask each and every one of you many questions about your opinions regarding the happenings at Maskelyne Hall exactly fourteen years ago when the magician father of this house was inexplicably struck down. May I suggest it is now time to put your questions to him!'

Chapter 11
CIRCLE OF SUSPECTS

Every person that was present at Maskelyne Hall, fourteen years ago, now sat around the polished mahogany drop-leaf table or was in the room watching them; every person, that is, except Jack Ramsden, erstwhile cabinet maker, magician and illusionist, husband and father. And Jack Ramsden, who died from a gunshot wound on Allhallows' Eve in 1952, was now to be summoned to account by those taking part in this charade in a macabre attempt to glean the truth about the events of that night that had, so far, remained an unsolved mystery to all but at least one of them.

With his hands dug deep in his trouser pockets, Giles, who had declined the invitation to join the group, stood with his back to the log fire and watched as Victor organised the seating arrangement of the nine people associated with the household.

It had been unanimously agreed that an independent observer should make the number up to ten and Freddie had consented to participate instead of The Prof, who was convinced that his long-time friend would not only make the perfect understudy but was the only person at the table he could unequivocally rule out as a potential suspect of any crime that may have been committed in the house all those years ago.

After some amusingly chaotic movement reminiscent of childhood musical chairs Victor finally had everyone seated to his satisfaction.

Isabella was on his left farthest away and facing directly towards Giles. She sat straight-backed and tight lipped with her hands folded together on the edge of the table in front of her. Giles was rather surprised that she had consented to take part in the experiment and scrutinised her features for any signs of explanation. There were none. She was impassive.

Next to her sat groom and handyman George Gardner, looking decidedly uncomfortable, his weather-beaten craggy face and white hair in stark contrast to the pale features and fiery auburn hair of Laura who was seated on his left.

Beside her, Freddie was relaxed and in conversation with Conrad's wife, Mabel, who, along with Edgar who was next, had their backs to Giles.

Doreen Gardner, cook and housekeeper for as long as anyone could remember, fidgeted with her hair and seemed a little agitated as she sat between Edgar to her right and Conrad to her left. Completing the "circle" Sally sat silent and composed as she listened to Victor offering some advice.

Victor looked up and rapped loudly on the table making Mabel jump a little. 'As we all seem to be ready let me explain what I want you to do. Before we start each of you must place your right forefinger on the base of the upturned glass and keep it there, no matter what happens. I shall ask the first question and we'll wait to see what happens. If the glass moves and spells out a word that makes sense we're in business. After I'm finished each of you may ask a question but keep them short and look for answers such as yes or no. If nothing happens we'll call it a day! Does that seem reasonable?'

'I'm sure everyone is satisfied with that,' Isabella confirmed as she acknowledged the nodding heads. 'But I trust that, no matter how everything progresses, you will all excuse me when it comes to my bedtime as I wish to retire before midnight.'

'There will be no problems there,' Victor assured her. 'Before we begin, however, I must ask you all to remain silent if the glass moves and not to press too hard with your fingers.'

There were murmurs of consent all round.

'Will you now place your right index finger on the glass.'

Silence descended and the only sounds audible were those of increased breathing and the burning logs in the fire that were creating flickering images across the expectant faces around an alphabet of playing cards placed on the reflective mahogany surface.

Ten fingers were placed on the upturned wine glass and Victor took this as a signal to start proceedings.

'Is anyone willing to speak to us from beyond the grave?' he asked. As if on cue his question was punctuated by a crack of thunder that seemed much closer than before.

Giles kept his eyes firmly on the glass but, other than an imperceptible tremble, there was no movement.

Ten pairs of eyes made involuntary and fleeting contact with each other around the table before Victor asked another question.

'Is there anyone there?'

This time, after a brief pause, the glass moved slowly on the spot as if trying to ascertain just how smoothly it could travel before gliding towards George and settling finally at the letter…Y. The look of wary incredulity on the face of the little groom as he crinkled the outer corners of his eyes and the ice-cold scowl of Isabella had just enough time to register with Giles before the glass moved hesitantly across to Sally and the letter…E. It barely stopped before gliding at speed towards the…S, close to where Freddie sat. He stared at the Lexicon card then glanced sideways at Giles and smiled. Both men had attended similar bogus meetings of this nature to conclude that someone was pushing the glass. That much was obvious! But the question was…who? And why? Was it a prank? Or was it a carefully orchestrated effort to confuse The Prof and throw him off the scent. Someone – perhaps more than one – was conspiring to play a game with him? If so it was a game he dared not lose! It was a time for vigilance!

'Who are you?' Victor's question interrupted his thoughts.

The wine glass hardly faltered as it slid across the table spelling the letters J-A-C-K.

Giles watched the path the glass took and each of the ten players but came to no conclusions. Any one or more could have wished to spell the name for a variety of reasons.

Victor removed his finger from the glass and invited the others to do the same.

'We all deserve a short respite,' he said 'but now that we've made contact I have two more questions to ask after which, if any of you wishes to put a question, the floor is yours – or should I say, the table! The ripple of muffled laughter lightened the mood of possible impending doom.

When Victor replaced his finger on the glass everyone followed suit. There was a brief pause before he asked the next question.

'Was the rifle meant to play a part in your illusion?'

The glass moved in the direction of Conrad, settled in front of the letter...N, then immediately travelled to the card next to it...the letter...O.

'I only have one more question. Were you alone in the library?'

The wineglass, like a dodgem car at the fairground, slithered across the mahogany surface making slight clicks as it crossed the small gaps between centre and hinged leaf ends spelling out the word Y-E-S in the process. The firelight catching the intricate shape of the glass created the colours of the spectrum and with ten arms extending from its sparkling body The Prof got the impression it resembled a Giant Squid seeking its prey.

'Has anyone else a question?'

'Yes, I have one!'

Laura, who made the statement, appeared to have recovered some of her ebullience.

'Go ahead, but please keep it simple!'

Laura leant forward in her chair.

'Were you expecting someone to come to the library?'

The glass, seeming to have a life of its own, moved without the noise that had been apparent earlier. The Prof watched as it tracked its familiar route to spell the word Y-E-S and he thought back to when Laura had entered the library while he was attempting to open the safe. There was something strangely sinister about the similarity of movement. He was still making mental comparison of the two incidents when Laura's strident voice rang out.

'Who were you expecting?'

The light squeak of glass on polished wood became evident once again as the crystal goblet that was an extension of ten arms moved across in front of her and to her right resting lightly at the...Y before moving back across in front of her and going left to the... O. Without stopping it travelled towards the centre and moved directly towards her...but never completed its journey!

Spinning out of control it crashed sideways and smashed into several shards as nine hands made futile efforts to prevent the catastrophe caused when Laura collapsed forward and fell with her head sprawled on her outstretched arm. The ensuing chaos lasted the best part of a minute as members of the family rushed to her assistance, checking for possible cuts and replacing fallen chairs.

Doreen Gardner swept up the broken glass and Freddie and George helped Laura into a comfortable easy chair. Victor quickly produced a brandy for her; Sally comforted Mabel who seemed to be suffering mild shock and Conrad and Edgar checked on Isabella to see if their mother was all right before she announced she was going to bed and, without further comment, retired for the night.

The Prof watched the entire scene played out in front of him and determined to have a private word later with Freddie to find out what he made of it all.

'It's been a long day and a hectic one,' George, the groom, said as he put a few more small logs on the dying embers of the fire. 'So, if you don't mind, I'll pay a final visit to the stables and make sure *Samson* and *Delilah* are bedded down for the night, then I'll turn in!'

The little white-haired man straightened up and went over to Laura who appeared to have perked up.

'Can I do anything for you?' he asked.

'No, Gee-Gee! But thanks for everything! You've been most helpful!'

He squeezed her extended hand and, with a nod to the others, left the room.

Laura arose from her cosy armchair a little unsteadily.

'I think I'll follow his example and hit the hay!' she said.

Doreen, the cook, went over to her and offered a supporting arm.

'I'll help you up the stairs, my dear, and when I come down I'll make a fresh pot of coffee!'

'Great idea!' Victor announced with gusto. 'After that little game I think we need a winding down period.'

'Well it was your idea to play the game!' Edgar chided him.

'Out of the mouth of babes!' Victor retorted sarcastically and lit a cigarette.

'Laura,' Giles got up and approached her as she was about to leave the room. 'If you feel up to it in the morning, I'd like to talk to you, privately, in here say at around 9.30. After that I'll have a word with Sally then you can both get on with what you have to do for the evening performance!'

'Fine, Giles! Whatever you say! Goodnight everyone!'

The Prof returned to the others.

'Will that be all right with you, Sally? It won't take more than a few minutes!'

'I'll be ready and waiting, Mister Professor!'

Giles smiled and turned to Victor who was blowing smoke rings into the air.

'So what did you really find out during your game tonight?'

'About as much as you did with your confidence trick with the words last night!'

'Well at least my little experiment produced no serious mishaps to body or to property!'

'I don't think you should count your chickens too soon, Giles!' Edgar counselled. 'We have still to see the outcome of that lie-detector test of yours. None of us have any idea what repercussions may still emerge.'

Mabel, who had been silent for most of the evening, addressed the group in general and The Prof in particular.

'Before we leave the subject of tonight's séance there is something I've been meaning to ask Giles for some time. When you were introducing us to the strange happenings of coincidence, in this very room the other day, you mentioned that you and your friend, Mr. Oldsworth, were members of the Ghost Club.'

'That's right! So I did! So I did!'

'Well what I'd like to know is what is it...the Ghost Club, I mean? And does it have any connection with what we were supposed to be doing tonight at the séance?'

'I would have to say yes to the second question, Mabel, but perhaps a short explanation can help to explain the first one!'

'I'm sure we'd all like to hear what you have to say!' Sally said with more enthusiasm than she'd displayed after Laura's collapse at the table.

'O.K. then! Here goes! The Ghost Club is the oldest organisation associated with psychic matters. Founded over a century ago, before Disraeli became Prime Minister, by a select number of London gentlemen, it was set up to investigate psychic phenomena and unmask false mediums. It was wound up sometime around the early years of the First World War then renewed once more in 1938 by a certain Harry Price when women were admitted for the first time! It was a great success!'

'I'm just wild about Harry!' Sally sang. 'Someone should strike a medal for him!'

'That would have been the Price of success!' Mabel exclaimed with a chuckle.

'Sounds like somebody has been giving my wife too much to drink!' Conrad joked.

'I agree with both ladies,' Giles said amidst the laughter, 'but I'm afraid it's a bit late for that. Harry Price died suddenly in 1948 and the meetings stopped after that.'

'So how come you are still members?' Sally asked.

'I'm sorry; I should have made that clear! Perhaps Freddie can take over and clarify things!'

'I'd be happy to oblige!' Freddie said looking pleased to play his part of the double act.

He took out his reading glasses and placed them in position as if preparing to read from a script then thought better of it and held them in one hand much to the amusement of his audience.

'After his death the Club remained defunct for about six years before being revived again. Membership now consists of many eminent people including judges and successful authors and meetings are held where members and guests can exchange ideas on psychic investigation!'

'And what more can you tell us about this Harry Price?' Sally probed.

'He was a bit of a Jekyll and Hyde, I believe! Please don't get me wrong! I don't mean that in the sense that he possessed an evil side. He was a very knowledgeable man and the Ghost Club was very close to his heart but there is some evidence to suggest that, although he devoted much of his time and spared no expense in the pursuit of psychic research, he was also capable of being two-faced and malicious. Nevertheless he probably did more to make people aware of his subject than any other person – before or since. He was quick to expose those he came in contact with whom he considered to be frauds yet at the same time was quite prepared to give credit to others he believed genuine. Oh, and one final, but interesting fact about Mr. Harry Price, he came to be involved in psychical research through his love of *conjuring*. So you can probably understand why Giles and I are rather sceptical about such games as happened here tonight. But tonight was just a bit of fun…wasn't it?'

He placed the spectacles back on his head and looked around.

'Just a bit of fun? I suppose you could say that! At least it was until Laura spoiled the whole thing by sprawling all over the table!' Victor said with tongue-in-cheek. 'Aah, here's refreshment!'

Cook entered the lounge with a trolley.

'I'll clear up before I go to bed.' she said and prepared to leave the room.

'How was Laura when you left her, Doreen? We need her for tomorrow's show!' Sally asked anxiously.

'She was quite composed when I left her and should sleep the night through, if I'm any judge!'

'Good!' said Conrad preparing to pour the coffee.

Mabel assisted by passing cups and saucers around and everyone settled down to drink coffee and become involved in small talk.

Amidst the social clatter and chatter of cups and voices The Prof announced that he was going outside for a final constitutional and Freddie agreed to join him.

With a multiple chorus of goodnights the three brothers and two sisters-in-law were left to finish off the evening as they so often did on such occasions. Only Laura was missing from this younger section of the family, and she was safely tucked in bed.

With overcoat collars raised against the chill night air Giles and Freddie left the Hall by the main front door and started to circle the house. Underfoot the gravel crunched as they worked their way around the south-facing façade and along the east side passing the billiard room where Jack Ramsden had introduced Giles to the game he later played with his own dad as he waited to return to his RAF base after welcome "leaves" at home. As he came to where the billiard room adjoined the library, the latter building jutted out some fifteen to twenty feet and contained the large sash windows that "old" George had patrolled on the night of the…? The…what, he asked himself?

'Accident, suicide or…murder ?'

'You're talking to yourself again, Giles!'

The Prof stopped in his tracks, looked at his companion and nodded in agreement.

'This was roughly where George Gardner was when the shot was fired that night!' he exclaimed. 'And where he could also keep an eye on the rest of the windows on the east side!' he muttered softly and started walking again.

Freddie shook his head, smiled and scampered after him, almost bumping into his friend as he stopped approximately where the painting of the Spanish Dancer would be hanging inside on the library wall. The Prof had turned to look upwards to where the chimney of the library stretched into a pale moonlit sky. He studied it for some moments deep in thought until light flecks of rain fell on his upturned face. He brushed the moisture away, dug his hands into the pockets of his overcoat and walked on past other windows that he thought belonged to a storeroom or something similar.

A few yards on, the path branched to the right towards the stable yard where were housed the two magnificent hunters;one that had left him satisfied but sore and the other that had been the mount of Laura before her extremely serious fall. But what had caused her second fall during the séance. Was it a relapse after her earlier mishap and medication or was it to do with something that happened or was about to happen after she asked if her father had been expecting somebody to come to the library just before he died?

Giles looked at Freddie as if anticipating a reply to his questioning thoughts before continuing his tour past the back door and the kitchen area where the lights were still on.

At the back of the house he descended the steps leading down to the entrance to the cellar and tried the door handle. It was locked. He looked up at Freddie who stood at the top of the steps with raised eyebrows. No words passed their lips. He climbed the steps and moved round to the west side of the house.

Passing a laundry room and the comfortable games room where he and Laura had lost at Contract Bridge he motioned his friend to follow him past the dining room and on to the lounge where Laura had collapsed during the séance. He couldn't make up his mind about her eventful day but under the circumstances was sure she had done the right thing and, like her mother, gone to bed early.

There were lights still on in the lounge; the heavy curtains didn't quite prevent that fact becoming evident.

'Something else is certainly not evident though!'

'You're-talking-to-yourself-again!'

Freddie's singsong ditty alerted the dreamer for the second time during their evening stroll.

'Look Freddie we must have a talk. I want...! No that's not quite true...I need your opinion and I suggest we retire and have that little communication upstairs...right now!'

The two men stopped outside The Prof's bedroom. Giles put his ear to the door and listened then grabbed Freddie by the arm and gestured with his head to move on along the corridor. They passed the main bathroom and continued to Freddie's room.

When they were inside Freddie turned on his pal.

'What was all that about, Giles?'

'I'm not sure, but I suspect that someone was in my room!'

'But why?'

'Again I'm not sure but I wouldn't mind betting that, whoever it was, he or she was looking for something...something they believe I may have, in writing, that could incriminate the person responsible for what happened here all those years ago!'

'What have we got here? Who's the betting man now?' Freddie said with a smile and a wink.

'The guilty person was sitting amongst our circle of suspects and playing a game with me at the séance tonight. Whoever that is may have decided to enter my room but they will be disappointed! Nothing will be found, though it does mean that someone is as worried as I am!'

'But surely, Giles, every other person in this house could have a legitimate reason for going into your room. They are part of the family, after all, and anyway how can you be so sure that nothing incriminating would be found there?'

'For the simple reason that my notes...my real notes, you understand, I keep in my head!'

'Look, Giles, I hope you're not becoming too melodramatic about this whole affair. Anyway if we're going to have a chat about what happened downstairs tonight, may I offer you a little of what I have in my travel bag?'

He produced a small bottle of Drambuie and ordered Giles to sit and relax while he went to the bathroom to get a couple of glasses.

Opening the large bathroom cabinet Freddie rummaged amongst the contents and found two small glasses that suited his purpose. He closed the cabinet and left the bathroom but instead of turning towards his own room he went in the opposite direction and paused outside the door of Giles' bedroom.

He listened for a moment, turned to leave then stopped and turned back. Taking the glasses in his left hand he knocked on the door with his right. He turned the handle, opened the door and switched on the light. The room was empty. Switching off the light he closed the door and walked along to his own room.

Giles was standing by the window and looking out to the stables. It all seemed such a long time ago, he thought.

He turned as Freddie poured a little of the amber liqueur into each glass. When he heard the tale of the entry into his room all he said was, 'Aah!'

He emptied his glass in one gulp, grinned for a brief moment then became serious.

'What did you make of the charade tonight?'

'Well, one thing is certain, the glass was being pushed, but unless you saw more than I did I haven't a clue who was doing it!'

'You were sitting amongst them. Did nothing make an impression? Nothing at all that could point to the identity of the culprit? I mean it could have been a prank by someone who wished to have fun at my expense or it could have been an attempt to call my bluff!'

'Sorry, Giles! I'm afraid I can't help you there. But I can be a bit more explicit about the pushing!'

'Go on!'

'The glass was pushed by more than one person – I'm as certain as I can be about that – and, what's more, they weren't sitting together!'

'A splendid observation, Freddie! This really gets better by the minute!'

He thought he sounded a bit like Arthur Conan Doyle's creation and he smiled at the dream.

'Yes I do, don't I? I most certainly do!'

He rubbed both hands together.

'Careful, son, I believe you're talking…?'

'To myself again! Yes I know! Isn't it wonderful? Look Freddie, thank you again for the drink. You get some sleep. I have something to check out before I turn in!'

With that he was gone.

Slipping off his shoes and placing them neatly under the bed Giles closed the door to his room and padded along the corridor in his stocking soles. Why hadn't he thought of it before? He'd been here more than two full days and only now were childhood memories returning. Memories of hiding in the attic. The attic! The entrance was along here towards the back of the house.

The door opened when he turned the knob and the stairs facing him in the dark were those that led up to the attic. His memory had not let him down. He reached for the light switch. Above him a gentle light illuminated the floor space at the top of the stairs. He climbed to the top and looked around him. He knew what he had come for but was temporarily sidetracked when he spotted several interesting objects.

A small card table with a green baize top and on it a black cane and white gloves reminiscent of evening wear of a bygone era and, beside them, a circular hatbox. Inside, when he opened the tissue paper, he found what he had missed when he'd explored the cellar full of magical props. It was a black silk top hat; the collapsible kind. With the cane and gloves these were the kind of props used by magicians; they were also the props that were seen in the Spencer Tracy movie Dr. Jekyll and Mr. Hyde and, more significantly, were the hallmarks of Hyde!

Registering that fact he spotted something in a corner. He bent down and examined a portable record player and a case of vinyl records. As he straightened up and swung round he came face to face with an unexpected visitor with arms raised in a threatening manner. Instinctively he'd already raised his arms to defend himself and, as the figure advanced towards him, he reached for the only weapon available. A fire bucket full of sand, a remnant of the war years, which he lifted above his head. He was about to hurl this relic of the past at the intruder when, in that split second as he froze in time, he realised the figure opposite him was about to do the exact same thing. It suddenly dawned on him that he was confronting his own reflection in a full-length mirror!

He placed the bucket, which George had maintained faithfully throughout the war, gently on to the floor and wiped the cold sweat from his brow. He grimaced a little as he touched the part that had received the blow in the cellar the previous day. With his heart rate returning to normal and only his pride hurt he put two and two together. The full-length mirror, the record player, records and formal props entitled him to conclude that perhaps Laura might have used this area to rehearse choreographic routines. He made a mental note of everything but that wasn't what he'd come for.

The attic ran the full width of the house and he examined the brickwork that was part of the chimney that linked to the library. He satisfied himself that the entire chimney was sound and intact. There was no means of entry there, which seemed to rule out the chimney as a hiding place, at least for the time being. He looked at his watch. It was almost one o'clock!

He descended the stairs and switched off the light. He carefully opened the door to the corridor. Everything was dark and quiet. He shut the door and tiptoed back to his bedroom where he mulled over the events of the day before deciding that sleep beckoned once more.

It was only when he stretched out under the bedclothes that he understood how sore he was after riding the hunter that morning. He ached in more muscles and joints than he cared to admit. The soreness had become so intense he'd almost forgotten about the contusion on his forehead after yesterday's escapade with the Iron Maiden in the cellar.

Gradually he found a position that eased the pain and as he relaxed he began to look forward to discovering more about his circle of suspects when he could talk to them individually in the morning. But all that could wait. He was soon fast asleep.

He hadn't a clue what time it was. It was still very dark and the house was quiet...but something was wrong. Something was very wrong! He wasn't alone in the room! Someone else was there! Someone or something! His imagination was starting to work overtime and he could detect the perspiration beginning to reappear on his forehead.

He tried to raise his head and lever himself up on one elbow. The next thing he knew...there was a hand firmly clamped across his mouth and nose and he was fighting for breath!

'Don't move or speak!' A voice whispered. 'Just shut up and listen!' He struggled to pull the hand away and, in doing so, fell back flat on the bed. His heart was pounding.

The voice whispered again, 'Just lie still, Giles, and everything will be all right!' He nodded and the hand released the pressure on his mouth.

'Is that you, Laura?' he murmured quietly.

'Yes!' She was in the bed lying beside him, her mouth pressed close to his ear. 'I couldn't sleep! I had to warn you!'

'Couldn't it wait?'

'No! You see, someone was pushing the glass!'

'What?'

'At the séance, idiot, someone was pushing the glass!'

'I know! I was aware that might happen and Freddie confirmed that to me after you went to bed. Shouldn't you be in bed now?'

'But I am, silly!'

'What!'

'Shh! Or you'll waken the house! The point I'm trying to make is that someone was out to suggest that I shot Daddy and that person was shoving the glass around. And the seating at the table was so arranged that the guilty person must have been on the opposite side from where I was!'

'You're starting to shiver!' He put an arm round her and held her tight. She was causing him some torment and he began to ache in a very different way from when he'd climbed into bed.

'Why don't you try and get some sleep?'

She snuggled closer.

'No, not here! We'll get to the bottom of this I promise you!' He eased himself out of bed and went round to the other side. He desperately wanted her to stay but knew that, if she did, his entire concept of the problem of her father's death would immediately be compromised. It was something he must not allow to happen.

He helped her out of bed, opened the bedroom door and looked out. Nothing moved. He turned round and she was in his arms again. The strong desire to kiss her fought a brief battle with his distrustful mind ...and lost!

She was gone and the rear view he had of her in her black silk pyjamas in that darkened corridor was one of almost total invisibility. *Black against Black*. Chung Ling Soo again he thought– for he was the magician who'd evolved Black Art Magic.

He shut the bedroom door, climbed into bed again and wondered if she had really been there? He knew she had. Her side of the bed was still warm! He continued to wonder. More importantly, he wondered why she had been there at all? Now where had he had that feeling before?

Chapter 12
THE WHOLE TRUTH
AND NOTHING BUT…?

Victor, Laura and Sally were the only ones present when The Prof entered the dining room shortly before 9.00 a.m. on that last day of October 1966.

Having showered, shaved and removed the sticking plaster from the wound received in the cellar, he felt a touch better and more ready to interrogate potential suspects than he did when he first got up that morning but that did not conceal the fact that he still felt under the weather, slightly grumpy and, for no obvious reason that he could think of, apprehensive about the morning's questioning.

He had slept fairly well after Laura had left his room but it was she who looked totally rested whilst he, on the other hand, was probably suffering from the overworking of his subconscious; a condition Freud would have had something to say about had he still been alive.

He nodded to the others and went across to the heated breakfast trolley. A little sustenance might just be what was required to banish the collywobbles.

'You look a bit rough this morning, Giles! Get up on the wrong side of the bed, did you?'

Victor's acid remarks made Giles turn round. Laura was smiling coquettishly and he wondered if she had confided to her brother about her visit to his room? Or was it simply a coincidence conjured up by his self-reproach? Those blasted coincidences again he thought.

He turned to pour himself a cup of tea and spread some scrambled egg on a piece of hot buttered toast. He felt his neck redden but was determined not to let his emotions get out of control. He had to be alert and keep his wits about him ready to absorb the detail that might result from his extensive questioning, that was due to begin, in a few minutes time.

He carried his breakfast to the table and sat down.

'Did you sleep well, Laura?'

'Yes! As a matter of fact I did, believe it or not!' The smile was still there.

'Well, if you're ready by the time I've finished this, we can make a start!'

He wolfed down his scrambled egg on toast and washed it down with hot tea. He immediately began to feel infinitely better and started to look forward to confronting the entire circle of suspects, one by one and, who knows, filling in some of the blanks in his scenario of the events surrounding the death of Jack Ramsden. Metaphorically he commenced rubbing his hands.

He drained his cup and got up to leave. 'I'm just popping next door,' he said. 'I'll call you when I'm ready! I'll try not to keep either of you ladies hanging about!'

'That's very kind of you!' Sally said appreciatively. 'We are your humble servants, Sir!' She threw back her head and laughed.

Giles went into the lounge and closed the door.

Cook was on her knees in front of the fire.

'I'm just about finished!' She said, striking a match and setting the fire alight. 'It should be nice and comfortable in a wee while!'

She got to her feet.

'Good luck! I hope you get what you want!'

She turned to leave the room. 'I'll bring in some coffee and fresh baking later on!'

'Thank you, Doreen!'

The door leading to the hall closed behind her and The Prof sat down for a moment to gather his thoughts; most of which concerned the young woman he was about to question and her clandestine visit to his bedroom in the middle of the night. He was well aware that the only occasion he'd been so conscious of the close proximity of her body, apart from the skirmish in the stables, had been when holding her hand during a game of Sardines in a very confined space in this same house when she was no older than seven or eight. That seemed light years away…!

He went to the connecting door between lounge and dining room and opened it.

Freddie had joined the others and was asking Victor if he could have permission to use the phone.

Victor gave Giles a look before answering.

'Why, certainly, but I suggest you use the one in the hall. We don't want to disturb the professor now do we? And if it's your lawyer you're calling I reckon we could all do with legal representation when himself shines the bright light and gives us the third degree!'

Giles ignored the remarks and beckoned to Laura.

'Ready when you are!' he said.

'…Said the spider to the fly!' Edgar mocked as he entered from the hallway. 'Morning everyone! I trust the condemned have eaten a hearty breakfast! I'm starving!'

The Prof ushered Laura into the lounge and closed the door.

'Exactly what do you wish to know?' Laura asked as she sat down near the fire.

'I want to know everything that happened the night your father died but first of all can I say you look more rested than I expected…after last night!'

'And what do you mean by that?'

'Well, forgive me, but when you collapsed during the séance you were hardly a picture of health?'

'Oh, that! No I wasn't, was I? I'm sorry; I thought you were referring to something else entirely!'

'Aah!' With his hands behind his back he started to pace the floor. 'Why did you ask me to come here?' His tone was abrupt.

'I was convinced you were the right person to find out the truth about Daddy's death!'

'Yes, but what I can't understand is what made you doubt the findings of the Fatal Accident Inquiry following the post mortem? After all it is quite some time since your father died! Something must have happened to create this doubt, or have you always suspected the official verdict?'

'Yes, Giles, I have continued to believe there was something wrong since day one!'

'But why have you waited so long?'

'Because I'm sure no one would have taken me seriously. Certainly not the police!'

'Can you explain that?'

'No, I'm afraid I can't! Put it down to premonition, if you like. Lately I've been experiencing disturbing dreams. Dreams that have convinced me that Daddy intended to use one of us as his new assistant on that…final illusion!'

She hesitated before continuing.

'I genuinely believed he would ask me!'

'Why? What made you believe that?'

She hesitated once more before answering.

'…I was sure I fitted the ideal prototype!'

'How old were you at that time?'

'Nineteen!'

'And what were you doing at that time?'

'I was training as a dancer with a view to doing what I do now!'

'And what do you do now?'

'I'm a choreographer working with clients for film and stage and some television advertising!'

'Did your father ever invite you or even hint at the possibility of you acting as his assistant after his previous assistant left him?'

'No!'

'Were you angry at this snub?'

'How dare you!'

'Please, Laura, I'm trying to establish all the facts. The feelings and emotions of all concerned may help me arrive at the truth and, as I understand it, the truth is uppermost in your plans as well!'

'That is true! I'm sorry! You were asking?'

'Were you angry that your father did not make you part of his act?'

'No! Not angry, more confused and rather puzzled!'

'Why? Your mother suggested that after his previous assistant stormed out *he was going to alter his act to suit!* Isn't it possible he would do without an assistant or even ask one of your brothers to take part?'

'I very much doubt he would work alone and although it is just possible he might bring in another man for the Jekyll and Hyde illusion I have this uncanny feeling he wanted a female for this part to create a much stronger transformation.'

'Is it therefore possible that he might have asked either of your two sisters-in-law, Mabel or Sally?'

'But that's where it all goes wrong! Don't you see? Mabel hardly strikes me as the kind of person who would have made a suitable assistant to a magician and on the night of his death Sally had still to be introduced to Daddy. That was to be Edgar's surprise after dinner!'

'Hmm! On the night of the illusion why did you decide to take a bath instead of waiting to watch your father's presentation? Was this a display of childish petulance at not being taken into his trust to assist him? Or was there some ulterior motive in leaving the scene?'

'How…! Certainly not!'

'Then why were you so insistent that Edgar's fiancée, whom you had just met, should not use the main bathroom which had recently been refurbished?'

'Because I was feeling the need to relax and the new bath suited that need and, besides, the newly installed cabinet contained all the requirements for providing me with a relaxing bath!'

'Now then I want you to cast your mind back to that night and please try to be as accurate as you can.'

'I'll try!'

'Good! Now when you went upstairs to have your bath can you remember if the door to the other bathroom was open or closed?'

'It was closed and I could hear the shower running!'

'Did you hear a shot being fired?'

'Yes, I did! But this kind of thing was not unusual when Daddy performed one of his illusions and I really took no notice!'

'Where were you when you heard the shot?'

'I was in the bath!'

'When did you become aware that something was wrong?'

'I heard someone banging on the door across the corridor, then Edgar's voice shouting that there had been an accident or something. I'm not too sure of the exact words!'

'Please go on!'

'This was followed, seconds later, with Edgar banging on my bathroom door telling me to come downstairs because there had been an accident in the library!'

'How long did you wait before going downstairs?'

'Fifteen or twenty seconds at the most. I put on a bathrobe and went down in my bare feet!'

'Can you remember if the bathroom door opposite was open or closed?'

'It was open…and there was no sound of running water!'

'What did you see when you got downstairs?'

'Most of the family seemed to be crowding around the library door. I pushed my way through …Mother was kneeling beside Daddy who was lying on the floor. She looked up as I entered…I was numb with fright!'

'Thank you, Laura, that will be all for the present! I suggest you have another cup of hot coffee before starting any preparations for tonight. You can send Sally in if she's ready.'

Laura made for the door.

'Oh, there's one final question!'

She paused with one hand on the doorknob and looked back over her shoulder.

'Yes?'

'What did you do when you went into the library after coming down from the bathroom? And did you notice if anyone was missing from those gathered in or just outside the library?'

'I believe you have just asked two questions! The answer to the first is that when cook took mother away I helped Conrad look after Daddy until the ambulance arrived. As to the second question…!' She paused for a moment. '…I don't think anyone was missing. I can't be absolutely certain but when I looked up everyone seemed to be either in the room or hovering just outside!' Her voice trailed away to a barely audible whisper.

'Thank you, Laura! You may go now!'

When Sally entered the room The Prof was again struck by the similarity of the two women. Admittedly Sally's hair colour was nothing like Laura's. Sally was very dark and her eyes were blue, and she seemed a few years older. She did not quite have the soft lines in the face that Laura seemed to have, but the two women were strikingly similar in height and build, with figures matching in almost every sense and they both moved with the same ease and grace.

Sally sat down and crossed her legs. She inclined her head and looked upwards inquiringly.

Giles stroked his chin as if trying to figure out which parts of his face he'd missed when shaving.

'May I ask how old you are?' he enquired.

'You may!'

'Well, Sally?'

'Well, what?'

'Your age? How old are you?'

'I did say you may ask. I didn't say I would tell you!'

'Point taken! So you're not going to tell me?'

'Let me say that although I'm in the prime of life, I have not yet reached the age at which, according to popular belief, life begins!'

'That will do for the present! After all who am I to complain when others talk in riddles?' He paused. 'How did you meet Edgar?'

'We met at a party shortly after he finished at high school. I was a dancer then and young Edgar and I started going out together.'

'I understand you became engaged?'

'Yes!'

'When was this?'

'Late summer of '52. Towards the end of August. We decided that at another party!'

'Why did Edgar not introduce you to his family until the end of October?'

'He didn't think his father would approve. He was not yet eighteen and we decided it might be better to wait until the night of the birthday performance before we revealed our plans. He secreted me into Maskelyne Hall earlier that day knowing his father would be busy in the library. I was taken to meet the rest of the family and shown round the house. We were to meet Jack after the illusion was over but, as you know, we never did! Edgar kept me in the background during the time Jack was briefing everyone about his intended performance!'

'Was that why you decided to wash your hair when Mr. Ramsden was preparing everything in the library?'

'Yes!'

'When you went upstairs where did you go?'

'I went to the smaller of the two bathrooms.'

'Why?'

'Because Laura warned me not to use the other one as she intended taking a bath!'

'You washed your hair?'

'Yes, but took the opportunity to have a shower as well!'

'Did you hear an explosion?'

'Yes! At least I thought I did! The shower was full on but I heard the sound of a gun being fired. That's what it sounded like. I'd been warned to expect strange goings-on so didn't take much notice!'

'When did you become aware that something serious was wrong?'

'When Edgar banged on my bathroom door and shouted there had been an accident!'

'What did you do then?'

'I switched off the shower and put on a robe. I covered my head with a towel and dashed down the stairs behind Edgar who had been hammering on Laura's bathroom door!'

'Did you close your bathroom door when you left?'

'No, I must've left it open! I was in such a hurry!'

The Prof nodded.

'Before you go, Sally…when did you marry Edgar?'

'The following April when we set up our Magic Supply business in Manchester.'

'Are you still involved in that?'

'It is mainly Edgar's hobbyhorse. I concentrate on my Studio and Agency!'

'I'm not sure I understand! About this Studio and Agency, I mean!'

'I act as a go-between for young hopefuls looking for work in modelling, photographic and fashion. I can also offer help to suitable candidates lacking the necessary deportment or posture required for professional work as, for example, magician's assistants, though there is not the same demand for this as there used to be!'

The mischievous glance she gave him suggested she was enjoying the game; with he as the puppet and she manipulating the strings.

'Thank you, Sally! You have been extremely helpful! It's now time for you to go and help Laura with your preparations for tonight! You can send Victor in!'

When Victor entered he immediately took out his cigarette case, removed a cigarette and tapped it three times on the outer shell of the silver case before popping it in his mouth.

'I hope you don't have any objections if I smoke in my own lounge?' He drawled out of the corner of half-closed lips. 'I could offer you a cigar if you feel as stressed out as you look!'

'I'm not sure I could use one this early in the day but I have no objections with regard to yourself!'

'That's bloody obliging of you!'

'Look, Victor, you have no reason to be stroppy with me...unless, of course, you have something to hide!'

'What the hell do you mean by that?' Victor challenged, lighting his cigarette.

'You tell me! Unless you know exactly what went wrong the night your father died I'm sure you must be as anxious as I am to discover the truth and give this whole affair a decent burial! What I want is your version of the events leading up to the firing of the gun and you can then allow me to arrive at my own conclusions! Have I made myself clear?'

'Crystal clear, Giles!' Victor said pointing a finger. 'But I warn you that you mustn't expect me, or any of the others for that matter, to sit back and accept your findings without the proverbial pinch of salt!'

'Crystal clear, Victor? As clear as the wine glass you introduced last night before your distraught sister shattered it? Now I wonder if that is too much to hope for?'

'Why don't you get on with your questioning then *you* can be the judge!'

'That's better! I wondered when you might come round to my way of thinking?'

Victor grunted and flicked ash into the fire. Giles smiled and continued his attack.

'Before you change your mind,' he said, 'please tell me what you were doing in 1952? As far as a job is concerned, that is!'

'It won't sound nearly as impressive as your verbal C.V. the day you arrived but it suited my purpose!'

Giles nodded approval and motioned Victor to continue.

'You and I were always of an age, one of the reasons why we were always so competitive I suppose. Anyway I was not called up for the forces, I won't let you into my secret about that, but I occupied my time assisting a local farmer until I went to university in Edinburgh. The student life appealed to me but not the studying; too much like hard work...I think even you can understand that!'

Victor drew heavily on his cigarette and appeared to be unsure of his next offering. After a short pause he continued.

'I got heavily involved in theatre and the enjoyment of cheap foreign films of the more risqué variety, met and married a young dancer of the exotic genre which lasted a few months and ended in divorce. I gave up university and nothing I was doing seemed to meet with the approval of my father who threatened to cut me out of his will. I make that quite clear to you because you would eventually ferret that information out for yourself and no doubt come to all the wrong conclusions. Anyway I managed to wangle myself a job in a film distributor's office; remember we used to be given trade show passes to cinemas in Glasgow where we sampled top movies before their release. I am now a respected leading light in film distribution. Changed days since my father...! He would've been quite proud of the black sheep of the family if...!'

'To get back to the night your father died. Did you attend the briefing he gave in the library when he was explaining about the necessity of examining the room and ensuring that there were no hiding places and that he was the only one left when the door was shut?'

'Yes!'

''So where did you go and what did you do after your mother closed and locked the library door?'

'I came along here, where we are now. There was a fire on and I wanted to be alone!'

'Aah, like Greta Garbo?'

'Don't try to be facetious, Giles. It really doesn't become you!'

'Touché, my friend! So what did you do here?'

'I poured myself a gin and tonic! I knew father would let everyone know when he was ready to present his illusion.'

'And were you alone?'

'Yes!'

'Did you hear the shot?'

'Yes! I assumed it was the signal to return to the library!'

'So what did you do then?'

I drained my glass and left it on the drinks cabinet. I was on my way back to the library when Edgar dashed upstairs shouting he was going to warn the girls!'

'How long were you in here before you heard the shot?'

'Several minutes, I'm sure of that. Long enough to pour myself a drink and enjoy a bit of solitude.'

'When you reached the door to the library what did you see?'

'Mother was kneeling by my father and I could see the blood as he held his chest. I turned and went to the telephone in the hall and dialled the emergency number and asked for an ambulance. When I explained the situation I was told that the police would also be informed.'

'What did you do then?'

'I think I had a word with "old" George. It was he who suggested that his wife should escort my mother to the lounge. Laura and Conrad stayed with father and I warned the others not to touch anything!'

'*Did* you touch anything?'

'Whatever do you mean by that?'

'Well, did you move anything in the library? For example, did you touch the curtains, rifle, even the fire screen or, perhaps, remove anything lying on the floor? Or maybe you went over and touched the safe? Do you see what I'm getting at?'

'No, I don't see what you're getting at and, what's more, I don't care for your tone!'

'But you did go over to the rifle on the stand?'

'What the devil makes you think I did that?'

'Nothing – just curious, that's all!'

'I think I've told you all I know so can I go now? I have a rather unpleasant taste in my mouth that requires immediate rinsing!'

Victor turned and headed for the door.

The Prof stopped him in his tracks. 'Were you a beneficiary in your father's last will and testament?' he barked.

'Yes, but so was everyone else in the family except, that is, Sally, whom father was unaware of at the time of his death.'

'Right then, that seems to be all, Victor, at least for the present. When you go you can tell your young brother I will see him now!'

The Prof turned his back and went over to the windows to look out on an autumn landscape that was giving way to winter. On the way he renewed his questioning.

'Victor?'

'Yes?'

'There is one more piece of information I'd like to have!'

'Yes?'

The Prof turned to face his schoolboy adversary.

'Can you think of anyone connected with the household who may have had good reason to wish your father dead?'

'I wondered when you might get around to asking? God almighty knows, he was a good father in many respects but he could be an arrogant bugger at times and he'd be the first to admit it. Why don't you ask George? I believe he was about to be relieved of his services at the end of that summer. After being with the family for what must've seemed a lifetime that could always be construed as a valid reason for wanting to…! And Mother, bless her heart, wasn't too enamoured when rumours persisted that *her* Jack was having an affair with his assistants from time to time. Good old Jack!'

'Thank you, you've been most helpful!'

There was a light tap on the door to the hall and cook came in with a trolley.

'You're on your own I see!' she said. 'Are you finished already?'

'No, Doreen, I'm waiting for Edgar. He should be here in a moment!'

'Did I hear someone mention George before I came in?'

The Prof was caught on the defensive like a small boy with his hand ready to invade the sweetie jar.

'Victor was just pointing me in the right direction in answer to a problem I had. He was positive that your husband could clarify things,' he stated rather lamely.

'I've brought some fresh coffee and baking as I promised. Just leave things when you're finished!'

As she returned to the hallway he wondered how much more of Victor's assertions she had heard when eavesdropping at the door. He had no time to pursue the matter. The other door opened and Conrad entered dabbing his mouth with a napkin.

'You wanted to speak with me?' he said.

Chapter 13
THE PRIEST-HOLE

Tossing his napkin in the air Conrad closed the lounge door with a bang. 'You wanted to have a word with me?' he persisted as he caught the piece of linen and proceeded to fold it with precision,

The Prof looked a little nonplussed as he stared back.

'Aah, yes I suppose I did! Please excuse my rudeness; I was expecting Edgar but not to worry you are more than welcome!'

'Is that some fresh coffee?'

'Yes! Mrs. Gardner brought it in a moment ago. Why don't you help yourself?'

'Thanks! I don't mind if I do!'

Conrad poured himself a cup, added a little cream and stirred the contents.

'Before you start asking any questions do you mind if I ask you something?'

'Not at all, be my guest!'

'You have already told us you believe you know who fired the gun that killed my father! If that is the case can you tell me if you are any further forward in those beliefs after interrogating more than half the family, plus one of our loyal staff I might add? Or do you now expect everything to fall into place when you put Mabel and I under the microscope? I can tell you we have little or nothing to contribute to what the others have said and, if my arithmetic is correct, that leaves Edgar and perhaps "old" George to give you their versions before you're left "singing in the dark." Or do you expect your favourite ally, coincidence, to come to your rescue like the cavalry in those old Westerns we used to watch?'

'For what it's worth, Conrad, I am unfortunately no closer to the truth regarding your father's shooting than I was before but, like the jigsaw puzzles we used to enjoy on wet Sunday afternoons, the whole picture will only become clear when the final piece is firmly in place. What I don't want repeated are those occasions when pieces were missing. That mustn't be allowed to happen here! So, if you don't mind, I'll begin by asking about your occupation …then and now!'

'I work as a freelance photographer and have a small but successful business in Carlisle! I was, as you know, always interested in the camera which, like me, as you also know, doesn't lie!' Conrad paused for effect before resuming.

'After completing my two year conscription period in 1949 I joined a local newspaper as a photo-journalist!'

'Let me just interrupt you there for a second!' Giles said eagerly.

'During conscription did you learn to fire the Lee Enfield rifle?'

'Yes!' Conrad said with a smile before taking a sip of coffee.

'Please go on!'

'I was still working with that local "rag" when I married Mabel. That was in 1951 and we'd been married just over a year when the incident in the library happened. I'd been seriously thinking of setting up business and becoming freelance but obtaining suitable premises was to cost a fair bit of capital so Mabel and I decided to stay here at Maskelyne Hall for a spell and save some money.'

'I see! So the death of your father, however regrettable, worked out for the best?'

'I suppose that is one way of looking at it!'

'I am trying to look at it from as wide an angle as possible, you understand, similar to you using a fish-eye lens I suppose.'

'Not really, Giles! You'll find the fish-eye lens, though giving a wide angle as you say, distorts the view and I would advise that you do not let that happen in your delicate suppositions!'

'Hmm! On the night your father was shot did you attend his pre-illusion lecture?'

'Yes!'

'What did you do when the lecture was over?'

'Mabel and I decided to take a walk around the house until we were called back.'

'Did you meet up with George? He was to be in position outside the south-facing library windows.'

'No! As a matter of fact we didn't! We went round the other side of the house, past the lounge windows.'

'Were the curtains drawn?'

'Yes, but we thought we heard a noise and tried to peer inside.'

'Could you see anything?'

'The curtains were not quite together and, although it was difficult to see clearly, it was evident that Victor was in the room. He seemed to be on his own and he was pouring himself a drink. Clever old Victor!'

'Where did you go then?'

'We went on round to the rear of the house. I thought I heard a noise coming from the cellar so I went down the steps and tried the door. It was locked!'

'And?'

'We were there for several minutes, just chatting.'

'Did you hear the shot?'

'Yes! There was a wind blowing but we were sure the noise we heard was a gun being fired! We moved to the back door leading to the kitchen thinking that was the quickest way back into the house, but cook must've locked the door. We raced round towards the front of the house along the east side and saw a figure disappear round the corner of the building. When we finally got into the house there was a group at the library door. I think you know the rest!'

'Hmm! Not quite!'

'Laura asked me to help look after father. Mrs. Gardner took mother away and "old" George looked after Mabel, who wasn't too keen on the sight of blood!'

'Did you see Edgar and Sally?'

'Oh yes, but they kept well back, out of sight really. You know that Sally had never been introduced to her prospective father-in-law, and it began to look as if she never would!'

'Is there anything further you wish to add?'

'Only this! If you're searching for potential suspects for your so-called crime you can eliminate us right away. We were the furthest from the scene when it happened! By the way, thanks for the coffee!'

Conrad turned and as he left the room he called back. 'You're on your own, squire!'

'My brother mentioned you had fresh coffee in here.' Edgar intoned as he entered the lounge. 'You don't mind if I help myself?' Without waiting for an answer he started pouring. 'Now where do you want me to begin?'

'Let's start in the summer of 1952 at the time you met Sally!'

'That sounds fine by me. I couldn't wait to leave school and become…!'

'A man of the world, Edgar?'

'Yes, why not! It was party time for me and we met at one of those. It was love at first sight; a much maligned cliché, but true in our case!'

' You didn't take her home to meet your parents! Why not?'

'For the simple reason…!' Edgar started but got no further as seemingly he thought better of what he was about to say. '…They wouldn't have understood! They were rather old-fashioned about relationships. It was then that we…hatched a plan! We agreed that we would come clean about our affair at the Hallowe'en birthday party. We were denied that delight by circumstances…beyond my control!'

'On the night of that party you elected to remain outside the library door with your mother. Why?'

'I would've thought that was obvious? Someone had to ensure there was fair play. I took it upon myself to adopt that role, and just as well I did!'

'Why do you say that?'

'Didn't Mum tell you? She almost went into a coma when the shot was fired. I had to virtually force her to open the door!'

'What did you find when the door was opened?'

'Jack…that is…Dad was lying on the floor clutching his chest. It was obvious he'd been shot; his eyes were glazed and blood was oozing between his fingers!'

'What did you do then?'

'I thought I'd better alert the girls. Everyone appeared to be gathering from all directions, that is everyone except Sally and Laura who were upstairs.'

'Why didn't you phone for an ambulance?'

The Prof's intervention silenced Edgar who struggled to appreciate the importance of the question.

'What?'

'I said why didn't you phone for an ambulance?'

'I…I can't remember! It just seemed natural to call the girls and I suppose I assumed that Victor would…!' A puzzled frown dominated his forehead and fear showed in his eyes.

'Go on, Edgar! You dashed upstairs?'

'That's right! I went to the bathroom where Sally was washing her hair and banged on the door. The shower was still running so I shouted that there had been an accident. I did the same at the bathroom where "Sis"…I mean Laura, was and she said she'd come down straightaway. As I ran back down the stairs I heard Sally following me. I believe big sister was down soon after.'

'What did you do when you got back downstairs?'

'I looked after Sally. It seemed the wrong time to reveal identities and the poor girl was cold and her hair was wet!'

The Prof pursed his lips and placed his fingertips together. He studied the man in front of him and was struck by his likeness to the small boy up before his headmaster for a misdemeanour in school, a position he reckoned Edgar had previously experienced on more than one occasion.

'Can I go back to the time between the locking of the library door and the shot being fired? Did you hear any sounds coming from the room?'

'Jack seemed to be talking to someone and warning, whoever it was, not to touch…!' He shrugged his shoulders. 'It was all a bit confusing and I can't remember exactly what he said. It was then that the gun went off! After the shot I heard a thump and his voice saying something about keeping a secret. I had to push mum towards the door. She didn't seem to know where the key was. Then, when she discovered it was still in her hand, she couldn't get it in the lock!'

'Did you…and I urge you to think very carefully about this…did you hear anyone speak to your father before, or after, the shot was fired?'

'No, I don't think so! But I got the distinct impression that he…knew the person he was speaking to!'

'What makes you say that?'

'Well, it wasn't *what* he said, it was *what he didn't say*!'

The Prof's blue eyes lit up with youthful exuberance.

'Now that is interesting, young sir! I wonder if you appreciate the full value of what you've just told me?'

'I'm not sure I do!' Edgar remarked in a distinctly puzzled and wary voice.

'You will, in due course! I recommend that you read one of the short stories from The Memoirs of Sherlock Holmes entitled Silver Blaze. In that the Inspector asks Holmes if there is any other point to which he would draw his attention and Holmes replies,*" To the curious incident of the dog in the night-time."* When the Inspector retorts,*" The dog did nothing in the night-time,"* Holmes remarks,*" That was the curious incident."* Now do you follow me?'

'No, I'm afraid not! You're talking in riddles again!'

'Of course I am! Read and understand!' The Prof chuckled and rubbed his hands together. 'Will you now explain to me what your father didn't say?'

'He didn't use any bad language, you know, the kind of Yorkshire expletives he would have used when confronting an impostor!'

'Well done, Edgar and full marks to Sir Arthur Conan Doyle. Our little discussion has been very productive though I see by your expression that you are still a trifle perplexed. Never mind, I don't need to detain you any longer. Thanks for your help and remember…*read and understand*!'

Mabel slinked seductively into the lounge and draped herself against the door, 'Here I am, Professor. I just knew you'd save the best till last!' she said, giving a fair interpretation of a femme fatale Bond girl in the latest of the 007 movies to hit the screen. Giles knew that shy, reserved Mabel was playing a part with him. This demure young woman who, according to her husband, loathed the sight of blood, was acting out her role unassisted by the evocative music of John Barry and he inwardly applauded her audacity. He immediately warmed to her, though he was hard pushed not to burst out laughing.

Restraining himself as best he could he was able to utter just one word, 'Spooky!'

'Well thank you, Professor Dawson. It's flattering to know that you are so stirred!'

'But not shaken, ma'am, more shaking!'

'Shouldn't it be the other way round, Giles?'

'I do believe you're right, Mabel. Anyway welcome and please make yourself at home! There's fresh coffee and some of Doreen's newly-baked scones.'

'Cook says the secret of a successful scone is sour milk and she certainly knows what she's talking about. Unfortunately I'll have to decline the invitation, it can play havoc with the figure, you know!'

She sat down near the fire, placed both knees together and rested her hands neatly in her lap. She was wearing a tailored grey skirt and pink sweater with a single string of pearls and, although the whole ensemble added to her coyness, there was an aura of provocative sensuality about her that seemed ready to explode.

'I want to be serious for a moment,' The Prof began. 'I want to go back in time to the night of 31st October 1952. You'd been married to Conrad for a little over a year.'

Mabel nodded.

'What were you doing at that time?'

'I was trying to gain some recognition as an artist working mainly with pen and ink. It wasn't easy but I gradually progressed, providing simple film posters for a small cinema and leading up to what I am doing now.'

'And what are you doing now?'

'I'm an illustrator of children's books. The *Punch* magazine, towards the end of the war, is to blame for that! The cartoons of Bernard Partridge and E.H. Shepard have a lot to answer for! Shepard, incidentally, was the illustrator of the Winnie-the-Pooh stories! Did you know that?'

'Oh yes, I know he was, Mabel. But we digress!'

The Prof cleared his throat.

'On that fatal evening in 1952 what did you do after your father-in-law ended his lecture about the proposed performance?'

'I stayed with Conrad and we took a walk outside.'

'You went down to the stables, I understand?'

'No! Whatever gave you that idea? Didn't Conrad tell you?'

'Yes he did, but I wanted to hear it from your own lips!'

'I see! Well you must know that we went round the house …along that side,' she pointed to the lounge windows. 'We were naughty and looked in through the closed curtains. We could just make out Victor helping himself to a drink.' She stopped abruptly and put a hand up to her mouth. 'I hope I haven't given the game away!'

'No, no, that confirms what I already know! When did you hear the gun being fired?'

'It was when we stopped at the steps leading down to the cellar at the back of the house. We thought we heard a noise but it might have been coming from the heating system. Anyway it was while we were chatting outside the cellar that we heard the sound of the gunshot. We started to run round to the front of the house…!'

'By the same way as you came?'

'…No, by the back door! We tried to get in that way but the door was locked so we went round past the library windows!'

'Did you see anyone there?'

'No, but what we did see was the outline of a figure disappearing round the front corner of the house!'

'Could you tell if the figure was male or female?'

'Not really, but if I had to guess I'd say it was a man. I think Conrad and I agreed it was probably George.' ·

'When you eventually got back into the house what did you find?'

'Everyone was crowding round the library door and, when I got there, all I saw was the blood! I felt sick and George helped to calm me down.'

'Were you aware that any members of the household were missing?'

'I'm so sorry! I couldn't be sure. I didn't recognise anyone or anything…except the blood!'

'I regret having re-acquainted you with the terrible trauma of that dreadful experience, my dear. I don't think we need delay your return to…!'

It was at that point that cook burst through the connecting door from the dining area and almost collapsed into The Prof's outstretched arms.

'Thank goodness I've found you, Mabel!' she blurted out. 'Isabella has suddenly taken a turn for the worse while she was getting out of bed. I think you should come. I can't find Laura or Sally…they must be down in the cellar!'

Without any further warning Giles was once again on his own!

It didn't take long for The Prof to realise where he might be going for, soon after leaving Maskelyne Hall and passing through Lockerbie, he was turning on to the Dumfries road and travelling a route he had regularly used during his senior school days in the early 1940's.

To be heading in this direction, in the rather noisy comfort of Freddie's car, was a welcome relief to the morning of prolonged intensity extracting details from the group that had been present the night, fourteen years ago, when his childhood mentor had died in strange circumstances whilst preparing to perform what he loved doing most...*magic!* Although still unable to satisfy himself exactly what had taken place, and why, he was, more than ever, sure that Jack Ramsden had been *murdered!*

'So where are we going? And don't be smart and say we're going to Dumfries - because I know that! What I'd like to know is...why?'

'I'm taking you to meet a good friend of mine; I phoned him while you were playing Hercule Poirot in the lounge and thought you might enjoy a breath of fresh air and a change of scenery. He sounded quite eager to meet you and I have an idea he might be of immense help.'

'Good for you, Freddie. I must admit I'm relieved to get out of the house for a short spell and get a chance to recharge the batteries. It wouldn't be a garage we're going to, would it?'

'Eh! Ah, I see. You're having your little joke! No, Giles, patience please! Oh, by the way, I was in conversation with Conrad at breakfast and we were discussing my family. Did you know that he and Mabel can't have any?'

'Any what, Freddie?'

'Family, you dope! Sometimes I despair!'

'No, I didn't know that! Good job I never broached the subject!'

Giles fell silent as the Spitfire sped towards the *Queen of the South* and when Freddie glanced across at him he was fast asleep.

Giles awoke with a jolt as the car juddered to a stop outside a red sandstone villa overlooking the river on the outskirts of the town. As he got out and stretched his legs the door to the house opened and a giant of a man stood on the doorstep.

Bulky, in every way, the man, who must've weighed nearly 300 pounds, wore corduroy trousers an open-necked shirt and tweed jacket. He was in his early sixties, had a broad forehead, a receded grey hairline, and slightly hooded eyes with dark eyebrows flecked with white, and a thin mouth.

Strangely enough his sinister appearance gave way to obese jollity at the sight of Freddie. In his left hand he carried a walking stick, which he used to support his weight while, with his right, he welcomed them both with warm handshakes. In a strange way Giles couldn't help feeling he'd seen this man before.

Once inside the hallway they removed coats and were ushered into the living room where a large coal fire was burning.

'Giles, I'd like you to meet an old friend of mine, ex Detective Superintendent Martin Drummond, known as "Bulldog" by his friends and probably by his enemies as well!'

'Glad to make your acquaintance...may I call you "Bulldog"?'

'By all means! Any friend of Freddie's...!' "Bulldog" motioned the others to sit down.

'Martin was at The Yard until he took early retirement and established a security team for North of England racecourses. That was how we bumped into each other.' Freddie grinned and Martin chuckled joyously as both men relished the thought of bumping into each other.

'Your friend explained quite a bit about why you are back in this neck of the woods when we spoke on the phone this morning,' Super Bulldog said, opening the conversation, 'and I will try my best to give you any helpful advice I can.'

'I will appreciate all the help I can get.'

'I'm not entirely sure how much you know of procedure in cases such as you're involved in but I'll take you through, step by step.'

'When death is sudden or unnatural a pathologist may be asked to examine the deceased by holding a Post Mortem, after which the findings will be reported to the Coroner who holds an Inquest. That is the case in England but in Scotland things are slightly different. Here the Sheriff has responsibility with The Procurator Fiscal having the key role in a Fatal Accident Inquiry, which is roughly equivalent to a Coroner's Inquest. Are you with me so far?'

'So far, so good!'

'I remember this particular death quite well and, though I didn't know the gentleman concerned, I knew of him. I talked with colleagues at the time, as it occurred in familiar territory, and it was fairly obvious that the death was unusual, to say the least! It was sudden and certainly not of natural causes.'

'The pathologist confirmed that death had resulted from a single gunshot wound from a Lee Enfield rifle that belonged to the deceased. No fingerprints were found on the gun except those of the magician. On further examination the gun was found to have had a slight modification producing extreme accuracy over short distances allied with a reduction of recoil. There were the usual marks around the wound in the chest consistent with being fired from a distance of several feet and there was no exit wound, thus the bullet remained in the body.'

'At the Fatal Accident Inquiry the Procurator Fiscal concluded there was no evidence to suggest foul play. Murder wasn't contemplated and Culpable Homicide, better known as Manslaughter, was also ruled out. Suicide was a possibility but all the signs were against it. Had any of those verdicts been implied the police would've been asked to investigate. As it was, an "open verdict" of "death by misadventure" was brought in signifying it could have been due to any number of possibilities but, more likely, that it was due to an accident. In a nutshell that is what it amounted to but now I understand you doubt the correctness of that verdict.'

'Yes!'

'That means you possibly have good grounds for such doubts and I'd be interested to hear what you've come up with so far.'

For the next thirty minutes, accompanied by the regular ticking of the clock and the irregular noise from the coal fire, Giles gave a fairly comprehensive account of events as told to him by the various members of the household at Maskelyne Hall. During the prolonged explanation Drummond offered his guests a cigarette which they refused. He himself lit a cheroot and puffed away quietly throughout.

When the story had finally unfolded "Bulldog" sat back and nodded.

'Compelling stuff! I grant you that! And even if you fail to prove the original verdict wrong, the very fact that a master magician conceived everything creates the possibility that nothing is as it seems and gives you a reasonable chance of unearthing something extraordinary, especially with your background knowledge of the history of magic. There is one statement, which you said was made by his wife when she knelt down by his side, which especially intrigues me!'

'What was that?'

'Apparently one of the last things he said to his wife was *"I didn't mean it to end like this!"* I know that is open to all sorts of interpretation, but to my way of thinking it hints that, as a magician, he regretted a well-planned trick had gone wrong...and that you may therefore be right in your assertions. Quite how you prove it, beyond reasonable doubt, is another matter!'

"Bulldog" threw the remains of his cheroot into the fire.

'I intend going across to America in the very near future,' The Prof said, by way of explanation. 'I want to visit Boston, where Jack went some months before his death. There are some things I have to get clear in my own mind before I start to put the whole puzzle together.'

'I may be able to help you there. I'll confirm that before you leave here! To get back to the planned illusion that might just have gone wrong, doesn't it hinge on this magician conceiving a secret means of entry into the library where another person could be concealed...perhaps more than one?'

'Agreed!'

'A kind of *priest-hole?*'

Freddie, who'd remained silent throughout this two-way conversation turned to look at Giles.

'I'm not sure I'm conversant with that term as a magician's device. Would someone please explain?' he said.

'I do recall some history lectures using the term which had a religious connotation but I'll leave the Super to bring us both up to date,' The Prof added for good measure.

'By all means!' The Inspector agreed, heaving his bulky frame out of the chair to reach down and grab a poker with which to disturb the fire.

'After the English Reformation, Roman Catholic priests and others attempting to flee from persecution often sought refuge in small secret holes or spaces created as hiding places in large English houses. Those hiding places were known as priest-holes! I hardly need to remind you of how little space is required to conceal a human being?'

'The secret of so many of the great illusionists!' added The Prof respectfully.

'Just so! Very little area is needed to conceal a human being…or an inhuman one, I might add!' "Bulldog" paused before continuing. 'Have you considered the use of the fireplace, behind the safe, as such a hiding place? A priest-hole with access being gained from, *under the library via the cellar*?'

'Worth considering! Yes, definitely worth considering!'

'There is one other way…! Simplest of all, and the way most of us overlook when attempting to outsmart the complexities of the professional magician!'

'O.K. I'll buy it!'

'Entry by the library door! That would, of course, presume collaboration by the two people waiting outside. Far fetched? Maybe, but not entirely impossible…or is it?'

'Food for thought!' Giles assured the genial giant who rose when his wife entered the room carrying a tray.

'A spot of afternoon tea, gentlemen?' she said, handing the tray to her husband before placing a small coffee table in front of him.

'Allow me to introduce you to my better half, though half is hardly what you get if you compare us by size!' Drummond guffawed as he laid the tray on the table. 'Meet my wife, Anna! You know of Freddie and this is his friend Giles Dawson, a Professor of History, my dear. More than that he's a professor of magic so don't get too close or he may saw you in half!'

'If that happened there would be even less of me for you to worry about, Martin!' she said and gave a nod and a wink before leaving.

Anna Drummond, in her late fifties, was petite beside her enormous husband but in the short time that she'd been in his presence, Giles was overwhelmed by her stature and regretted the brevity of their meeting.

'Tuck in lads!' "Bulldog" advised with enthusiasm. 'And if you'll excuse me for a couple of minutes I'll go and see if there's anything I can do.'

When the ex-detective returned Freddie and Giles had demolished most of the buttered gingerbread, fruitcake and assortment of biscuits and cheese.

'It's all set! I've been on the "blower" to Boston and managed to have a word with an old chum of mine before he went to work. If you decide to go to Boston give this guy a "buzz" beforehand. He and his wife will be glad to act as hosts and I'm positive you'll be well rewarded. You see Alan Berkeley is also a Professor. He's a Professor of Criminology at Harvard University and his wife Jennifer is a qualified criminal attorney!'

"Bulldog" started shaking with infectious laughter as he gave more information about the Boston professor.

'Some of the law students at Harvard claim they are on the ABC course; the Alan Berkeley Criminology course!'

The laughter subsided as he passed over a folded piece of paper.

'I've listed the phone number for you to give him a call, Giles. Alan will fill you in about essential details and when you decide to go he'll meet you at the airport. He thought around "Thanksgiving" might be a good time. Oh, and when you meet him, you'll get the shock of your life! I promise you! The shock of your life!'

He broke off and whispered something in Freddie's ear.

'Yes! The shock of your life! You'll recognize him the moment you clap eyes on him! Freddie will explain later!'

Ex Superintendent "Bulldog" Drummond bubbled over with convulsive laughter. Everything about the man, from the moment they'd met, had reminded Giles of the great Sydney Greenstreet who, at the age of 61, played his first film role in *The Maltese Falcon*. He was still bubbling with laughter when the two men left in the Spitfire to return to Maskelyne Hall.

Chapter 14
TUNNEL OF WITCHCRAFT

The daylight was fading fast when the red Spitfire crunched to a halt on the gravel path outside the Hall. The Prof dashed out, leaving Freddie to park the car round the back of the house, and immediately made a beeline towards the kitchen where he found Mrs. Gardner preparing ingredients for the evening meal.

'Have they finished yet?' he asked as he barged in.

'Slow down, Giles!' Doreen Gardner insisted with what closely resembled a scream as she brandished a large kitchen cleaver in his face. 'Have who finished? And finished what, may I ask?'

'I'm so sorry for rushing in like this!' he said pushing the glistening blade gently to one side. 'I should have explained! What I meant was have Laura and Sally finished working between the library and the cellar, you know, for tonight's performance? I was hoping to pay a visit to the cellar; there's something there I'd like to take a look at!'

'The cellar, eh? Well why don't you just try the door? I would've thought that was the easiest way to find out if they had finished!' she said as she crashed the lethal weapon into the chopping board with a spine-chilling thump making The Prof jump backwards in tremulous fright.

That settled it. He wasted no time in leaving cook to get on with her preparations for dinner and quietly closed the kitchen door.

As soon as he tried the handle of the door leading to the cellar he knew he was in luck. It opened immediately and the lights had been left on. So, he thought, the girls were still paying visits.

First examination revealed that the room was empty. He descended the steps and started to move along the assortment of magic props trying, as he went, to establish where the library fireplace was in relation to the cellar.

Once he was reasonably satisfied it was obvious a pair of portable steps were needed if he was to get close enough to the ceiling for a proper inspection. He searched around the maze of objects and, after several minutes, found some ladders of varying sizes plus two sets of portable steps. He chose the set that appeared to suit his purpose and carried them over to the area he'd earmarked for examination.

Once they were firmly in place he climbed upwards and started to scrutinise the ceiling above him. After shifting the steps a few times he was fairly content that there was no evidence of marks in the plaster conducive to the possibility of what jovial Super "Bulldog" Drummond had suggested. There was no way into the library from below, it seemed!

'That puts paid to the priest-hole!' he muttered bringing his head back to the vertical from the aching bent-back angle it had been in to gaze at the ceiling and, in the process, experiencing a touch of vertigo as he teetered on the top step.

The voice that answered him almost brought disaster as the steps rocked unsteadily and threatened to topple over.

'What on earth are you up to now, Giles?'

Unable to look down at the source of the question, The Prof clung desperately to the wooden sides until gaining confidence and virtually sliding down the steps to the ground where he began massaging his neck.

'Oh, it's you, Laura?'

'Yes, it is! And I was asking what you were doing. I'm not too sure I want to know the answer to that if you don't mind. You were talking to yourself again and, if you'll pardon me saying so, you sounded quite irreverent!'

'Aah! You mean the bit about the priest-hole?'

'Please, Giles! Stop right there! I don't want to hear any more!'

'Well if you really want to know I was getting a crick in my neck!'

'If you ask me, this place down here doesn't seem to be terribly good for your health! I'd try to avoid it in future if I were you! Now are you coming upstairs? We seem to be finished down here!'

At the library door The Prof left Laura to complete her final planning in collaboration with Sally for the forthcoming birthday illusion then walked out of the house, by the front door, and headed for the stable yard at a brisk pace.

To meet with and talk to George in his own environment, without the intimidation of the interior of Maskelyne Hall getting in the way, was too good an opportunity to miss.

When the low tones of the little groom floated out on the night air, as he talked to one of his horses, they came as music to The Prof's ears. His discreet cough signalled his presence.

'That you, Giles? Come on in but mind your step! I'm just putting my babies to bed for the night!'

'Sorry to disturb you, George, but I wanted a quiet word with you!'

'That's all right, lad. I'm just about finished with this one. Steady Sam, that's a good boy! He's been a right bugger today! Steady now! That's better. Right then, what would you like to ask me, lad?'

The Prof stepped nimbly out of the path of the restless hunter.

'On this night, fourteen years ago, you were stationed outside the library windows when your employer made his final preparations for the birthday illusion, I believe?'

'That's correct!'

'Did you see anyone during the time you were there?'

'No! Not a single soul!'

'That was very convenient for you?'

'What are you driving at?'

'Well didn't that give you the opportunity to…?'

'To what?' The little groom, his jaw clenched tightly, removed his cap and scratched his head.

'Why, to open the library windows, climb inside, grab hold of the rifle and shoot your employer, Jack Ramsden, in the chest!'

The silence, followed by the spluttering and outpouring of disbelief from the small broad-shouldered man, lasted no more than a few seconds.

'Bloody hell, you've got some imagination, I warrant you that! How the hell could I have done that when the windows were locked?'

'Easy! Your good wife could've left the windows unlocked. One of them might even have been left open, behind the closed curtains!'

'I don't believe what I'm hearing, son! Anyway why would I want to do that? I had no reason to bring an end to Jack's life!'

'No! No, of course not! Unless…?'

'Unless, what?'

'Unless you were about to be given the sack! Were you about to be dismissed?'

'Good God, no! Who gave you that idea?'

At that same moment the edginess of the little groom and that of his partner, the massive *Samson*, subsided in unison.

'Oh, now I can guess…! Victor!' he asserted under his breath.

'No smoke without fire, George! No smoke without fire! But whatever would prompt Victor to suggest that about you?'

'I'd rather not say!'

'I'd guess it would be in your own best interest, old fellow, but if you'd rather keep it to yourself…!'

George Gardner licked his lips apprehensively and the muscles in his face showed the tension in his jawbone.

'Victor was in one of his moody phases at that time. For some reason or other he imagined I was poking my nose in where I had no right. He found me checking those same library windows one night when Mr. Ramsden was working in secret with his assistant; that was before he had a barney with the girl and sent her packing. He all but accused me of playing Peeping Tom and threatened to tell his father and have Doreen and me as the next ones applying for a job. Victor wasn't flavour-of-the-month at that time and was trying to curry favour with his father. It was then that a rumour started that Mr. Ramsden was having an affair with his assistant when she came to the house for rehearsals. I'm sure Victor was behind that as well. Anyway it all died down after his father died and he's never been vindictive since then! Not that bad, anyway!'

'No comment! Except to say that I firmly believe everything you've said, old friend!'

'So why the hell did you accuse me?'

'I didn't, George! I merely put the possibility forward in order to get your reaction and perhaps collate some information. I'm more than satisfied with what you've told me! A couple more questions before I leave you to finish in here. Before the shot was fired, that night, did you hear voices coming from inside the library?'

'I heard Jack speak but couldn't make out what he said. He was shouting some kind of warning – I'm sure of that!'

'What did you do when the shot was fired?'

'I ran towards the front door!'

'Why? Why did you run?'

'Because I knew something was wrong!'

'Thanks, old fella! Will I see you at the birthday do?'

'Yes, if I can get finished in here! How long have we got?'

The Prof checked his watch.

'About an hour and a half so I'll let you get on with things in here!'

As he turned away the little groom grabbed him by the arm and the muscles in his face relaxed as he looked up into The Prof's eyes.

'Thanks for the talk, lad!'

On the way back to the big house The Prof went to the kitchen door and crept into cook's domain to find Mrs. Gardner with her back to him. Reluctant to cause her a second shock of the evening he kept well back and cleared his throat. Without turning round she straightened up from her chopping board and sighed.

'That you again, Giles? What is it this time?'

'I dropped by to apologise for almost impaling myself on your machete earlier this evening!'

Cook laid her knife down and slowly turned to face him.

'You are forgiven but you came mighty close to giving me a heart attack, young man!'

'Truce?'

She nodded and picked up the knife again as he moved towards the door.

'What are we having for dinner?'

'Isabella's favourite! Jack's as well, for that matter! Roast beef and Yorkshire pudding! She loves to have that on her birthday!'

'I thought I recognised the smell, Doreen. Damn, that reminds me; how could I be so stupid...I've forgotten to bring her a present!'

'Didn't Laura tell you? Isabella asks for nothing apart from her annual illusion and her special dinner, with her family gathered around, to bring back memories of the old days.'

'How is she? She didn't seem too well this morning when you rushed Mabel away from me!'

'She's much better, I'm pleased to say, and should be able to enjoy her evening. Now, be off with you, or I shan't enjoy mine! Oh, Giles!'

'Yes?'

'The best present you could give her would be...!'

'Yes?'

'...A solution to the puzzle that has troubled her for the past fourteen years! Can you oblige?'

'Hmm! I'll do my best!' he said thoughtfully and departed.

Having showered and changed The Prof went down to the lounge where Freddie was being entertained by most of the suspects he'd interviewed earlier that morning.

Victor approached him with a crystal tumbler and a decorative square-shaped crystal decanter.

'Is it a Scotch for you, Giles?'

'Yes, thank you!'

The Prof took the heavy glass and, as Victor poured a sizeable dram of whisky, became aware of the broad smirk on the eldest son's face.

'Your friend has been telling us that you visited a real-life investigator this afternoon!' Victor announced, the smirk widening.

'A crash course in detection, was it?' Conrad continued with the ribbing.

'You didn't need to go all that way, Giles! If only you'd asked, we could have played a game of *Cluedo*!' added Edgar, much to the amusement of the others.

Mabel came across wearing a red dress and carrying a container of ice.

'Say when, Giles!' she advised, helping him to a couple of cubes.
'When!'

'Edgar is spot on!' she said. 'A game of *Cluedo* might have revealed the murderer to be…!'

She was not allowed to finish.

'Professor Plum, eh Miss Scarlet? Wouldn't it be a surprise if I…?'

Giles raised his glass towards the lady sitting quietly by the fire.

'I sincerely trust you are feeling better, Ma'am! I am delighted to drink to your good health! Happy birthday, Isabella!'

The high-spirited hilarity died down and glasses were raised all round followed immediately by a chorus of "Happy birthday."

As if on cue Mrs Gardner entered the lounge to let everyone know that Laura was ready to begin the first part of the programme to celebrate Isabella's seventieth birthday.

The illusion, to be performed in the library, would be followed, shortly afterwards, by dinner.

George, who was waiting outside the library door like a genial commissionaire without the uniform, opened the door to allow everyone access.

Inside Laura was standing in front of a long box-like structure on wheels that was open at both ends. The structure resembled an open gipsy caravan and the wheels allowed a complete view of everything underneath. The main lights in the room were switched off and the only illumination came from two standard lamps strategically placed and cleverly angled towards the front of the caravan.

Laura was wearing a neat black dress, dark stockings and black shoes. Incongruously she also wore long elbow-length black gloves with which she gestured everyone to become seated on a row of chairs to the right of the door.

'Welcome to the Tunnel of Witchcraft!' she invited her audience in her perfect diction.

'What you see before you is an elongated narrow caravan raised from the ground on four wheels allowing total visibility above and below. There are steps at each end and the caravan is hollow with the inside painted black. You can see right through from front to back and, as I move along one side and round behind, you can see me pass the opening at the rear as you look through the tunnel.'

All the while she was speaking Laura moved round the back of the caravan crossing in front of a large screen and appearing on the other side. As she came back towards the front Giles started to recall a memory from the past.

Laura climbed the steps leading to the front opening and pulled out some black clothing that had been concealed by the dark interior of the tunnel. She then fixed what seemed to be a sheet of black paper over the opening covering it from top to bottom before descending the steps.

When she reached ground level she took the clothing and put on a black cloak that reached the floor and finally, over her head, she pulled on a black hood that had a macabre painting of a skull in white over the face part of the hood.

Without any further speech she glided once more towards the rear of the caravan, moved behind and reappeared round the other side. Because of the material covering the entrance it was impossible to see her figure through the hollow tunnel but she was out of sight for only a second.

She continued along the other side until she had completed a full circuit and was once again standing in front of her audience. She stretched both arms wide then turned and began to climb the steps.

At the top she removed the skull from her hood and appeared to stick it on the sheet of black paper covering the entrance. She descended the steps, turned to face her audience, bowed then left the room by the library door. It took several moments before it dawned on the seated group that the macabre image of a skull that was stuck on the black cover at the top of the steps was beginning to move.   A figure in black slowly emerged from the tunnel, descended ˙ the steps and stood before the audience. The arms were outstretched briefly before grasping the hood to wrench it away from the head and reveal the person who had seemingly just left the room – Laura!

A smiling Laura received the spontaneous applause when the door to the library was thrown open and Sally, dressed in a simple black ensemble, entered and breathlessly asked 'Am I too late? I'm afraid I was busy doing something else!'

'No, you're not too late, Sally dear! In fact you're just in time; I couldn't have done it without you!'

The plate-size Yorkshire puddings with a pouring of roast beef gravy made a superb starter for what was to follow at dinner.

Victor carved the succulent beef to perfection and, together with the selection of vegetables, roast potatoes, gravy, mustard and the sharp-tasting horseradish sauce, it provided a main course to savour. As a very special addition to the meal Laura had obtained two bottles of Château Lafite and George was asked to charge everyone's glass before Victor proposed a toast to his mother and the group rose to the occasion.

The next hour of the birthday banquet, which came to a climax with the rich chocolate orange mousse, passed enjoyably without tedium. The gourmet eating of good food, accompanied by fine wine and pleasant chit-chat, made the evening go with a swing, until it was time for the biscuits and Lockerbie cheese, plus the coffee and liqueurs, in the cosy warmth of the lounge.

'Will you tell me something, Giles?' Isabella asked when she was seated in her comfortable armchair by the fire.

'Of course! Ask away!'

'As someone who has delved into the history of magic can you give your valued judgement about the illusion you watched in the library tonight and do you have any more anecdotes regarding unusual coincidences that can add to the enjoyment you have given me since your arrival?'

Giles thought for a moment before answering.

'The whole undertaking was ultra-professional,' he stated assuredly. 'And I congratulate your daughter for putting on a demonstration under the extremely difficult conditions that the stage magician can avoid in a theatre. It was brave of Laura to attempt such a performance and I extend my congratulations to Sally who helped set up the Tunnel of Witchcraft. Her assistance was essential to the success of the project – as Laura acknowledged at the end of the illusion!'

Both young women stood and bowed theatrically then expressed, in unison as if it had all been rehearsed, 'You are most generous with your praise, kind sir!'

The Prof shook with laughter before responding.

'But there is more!' he said. 'In answer to Isabella's request about coincidences I think you might find, what I am about to say, remarkable in the extreme! Not only that – it has a bearing on the illusion of tonight! Do you wish to hear my tale?'

'Indeed I do, Giles! It sounds most intriguing! Please go on!' The matriarch of Maskelyne Hall glared around the room as if daring anyone to contradict her.

The Prof took a deep breath.

'The story I'm about to tell you is true – in every detail! I have to go back in time to the early war years. In September 1941 a magician named Cecil Lyle opened his Cavalcade of Mystery as The Great Lyle at the Aldwych Theatre in London then a year or so later toured the country and appeared in Glasgow where I went to see the show.'

Giles looked around the group who seemed to be listening attentively.

'Lyle was the first professional magician I saw perform on stage and on that night I took a friend with me. Her name was Janette and I met her when she was sent from Glasgow to Lockerbie as an evacuee.' He rubbed his chin. 'I ask you to remember her name because it is central to my story.'

'That night in Glasgow I saw an illusion so similar to tonight's offering by Laura that as I watched the Tunnel of Witchcraft in the library my memory went back twentyfive years and I was able to assess and compare the two performances.'

'As friends often do when growing up, Janette and I lost touch with each other – until some nine or ten years later when I met her again in a fashionable Glasgow ballroom. I was there with my fiancée to celebrate our engagement and Janette was with her doctor husband. After introductions were made I was told that Janette had three young daughters whose names were Patricia, Linda and Helen, in that order. When I tell you that my fiancée, whose name was Linda, was one of four sisters with the following names, in order of birth, Janette, Patricia, Linda herself and lastly Helen, corresponding exactly with the very same sequence, you'll understand how strange a coincidence that is. The odds against that happening in two families have to be a long shot in Freddie's parlance. In terms of coincidence they are astronomical!'

172

'Well I never!' Isabella uttered in a way that suggested she was hoping for some other facts to emerge to make them even stranger than any fiction.

'Spooky!' Mabel declared in her own inimitable style.

'However…' Giles added with deliberate emphasis as he sensed the approval on Isabella's features, '…that is not quite the end of it! You see when I studied the history of illusion and professional Magic I came across a further bizarre coincidence that defies belief. Researching the life and death of the magician who appears on the poster in your library, the one and only Chung Ling Soo, real name William Ellsworth Robinson, who was killed performing the Bullet Catching Trick at the Wood Green Empire in suburban London on Saturday March 23rd 1918, I encountered a further coincidence. In his dressing room prior to the last performance of the evening the magician was loading the muskets with gunpowder in the presence of a young soldier who was in his early years as a stage magician. In deference to the great Chung Ling Soo the soldier magician did not watch the front-loading of the guns but, instead, turned his head away. The "Chinese" magician had to leave the dressing room to sort something out with a stage carpenter and left the soldier behind. The young soldier was still there when the magician's wife came to collect the guns for the trick and he then decided to watch the show from the front of the house. It was from there that he saw Chung Ling Soo being shot and fatally wounded!'

The Prof paused for dramatic effect.

'The name of that soldier was Lance Corporal Cecil Lyle! The same Lyle I saw in Glasgow perform the illusion you all saw tonight!'

The fire produced the only sound to be heard. The only sound, that is, until Victor started his slow handclap.

'You are a damned fool if you expect us to be taken in by this manufactured mumbo jumbo and contrived claptrap of yours!'

'Please yourself, Victor! I was asked to give another example of coincidence and this I've done. If you choose not to believe it that is your prerogative. The latter part of the story concerning Chung Ling Soo and Cecil Lyle can easily be checked for authenticity by consulting the records. The earlier part about the girls' names, I'm afraid, must be taken on trust and that has been in short supply between us for some time – but, and I stress this, I assure you it is the absolute truth, another commodity I continue to search for.'

'Well said, Giles, though I too must admit that your tale is nothing like as easy to swallow as cook's sumptuous meal at dinner!' Conrad's declaration was expressed in good humour.

'Don't listen to the boys, Giles! I asked for it and I certainly got it!' Isabella said, tongue-in-cheek.

'Come on, Freddie! Where's your loyalty? When are you going to stand up for your friend?' Laura asked defiantly.

'Hold on, you lot, I've known Giles long enough to discover he's thick-skinned and can stand up for himself!' Freddie answered defensively.

'Oh, come on,' said Sally entering the discussion. 'I'm sure even you have to admit that, in telling his stories, he does embellish things?'

'That may be so,' Freddie said glancing across at his friend 'but what I can say about this particular story is that I knew his fiancée before her...tragic accident...and they both told me the strange facts about the sequence of names in the two families. I have no reason to believe they were making it up. Why should they?'

With the genial nod of the head from Giles Freddie continued the verbal defence of his friend.

'As far as the other part of the coincidence is concerned – about the two magicians – I was unaware of that until tonight simply because it had no relevance to the original story until the illusion by Laura and the fact that, as I understand it, Mr. Jack Ramsden had considered the thought-provoking Bullet Catching Trick as part of a future act. As you have already had it explained all you have to do is check the facts! By all means continue the banter, folks; my friend can absorb all the flak he gets!'

'What is flak?' Mabel enquired.

'Hostile criticism!' Victor said instantly. 'That's what it is – the kind of stuff I've been handing out since the professor arrived!'

'I know that! I have heard the term before, but where does it come from, know-all?'

'It was a wartime expression describing anti-aircraft fire from ground-based guns. Most of them probably in the London area during the blitz! Are you satisfied?'

'Roger!' said Mabel in her clipped enunciation, sounding suspiciously like a member of Bomber Command. 'Same as all those newsreels they showed of the Queen Mother visiting the East End with pictures of barrage balloons attached to long wires and so on!'

'That takes us back, doesn't it, Giles?' Freddie reminisced.

'You're no doubt referring to Cardington, I suppose?'

'You're talking in riddles again, Giles! Who or what is Cardington?' entreated the bemused Laura.

'Cardington is not a who, but a what!' The Prof explained. 'It was the RAF station near Bedford where we trained in the huge hanger that had been used for those barrage balloons, I believe, but had originally been the place where one of the largest airships, the *R-101*, was built!'

'Wasn't that the airship that was destroyed by fire?' Conrad asked.

'Yes, that's right!' said Freddie. 'That disaster in 1930 and the later destruction of the *Hindenburg*, in the same decade, spelled the end of airships as a mode of transport!'

'Weren't there some stories about people having premonitions about both of those tragedies similar to your accounts about the *Titanic*?'

The Prof looked across to Conrad who had posed the question.

'You're absolutely correct!' he said. 'Many cases of good and bad luck have followed events of appalling loss of life – many of them due to alleged premonitions.'

'Are you all right, Edgar?' Isabella asked anxiously. 'You are very quiet and any colour you had seems to have gone. I hope it isn't to do with anything you've eaten!'

'No, mother! It has nothing to do with anything I've eaten, I assure you! Cook's effort was wonderful!'

'Oh, my goodness, I almost forgot!' said a suddenly apologetic Mrs. Gardner, rising and scuttling away to the dining room.

She was absent for only a few moments and when she came back she was carrying a magnificent birthday cake and seven lighted candles.

Everyone burst into song.

'Happy birthday to you – happy birthday to you!
Happy birthday, dear Isa! Happy birthday to you!'

Isabella had to dab her eyes with her handkerchief as she rose to blow out the candles.

'Remember to make a wish!' her eldest son advised.

Isabella took her time and beamed with a kind of childish delight when she'd finished.

'Did you make a wish?' Sally asked.

'What? A wish? A wish, did you say?' The old lady sniffed and raised her hanky to her nose.

'Oh, yes! I made a wish!' she said endearingly as nostalgia spilled from moist eyes. 'I am, however, a little tired tonight so, if you'll excuse me, I'll head for bed! Thank you all for such a lovely time! Oh, Giles, can I have a word with you before I go upstairs? We can talk in the dining room!'

She gathered her things together and The Prof followed her next door.

'You are leaving tomorrow?' she asked when they were alone.

'Yes!'

'What are your plans, may I ask?'

'I have some lectures arranged and then I'm off to America where I hope to learn what evoked so much enthusiasm in your husband during his visit. After that I believe I may be better equipped to solve the mystery of what happened in this house fourteen years ago. It would help if I could take your husband's diary! May I?'

'Please do and I hope you find what you are looking for! That was my wish when I blew out the candles! Whatever you find please keep in touch with Laura and…come back and see us soon! I'll be there when you leave in the morning. Goodnight, Giles!'

The Prof returned to the lounge sampled a piece of birthday cake and more harmless repartee before deciding to retire for the night.

Outside his bedroom he looked at Freddie who had also elected to call it a day and both men stared as if reading each other's thoughts.

'What did you make of young Edgar tonight?' Freddie asked. 'He seemed to be afraid of something, didn't he?'

'I knew you were going to ask that! My thoughts exactly! But, for the life of me, I haven't a clue what's bothering the lad – but, of one thing, I'm certain! I'm going to find out! That, I'm afraid, will have to wait for now! See you in the morning!'

Chapter 15
ATHENS OF AMERICA

The Prof welcomed the beginning of November as a time for reflection – a chance to take stock and sort things out in his own mind.

The journey south in Freddie's red Triumph Spitfire on the Tuesday morning had followed a brief cheerio with each of the household at Maskelyne Hall, most of whom were also returning to their normal routines, after the Hallowe'en birthday party. He promised to contact Laura as soon as he had something definite to report and particularly when he required everyone to return to the house for a conclusion.

When he considered the maze of enigmatic brainteasers he'd already encountered a conclusion seemed a long way off, but two whole days in the company of Freddie and his wife Penny and their young family, at their home in the Cotswolds, with barely a mention of Maskelyne Hall, worked wonders – without throwing up any answers. The missing pieces in the jigsaw might be found in the United States and he looked forward to his trip with interest. That, however, would have to wait for another three weeks during which period he had to prepare and deliver lectures to a group of enthusiasts including an informal meeting with The Magic Circle.

Back in his South Kensington flat, after his relaxation in the Evesham area, he found time for research at The British Library where he consulted the *Life and Cases of Bernard Spilsbury*, the eminent pathologist.

Ploughing through the intricacies of forensic science, gunshot wounds and suicides until his head buzzed with factual information, surmise and speculation, he was soon ready for making plans for his visit abroad.

Seizing the opportunity to sit down with a drink he reached for the phone, scratched around for the piece of paper given him by Superintendent Drummond, ex of The Yard, and rang the number in Boston, U.S.A. As it was ringing he tried desperately to work out what time of day it was in Boston, making a pig's ear of comparing the end of British Summer Time with Eastern American.

When a female voice eventually answered he was momentarily taken aback until he established the owner of the voice to be none other than Jennifer Berkeley, wife of the Professor of Criminology at Harvard. A.B., as she called him, was out and she was about to leave to attend the law court so he was lucky to find someone to speak to. The upshot was that she and A.B. would be delighted to have him as a guest during the week of *Thanksgiving* if he'd give them a call nearer the date and confirm travel arrangements.

When he put the phone down he fixed himself another drink and settled back to mull over his imminent visit to the *Athens of America*.

The week before leaving for the States The Prof made three important phone calls. The first was to the Boston number when he again talked to Jennifer Berkeley confirming he would be travelling on Tuesday 22nd November on the evening flight from London, Heathrow. The second call was to the "Bulldog" in Dumfries to thank him and make clear that all was set for his few days on the other side of "the pond".

His third call was to Freddie to arrange a get-together before he left in order to exchange ideas and compare notes. It was at that meeting that his friend had disclosed everything Drummond had said about the Boston Professor, regarding the unmistakable identity of Alan Berkeley, that had caused him to display the chuckling outburst. His final statement being, " The Prof's love affair with Hollywood movies would be all he required!"

From his window seat Giles watched the twinkling lights of Boston as the evening flight, from Heathrow Airport, approached the Massachusetts coastline. It was late afternoon on this side of the

Atlantic and he sat, lost in thoughts, paying little or no attention to the announcements being relayed to passengers as the Boeing-707 descended and prepared to land at Logan International Airport.

Internationally accepted as the "Athens of America", Boston was a part of the United States he had not visited before and he had a strong gut feeling that perhaps the next few days would provide many answers that might reduce the complexity of the mystery back in Scotland. The first puzzle though was to recognise his host, from the description given by the "Bulldog", who had arranged the visit.

When the aircraft taxied and finally came to a halt, passengers around him rose from neighbouring seats and collected hand luggage. Giles, despite strenuous efforts to gain a vertical position, discovered, with a quickening heartbeat and a cold sweat on his forehead, a complete inability to rise.

He immediately put it down to a combination of flight inertia and the onset of cardiac arrest – until being told he'd forgotten to unfasten his seat belt. He looked at other passengers in a suitably embarrassed manner but nobody seemed to have taken a blind bit of notice of his temporary predicament.

Having retrieved his bags and negotiated passport control Giles scanned the faces waiting for visitors in the main concourse wondering what he would do if his host didn't show up displaying some form of identity. His concern was unfounded as he recalled the words of "Bulldog" relayed to him by Freddie, "Just remember," he'd said, "if you are half the movie buff I believe you are, it will be entirely unnecessary to add the tweed clothes and deerstalker hat in order to pick out this Professor of Criminology!"

Undeniably prophetic words as it was about to turn out; for Giles, with outstretched hand in readiness to greet an icon of the cinema, was already approaching the tall lean gentleman in the navy overcoat, black Homburg and red and white candy-striped bow tie who was carrying a walking cane that could have doubled as a swordstick. With his aquiline features he was the definitive Sherlock Holmes, Basil Rathbone or a very impressive facsimile of the great actor.

'Professor Berkeley, I presume?'

'Giles Dawson, if I'm not mistaken! At your service, Sir. Welcome to Boston!'

179

The handshake was firm and friendly and Giles was instantly aware that his few days in this New England city could well prove to be a rewarding experience.

Logan International Airport, 3 miles from Downtown Boston, is closer to town than any other major airport in the States and yet Professor Berkeley, driving his old but well-preserved Cadillac, still took a little longer to travel the short distance than the mileage suggested, despite avoiding the traffic jams at the tunnel and deciding, instead, to use the bridge. Nevertheless this delay allowed the two men to become better acquainted.

'We're heading for the Back Bay area of the city,' A.B. exclaimed as he swerved to avoid a taxicab 'and Jenny will be cooking up something to eat when we get there. After that you can put me in the picture regarding this problem of yours and we can take it from there!'

'Having twice spoken to your wife on the phone, I'm really looking forward to meeting her, but I hope you can assure me she does not resemble Dr. Watson!' Giles said, tongue-in-cheek.

'Not in the slightest!' A.B. replied chuckling. 'But I know what you're thinking of – that's "Bulldog" for you! He's quite a guy...and a damn good cop!' he said renewing his chuckle as he negotiated traffic. 'Did you have a good flight?'

'Yes! As a matter of fact I did. The weather was fine and we were up to time!'

'I have news for you! The forecast is for dry weather and sunshine for the next few days and our city is just made for walking so wherever you want to go it will be very pleasant for you.'

'There are several places I need to visit and the first of those is your library.'

'You're in luck again! We're only a few blocks away from the Boston Public Library and you can go there first thing in the morning. I'll fix you up with a map and you'll find the staff very helpful. On Thursday I'll take you over to Harvard and let you see where I expound my theories to unsuspecting law students; *Thanksgiving Day* is a public holiday so we'll have the run of the place. In the evening we'll have the traditional dinner and drinks and take an inventory of the progress you've made up till then.'

'Sounds fine by me!'

'Hold on – we're almost there!'

The car turned into a wide avenue of beautiful town houses split by a tree-lined central mall.

A.B. parked and, as both men got out, he announced, 'Here we are! This is Commonwealth Avenue and that name ought to make you feel quite at home! Let's go in and meet Jenny!'

The cool night air smelled good, with the trees in the centre of the mall adding their own quality to the evening freshness and, as Giles stepped across the broad sidewalk towards the front door, he believed this journey of discovery would reveal answers to the many questions that eventually ought to unmask a fiend still cloaked in respectability.

Inside, the house was spotless and friendly and smelled of fresh polish; the radio was on and Sinatra's "Fly Me to the Moon" filtered through to the hallway as A.B. placed his hat and cane in the stand, removed his overcoat and slammed the front door.

'Is that you, Alan?' The voice The Prof had heard twice on the phone now reached his ears from a much shorter distance.

Before her husband could answer she appeared from an open doorway. She wore a dark blue skirt and pale blue blouse; dark stockings with shoes to match her skirt, a skirt that was covered at the front with an apron imprinted with the stars and stripes. Her hair was dark-honey in colour and her eyes were jade green. She held out a small hand on a slim wrist and she smiled a smile that lit up her face and would surely capture the attention of any jury in the land.

'It's so good to meet the owner of the voice that offered me transatlantic heavy breathing by cable!'

'My pleasure, entirely!' Giles said as he held the proffered hand.

'How do you like your steaks done, Giles?' she said and, like jesting Pilate, the Roman Procurator, didn't wait for an answer.

A.B. shook his head and smiled, 'We'll go and see how she's getting on!' he said.

'You *are* a busy couple,' Giles remarked, grabbing the American by the arm. 'How do you manage to hold down two important and onerous jobs, yet find the time to run a home and accept a stranger with more problems?'

'The two of us become three most days – when Millie comes in and "does" for us. She'll prepare Thanksgiving Dinner on Thursday –

you'll meet her then! As for you, just let me say Jenny and I love a good mystery, especially one straight out of Ellery Queen, and the call from "Bulldog" more than hinted we might get that in abundance. Let battle commence, I say! Now I'll fix us all a drink!'

After grilled steaks and cold beer the Harvard Professor of Criminology and his Attorney wife kicked off their shoes and curled up on a couch in front of a roaring coal fire to listen to the History Professor of Magic and Illusion telling his story of events at Maskelyne Hall in faraway rural Scotland.

'That's quite a brief you have there!' said Jennifer when it was finished. 'Like something from an Ellery Queen mystery novel!'

'Coincidence rearing the head again!' The Prof commented excitedly. 'Your husband mentioned Queen when we were hardly in the house tonight and I have a passion for coincidences!'

'I reckon A.B. has a few strange stories you'll enjoy, especially about some of our Presidents he uses in lectures over in Cambridge. That's why he's sometimes known as Abe in College.'

'Yes! said the American with a nod. 'I'll be delighted to oblige, but that will keep till later. Here we definitely have a problem to solve – and that's where we both come in. I think we can help! Firstly we'll cover the motives for murder and see if any tie in with those on the list of suspects. Later on I'd like to take a look at the results of that word game you mentioned in your chronicle of events, but first things first!'

A.B. produced a memo pad and pen and started to jot down a few notes.

'Murder in the United States,' he said, continuing to write, 'is classified by degree of seriousness; murder -1 being the most serious, though that is for the purpose of handing out a sentence once guilt has been established in a court of law.'

'That's all very well, Alan, but it doesn't cut any ice for the victim – when murder can be *deadly* serious!' Jennifer's one-liner brought smiles all round.

She glanced over Abe's shoulder as he continued to scribble, nodded and looked up at Giles.

'What we'll do, when Abe has completed his list of motives, is take each of your suspects and try to match them with four trump cards.

Motive, Opportunity, Capability to kill and Capability to commit this particular crime i.e. Method.'

A.B. passed the pad across to Giles who scanned down the list.

Motives for Murder

Money – financial gain
Power
Fear
To preserve status, position or rank
Revenge – a powerful motive for murder!
Religious belief
Anger
Vanity
Jealousy
Protection of someone you love
Protection of yourself
Principle
Retribution – for previous humiliation
To overcome a barrier to sexual happiness
To eliminate someone capable of identification
To stop someone talking and giving show away
Insanity
To kill – just for the hell of it!

With memo, pad, and pen at the ready, Alan Berkeley began by writing a name down.

'Let's go through your list of suspects, one by one, starting with the lady of the house, Mrs. Ramsden. If you spot a convincing motive I'll make a note of it and we can see if any of the remaining trump cards match. That ought to produce something significant and, who knows, we might be able to reduce the list to a select few.'

'Agreed!'

'Here goes! Isabella Ramsden?'

'How's about Jealousy or Anger, if the rumour about her husband having an affair was correct?'

'Okay, but it was only rumour, remember! Opportunity?'

'Fairly obvious, she being outside the door with the key, but improbable unless Edgar was in cahoots!'

'Capable of murder?'

'She can be a feisty lady but I doubt murder would be in her repertoire!'

'Is she capable of killing the head of the family?'

'I would say not, but that might also apply to every one of our suspects!'

'Victor next! Motive?'

'Hmm! Difficult one this! Black sheep of the family and a disappointment to his father after his shenanigans at University and involvement in a marriage that was so ill conceived. To preserve status or even retribution for previous humiliation, but a question mark there!'

'Opportunity?'

'I can't see how! He seems to have a cast iron alibi; he was in the lounge when it happened and that is corroborated by two others!'

'Fine! Is he capable of killing?'

The Prof looked up from his list and thought for a moment before answering.

'I knew him as a boy and he can be very belligerent. He hasn't changed and, if I were pushed to answer, I'd say categorically that he's capable of killing, but killing his father? I think there has to be a doubt about that!'

'The four trump cards concerned with Victor are answered so we can move on to Laura. Before you comment please cast your mind back to those ancient Freudian riddles she sent you in her original letter. She had to be well aware of their significance suggesting a hermetically sealed chamber and, if she was privileged to have insider information about entry to the library but was then denied such entry by her father's change of heart, for whatever reason, might that not have been why she decided to take a bath? On the other hand she may well have decided to go through with the illusion and kill – in *Anger*! What do you say?'

'Although reluctant to admit it, I agree that could be a possible motive!'

'Opportunity?'

'If she knew the secret way into the library she would obviously have had opportunity but, if she did enter, there appears to be no reason why anger should be her motive for murder because being in the room with her father suggests she was there with his approval. It just doesn't make sense – there's something we're missing!'

'Leave that for a moment, Giles, is she capable of killing?'

'Laura is a beautiful woman who has demonstrated, in moments of stress, a fiery temper…!'

'It goes with the red hair, Giles!' said Jennifer with perfectly timed interruption. 'But is she capable of murder?'

'Maybe! He declared hesitantly. 'But I doubt she could ever commit patricide!'

Jennifer Berkeley uncurled herself from the sofa; 'I'm going to make some coffee!' she said and went off to the kitchen.

The Harvard Criminologist put a little more coal on the fire, said, 'I shan't be a sec!' and disappeared.

He returned with a stylish wooden box suitable for containing something larger than cigarettes, opened it and passed it across.

'A little bird told me you might enjoy one of those, especially when you're concerned. Care to join me?'

The Prof smiled and reached for one of the special Havana cigars.

'Those are very hard to come by if the reports coming out of Cuba are anything to go by,' he said rolling the cigar between his fingers before removing the band.

'Yes, you're quite correct; in fact they might be impossible to get shortly but I have a special contact who doesn't often let me down.'

Giles, noting the end had already been conveniently cut, put the cigar in his mouth and lit it with the monogrammed lighter offered him by his host.

Both men were lying back and blowing smoke into the air when Jennifer Berkeley returned with the coffee.

'A man's gotta do what a man's gotta do!' she drawled in Mae West fashion. 'If you can't beat 'em, join 'em!' she said, reaching for the cigar box and lighting one of the Havana's.

'Okay, guys – coffee break over – now where were we?' A.B. said between puffs.

'Three down, six to go, I think!' said his wife.

'Conrad is the next one to consider!' said an extremely relaxed guest who was almost asleep.

'Conrad it is then!' said A.B. 'Motive?'

Giles pondered for a few seconds before answering.

'Money! He and Mabel were a bit strapped for cash at that time and, by his own admission, the death of his father came as a kind of welcome relief.'

'What about opportunity?'

'They went for a walk, so they say and, although they claim to have seen Victor in the lounge nobody saw them – or where they went to! They could've gone anywhere and done anything if they knew the secret of the priest-hole. The problem is did they know? There has to be a question mark against opportunity!'

'What about capability to kill?'

'Doubts on both counts! The stumbling block could be Conrad's wife. If she remained with him she would be an accessory – and I have reservations about whether she has the stomach for a crime like this. One final thought; it's questionable whether they had enough time to perpetrate the shooting and arrive on the scene for Mabel to collapse at the sight of blood!'

A.B. nodded as he completed his notes. 'We can assess his wife, Mabel, now,' he said taking another puff of the cigar. 'Motive?'

'Money, I suppose – same as Conrad! But not a very strong one! Her testimony mirrors that of her husband and any opportunity she had must surely be identical to his!'

'That just leaves the capability factor. Have you anything to say on that?'

'Speaking as a lawyer,' Jennifer declared with some conviction. 'Mabel doesn't sound to me like a cold-blooded murderess or an accessory before and after the fact. She seems a sensitive human being who would abhor murder though still enjoying a good ghost story. But, in a way, so did Lady Macbeth – devoted to her husband and deciding the king must be removed for him to achieve the throne!'

'Hmm! An interesting analogy!' Giles said with a wry smile. 'And well worth keeping in mind!'

'Edgar is the next one in the ball game.' A.B. said, removing his bow tie. 'Any motive you can think of?'

'The only one that comes to mind,' Giles said scanning the list of motives. 'To get rid of the barrier to sexual happiness! He was intent on getting married and his father was set against this happening because of his youth. On the other hand Edgar was meaning to introduce Sally to his father at the birthday party after the illusion had ended and, if he had a motive for murder, wouldn't you think it doubtful he'd introduce his intended bride to all the rest of the family as a prelude to showing her off to the king? After all Sally was only a fiancée and it might have been long enough before a wedding took place and Edgar much older by then! Anyway the old man might have been taken with the young woman – she was not unlike his own daughter!'

'Okay, motive or not?'

'Possible but questionable!'

'We list that as a near miss then! What about his wife who, at the time of the shooting, was his fiancée?'

'Sally, by her own admission,' said Giles with a sigh, 'suggested the reason she was not brought home to the family until the end of October was because Edgar didn't think his father would approve. Now, if Sally *had* a motive it had to correspond to that of her fiancé at the time – namely to protect a loved one! But I'm clutching at straws; there may be other motives but I cannot fathom them out for the moment!'

'Opportunity?'

'We know she went upstairs to wash her hair and presumably took a shower locking the bathroom door until she was alerted by Edgar about the shooting downstairs. She was, therefore, beyond the scrutiny of anyone until Edgar banged on her door and, if she had the insider information about a secret entry, I suppose she could have used it! But I fail to see how she could have had that information when she was visiting Edgar's home for the first time!'

'Okay, again! A question mark against her on that score, leaving us with the issue of probability, Giles?'

'I guess Sally would support Edgar but only in a secondary capacity. Unless evidence to the contrary is produced the probability of her committing murder and, more importantly, killing her prospective father-in-law must be put on the back burner for a while longer!'

'If you'll excuse me, boys,' Jennifer announced with a stifled yawn. 'I have to be in the Courthouse tomorrow, so I'll clear things up in the kitchen and go to bed!'

'Giles and I will finish this list of suspects, darling, then put this to bed as well. See you in the morning!'

When Jennifer had gone A.B. poured a couple of bourbons and both men, friends for only a few hours, settled down to finish their smokes and analyse the last two on the list of suspects – the retainers George and Doreen Gardner.

'From what you said in your account of the happenings at Maskelyne Hall, George and Doreen have been with the family for three decades or more and appear to be a devoted pair who enjoy the atmosphere of the place. In your opinion do either of them have a motive?'

'I did think so at first, but on further examination I'd have to say…no! Unless the rumour that George was to be sacked had some foundation, in which case his wife would have been dismissed as well. There doesn't appear to be any strong reason for murder. But, as I've said before, there's no smoke without fire. The murder of Jack Ramsden, in order to prevent being fired, was no sure thing with such a close-knit family!'

'The description of their duties on the night of the illusion, gave both George and Doreen ideal opportunities to have full control over entry.' said A.B.

The American Professor picked up the memo pad once more and scribbled a few lines.

'Had Doreen left the windows unlocked it is fairly safe to assume they would go unnoticed by the magician,' he continued outlining his premise. 'And by locking them immediately on her return to the library she would've created the hermetically sealed chamber effect. The other means of entry, the door, was in fact locked from the outside, by the magician's wife, who was supervised by his youngest son. George, who was the only one outside those windows, was able to gain entry, do whatever had to be done, and get out again. His actions would be undetected unless, of course, some other member of the family happened to be in the vicinity and that is something over which he had no control.'

'Yes, but why take a chance that no one else came on the scene? Nevertheless, there were two very simple and obvious means of entry, as you correctly point out – the door and the windows – and all the time I've been searching for a complicated way in. I believe I've already considered those and rejected them but I do agree they demand extra investigation.'

'Taking the hypothesis a little further there are several pieces in your story that also demand more scrutiny.' A.B.said as he made additional scribbles on the pad and Giles tried very hard to keep awake.

'Who suggested you go riding with Laura? Answer – George!'

'Who had the opportunity to tamper with the stirrup leathers? Answer – George and Laura!'

'Who was in the cellar when you had your encounter with the Iron Maiden? Answer – George (who admitted being there attending the central heating) and don't forget Laura who assisted you out of the place!'

'Who were diagonally opposite at the séance table and were able to move the glass to whatever position was required? Answer – George and Doreen!'

'Look over that list and who is the common denominator? Answer – George! With Laura and Doreen coming second and third!'

'Coincidence rearing the ugly head again?' Giles insisted with a questioning smile.

'Maybe! Maybe!' Abe Berkeley said slapping his hands loudly on both thighs. 'I was going to let you into my secrets about coincidences involving renowned leaders of our great Constitution but they can wait!'

Berkeley rose and casually poured two more drinks. 'Look, Giles it's getting late and you've had a long day, let's have "one for the road", granted that the road we'll be taking is the short one to our respective beds. Tomorrow is another day!'

Stubbing out his cigar and draining his glass before being overcome by the oncoming sleep, Giles was a compliant participant when shown the way to his bedroom where he could lay down undisturbed and unmolested for a good few hours – or so he thought!

'Are you asleep, Giles?'

Being roughly shaken in the middle of the night in a strange bed was not an idea he was particularly enamoured with.

'I don't think so, Holmes,' he said, trying hard to sound jocular. 'But God knows I should be! I was dreaming about Conan Doyle's excellent sleuth until I was rudely interrupted!'

As soon as the bedside lamp was switched on the sight that met his eyes was of a tall lean man with aquiline features dressed in a long Cashmere dressing gown, the spitting image of the person in his dream.

'Is there something wrong?'

'No, not wrong, but I couldn't sleep! My brain was ticking over and I have an idea. So preposterous it might, conceivably, be the elusive answer you've been chasing. D'ya wanna hear it? Here grab this, and come on through.'

Throwing a dressing gown on to the bed the American turned and made for the door. 'I'll make fresh coffee!'

'Much of the graphic happenings of your week-end in Scotland have been going round and round in my head and I've been trying to make sense of something!' A.B. said as both men sat drinking coffee.

'This preposterous idea of yours; what is it?'

'It's only a hunch, mind you, but let me ask you a question first. What kind of a man was he?'

The Prof, looking decidedly bleary-eyed, could utter only one word, 'Who?'

'Your magician friend, Jack Ramsden! Drink up your coffee!'

'How do you mean – what kind of a man was he?'

'Well, wasn't he badly let down by his assistant shortly before the illusion was due to be performed? I just wondered if he'd bear a grudge?'

'He could be bloody-minded, that's for sure, but bear a grudge? Possibly! What are you hinting at?'

'What if Jack planned to get even by throwing suspicion on his ex-assistant by arranging a failed suicide that subsequent investigators could be persuaded to believe was a failed attempted murder!'

'I'm not sure I follow!'

'The magician might have entrusted one of the family or one of the retained staff to enter using the hidden route and with the rifle and stand mathematically in a position to be fired to hit a position on, say a shoulder to wound and not kill, the new assistant could remove any evidence of a suicide attempt leaving the wounded man in what appeared to be a sealed chamber. Had the magician survived, as he expected, he could accuse his former assistant with the damning evidence that she was the only one in possession of the secret entrance to the library and was therefore the only one who could have carried out the shooting.'

'But how could Jack be sure the gun was aimed at a non vital spot?'

'He couldn't, but I'm certain that in history you can produce examples of magicians working with crossbows, firearms, tomahawks and throwing knives calculated, within an inch or so, to hit or miss a given target and, although I accept that my idea is a little extraordinary, I believe so was Jack. I did say it was preposterous – but not impossible! Even if the ex-assistant had an alibi she would be hard-pressed to provide a believable case for her successful defence!'

'So you think it might have been an attempted suicide made to appear as attempted murder – an audacious plan that went badly wrong and, of course, whoever had been a party to the plan on the night would be unable to make such an accusation with the magician dead?' The Prof took a sip of coffee and his eyes showed the wheels in motion.

'But whatever made you contemplate such a preposterous idea?'

'Why, it was one of the last things Jack said to his wife before he became unconscious.

"I never meant it to end like this!"'

Chapter 16
HOW A BOTTLE OPENER CAN OPEN
MORE THAN BOTTLES

The Prof checked his watch shortly after leaving the 19th century town house as he strolled along the French-styled boulevard in the warm hazy sunshine of Boston on the morning before Thanksgiving Day.

After a breakfast of wild blueberry pancakes in a stack with butter and blueberry syrup, freshly squeezed orange juice, and coffee, he felt equipped to make a start at interpreting some of the notes he'd found in a dead man's diary of fourteen years ago.

He removed the white linen handkerchief from the trouser pocket of his dark grey three-piece suit; a handkerchief knotted in three places to remind him of important things to do, and instantly recalled his first port of call as the Boston Public Library.

The second knot, he was sure, had to be The Statler Hotel and the third knot…? Hmm…perhaps the third one was to remind him not to forget what the other two were for?

He checked his watch again. He'd more than three hours before he was due to meet his American host for lunch…time enough to *put a toe in the water* and get cracking on the final phase of his quest for a solution to the mystery of Maskelyne Hall.

With overcoat open and hands in pockets he sauntered past the seated statue of abolitionist William Garrison, one of about half-a-dozen statues in the wide mall, with two lines of trees desperately clinging to the last of their leaves splashed with striking autumnal colours.

At the corner of Commonwealth Avenue and Clarendon Street he wandered past the Romanesque Style First Baptist Church, stopping briefly to admire the square bell tower with the decorative frieze modelled in Paris by Bartholdi, the sculptor who created The Statue of Liberty.

The faces on the frieze, depicting the sacraments, were of some prominent Bostonians, including Henry Wadsworth Longfellow whose poem about *Haunted Houses* had been quoted by Mabel during an evening discussion at Maskelyne Hall.

Was this another of those coincidences...or an ominous portent perhaps? The Prof smiled and walked on.

He turned right into Newbury Street, the name of which brought back vivid memories, whilst in the RAF, of watching racehorses exercising on the downs near Greenham Common, Newbury, at a time when he himself was engaged in target practice.

Newbury Street was a place of art galleries and sidewalk cafes and, as he passed the Café Florian, Boston's oldest and most authentic coffee house, he was immediately reminded of that third knot in the handkerchief – he was due to meet A.B. there, later on, for a spot of lunch.

Consulting the map, given to him by his host at breakfast, he turned left into Dartmouth Street and was soon approaching Copley Square to his left and, facing the square on the opposite side, the magnificent structure of the Boston Public Library.

He crossed the street and walked towards the building constructed of Milford granite blocks set on a broad granite platform. The greyish-white stone reflected faint pinkish lights and the ornamental cornice above the frieze at the top of the façade, where it met the red-tiled roof, was topped by a green copper cresting.

As he climbed the steps leading to the three entrance arches flanked on either side by two seated female figures in bronze representing Art and Science, he glanced up to the keystone above the central arch on which was sculpted the helmeted head of Minerva, goddess of wisdom.

Above that he read the words FREE -To-ALL then, with a quickening heart beat he moved forward into the vestibule and took the first steps towards finding out what Jack Ramsden found in this beautiful city fourteen years before that sparked off the excitement that ultimately led to his death.

Inside the building the walls and vaulted ceiling were of pink marble with the floor inlaid with patterned marble and, from a knowledgeable attendant, he learned that the three doorways leading to the Main Entrance Hall were copied from the entrance to the Acropolis of Athens; one of the reasons, he thought, why Boston was accepted as the Athens of America.

In the deep niche, on the left as he entered, was a bronze statue of a dashing aristocratic cavalier who had been beheaded in England in mid to late 17th century for *rebellion against the king* and The Prof reflected on the possibility of another *rebellion against the king* at Maskelyne Hall being yet one more coincidence that would eventually take a hand in exposing an ingenious murderer who'd stop at nothing in order to kill in cold blood.

He checked his watch again and decided he'd better get a move on.

Heading for one of the three doorways leading to the Main Entrance Hall he was stunned when he learned, from the same obliging attendant, that each of the six doors, made of bronze, weighed fifteen hundred pounds. Symbolic figures sculpted and arranged in pairs represented Music and Poetry, Knowledge and Wisdom, and Truth and Romance and, once again he saw the figures as epitomizing much of what he sought on both sides of the Atlantic.

He asked where he was able to examine copies of newspapers and was directed to a small flight of stairs just off the first floor entrance.

Further information that original paper copies in bound volumes might take a day or so to be delivered from an off-site depository was less encouraging, but those were available on microfilm for reading without much delay. It all depended on the titles required.

Upstairs he was well received by a capable young woman who advised him that a search of the *Boston Globe* or *Boston Herald* might reveal details of the 1952 magicians' convention, but they were on microfilm.

They were, however, available in bound volumes, which were stored in the library basement and could be retrieved on presentation of a call slip and a valid library card. When he asked how these could be obtained he was told he'd have to produce identification and be vouched for by some person known to the library.

Gentle persuasion and a short call to Harvard College by the librarian on his behalf did the trick.

After a short wait bound copies of both newspapers for May and June 1952 were brought to him and he started to look through them for articles relating to the Convention.

For the best part of one and a half hours he waded through page after page but to no avail.

Totally disconsolate he returned the non-productive volumes to the librarian and was ready to leave when he was called back.

'Excuse me sir,' she said, but there's an outside chance you might find what you're looking for in the *Boston Sunday Globe*. Would you like to search?' Her smile was irresistible and the decision to hang on a bit longer wasn't difficult to make.

Going straight to the *Boston Sunday Globe* of June 1, 1952 he scanned each page in turn until the article on page 37 caught his eye.

Nothing to Hide!

Magicians Say It's Fraud, But Who'll Believe 'Em

By PAUL BENZAQUIN

BULLETIN – The Statler Hotel, headquarters for the American Society of Magicians' convention disappeared in a puff of blue smoke last night. It was later found in the bottom of a silk hat beside a small rabbit. Police with-held details and it was rumored their report had been changed into a three-dollar bill by one of the delegates.

The remainder of the article detailed many of the close-on manipulators and sleight of hand experts including the great Chanin – "openly regarded as the best."

There was no mention of anyone with the initials K.A. but The Prof was more than satisfied with the facts already obtained.

He thanked the librarian for her splendid assistance, checked his watch again and, leaving behind the classical elegance of the Boston Public Library, headed for Newbury Street and the Café Florian for his lunchtime meeting with Professor Berkeley.

'I take it you were successful in reading our local journals.' Abe Berkeley said as the two men sat down to lunch. 'The young woman I spoke to, on the phone, seemed satisfied with the credentials I presented on your behalf!'

'Oh yes! I was treated with the utmost courtesy and, to my knowledge, at no time did they call out the FBI!'

'Super news - I'm relieved to hear it!' Berkeley replied snapping his fingers to get the attention of a waiter. 'What's next?'

'The Statler Hotel, where the Golden Anniversary Convention of the Society of American Magicians was held.'

'The hotel you're looking for has changed hands since 1952; it is now owned by the Hilton Hotel chain and goes by the name of the Statler Hilton. You'll find it in Providence Street and, although there's been a change of name, many older residents of Boston still refer to it as the Statler.'

Giles brought out the map and A.B. pointed to a place not far from where they were sitting.

'It overlooks the Public Gardens and you'd normally have a good view of the Swan Boats but unfortunately they've been put away for the winter season.' he said.

Giles folded the map and stuffed it in his overcoat pocket.

'I seem to be in luck again.' he said cheerfully. 'It looks as if it's only a short walk from here and that will give me time to dig around for the clues I need.'

'You have all afternoon to explore and ask questions and we'll have dinner in town. I've been in touch with Jenny and made arrangements for us all to dine at the Café Rouge this evening; you'll find it in the Statler Hilton so you won't get lost and Jenny will meet us at about 7.0 p.m. and we can take it from there. Now!' A.B. said rubbing his hands. 'Can I interest you in a bite of lunch? Oh, and before I forget, I have a tip for you...don't ignore the hotel doorman – he's often the best source for information!'

A light but satisfying lunch later The Prof, armed with his street map, headed for the Statler Hilton Hotel on Providence Street and, after speaking with the smart and obliging uniformed doorman, made his way to the Main Lobby where he was completely mesmerised with the décor.

The lobby was enriched with the Spanish Renaissance motif, the painted and gold-leafed coffered ceiling and the Terrazzo and carpet flooring.

The walls were panelled in rich, dark American Walnut that enhanced original artwork and period antiques throughout the nerve centre for guests and visitors alike.

He had a word with receptionists, attendants and the Head of Sales and Marketing; he was invited to go upstairs and downstairs where he met and talked with an attendant on each floor, but not a single person remembered or had even heard of a magicians' convention taking place in the vast complex in 1952 or any other year.

There was no doubt in his mind that the event had been held in the hotel, the newspaper article confirmed that, it was simply that nobody could recall any details that could help.

It was as if, like the first lines in the *Boston Sunday Globe* report, the Golden Anniversary and the Statler Hotel had disappeared in a puff of blue smoke

Was his mind playing tricks again? Surely the Statler Hotel and the Magicians' Convention couldn't vanish like the murderer in the library at Maskelyne Hall?

Up a flight of stairs from the lobby the Mezzanine level was hung with original artwork and decorative effects that evoked the magnificent opulence of the chandeliers hanging over the Main Lobby.

From conference facilities and ballrooms, dining rooms and domed ceiling theatre restaurants and cafes, the building lived up to the hotel's original mission to be a "city within a city."

Everywhere he went he was greeted with charming courtesy. On one of the floors he met a mature employee who had some recollection of the magic convention being held for a few days but couldn't put a date on the event.

At the mention of a bottle opener he was told the hotel did possess the equipment in some of the rooms and he was kindly allowed to see for himself but was none the wiser. The bottle opener had no significance as far as the employee was concerned and neither had the initials K.A. Giles was drawing a blank and getting nowhere fast – but *nil desperandum,* as his Latin tutor once cajoled him.

He was sure he'd have been totally depressed by this stage, had it not been for the splendour of the place.

As it was he was convinced that, if he remained long enough and soaked up the ambience that had been the brainchild of E.M. Statler, one of America's most visionary businessmen, some coincidental twist of fate would come to his rescue.

He gawked when he was invited to explore the Palace of Versailles styled room in black, turquoise and gold with a parquet floor, Bacarat crystal chandeliers and velvet draperies.

History dictated that the Palace of Versailles had been built for Louis Quatorze, the sun king in the 17th century but, as yet, the only sun The Prof could count on could be seen outside this magnificent palace shining hazily on the streets of Boston

With the compliments of the hotel, afternoon tea was served to The Prof in Swan's Court and that gave him the chance to have time out to evaluate his progress so far.

He questioned a waitress who said she believed the doorman was a bit of an amateur in magic; he was always ready to entertain her with his disappearing coins. She thought he might have sources that could take the gentleman a bit closer to knowing what had gone on in the hotel over the years.

What a fool he'd been...hadn't A.B. warned him not to ignore the doorman? Wouldn't it be ironic if the amiable person in uniform, who had been the first person he'd met at the hotel, now turned out to hold the secret he was looking for?

He finished and left Swan's Court, moved through the Main Lobby and out to the Main Entrance where the friendly doorman asked if he wished a cab.

The doorman's name was Eddie and he was, as the young lady in Swan's Court had said, a keen amateur in the field of magic. Yes he did remember the Magician's Conference – "Wow! Was it that long ago?"

His memory was a bit sketchy but he did recall a professional dealer in magic who'd caused quite a stir. His name had been Allen – that was his surname – and the name had been easy to remember. Why? Because it sounded the same as the middle name of the gentleman whose birthplace wasn't far from Fayette Street where he lived in Boston.

What significance could a middle name have to imprint itself so indelibly in the memory of an amateur magician? "Why, that was easy! It was the middle name of the man who wrote what was considered by many to be the first detective story and, almost certainly the first locked room murder – *The Murders in the Rue Morgue"* – *Edgar Allan Poe!* You see – the names had almost identical spelling!"

The doorman's words reverberated in The Prof's head. Yes, he *could* see; in fact he was beginning to see a lot clearer now. The fog was dispersing. He cursed himself for not conversing with Eddie in the first place. But then he might have missed...? Never mind! The end of the tunnel was coming into view.

Now Eddie wasn't sure if the dealer with the surname Allen was of any importance but he'd been all the rage at the time..."Was it that long ago?"

No, he didn't remember Allen's first name. He might be the K.A. he was looking for but there was someone else who might just be able to help him there. In Boylston Street there had been a famous shop called Max Holden's Magic Shop, run by Herman Hanson, who'd been the chairman at the Convention. Mr. Hanson had been a renowned professional in magic and Eddie used to buy some small items of hand magic there.

It was there he met another magician who was now a Sergeant in the BPD – the Boston Police Department to give it the full title. No, he didn't think Max Holden's shop was still in Boylston Street but he was sure Sergeant Anderson was still at the Police Department.

The handshake was as substantial as the tip The Prof tendered at the end of a brief encounter and, as he buttoned up his coat and wandered on to the sidewalk, his smile ironed out all the frowns that had been gathering on his forehead. He wasn't too clear in which direction he was walking but he didn't care. He started whistling *"Fly Me to the Moon"* and was almost certain he could see the Swan Boats – even though he'd been told they were now away in winter quarters.

The Café Rouge was becoming busy when The Prof walked in and removed his coat. He was shown to a reserved table set for four, which he thought was rather odd, but had little time to dwell on that trifling problem as A.B. and Jennifer Berkeley approached.

When the lady was properly seated at the table four menus and a wine list were produced.

'So, my friend, did you score in the Statler with the same amount of success as you did at the Library?' A.B. asked with a wicked twinkle in his eyes.

'Yes, I'd love to hear how your day has gone!' his lawyer wife added.

'I've had a bit of good luck,' The Prof began earnestly. 'I may have cracked the code regarding the initials K.A. although I have to admit that I'm still none the wiser about the cryptic "bottle opener" quote!'

He scanned the menu as he continued. 'I also have to admit I almost didn't take your advice – about the encyclopedic doorman, I mean! Good job I did! Eddie, that's the doorman, was a mine of information; he mentioned a Sergeant Anderson of the Boston Police Department as a possible extra source of info about what happened here and I wondered if you might just be able to make things easier for me by...?

The Prof's appeal was cut short by A.B.'s interruption.

'Well I sure am glad you took that advice,' said the American, rubbing his hands, 'I'd be glad to help...in fact I have news for you. On the recommendation of one of our tweedy Profs at college I was on the phone to someone who can help and he has agreed to join us here sometime this evening!'

'The reason we are set for four and not three I assume,' said Jennifer placing her napkin over her lap and indicating the place settings and additional chair at the table, 'Are we ready to order?'

'Your assumption does your legal powers of deduction proud, my dear,' said A.B. 'I'm famished and I suggest we have the Clambakes and a bottle of Chardonnay and I do commend you, Giles, for your astuteness in asking...who was it, Eddie, about...?'

'More coincidences A.B. – you seem to be one step ahead all the time? You never cease to amaze me, but I'd like to hear more about yourselves. Did you happen to meet at College, 'cause that would be romantic?'

'No, sorry to disappoint you Giles, but as a matter of judicial fact, Alan and I met in the D.A.'s office, purely by chance one morning about ten years ago, shortly after I started practicing in Boston!'

'Aah! So you didn't actually meet at Harvard?'

'No, I'm afraid not,' Abe Berkeley replied. 'Jenny would've had to impersonate a man in order to do that and all would have been revealed in the showers after the ball game – you see Harvard, has never admitted females to the College; I'm sure that's gonna change in the next three or four years! I certainly hope so!'

'I didn't know that!' The Prof's words showed his disappointment as he gazed at Jennifer. 'So it obviously hasn't been too easy to become a female attorney?'

'No!' Jennifer conceded. 'I gained my *juris doctor* at George Washington Law School and was admitted to the D.C. Bar shortly after. Three years later I was granted admission to the New Mexico Bar as one of the earliest female attorneys – a bit of a man's world, I'm afraid – but I'm steadily climbing the ladder!'

'So I suggest,' said the Harvard man, grabbing The Prof's arm and giving it a firm squeeze, 'that you keep in with Jenny; you never know when you're gonna need a good lawyer – and she's one of the best!'

'Flatterer! Can I have that in writing?' Turning to Giles, she asked, 'Have you, by any chance, had a problem with the English language, as it is spoken by some of our inhabitants?'

'No, I can't say I have,' said The Prof with a puzzled look on his face. Everyone has been so pleasant and easily understood – even the friendly Eddie at the door. Why do you ask?'

A.B. guffawed, fit to burst and the tears started to roll down his cheeks.

'Oh, yeah!' Jennifer Berkeley drawled in a strange dialect and wiped her husband's eyes with her lace handkerchief. 'No reason except that Alan says there's a saying used in jest at the College that typifies some of the local dialect. It goes something like…well you tell 'em pahdner!'

The Professor of Criminology controlled his laughter long enough to spout – 'Ya can't pahk ya cah in Harvihd Yahd!'

'Which loosely translated means – you can't park your car in Harvard Yard!' Jennifer said, joining in the laughter.

Giles nodded in amused appreciation as he spread his napkin on the table to use as a substitute map and, pointing with his index finger he said, 'With the help of Abe's map today I was able to get from theah to theah!'

All three were still bubbling over when a perplexed waiter poured the wine and the main course was served.

When the coffee was brought to the table Alan Berkeley was called away. On his return a blue-uniformed officer in the Boston Police Department accompanied him. Both men looked suitably stern.

'Whatever it is you've been up to, Professor,' A.B. announced, 'I do hope you've taken my advice and fixed yourself up with the services of a good lawyer. The lady seated next to you looks familiar as a criminal attorney – so allow me to introduce the gentleman I spoke to on the phone this afternoon; Sergeant John V. Anderson of the BPD.'

At an indication from the criminologist the police officer sat down and produced four compact magazines and placed them on the table in front of him.

The Prof could see that each of the magazines was headed M – U – M representing Magic – Unity – Might; The Society of American Magicians published them monthly.

Giles picked up the April, 1952 edition. It was the Boston Issue and had a picture of three magicians on the cover, including that of Herman Hanson – the Boston Convention Chairman.

He waded through page after page, much of it covering the forthcoming Convention, with mention being made of Milbourne Christopher, "the magicians' magician of the year", as one of the many glittering entertainers set to appear in the Hotel Statler's great ballroom.

A search of the May and June issues was made while Alan and Jennifer Berkeley were engaged in conversation with the police officer and a fresh supply of coffee was ordered. He finally picked up the July, 1952 issue and noted that the opening articles covered the Golden Anniversary Convention. This was more like it, he thought.

The names of Long Tack Sam, The Rigoletto Brothers, Ace Gorham, Slydini and John Scarne read like a "who's who" of magic and The Prof almost forgot what he was searching for then, turning page after page finally there it was on page 37 - in black and white, at last, under - Contest Winners.

Page 37 again – same as in the *Boston Sunday Globe*!   Yet one more strange coincidence in the entire chapter of events that continued to play havoc with the historian's brain.

For what seemed an eternity The Prof read and reread the line that leapt out at him from the magazine.

"…Ken Allen won the professional trophy…"

K.A. was no longer the mystery man – but his illusion had still to be revealed. Even so The Prof could not contain his elation and his facial expression must have given the game away as Sergeant Anderson looked up from the others and asked 'Have ya found what you were looking for?'

'Yes and no!' replied The Prof. 'The name of Ken Allen is there but there's no mention about the illusion he performed!'

'Oh ya mean the guy who won the trophy? Ken Allen, the dealer! I can fill you in on that,' he said. 'Ya see I was theah!'

Alan and Jennifer Berkeley glanced at each other as the pronounced dialect made an impact and they struggled to suppress their glee.

'I'm listening!' said an expectant Giles in anticipation.

The tale that ensued from the policeman-come-magician held the attention of both Professors and the lady Attorney.

It sounded like a chapter from the writing of Clayton Rawson or John Dickson Carr.

Whilst attending the trade fair that was part of the Conference in 1952 John Anderson had heard, on the grapevine, that a leading dealer in magical apparatus was performing a brilliant illusion in one of the bedrooms set aside for the Golden Anniversary. As the dealer had apparently performed the demonstration more than once the policeman was determined to catch the act and see for himself.

The dealer's name was Ken Allen and, in this particular hotel room there were no windows and the door to the hotel corridor was locked after his audience was inside.

Allen then invited two friends to hold up a blanket and screen him from view and, when the blanket was dropped, after a short length of time, he was nowhere to be seen – he had completely disappeared!

The two assistants invited the astounded onlookers to examine the entire room and the adjacent bathroom, including all the closets and, when no sign of the dealer had been found nor any evidence of how the disappearance was enacted, the assistants held up the blanket once more and, on the dropping of the blanket for the second time, Allen walked out from behind to breathtaking applause.

It was unquestionably, an award winning performance – even more so when he revealed how it had been done!

It seems that a day prior to his first effort in front of an audience Allen had attempted to open a bottle of beer using a bottle-opener attached to a cabinet over a washbasin in the bathroom. When the bottle top wouldn't come away, Allen pulled harder and the cabinet swung away from the wall where it was hinged on one side. When it was against the wall there were no signs of the hinges or fixtures but when pulled out it revealed a square opening on to an airshaft that ran the full height of the hotel.

Inspired by the possibility of creating an ingenious illusion the dealer cleaned that part of the airshaft and devised a method of holding the cabinet in place once he was inside. Using rubber-soled shoes to give him a grip against the opposite wall of the shaft and prevent falling, he demonstrated a disappearing act of mind-blowing proportion that displayed the nerves normally required of a steeplejack.

To repeat the feat several times, that could've cost him his life, earned Ken Allen a reputation that was unique!

The stunned silence around the table at the conclusion of Sergeant Anderson's account was broken when the police officer looked at a bemused Giles, snapped his fingers twice and asked, 'Does that answer the question you've been asking yourself, Professor?'

Three pairs of American eyes stared at Giles as they waited for his reply.

'Hmm, yes!' he said. 'How a bottle opener can open more than bottles?' he muttered to himself. 'Indeed it does, Sergeant! Indeed it does!'

Chapter 17
THE STATUE OF THREE LIES

"All that we see or seem is but a dream within a dream".
Edgar Allan Poe

The Prof couldn't quite figure out what had caused the overwhelming feeling of tiredness that had come over him when he got back to the Berkeley's place in Commonwealth Avenue.

He remembered indulging in a few more drinks after Sergeant Anderson of the BPD had left following his tale of a dealer's illusion in a hotel room. There was almost a feeling of anti climax when, at long last, he knew the secret that Jack Ramsden took with him on his return to Maskelyne Hall after the magicians' convention.

The celebratory drinks had been a little premature – he admitted that to himself – for knowing what he did now and being in possession of many missing clues did not, necessarily, give him the complete picture. There was still work to be done but there seemed to be no harm in a little indulgence in the company of his two hosts particularly as he'd achieved so much on his first full day in Boston.

No, it couldn't have been the alcohol that made him so tired – he remembered leaving the hotel and the doorman calling a taxicab; the doorman wasn't Eddie though, he'd never seen him before in his life, but logic told him the Statler Hilton had more than one doorman. In fact he thought he could remember seeing several of them all lined up at the entrance just as he was bundled into the cab.

Back at "chez Berkeley" gallons of black coffee accompanied by a showing of the late night movie, Hitchcock's "Vertigo", made for a perfect end to the evening. A.B. reckoned that the Thanksgiving holiday allowed them to relax at the end of an exhausting day and enjoy a long lie in bed on the following morning when he would take

Giles over to Cambridge and Harvard University, after which they could all engage in a bit more sleuthing – the word association game being of particular interest to the criminologist.

The Prof couldn't be positive he'd watched the end of the film but there was no doubt he'd fallen asleep immediately his head touched the pillow…but where was he now? He thought he could feel a current of air on his face but his shoes didn't have the grip on the opposite wall that would make him feel secure.

He was slipping! He looked down but couldn't see anything. It was much too dark! The semicircular canals in his inner ear were experiencing a problem. He was beginning to suffer vertigo. He shouldn't have looked down. Jimmy Stewart's role in the movie should have told him that. Oh, God, he knew where he was – he was in an airshaft and one that ran the entire height of the hotel, about 150 feet or more. Was the sensation of dizziness due to disease of the inner ear or were parts of his brain deteriorating?

There was something else seriously wrong – he was unable to get out of the shaft. Please, God, don't let him stay entombed…like Poe's Fortunato in The Cask of Amontillado! Surely there was an audience waiting for him to appear from behind a blanket – or was it a large Japanese fire screen in front of a safe?

Safe? Was that possible? Could he be safe? A light filtered across his face – a door was opening and that meant…?

'Come on, sleepyhead! Rise and shine like our Boston weather! I fear it may not last much longer!' Abe's melodious tone was a welcome relief from a long lingering…?

The Prof joined the others and had a refreshing glass of orange juice.

'I think it's a good job you woke me out of my nightmare,' he said, rubbing the stubble on his chin. 'I couldn't get that death-defying stunt in the airshaft out of my subconscious – no wonder Jack Ramsden returned to Scotland with tremendous plans for his future illusions.'

'You can say that again!' A.B. said, padding around in his bare feet. 'Anyway I have a suggestion to make. What about going out for breakfast this morning? Jenny wants us out from under her feet today – she has some catching up to do on legal work and, when little Millie comes in later, the two of them intend to get everything ready for Thanksgiving Dinner.'

'Sounds fine by me!' said Giles.

'Sounds swell by me as well!' said Jennifer Berkeley.

'You were on a first, Giles, when you visited the library yesterday, the first free library in the United States, so here's the plan; this morning we'll travel to Cambridge on what was the *first* subway in the U.S.'

'Yeah, ya can't pahk ya cah in Harvihd Yahd!' Jennifer quipped, with a nod and a wink.

Everyone fell about laughing.

'After that we'll have breakfast in a diner I use quite often,' said A.B. wagging a finger at his wife, 'then I'll show you around the earliest University in North America – Harvard!'

'In that case I may just use the auto and pick something up at the grocery store for this evening,' Jennifer said. 'Now why don't you both get washed and dressed and get out of here before I have you arrested for loitering?'

Less than an hour later the Professors were ordering bacon, eggs, hash browns and toast with an unlimited supply of coffee, after which, a short walk from the diner took them through the Johnston Gate, erected in 1890 and the first University structure to use handmade and wood-burned Harvard Brick to simulate the material used in earlier buildings, then on past the ivy-covered Massachusetts Hall into Old Harvard Yard. The elms in the normally leafy yard were beginning to look a little bare but in summer and fall they must have provided a wonderful area where students could meet and chat.

A stroll across the yard brought them to the granite building of University Hall in front of which was a bronze statue of John Harvard. The seated figure of the robed benefactor appeared to be the focus of attention for graduates and visitors with cameras, and Giles was studying the bronze with interest when Berkeley took him aside and pointed to the statue.

'That,' he said, 'is often nicknamed *The Statue of Three Lies*!'

Giles looked at the criminologist, 'Now that is intriguing! I'd like to know more!' he said.

'Most visitors do! Lie number one: Because there were no known portraits of John Harvard, the sculptor used an undergraduate as a model when the statue was cast in 1884 – so it is not John Harvard, but a student.'

'Lie number two: The inscription refers to John Harvard as the founder when he really was the first major benefactor in 1638, and certainly not the founder.'

'And Lie number three: The statue refers to the founding of the College in 1638, which was the year of John Harvard's bequest and not the founding which was two years earlier in 1636!'

'Hmm! Now that is food for thought!'

'You're miles away, Giles!'

'Yes, and you're not the first person that's told me that!'

'And I probably won't be the last either!' said the Harvard man.

'Do me a favour!' Giles pleaded. 'Remind me of that statue after dinner tonight. I have a strange feeling that lies, fabrications and deceptions may have played...'

'There you are, Giles – you're doing it again! You're miles away!'

The Prof smiled knowingly as the two men moved on and continued their tour of the historic buildings.

Despite the excellence of the guided tour provided by A.B., Giles couldn't get the Statue of Three Lies out of his mind; everything else seemed to take second billing until he found himself inside one of the buildings and following the criminologist into his private study.

'Have a seat!' he was told.

A.B. then went to a bookshelf and picked out a well-thumbed copy of a novel before handing it over. It bore the title: "The Three Coffins" by John Dickson Carr and was published by Harper and Brothers.

The Prof knew it better by the English title: "The Hollow Man" published by Hamish Hamilton, but he also had a good idea why it was in Berkeley's study and, more importantly, why it was well thumbed and dog-eared.

Both professors faced each other and, in perfect unison, muttered the words "The Locked-Room Lecture"! The laughter that followed was of mutual understanding.

'Yes, you've guessed it,' the criminologist admitted. 'I have learned that all the points made by Dr. Fell in the lecture provide me with excellent material to set student minds in motion.'

'I agree!' said Giles thumbing through the pages that seemed to be turning themselves. 'The stuff to inspire budding criminologists!'

'Or aspiring writers of detective fiction!' A.B. added.

The Prof skipped over the sections titled First and Second Coffins then on to the Third Coffin and the chapter with the heading "The Locked-Room Lecture". He scanned each page with obvious delight but his demeanour changed when he came to the end of the chapter; he paused and his eyes narrowed. He looked up at the American. 'This is interesting,' he declared. 'I don't remember this. What do you make of the title to the next chapter?'

He pointed to the page and Berkeley looked at the words: The Chimney.

'Another coincidence, my friend!' A.B. remarked with emphatic conviction.

'More coincidences than I know what to do with!'

'The Chimney?' said Berkeley taking hold of the novel. 'That's more than just interesting! But that would mean...!'

'Yes I know what that would mean...!' The Prof said, with a deep sigh. 'If that was the way it was done it must surely mean...!'

'You won't know until you get back to Scotland and can go over everything with a fine tooth comb but, as you say, if that was the way it was done, and it would make sense, you may find you have a problem if you allow your heart to rule your head!'

A.B. moved to a closet and brought out a box of cigars. 'Please join me in one of my specials, Giles,' he said. 'I keep them for moments such as this and it will give me an opportunity to deliver my thoughts and explain why you should beware of allowing your heart to rule your head – difficult though it may be.'

Without so much as a momentary hesitation The Prof had the cigar between his lips, had it lit and was lying back puffing the object in an almost provocative position.

'I have a little story to tell that I often use in my work. I'm not aware of the origin though it may have evolved from some vaudeville routine. It concerns a small boy of a certain faith who, when told to jump off a wall and be caught by his father, is allowed to fall to the ground. When he picks himself up and dusts himself down his father tells him he has just learned one of the most important lessons in life – "Never trust anybody," he's told. "Not even your own flesh and blood!" I use this comparison because statistics show that in murder people, known to the victim rather than total strangers, commit the crime more often. In spite of the old adage, you are often more secure in the company of strangers than in the presence of friends or family. There are, of course, exceptions and occasionally the converse is true; it is then we have to decide what to ask and where to look – and there are times when friends or family turn out to be…not what they seem!'

The Prof shuffled a little in his chair and knocked cigar ash into an onyx ashtray on the large desk beside him.

'The problem so many investigators have when they are trying to find reasons for every action or event they happen to see or encounter is that they are inclined to create a problem where none exists. Take this cigar, for example,' A.B. said, holding the smoking object up in the air. 'When Freud, who smoked especially large cigars, was once asked by one of his students if there was any significance in their size, he replied that "Sometimes a cigar is just a cigar!" We ask the wrong questions and we dispute the answers when they are freely given. We do not see the importance of apparently meaningless gestures, expressions, comments or behaviour. We distrust the truth and accept downright fabrications. More often than not we are reluctant to suspend our disbelief. We are easily duped by the plausible; witness the accounts of the smooth talking travelling salesmen peddling their bottles of elixir – the miraculous cure-all – in the not-so-distant past!'

'If we like someone we take them at face value!' The Prof said in agreement with everything that was being expounded.

'Yes! And if we *love* someone we refuse to believe the truth when they turn out to be a wrong'un!' added The Harvard man, bringing his fist down hard on the leather topped desk.

'I have another little tale to tell,' A.B. said, picking the detective novel up again, 'but, before I do, I want you to consider much of what is in Dr. Fell's Locked-Room Lecture. There is murder that is not murder but a series of coincidences ending in an accident that looks like murder; murder that really *is* murder but where the victim, because of circumstances that he or she is unable to cope with mentally, is actually forced to murder himself – or herself as the case

210

may be, in other words suicide. There is murder by mechanical means using gadgets; suicide that *looks* like murder; murder where time of death is confused, due to the tampering of clocks, and so providing false alibis; murder where there's jiggery-pokery of keys, hinges, bolts, locks, doors and windows where even whole panes of glass have been removed; murder using ice as a weapon that disappears as it melts – the list is endless. We also have murder derived from illusion and impersonation and that's where my little tale comes in.'

The Harvard Professor slipped off his shoes, sat in a chair and placed his stocking feet on the table in front of him. He puffed at his cigar and then began his story.

'A young man accepts a wager made by his friends who bet he cannot spend a night alone in a locked room with a coffin containing a dead body. When the coffin is in place, the lights switched off at the mains and the door finally locked, the young man settles down for the night confident that it is only a matter of time before he collects a substantial reward.' The Harvard Professor took another puff at his cigar.

'During the night, however, he hears strange sounds coming from the direction of the coffin; the sounds are human and are followed by the creak of the coffin lid opening. Keeping his nerve he listens in the dark until he feels someone touching his arm; at that moment he tries to scream, but the scream dies in his parched throat…! In the morning when the door is unlocked the young man is found slumped in his chair – close to death.' The American paused for effect.

'He's a changed man; his hair has turned pure white, his breathing is shallow and laboured, and his pulse is weak and irregular. When the friends, who had made the bet, open the coffin they discover the man inside is dead. He is not only dead but he is not the same man who started the night in the casket as part of the prank – *he is the young man who accepted the bet*! The man who had been inside the coffin to start with and had played the trick was now the one in the chair – they had changed places!'

Giles' face lit up. Something had stirred in his brain – a recognition …'Do continue.' he said with a smile.

Abe smiled back. 'You see after he'd climbed out of the box and touched the man trying to win the bet he discovered that the man in the chair had died from a heart attack. He put the body inside the coffin and closed the lid and settled down to spend the rest of the night alone in the room with the dead body – the tables had turned, the innocuous jest had backfired! By morning the man's hair had turned white with shock and his cardio-respiratory system had been virtually destroyed. So beware, I say; beware the impostor! Question impersonation and substitution and don't accept that friendships are necessarily for ever even though they last for life – or, at least, until life is…extinguished!'

'No wonder your students enjoy their ABC Course as your "Bulldog" friend christened it!' Giles said. 'I myself wouldn't object to being a fly on the wall at some of your lectures! It seems to ring a bell, however, the story I mean! There is something familiar about it!'

'I'm not exactly sure', said the American, 'but the story may have been one of Carr's creations that was broadcast as a play on the CBS *Suspense* radio show. Anyway it is enthused about in these circles.'

'It's not difficult to see why.'

'You're very kind, Giles, but don't you see that your involvement in the history of magic and illusion must make you understand the importance of deception and the creation of diversion – one of the great art forms, the Art of Misdirection. If we look in all directions and take the trouble to examine every possibility there is a good chance we may spot the vital clue that will unlock the last door to the final solution. Somewhere amidst the bits and pieces of extraneous matter there lurks a single fragment that is of monstrous importance if only we can recognise it.'

The criminologist puffed at his cigar that had almost gone out.

'We must also avoid being sidetracked…you see if it looks like a duck, waddles like a duck and quacks like a duck there's a damn good chance that, perhaps, that's what it is – a duck! As I said before don't let your heart rule your head and, if the bottle opener, airshaft and the coincidence regarding the chapter title The Chimney, are anything to go by, I'd say you'd be in danger of falling into that trap!'

'I promise I won't jump to any conclusions,' Giles said with a degree of humility. 'And I can assure you that, whatever the outcome, I will pursue the culprit without fear or favour.'

'Good! After dinner I would like to examine the results of your word game and we can also explore those possible lies that our statue may have implied. Now it's time, I think, to clear up here, make a final round of the College and then get back to Jenny and a Thanksgiving Dinner.'

The daylight had already gone by the time the two Professors ended the tour of Harvard; a tour that included a visit to the third oldest building in the Yard, Holden Chapel, and a look at the world's largest academic library, the Widener Library which had been constructed in 1914 and funded by Eleanor Elkins Widener in memory of her son Harry Elkins Widener, Class of 1907, *who died in the Titanic disaster.*

When they arrived back at Commonwealth Avenue the mouth-watering smell of roasting turkey met them at the door.

Inside, the table was set for three; Millie had gone home to complete preparations for her own family meal and Jennifer was in full control and had everything at the ready for the apéritifs.

'Did you use the car, darling?' A.B. asked after kissing his wife.

'Yes I did!' she replied. 'And I'll give you three guesses as to what happened!'

'Don't tell me! You didn't, by any chance, have trouble on the rotary again, did you?'

'Yes, I did! And you can wipe that grin off your face! I can never be absolutely sure who has the right of way!'

'The rotary?' Giles queried.

'Something similar to your roundabout back in Britain but here the traffic circle is called the *Suicide Circle.*' A.B. said with a resigned shrug of the shoulders.

'And who does have the right of way?' The Prof asked.

A.B. looked at his wife before answering, a playful smile creating soft lines around his mouth. 'Senior residents claim the right of way belongs to the oldest car with the most bumps!'

'They're not far wrong!' said Jenny with a broad smile as she turned towards the kitchen.

'How's dinner coming along?' her husband said, patting her bottom. 'Smells fabulous!'

'It won't be long but you've both got time to freshen up...and drinks await!'

Thanksgiving Dinner, of Roast Turkey with all the trimmings followed by Pumpkin Pie, was a truly memorable occasion that The Prof enjoyed, with his genuine friends of only a few days, without thoughts of a faraway killer flitting in and out of his fertile imagination. All such thoughts were exiled for the duration of the meal and only when the washing up was finished and coffee introduced did any of the threesome broach the subject of murder.

'Did Alan do his party trick for you this afternoon, Giles? Did he entertain you with the bizarre coincidences of two of our popular Presidents?'

'No, as a matter of fact, he didn't – he did, however, recount intriguing and important anecdotes for which I am greatly indebted. I think he was saving the other stuff until later!'

'Well, it's now later so, I'm certain a minor twist of the arm is all that's necessary for us to hear what I consider to be fascinating – so much so I don't mind hearing it again and again! What do you say, Abe?'

'The minor twist of the arm is not necessary but I wouldn't say no to a drink and a twist of lemon – to lubricate the larynx, you understand!'

The Harvard man, who was relishing a busman's holiday in the confines of his own home, took the glass his wife handed across to him. He took a sip before starting to speak

'When Jack Kennedy, one of our most popular Presidents was assassinated in Dallas three years ago, this very month, certain historians began to note many weird connections between that killing and the murder of another American President, Abraham Lincoln, almost 100 years before. Weird connections, I believe I said! I'll let you be the judge of that!' he murmured softly.

'1. Both Lincoln and Kennedy were shot in the head on a Friday, in the presence of their wives.' A.B. held an index finger aloft to emphasize the point.

'2. Abe Lincoln was in a theatre when he was shot by a man who hid in a warehouse and Jack Kennedy was shot from a warehouse by a man who hid in a theatre.'

'3. John Wilkes Booth, who shot Lincoln, was born in 1839 and Lee Harvey Oswald, who shot Kennedy, was born in 1939. Both assassins were from the South and in their twenties – and both men were shot dead before they were brought to trial!' A.B. raised two more fingers.

'4. Lincoln's secretary, whose name was Kennedy, advised him not to go to the theatre while Kennedy's secretary, whose name was Lincoln advised him not to go to Dallas!' Berkeley now had four fingers in the air.

'5. Both Presidents were succeeded by men called Johnson – Andrew Johnson followed Lincoln and Lyndon B. Johnson came after Kennedy.'

'Give me five, pal!' Jennifer said as she and her husband placed open palms together.

'6. Abraham Lincoln was elected in 1860 and Jack Kennedy in 1960. Andrew Johnson, Lincoln's successor, was born in 1808 and Lyndon B. Johnson, Kennedy's successor, in 1908.' Abe's triumphant whoop of delight made a barnstorming finish.

'And if that doesn't satisfy your hunger for an amazing set of coincidences…' Jennifer declared. '…Now hear this!'

'Jack Kennedy,' The American said, looking as if about to pull a rabbit out of a hat. 'Jack Kennedy was shot while he was being driven in a Lincoln car!'

He paused to allow the anticipated applause that invariably followed his collection of coincidences at Harvard, before concluding, 'Unfortunately, try as I might, I haven't been able to produce any evidence that Lincoln was shot in anything remotely resembling a Kennedy theatre or anything else with the name of Kennedy attached to it. But, never mind, the entire catalogue of coincidences are uniquely bizarre – don't you think?'

The Prof had a little chuckle at this last observation and was then reminded, by the criminologist, that this wouldn't be a bad time to have a look at the results of the word game he'd conducted back in Scotland. He nodded and left the room.

When he returned he was carrying a large sheet of paper folded in four. A.B. was standing with his back to the fire and, as The Prof unfolded the sheet and spread it out on his lap, Jennifer produced a coffee table and the paper was moved to the flatter surface.

'I thought it best to transfer all the results to a single sheet that would make comparison easier.'

'Good thinking, Giles,' A.B. said. 'I hate working with tiny bits of paper!'

'I'm not sure if this little experiment has produced anything significant but I'll be glad to know what you think, especially as regards the answers covering the Boston question. One member of the group, taking part in the game, asked if it was a sort of lie-detector test without the machine, so I'd also be interested to have your opinion on the value of such a test.'

'I intended doing that anyway, Giles!' said the American taking a deep breath. 'Before I take a look at your findings it is important that you are aware of the track record of the "polygraph" as an instrument of scientific accuracy.' The criminologist was back in the lecture theatre.

'As you may know, it is an instrument for measuring responses of the autonomic nervous system by recording blood pressure, pulse rate, respiration and electrical impulses of the skin but, as a means of determining if a person is telling lies or not, it seems deeply flawed. The theory is that when someone tells a lie certain uncontrollable reactions take place and, by measuring the electrical conductivity of the skin which we call the galvanic skin response, shown by such things as sweating and increase in blood flow that are linked to very strong emotions such as fear, we can come to a conclusion about who is lying and who is not.'

The criminologist shook his head acknowledging the grin from his wife. 'Unfortunately all it does is detect a change in metabolism and not whether a lie is being told. It's cumbersome and can only be used by an expert – and they are thin on the ground. And, when it comes to a question about a specific crime – as say a shooting in your case, it may not be able to differentiate between someone who may have committed the crime and someone who may have witnessed it or known about it. It's not reliable when trying to identify the mentally disturbed, the problem being identifying what is causing the disturbance nor is it of any use with the psychopathic liar. There are problems with those that are emotionally upset or those under medication and I'm afraid it only seems popular in detective fiction. In fact your word game may enjoy just as much success – if not more. So why don't we have a look!'

A.B. sat down to study the written document as The Prof moved aside to allow easier access; Jennifer came closer and looked over his shoulder.

Both criminologist and attorney studied the contents for some considerable time in complete silence. At one stage A.B. produced a pad and pencil and started making some notes. As he did so he occasionally passed the pad across to his wife, receiving a nod or shake of the head, before continuing to scribble.

When he was finished he placed the fingers of both hands on the document that read –

Word Association Game – Key Words

Isabella

Black	Fire	Shot	Thirteen	Boston
Widow	Brigade	Jack	Unlucky	Tea Party

Victor

Black sheep	Firearm	Film	Unlucky	Strangler

Laura

Magic	Escape	Gunshot	Diamonds	Tea Party

Conrad

Blackjack	Walking	In the dark?	Grand Slam	Red Sox

Mabel

Beauty	Fireside	In the arm	Unlucky	Paul Revere

Edgar

Blackout	Firebomb	Gunshot	Ides of March	Harvard

Sally

Blackmail	Fire Escape	Crack shot	Unlucky	Salem

George

Blacksmith	Firewood	Shotgun	Unlucky	Lizzie Borden

Doreen

Pepper	Extinguisher	Snap	Baker's dozen	John Kennedy

A.B. placed the fingertips of both hands together, rose from his seat and, without uttering a sound, started to pace up and down like a caged

---

lion. He stopped and turned, as if to speak, thought better of it and resumed pacing. Jennifer smiled the smile of resigned patience.

'Violence!' The words exploded from his lips. 'Violence, the inexplicable, and the downright erroneous! I'm so sorry for the outburst, my friend, but it seems Boston is a city of savagery, turbulence and cruelty, at least according to many of those who took part in your game – though to be fair, I must admit I'd have extreme difficulty in writing a word or phrase in answer to a question concerning Edinburgh or York in your fine Country.' He flicked cigar ash into the glowing fire.

'We are fascinated by the sensational. Historical events, particularly if they are a trifle gruesome or macabre, are the lifeblood of our journalists, poets, authors and playwrights. There's no business like show business and generally there's little or no news in good news. The first word that caught my attention was Isabella's *black widow* – perhaps a reference to the spider that has a reputation for eating her mate!'

'And supposedly just after making love!' Jennifer added with a touch of spice.

'I know the feeling exactly!' joked her husband, raising his eyebrows to the ceiling and gently shaking his head. 'The black column contains a few other words with violent tendencies, as one would expect since we normally regard black as the opposite of white, the symbol of purity and goodness; black, on the other hand, we accept as representative of dark or evil forces.'

'And then we are reminded of the white robes of the three K's!' Jennifer declared softly. 'The Klan!'

'Now where have I heard that expression before?' Giles questioned through partially closed lips.

'You're quite correct, Jenny,' A.B. conceded. 'But don't forget the Klan use white to imply goodness where little exists!'

'What other words set off alarm bells in the next three columns, Abe? And, while we're at it, I'd respect any input from our lady attorney.'

'I'm more interested in the last section – the one on Boston, but Jenny's shrewd observation may come up with something.'

'Yes! There's one comment I'd like to make,' she said. 'The *Ides of March* is not strictly correct – according to the ancient Roman calendar the ides is the fifteenth of March, May, July and October and the thirteenth of every other month. An understandable mistake but it does go to show how easy it is to register discrepancies. It is lucky for us that we can detect and identify those discrepancies!'

'And that's something the polygraph cannot do!' A.B. threw in for good measure.

'That statue in front of University Hall this afternoon…!'

'You saw our Statue of Three Lies, Giles? It does make you question everything, doesn't it?' said Jennifer.

'It certainly arouses my curiosity – that's for sure! Now looking down the Boston list, and that's the one where the two of you can probably be most helpful, I'd really appreciate any comments you'd care to make. I'm sure there's something there that ties in with the statue and the lies – something that can open a door…to a solution!'

Abe and Jennifer looked earnestly at each other.

'Okay!' said A.B. 'I'll bat first then Jenny can take over when I get to first base!'

'Let's play ball!' The Prof said, obviously enjoying the play on words.

'We can ignore the Tea Party – historically the most associated event connected with Boston. The Red Sox baseball team and J.F.K. are Boston institutions – we're proud to call them our own; the same could be said about Paul Revere and his midnight ride that was immortalised by Longfellow but, as in many similar works of literature, there are discrepancies in the poem. It may pay to scrutinise those witnesses' statements at home!'

'My turn now,' said Jennifer. 'Harvard, technically, is in Cambridge but accepted, the world over as part of Boston – on the other hand Salem is quite a way out of town!'

'It's all very intriguing stuff, I must admit. And, like the central character in *Oliver Twist*, can I have more please!'

'I expect Jenny will have the last word,' A.B. announced. 'I will, therefore, concentrate my profound wisdom on *The Boston Strangler*. The Strangler, who was cited by Victor, needn't concern us too much but a certain American psychiatrist, James A. Brussel, must receive a mention. He was the man who turned psychological profiling into an art form and who, two years ago, was largely responsible for the conviction of Albert de Salvo, otherwise known as *The Boston Strangler*. The Harvard professor was back in lecturing mode.

'Dr. Brussel, who was described by one reporter as the "Sherlock Holmes of the couch" and, by another, as the "Psychiatric Seer", did the reverse of most psychiatrists by deducing a person's characteristics through the study of that person's actions and responses and not the other way round.'

A.B. pondered for a moment and pointed to the sheet lying on the coffee table. 'I would suggest to you that a similar study of that paper, allied with the responses and actions you witnessed at the house near Lockerbie, could be very profitable! In due course it may turn out that the Coroner, or in your case, the Procurator Fiscal, may have been wrong – but it takes a good Coroner or P.F. to admit, about a death, *that perhaps he got it wrong!*'

The Prof nodded in acquiescence and his eyes narrowed as wheels started turning in his brain. The thought processes had barely started when they were suddenly interrupted.

'Gentlemen of the jury!' Jennifer proclaimed coquettishly. 'George D. Robinson probably used those words when he rose to deliver his closing arguments to the all-male jury in New Bedford in 1893 as he defended Lizzie Borden at her trial for the axe murders of Andrew and Abby Borden in Fall River, which is several miles from Boston, so no connection there, I'm afraid! Lizzie was acquitted of the murders, but a nursery rhyme was spawned even before she came to trial.

"Lizzie Borden took an axe and gave her mother forty whacks! And when she saw what she had done, she gave her father forty-one!"

This was popular with lots of school playgroups involved in rope jumps. My mother told me she used to skip to the ditty in an attempt to reach forty-one jumps but although the old nursery rhyme is easy to remember, it is inaccurate; according to the pathologist Lizzie's mother received nineteen whacks and her father only eleven! The real error though is in the identity of one of the victims! It wasn't Lizzie's mother that was killed! Not everyone is aware of the fact but – *Abby was her step mother!*'

Chapter 18
APPOINTMENT WITH DEATH

When he opened his eyes and glanced at his watch, lying on the bedside cabinet, The Prof knew, immediately, he had overslept.

He lay back on the pillow and grabbed his thoughts by the scruff of the neck.

He'd gone to bed feeling quite elated after hearing the comments about the word game. There was no doubt the bottle of Jack Daniels A.B. produced afterwards had a contributory effect but it was the distortions, falsehoods and inventions that materialized out of so many differing names and events that his brain grasped hold of and refused to let go.

He'd been ages falling asleep but the subsequent rest had been long and beneficial. Too long!

Downstairs the house was quiet except for a duet coming from the radio.

"Ol' blue eyes", Mr.Francis Albert Sinatra, was unmistakable as he sang *They Can't Take That Away from Me* but Giles couldn't put a name to the vocal backup until he had a back view of a petite blonde armed with a feather duster.

'The way you sing off key...the way you haunt my dreams...no, no, they can't take that away from me!' she sang as she swung round and planted the feathers on a stick smack on his face, right under his nostrils. The urge to sneeze, as the feathers moved back and forth across his upper lip and up his nose, was uncontrollable.

'A-tishoo!'

'Gesundheit!' the little lady declared without moving the irritating object. 'You must be Giles...I hope I didn't waken you with the vacuuming!'

'And you must be Millie!' he spluttered through multi-coloured feathers. 'No! You didn't waken me – it was time I was up anyway!'

'The others are out...they didn't wanna waken you and told me not to disturb you...and Alan left you a note!' She rushed her news out and dusted him down at the same time, in rhythm with the Nelson Riddle arrangement of the Sinatra ballad. She passed the note across.

We didn't wanna waken you, so take it easy for the day and make yourself at home.

If you decide to book a flight home try and keep tomorrow morning free – I have a surprise for you. Oh, and if you feel like a bath there's plenty of hot water. Anything else you need, just ask Millie. She'll take care of you!! See you later.

Alan.

He couldn't help smiling at Abe's use of the word *wanna* in anticipation of Millie's dialect.

'...*The way you sip your tea*!' Millie continued to harmonize with ol' blue eyes. 'Are you gonna take the bath, Giles? I can rustle up some eggs in...say, half-an-hour...and I can scrub your back if you like...you only have to ask!'

He tilted his head and smiled. This Millie was the nearest thing to perpetual motion he'd seen in a long time.

'I think I'll take you up on that, Millie!' he almost shouted. 'The bath and the eggs, I mean! But not the back scrubbing!'

'Spoilsport!'

The water was hot – and there was plenty of it. The bathroom was luxury plus and, as he soaked in the suds, his mind wandered across an ocean to another bathroom several thousand miles away; a bathroom he would have to examine in detail, when he got back, in order to make up his mind about...?

When A.B. had disclosed the facts about Dr. Brussel and how he'd reversed normal psychiatric procedure Giles had the strong determination to do something similar and reveal certain characteristics from the actions and responses of individuals he'd stored in his memory bank. Was it possible that by following Brussel's line of thinking he might be able to find answers that, so far, had remained a mystery? The clouds were beginning to roll away.

'It is just possible...!' he remarked to himself. But it would have to be verified by a visit to...only then would it start to make sense! 'Yes, it is just possible...!' he repeated. And if the long shot came up it could certainly clarify some of the statements that were made at the scene of the...what? *Murder?* There were at least three persons who had said things or been misquoted whom he would love to confront once more. He was confident that an entirely different slant on things could be achieved with the missing pieces in the jigsaw being found and ready to fit in place to complete the true picture.

It all depended on the visit to that important House in London – but that would have to wait until he was back home. The next step was to book a flight.

There was a hint of fog in the atmosphere as, a superb bath and two fried eggs later, The Prof made his way to book a flight home, armed with the directions given him by the cheerful Millie.

He was offered a late flight on that same day which he declined but decided to accept one on the Saturday. A.B. had said in his note that he had a surprise lined up and to keep the morning free for the following day – the flight booked for the afternoon would get him into London late on Saturday night and he could have a restful day on the Sunday and, first thing Monday morning, he could make that visit to the House.

Before that he reckoned a phone call to Freddie to arrange a meeting and plan a trip back to Maskelyne Hall would get the adrenalin going in no time at all.

He checked his watch and, with the main purpose of his visit to Boston now complete, he believed he could indulge himself in a leisurely wander around the city taking in many places of interest including the *Old Corner Bookstore* that had been a favourite haunt of the poet Longfellow and his friends.

'You met our little Millie then? I hope she didn't get up your nose!' The opening words from A.B. that met him when he returned to Commonwealth Avenue turned his smile into a broad grin.

'Not quite!' he replied, rubbing the underside of his nose with the backs of his fingers. 'She was very obliging! So much so I found it difficult to turn my back on her!'

Abe and Jennifer Berkeley looked at each other before bursting into laughter.

'That's our Millie for you!' Jennifer said. 'She's never been scared to get down to a bit of scrubbing!'

'Oh, Giles, I hope you don't mind,' A.B. said. 'But we have guests coming for dinner tonight. They're a fine couple and we're sure you'll enjoy their company!'

'I'm sure I will!'

'Did you get booked on a flight?'

'Yes, for late tomorrow afternoon!'

'Splendid! We'll take you to the airport but on the way I have a little surprise for you. If you're packed and ready to leave by mid morning we can make that trip.'

When the Cadillac turned on to the Highway 95, with A.B. at the wheel, and headed southwest on the road to Providence Giles, who sat in the back of the car with the attorney wife of the Harvard Professor, reflected on his few hectic days in the *Athens of America*, his good fortune at meeting two wonderful ambassadors of the United States and his genuine regret at having to say goodbye to the house in Commonwealth Avenue. Thanks to his introduction by the Super *"Bulldog"* Drummond he'd met two great friends and the wisdom of coming to Boston, in his search for answers to so many questions, had been more than justified.

The road sign to the town of Providence was surely another omen – suggesting care, guidance and good fortune, and he appeared to be the recipient of plenty of that.

His final evening with the Berkeleys and their two dinner guests had been a most enjoyable affair for, not surprisingly, neither murder nor killing had come up as a topic of conversation. And no wonder, for the male guest had spent part of his life, in the 40's, as a member of the team of someone who'd been a kind of boyhood hero of his. The man who'd led that team had been Frank Buck – the one who, in the 20's, 30's and 40's had brought back, from the jungles of the world, animals in prime condition for the zoos and circuses around the land…hence the title bestowed on him of "Bring-'em-back-alive" Buck!

Listening to his escapades had been real-life adventure and two things in particular had left a lasting impression; the knowledge that the black rhino, as opposed to the white variety, was more aggressive despite not being provoked and the old adage about the female of the species being *deadlier than the male*!

His thought processes had been working overtime.

He'd slept well and had completed his final packing in plenty of time for A.B. and Jennifer to get him into the car and set out for…? It wasn't Providence – that was some way off yet and they were slowing down and leaving the main highway. Apart from small talk Jennifer had remained silent for most of the journey but now an anticipatory smile was beginning to appear on her features as she turned to watch him!

They were approaching a burial ground!

It was Oak Grove Cemetery, Fall River!

A.B. parked the car and everyone got out.

'We'll walk from here,' he said. 'I want you to see something before you leave!'

They hadn't walked far before they came to a well-kept grassy plot where a piece of marble lay flat in the grass with a few simple flowers around it. On the curved top in capital letters and sculpted in relief was the single word – LIZBETH.

Giles glanced towards the criminologist and a glimmer of understanding started to wreathe his face.

The trio moved on a few steps to a large four-sided gravestone where, on one side, the following was engraved - CHILDREN BY
ANDREW J. AND SARAH A. BORDEN
ALICE ESTHER
LIZBETH ANDREWS
EMMA LENORA

Dates were listed for the three daughters (Alice had died in early childhood and both Lizzie and Emma had died in 1927 within days of each other) and the other sides of the gravestone showed the names of the father, Andrew, his first wife Sarah and his second wife, and step mother to the girls, Abby.

'I didn't want you to leave without sampling the after effect of a horrid murder!' A.B. said softly and with some reverence. 'Lizzie changed her name to Lizbeth but she was ostracized for the rest of her life by the community.'

'And the rhyme continued to have a following,' Jennifer said. 'Especially in the jump rope groups of young girls where they added – *Lizzie Borden took an axe and gave her mother forty whacks! Then she stood behind the door and gave her father forty more!*'

'The headless body of her father lies here,' A.B. said in a sombre tone. 'And so does the mutilated body of the other victim, her step mother!'

'It took the jury a little over an hour to acquit Lizzie!' Jennifer added in her best attorney manner. 'Had she been found guilty she'd have been the first woman to go to the electric chair that was a new device of execution, in 1893! But here in this quiet cemetery lie two people who were killed by person or persons unknown. This was a murder that has never been solved!'

'So return home, Giles,' A.B. said. 'And use your exceptional talents to bring your Scottish crime to a successful conclusion!'

All the way back to Logan International Airport The Prof remained silent and deep in thought for yet one more coincidence had occurred as he left Oak Grove Cemetery – the road sign for the town next to Fall River on the way to Providence had the name Somerset displayed on it…and that was the name of the place he had to visit when he got back to London…Somerset House!

When he said his brief goodbyes, before heading for the departure lounge at the airport, he was given a reassurance that the Berkeleys would welcome any future visit by him to Boston and, as he boarded the plane, he was able to appreciate the fact that any fogginess in the weather during his final two days hadn't clouded his judgement – he was more focused than ever!

On his arrival in London, Saturday night seemed cold and uninviting and, by the time he put his key in the door of his Kensington flat he was more than ready for a nightcap before retiring for the night. The Whisky Mac, to which he helped himself, on top of the in-flight booze, meant it would be well into Sunday morning before he surfaced.

He made one phone call before climbing into bed and that was to his "buddies" in Boston whom he thanked for their warm affection, generosity and wealth of information and enlightenment about solving crimes of apparent impossibility.

Sunday was spent collating his notes on the research he wished to cover when he visited the Record Office at Somerset House on the following day.

He sent out for a meal to be delivered and, to a background of his own L.P.'s of Sinatra, and with papers scattered over the floor, he scribbled, shifted scraps around and muttered to himself.

When, at last, he was left with a few blank spaces amongst his paper mosaic he filled them with written comments and question marks such as, "If A turns out to be the case after the records are checked?" or "B would make the whole thing possible, wouldn't it?"

He was totally heartened by what had been achieved but, at the same time, was mentally exhausted. It would now be up to the Records Office.

He gave Freddie a call at his home in the Cotswolds and made arrangements for a meeting the following evening for a special Roast Beef Dinner at Simpson's-in-the-Strand.

The last Monday in November 1966 was a dull start to the week ahead but that didn't matter to The Prof who was well aware he'd be spending much of the day indoors at Somerset House.

This giant square building around a central courtyard in the Strand and overlooking the Thames embankment dated back to the 16th century, some of it destroyed, rebuilt, refurbished or added to and now housing many governmental offices.

He wanted to search family records for answers to at least three vital questions and, if the answers were forthcoming, it would make his theory about the events of Hallowe'en 1952 at Maskelyne Hall very plausible and lend credibility to the belief that someone, who may have become an accessory to a prank, actually played an important part in what turned out to be – *cold-blooded murder!*

Most of the day was spent inside the building where the assistants were so helpful but were unable to undertake the research themselves. He examined endless lists of births, marriages and deaths until he had the information he wanted, making several phone calls to friendly associates in Fleet Street and, when he eventually looked at his watch, he realized he only had time to get back to his flat for a quick freshen up before rushing out to meet up with Freddie.

Outside the flat Freddie's red Triumph Spitfire was parked but, although he possessed a key, Freddie was nowhere to be seen. The Prof assumed he'd just parked the car and left for town on the presumption that a taxi would be the best mode of transport after a meal and a drink at Simpson's-in-the-Strand.

Freddie was waiting for him when he'd completed the five-minute walk from Embankment underground station and entered the Grand Divan Tavern of Simpson's-in-the-Strand.

The prestigious eating-place had been opened on the site of the Fountain Tavern in 1828 and had been the home of the former literary association – the Kit Kat Club. When a top caterer, John Simpson had joined founder, Samuel Reiss in 1848 the building, that had become the Home of Chess in the city, where top-hatted runners had carried news of chess moves to other competing coffee houses, was enlarged and underwent a name change from the Grand Cigar Divan to Simpson's Grand Divan Tavern and, thanks to the quality food and fine wine and beers that were served, became an attractive venue for men such as Gladstone, Disraeli and Charles Dickens.

'Great to see you again, Freddie. I was just thinking about the top-hatted gents that flitted in and out of this place many years ago relaying chess moves and was struck by the thought of another top-hatted gent, a magician involved in a chess game of a different sort and one where I require to break the stalemate and move into check!'

'And how far into the game have we moved, Giles?'

By the time the silver dinner trolley was wheeled to their table and the medium-rare roast beef was carved in front of them Giles was well into his extensive account of what had happened in Boston.

The succulent beef and red wine made for easy conversation or, in Freddie's case, listening to Giles as he recounted how things had gone on his visit to America and they were enjoying coffee when he was finally concluding his story with the visit to Oak Grove Cemetery.

'The Statue of Three Lies has a lot to answer for, Freddie! I've encountered and been made aware of so many lies, errors, deceptions and honest-to-goodness mistakes that I'm at the stage where I'm ready to discount almost everything I heard at the house in Scotland and name the killer based on what I *do know is true* allied with an intelligent use of what Poirot might have called the little grey cells! Even the gravestone of the Bordens listed the name of the murder suspect as Lizbeth Andrews when her middle name was Andrew, without the s on the end, or so I understand! It throws all the statements supposedly made on the night of the shooting into the melting pot and I'm reminded of the old vaudeville joke about the First World War problem of trying to relay a message without any loss of interpretation as it gets repeated along the line!'

'You mean the old chestnut about the message from the front to Headquarters?'

Yes, Freddie! "Send reinforcements, I'm going to advance!" ending up as "Send three-and-four-pence, I'm going to a dance! And one statement on that fateful night is in similar vein but without the comic tone.'

'Which one was that?'

'The one Jack Ramsden is purported to have asked his wife as he lay dying. "Did you see Dr. Hyde?" Now do you know what I think he said?'

'No, I'm sorry I don't – but I know you're about to tell me!'

The Prof leaned across the table and whispered in his friend's ear.

'You don't say!' Freddie began with surprise punctuating every word. 'Now that does throw a different light on things – and the cat amongst the pigeons!'

'I have a favour to ask of you!' Giles said. 'Will you drive me back to Maskelyne Hall and remain with me as back up?'

'Certainly – you know I will! When do you want to go?'

'Sometime this week, possibly in a day or so, but we needn't be there longer than a day if everything goes according to plan. You see I'm sure I can name the murderer but I'm not sure I can prove it – beyond reasonable doubt, that is! I have a plan...and it might just work!'

'What made your mind up? Was it something you were up to today?'

'Yes, it was!'

Freddie was then told everything that Giles had discovered that day.

'So you think that accounts for certain behaviour while you were at the Hall?'

'Yes, of course I do! And, if I'm not mistaken, it explains earlier behaviour as a child! I have to thank Brussel for this and it is one of the missing pieces in the jigsaw that gives credence to my theory about the possibility of this person being an accessory to a prank that ended in murder!'

'It makes sense but I don't see how you can arrive at an acceptable solution, so long after the murder was committed, when a straight denial by the murderer will leave you on a very sticky wicket!'

'Let's grab a taxi, Freddie, and get back to the flat. You'll stay the night, of course, and after I've made a call to Laura we should have a good idea of our timetable for the next day or so!'

Back in South Kensington Giles made the call to Maskelyne Hall and spoke to Laura for several minutes.

After a conversation, during which he gave nothing away, Giles knew he'd have to wait for confirmation that all of the suspects would be at the Hall on the same day. He'd asked Laura to repeat the Tunnel of Witchcraft illusion with Sally's assistance and to make sure all the necessary props were assembled in the library for the chosen day. He promised to call back the following evening and mentioned Thursday as an ideal day if everyone was available.

Next day Giles said he had something he wanted to check at The British Library and Freddie went National Hunt racing. Freddie promised to return for the evening and find out the result of the second call to Scotland. Giles managed to wangle two tickets for the St. Martin's Theatre and both of them had a night off at Agatha Christie's *The Mousetrap*, which was now into the fifteenth year of its run.

The call to Laura was fruitful – all was set for Thursday, so time was short. He and Freddie would be welcome on the Wednesday, if they could manage, and beds would be ready for them. The others would not be there until the Thursday morning but Sally had promised to assist with the illusion.

Freddie called home to tell his wife that he and Giles would be there for a few hours before going on to Lockerbie and they hoped to be back on the Thursday – but it could be late!

It was late, very late, but there was still a light on in the lodge as the red Spitfire turned off the road and went through the entrance gate to Maskelyne Hall on the Wednesday night.

Giles asked Freddie to stop the car while he went in to see if George was still up.

He was, but his wife had gone to bed, and the few words he had with the little groom were met with solemn understanding and a promise of total commitment.

Laura met them when they arrived; she told them they were in the same rooms as before and that Doreen had prepared some cold chicken sandwiches that would be waiting for them when they came down to the lounge.

The remainder of the evening with Laura was short; Isabella had already gone to bed and Victor, who had come home earlier that day, had also retired for the night.

The other four, Conrad, Mabel, Edgar and Sally would be there in the morning. Freddie was tired after his drive and decided to go up to his room leaving Laura and Giles together for a brief spell. It was then he let her know how he wanted things conducted on the following day without giving away any secrets about how he intended to proceed.

His closing words to her, before he went upstairs were – 'whatever I say or do after the illusion *I want you to remain calm and not lose your temper!*'

Shortly after going into his room he decided to go along to the bathroom where he made a cursory examination of the large cabinet that was fixed to the outside wall – but with no success! He brushed his teeth and went to bed determined to give the place a thorough going over in the morning before the others arrived.

He'd been tired, probably over-tired because he didn't sleep all that well and, when he awakened and got out of bed on that first day of December he looked out of the window at an overcast sky.

He padded along to the bathroom in his bare feet, locked the door and started to go over the wall cabinet inch-by-inch.

Everything seemed solid and secure. He pulled and pressed every small object he could see, but nothing moved.

He decided to shave and think things over and, as he made the final stroke with the razor, his thoughts turned to Dr. Brussel and Professor Berkeley and how they might have tackled the problem. He figured they would look for a fixture that nobody would want to have the wrong way round.

He splashed his face with cold water and dried it with the towel then returned to the cabinet to gaze at the structure. 'Now what wouldn't you want *the wrong way round?*' he asked himself out loud.

It stuck out like a sore thumb – the toothbrush holder; if it were the wrong way round the brushes would fall out. He might be wrong but it was, at least, a start.

He tried to rotate the object but it wouldn't budge. He tried turning it the opposite way and it responded after a little effort. The soft click, when he turned it upside down, was music to his ears.

He pulled and the whole of the cabinet swung away from the wall to reveal a fairly extensive square opening on to a shaft that extended vertically the entire height of the house – the chimney from the library.

Inside the shaft was a wooden platform, similar to a dumb waiter in a hotel, which appeared to be controlled by rope pulleys on the same lines as a block and tackle. He reached in and pulled on the rope and the platform moved silently downwards. He brought it back to the starting point and, after a few minutes more, decided he had seen enough to justify his theory – full marks to Brussel and Berkeley.

He swung the cabinet against the wall and covered the opening, rotated the toothbrush holder to its original position and put the toothbrushes back in place. It was logical to assume that once someone was inside the shaft the cabinet could be pulled against the wall and locked from the inside.

The locking device would be able to twist the holder into the correct position and everything would appear normal so long as brushes weren't scattered around the floor; simply removing any brush before starting

232

could easily prevent that. It was cunning, simplistic and required no death defying nerve that Ken Allen had displayed in the airshaft of the Boston Hotel all those years ago.

The chimney had obviously been reconstructed internally to allow easy passage of the platform down to the area behind the safe from where access to the library could have been achieved. The elaborate reconstruction of the chimney and the installation of safe, bathroom cabinet and pulley-operated dumb-waiter that had come from an idea born at a magician's convention had effectively been instrumental in causing the death of a master craftsman, who had remained alone in his library and awaited the secret entry of a fiend hell bent on his murder.

He dressed and went down to the kitchen and thanked Doreen for the sandwiches she'd prepared the previous evening. He also warned her that, whatever happened throughout the rest of the day, she should put aside all family loyalties and not become emotionally involved.

He accepted her offer of tea and hot buttered toast in the warmth of the kitchen then he went to the library where the props for the illusion were already assembled. He crossed to the fireplace and opened the safe using the Houdini combination and, as he replaced the diary he'd borrowed, he became aware that something was missing.

There was no sign of the long thin-bladed stiletto dagger!

The others started arriving just before eleven o'clock; Edgar and Sally were first followed shortly afterwards by Conrad and Mabel.

There was a strained atmosphere in the house that even the chitchat and small talk was unable to break.

Lunch was buffet style and when everyone had gathered around the table, prepared by Doreen, Giles made it clear that, as soon as it was dark enough, he wanted them to watch a rerun of the Tunnel of Witchcraft illusion they'd seen at Hallowe'en!

When he'd had a bite to eat he went upstairs to his room – it was a little after 1.30 p.m. There was a playing card lying on the floor just inside the door; it was face down and the red patterned backing looked ominously like a warning of danger ahead.

He picked it up and turned it over; it was the two of spades and, splashed across the white surface of the card, there was a message in red ink. It read: -

Meet me in the cellar at 2.0'clock. Come alone – I have something to tell you!

There was no signature, but wheels started turning in his fertile mind. 'Oh, God, no!' he said aloud. If, and it was arguably a big if, the playing card was being used as a means of fortune telling or Cartomancy, using normal playing cards instead of Tarot Cards, the card he held in his hands, the two of spades or "deuce of swords", signified deception!

He hurried downstairs and found Freddie mingling with the family. He took him aside and said he had something important to do and asked if he would cover for him should anyone ask where he was.

It was almost 2 p.m. when he checked his watch on the way to the cellar. The door opened at his touch but the place was in darkness. He tried the light switch but nothing happened – the cellar remained in darkness. He took out the small pencil torch that he'd thought he might need but it was only really effective at close quarters. There were no sounds in the place – no footsteps, no breathing – nothing! He picked his way along a row of familiar objects until he saw something that made him feel sick!

In the faint beam of his torchlight it looked like a bundle of clothes stuffed half in and half out of The Iron Maiden that was lying on the floor but the hairs started to rise on the back of his neck as he almost fell over the bundle – a bundle that was solid to the touch.

It was human and was lying in a grotesque position face upwards but the half-closed top of the Maiden hid the face. What Giles could see though was the long thin-bladed stiletto dagger that had been plunged deep into the chest, killing the person before the spikes could do the final damage.

'God, what a bloody fool I've been,' he said through clenched teeth. 'I should have expected this might happen – and now, dammit, I'm too late!'

He lifted the spiked top of The Iron Maiden and, with his fingers, gently closed the lids on the sightless eyes that stared in death! Eyes that, in life, feared the dark and, grim-faced, he turned and left those eyes in the dead body that had belonged – *to Edgar!*

234

Chapter 19
THE WOMAN IN BLACK

As dusk approached, on that fateful afternoon, the logs burning in the fireplace threw dancing shadows on the etched faces of those gathered in the lounge at Maskelyne Hall.

Everyone, who had been there when Jack Ramsden died from a gunshot wound on that last day of October fourteen years ago, was there now. Everyone, that is, except Edgar Ramsden.

Professor Giles Dawson and Freddie Oldsworth made the numbers up to ten. The Prof, still grim-faced and tight-lipped, took centre stage and started to address those around him.

'I have specifically asked you all to come here as I think it is now time you heard the truth.'

'I suppose you are going to tell us it was all done with mirrors!' Victor said in his customary petulant voice.

'You know,' Giles almost laughed with a quizzical look on his face, 'you might be a lot closer to the truth than even you believe! As we are all here...'

'I'm sorry but that's not true for a start,' interrupted Sally. 'Edgar has still to arrive! Don't you think it is only fair to wait for him? Surely you cannot be that desperate to bask in the limelight!'

'I agree with Sally,' interposed a quietly spoken Isabella Ramsden. 'After all, we have waited more than fourteen years for an acceptable explanation of my Jack's death. Surely a few more moments won't make that much difference!'

'I'm sure it won't, Mrs. Ramsden. However I'm equally sure that it is not entirely necessary for Edgar to be here. I ...' he paused, shrugging his shoulders as he sought the proper words, before continuing. 'I happen to believe that he is indisposed and may not be in a fit state to contribute much to what I am about to say.' He studied the sea of faces for any sign of response. No obvious reaction was apparent, yet someone in that group knew he'd been to the cellar and was aware that Edgar was dead!

'Does that mean we are going to have the kind of "dénouement" that Agatha Christie gets up to with her detectives at the end of her novels?' Mabel said, clapping her hands with excitement.

'I suppose so, Mabel. It'll look something like that by the time I'm finished.'

'Spooky!'

'Our amateur is hardly a Hercule Poirot lookalike though, is he, Mabel?' Conrad said.

'And he certainly doesn't fit the bill as a Miss Marple either!' Victor said as he joined in the playful banter. Even as boys they had continually poked fun at the thought of Giles ever becoming a renowned exponent of the whodunit variety.

Giles ignored the two brothers and turned towards Conrad's wife.

'To get back to what I hardly think is a laughing matter, Mabel; this is certainly going to be, to use your own description, the dénouement. Or something similar, I suppose! What I really want to do is get at the truth and that's been in rather short supply since I came back to Maskelyne Hall at Halloween. He pointed at Victor.

'You mentioned the use of mirrors a short time ago and I must admit the phrase has always been associated with the illusions of the stage magician. But what we tend to forget is that the mirror gives back an image of whatever is placed in front of it and although the mirror image is, of course identical, it is, nevertheless, reversed. That is why we must never believe all we see, or think we see; nor should we believe all we read and, more importantly, we should question all we hear especially when it comes to reporting such misconceptions to others as was done in this particular case...eh, Mrs. Ramsden?'

'How dare you, Giles! Are you insinuating that I have deliberately lied to you?' The resentment in her voice was mirrored by the indignation of the old lady's body language.

'On the contrary, Isabella. Everything you told me was, I believe, offered with the best of intentions. If it turned out to be not entirely accurate it was not wholly your fault!'

'You're talking in riddles again, Giles!' Isabella snapped back. 'I assure you that my account of what took place that night was the truth. So help me, God!'

'No need to swear on oath, madam. We're not yet in a court of law! It was all in good faith though…I grant you that!'

Giles paused and watched the matriarch of Maskelyne Hall as she squirmed uncomfortably in her chair.

'You see it took a trip to the United States to make me understand where I was going wrong and, even then, I stumbled on the circumstances that finally opened my eyes, quite by chance…but I am getting ahead of myself! Before I explain further I want you to witness a tableau of magic that should help to illustrate how I have arrived at my conclusions. I have asked Laura to re-enact the presentation she gave in the library on the evening of her mother's last birthday. The entire spectacle has to be an exact replica of what took place that evening.' He paused and looked at Laura who was nodding in agreement.

'I have also invited Sally to assist Laura in the preparation and execution of her illusion just as she did on that occasion.'

There was a sharp intake of breath from someone in the room as Giles mentioned the word "execution" but he was unable to identify the source.

'It seems as if we are almost ready to be entertained as a family again but, before I ask you to accompany me to the library we'll give Laura and Sally a few precious minutes to make sure everything is ready.'

Both women left the room without further ado except for a whispered conversation between Laura and Giles. Giles looked around the room as the door to the hall closed. Mabel, whose girlish enthusiasm for a Poirot style solution had subsided, was biting her lip; Mrs. Isabella Ramsden, her feisty temperament barely visible, looked decidedly frail; Mrs. Gardner held hands with her husband George, both housekeeper and groom looking apprehensive; their unease appearing to be contagious as Conrad, who was standing quite close to them, seemed edgy and on tenterhooks.

Across and to the other side Victor had lit a cigarette and was nervously removing a piece of loose tobacco from his pursed lips; his unblinking eyes stared incessantly at Giles as a snake does his intended prey.

Giles took it all in as his gaze moved to the reliable Freddie Oldsworth. Freddie was looking back at him in cool appreciation; the kind of look a maestro of the theatre might give to a fledgling actor who was giving the performance of his wildest dreams, but without saying anything. The imperceptible nod of Freddie's head, though, was reassuring. There was, however, no mistaking the anticipation in the clear steel grey eyes that more was to come from his professor friend and just how much he was looking forward to the final act.

Giles looked at his watch.

'Time to go!' he said and led the others in the direction of the library.

The library, despite the warmth from the central heating, had a sinister feel of impending doom. Laura was standing just inside the open doorway. As the others filed in from the hall she silently pointed to a row of chairs to the right of the door. The cocktail cabinet and writing desk had been shifted out of the way to accommodate the chairs and the long mahogany table and leather armchairs were now in front of the windows on the right wall where the framed poster of Chung Ling Soo still hung.

The rearrangement of the furniture allowed the audience, seated on the chairs, unrestricted vision of Laura and the tunnel construction behind her that was placed diagonally in the far left corner of the room where the bookcase wall met the wall containing the other windows and the portrait of the Spanish Dancer. The light from the standard lamps was directed away from the tunnel towards the audience.

Laura was dressed in a black frock and black stockings and was wearing elbow-length black gloves. Her shoes were also black and the rubber soles made no noise when she walked on the solid oak floor.

The tunnel was the one Giles had seen twice before. Firstly when he explored the magician's vast props cellar and then when he watched the illusion in the library on the evening of Mrs. Ramsden's 70th birthday.

When everyone was seated and Giles ready to address his audience he felt a tug at his sleeve. It was Freddie inclining his head in the direction of some empty chairs and whispering out of the corner of his mouth. 'Edgar hasn't shown up yet and George is missing as well.'

'That's quite all right. I'm aware of the situation,' he whispered back. 'No need to concern yourself!'

Freddie moved to occupy one of the chairs and Giles had a quiet word with Laura before turning back to his audience to announce the start of the presentation.

'Ladies and gentlemen,' he began rather formally, 'what you are about to watch you have seen before. This time however I want you to pay special attention to everything that takes place and make a mental note of anything that strikes you as significant. Please remain silent until the proceedings are over! Now sit back and suspend your disbelief!'

He gave the signal to start and Laura repeated her movements of the previous illusion. She circled the caravan until she was back where she started. Climbing the steps at the front she picked up the black gown and hood from the front opening before covering the open front of the tunnel with some black material.

She climbed down the steps and put on the gown that reached down to the floor. She then covered her head with the hood that had the macabre painting of a skull on the face and repeated her circling of the tunnel-on-wheels, crossing behind the caravan, and reappearing a moment later on the other side. She returned to the front steps having completed a full circuit of the object on wheels and faced her audience.

For a full ten seconds she stood, almost motionless, her head turning imperceptibly to allow the eyes in the painted skull to scan the seated viewers, before she turned to face the front steps. She climbed slowly and stood facing the black-screened entrance. Her gloved hands performed deft movements at head height as she stroked the area in the darkened opening and, as she stepped backwards, it was clear to see that she had transferred the image of the skull from her hood to whatever was now filling the area in front of her.

On reaching the floor the figure turned to show that her black hood was now minus the skull. She bowed, glided silently to the open doorway of the library, left the room and closed the door behind her.

Nobody moved; all eyes were focused on the white image of the skull floating ethereally against the inky blackness that was the front entrance to the box on wheels. The blackness with the face of a skull moved and started to descend the steps. In the diffused light from the standard lamps it was clearly a figure in black with eyes staring from behind the sockets of a skull. The figure stopped a few feet from the seated gathering; a hand moved upwards and, with a theatrical flourish, removed the hood. The figure in the black costume…was *Laura*!

It was Freddie who started the applause. The sheer professionalism of the performance had been quite stunning. Before the clapping had died down Giles spoke.

'Thank you Laura, that was deliciously baffling and something Jack Ramsden would have been very proud of.'

He gave that irritating little cough of his, the clearing of the throat that invariably preceded his important speeches, before continuing.

'Many magicians are opposed to allowing their secrets to be known and that is certainly understandable, but I have always been a great believer that the knowledge of how an illusion is performed does not necessarily detract from the enjoyment of that illusion so long as the stage presentation is of the highest.'

He cleared his throat again. 'I am always prepared to be baffled when, even though I know how it's done, I am completely unable to see the trickery take place. All the great illusionists of the past have my utmost admiration simply because of the sheer quality of their act. As soon as people thought they knew how a certain illusion was done along came another magician with a different version to baffle and entertain the audience. Entertainment has always been the keyword. The child in me wants to be baffled; the adult in me cries out to be entertained. What happened in this room on the night Jack Ramsden was shot was not entertainment by any stretch of the imagination. The illusion that allowed the crime to take place was baffling in the extreme.'

The Prof's words were being delivered like a barrister addressing a jury. 'I'm tempted to say this is the most baffling case I've ever had – and as this is the only case I've ever had that would certainly be true.' He paused and looked at the faces that watched him intensely. Then he smiled. 'You see how some statements can be misinterpreted.'

He reached into a pocket and produced a cigar. 'Isabella, I wonder if I may be allowed to smoke?'

'Certainly, Giles.'

'So the great detective is churning inside is he?' Victor bellowed as Giles started to light the cigar. 'Well if you feel like throwing up please try not to be sick or George might have to clear it up. Where is he by the way? That makes three missing, Edgar, Sally and now George. Surely to God if you're going to wave your magic wand and name one of us as the bloody murderer they should be here.'

'I'm sure I heard a car drive off a few moments ago!' Mabel announced. 'What are you up to, Giles?'

'All in good time!' Giles said, looking around for an ashtray.

'I want to take you back several years to the weeks before Jack died,' he said taking a puff from the cigar. 'He was, I understand, preparing a special illusion for Isabella's annual birthday extravaganza and, since he'd returned from the United States in June, Jack and his assistant had been rehearsing a Jekyll and Hyde transfiguration to be called Metamorphosis. That is,' he paused, 'until he and his assistant had, according to Isabella, an almighty row in this room during one of the rehearsals.'

He pulled a small notebook from his pocket and consulted it. 'September you said,' reading from his notes, 'it seemed they were disagreeing about money.'

'That's right!' said the matriarch of Maskelyne Hall. 'That was the last of Jack's assistant. We never saw her again!'

'So you said, Isabella! So you said!' A thin smile played for a moment on his lips as he consulted the notebook. 'You also mentioned, when questioned, that your Jack had always worked with a female assistant and that his assistant had always remained cleverly disguised or kept out of sight during rehearsals and, more importantly, that you were never aware of her identity.'

'That is so!' exclaimed the silver-haired lady.

'Well then it is surely not too difficult to assume that Jack would possibly turn to one of his family as soon as he knew he was without his regular assistant.'

He looked around for any sign of disagreement. 'After all it would appear that a great deal of spade work had already gone into making his birthday illusion something to remember, and it was much too late to start interviewing someone from outside.'

At this point Giles paused as if considering another possibility.

'Or could it just be that his assistant with whom he was having a heated argument was already a member of his family and the entire break up was a stage-managed charade as a lead to what he'd planned would follow. As he always chose a female for the role of assistant that left me with only five to consider; his wife Isabella; Mrs. Gardner the housekeeper; daughter Laura; Mabel his daughter-in-law, and Sally who was soon to be Edgar's wife.'

Giles looked at his cigar before taking a long and measured puff.

'I had no difficulty in eliminating Isabella Ramsden and Doreen 'Gardner,' he said, as he slowly exhaled, 'for the simple reason that, apart from the fact that Jack could hardly ask his wife to assist him when the illusion was for her entertainment, neither of the two ladies concerned fitted the type one normally associated with a magician's assistant. Sally had not yet been introduced although Edgar and Sally had been meeting for some time. It was Edgar's intention to introduce her as his fiancée on the evening of his mother's birthday. That left Laura and Mabel! Both girls matched the profile required but Laura was a professionally trained dancer and had theatrical experience. That clinched it for me! She fitted the bill admirably but I required further proof before I could be sure.'

The Prof took another puff from the cigar and brushed a few specks of ash from the lapel of his jacket. Holding the cigar aloft he looked around at his audience.

'This cigar should have been the catalyst I required all along,' he said. 'I should have known better! After all the riddle in Laura's original letter to me – the one that brought me here in the first place was alleged to be the work of Sigmund Freud, and I was informed by a Harvard Professor of Criminology of a story about the eminent man, who, when asked by one of his students about the significance of the size of the large cigars he smoked replied that " Sometimes a cigar is just a cigar!" You see we often place too much importance on trying to answer questions about extraneous matters that, in fact, have little or no significance and the distraction can prevent us from concentrating on things that really are relevant. The problem we have is how to differentiate between what is and what is not the important question that, if answered honestly, can lead to a solution to the puzzle.'

He took another puff of the cigar.

'The whole concept was a puzzle though. There was one question that had to be answered...how could an accomplice be admitted to a room that was, to all intents and purposes, locked and guarded from the outside,'

He paused. 'There was yet another complication to this scenario...the Lee Enfield rifle on a stand! Why was this in the room intended for a Jekyll and Hyde illusion? Could it be that Jack meant to do the Chung Ling Soo Bullet Catching Trick but then changed his mind after the visit to America when he saw something at the Convention of the Society of American Magicians in Boston? Or did he decide to link both illusions into one very special act? If so that would certainly explain why the rifle was in the room. It would also explain why he chose Laura to be his assistant...for Laura was single and unattached and, more importantly, she was a blood relative and the only female that met that criteria! Jack might have considered her to be a safety device against accident! His insurance policy! Unfortunately he did not heed the warning given to Houdini by the magician Harry Kellar!'

Giles glanced across at Isabella Ramsden sitting straight-backed between her sons Victor and Conrad. She was pale but otherwise showed little or no emotion.

'Don't try the bullet-catching trick,' Kellar warned. 'There is always the risk that some dog will job you. *Don't do it!* No matter what precautions are taken there's always the chance for an accident – or worse!'

'How dare you, Giles!' Quivering with rage the matriarch of Maskelyne Hall glared at him. 'You have the gall to imply that my only daughter may have violated the trust placed in her and caused her father's death. How dare you indeed! I wish you had never returned!'

'You are putting words in my mouth, Isabella. I suggest you hear me out and please remember who brought me here in the first place!'

'Surely that's just the point.' The buxom housekeeper entered the conversation for the first time. 'If Laura had shot her daddy why would she open the whole thing up by bringing you here to try and solve things? Have you thought about that?'

'Of course I've thought about it! It was one of the first things I did think about. The whys and wherefores of her intentions had several possibilities but I had to examine everything that might point me in the direction of a killer. Who would know there was a rifle in the library? Why...the assistant who was to help the magician, of course! A rifle without a bullet though would hardly provide an effective murder weapon so who would make sure to carry a bullet? Why...the same assistant, of course! But just supposing someone other than the assistant entered the room intent on murder, without being certain there was a gun there, he or she would have to take a weapon into the room unless...that person was aware that another weapon, capable of ending Jack's life, was among the Dr. Jekyll props lying on that table...the stiletto dagger that I found in the safe; the one used in the portrait of Isabella! So if someone, bent on murder, was unaware of a rifle in here it really wouldn't have mattered. A murder could still have taken place.'

'What makes you so sure it was murder?' Laura said questioningly. 'What about the findings at the fatal accident inquiry...?'

'Oh, it was murder all right, Laura! A cunningly-planned premeditated murder by an evil being. The Procurator Fiscal and the police could hardly have arrived at any other conclusion than an open verdict of "death by misadventure". After all the only fingerprints on the gun were those of the magician...the windows were locked and guarded...and so was the only door!'

'What about the other voice heard in the room? Plus the blood found on the safe?' Mrs. Ramsden had come to life again.

'Your own testimony suggested that one voice – and one voice only – was heard. The belief that Jack was talking to someone else was inconclusive as no reply was heard. Why?'

The word reverberated around the hushed library. 'There could be several reasons for this. The other person in the room might have been dumb, a theory so implausible as to be instantly rejected. Much more likely – *the person did not wish to be recognized by the magician in the room or did not wish to be recognized by those outside! Or both!'*

'And the blood on the safe? How was that explained?' Conrad and Mabel spoke in unison.

'As it was Jack's blood it could conceivably have been left there any time he'd used the safe – end of investigation!'

'Did you believe that explanation?' Victor asked in a more civil tone.

'No – and I'm just about to explain why.'

'The fingerprints on the gun were Jack's and only Jack's. Explain that, clever clogs!' Conrad ventured tauntingly.

'Simple!' Giles announced confidently. 'The person that fired the gun wore gloves as part of her costume…as Laura has just done in the illusion we've all been watching!'

His eyes narrowed as he searched for reaction to his statement.

'Everything began to point in one direction…Laura!' he said. 'It made sense that Jack and his daughter had agreed to work together and, if that were so, it meant that she was equipped with the knowledge of how to enter the room without anyone else knowing! Jack had planned the whole thing out and he was such a stickler for detail he wasn't likely to let things go wrong.'

Giles took another puff of the cigar.

'I required corroboration; yet something was wrong!' he said. 'All the planning and preparation depended on Laura co-operating with her father and from the evidence I was given Laura had seemingly decided, at the last minute, to go upstairs and take a bath. Why? Had they agreed that Jack should work on his own or was the bath part of the plan?'

Laura, who had carefully been removing her black gloves as she listened to the theories propounded by Giles, made an attempt to interrupt but was cut short.

'Not yet, Laura!' he said, 'You'll get your turn to explain!'

'In examining the possibility that Laura was to be the assistant she had to know how Jack had planned entry to the room so perhaps the pretence of taking a bath was her way of ensuring that she could disappear and be on her own; after all the bathroom is one place in a house that is left undisturbed when it is common knowledge that someone wishes it to be kept clear; it is also the one room in a house where the door can be locked without causing suspicion.'

Giles paused, licking parched lips, before continuing.

'Not only did Laura make her intention known but she also advised Edgar, in the presence of others, to tell Sally not to use the main bathroom when she was washing her hair. Why make such a fuss? To establish an alibi, of course, and then head for the hidden entry to…why this very room! The question that still had to be answered was where? How was entry made? The windows could conceivably have been doctored but that implied deception by George and his wife. The door was obvious but that would have required collusion between Isabella and Edgar who were waiting outside. None of these satisfied the premise that entry was to be the way it was always intended – and by the assistant! It wasn't until an arranged meeting with a racecourse security friend of Freddie that another point of access could be explored. This ex detective superintendent came up with the idea of a priest-hole…!'

'A what?' Mabel screeched with girlish delight. 'Tell me you're not serious Giles!' she giggled behind raised hands. 'This really is a hoot!'

'On the contrary, Mabel, I'm deadly serious! Let me explain.'

'I can hardly wait!' Conrad announced jocularly.

'The priest-hole was a small hidden room or space used as a hiding place in English Mansions for Roman Catholic priests and others trying to escape persecution after the English Reformation. Ex detective superintendent Drummond, nicknamed 'Bulldog' by his friends and now living in Dumfries, put forward a theory that the large fireplace with the built-in safe might provide just such a refuge; not the safe itself you understand but the space behind the safe with possible access from below. That would also explain the large Japanese screen, which would hide all movement of the safe itself, and also any person hiding behind it.'

The Prof looked around for the ash tray.

'The magician's props room in the cellar would have been an ideal place to have a secret entry to the library and any number of people had opportunity to find their way there unseen. Isabella and Edgar, who were stationed outside the door, were the only ones that really could be left off the list of suspects. Gaining access to the fireplace might be within the capabilities of most on that list but I doubt if many would lull Jack Ramsden into believing his assistant was visiting him. No…no…no! It all hinged on the assumption that Jack's assistant knew all the answers and that she…!'

The woman in black lunged at Giles in frenzy.

'Do you really know what you're saying?' she screamed. Restrained by Freddie and ably assisted by Conrad, who had rushed to his assistance, Laura shouted through her struggles. 'You idiot – you bloody fool! You haven't been able to understand – have you?' Her struggles subsided and she started to sob. 'I couldn't tell you! You wouldn't have believed me! You wouldn't have listened!'

A trickle of blood ran down the Prof's right cheek where Laura's fingernails had caught him with some force.

'Yes, Laura, I know exactly what I'm saying! I suggest you sit down,' he dabbed at his cheek, 'there, beside your mother. I'm sure Conrad won't mind.'

He dabbed at his cheek once more, then, discovering that, despite the events of the last few moments, he still held a cigar in the other hand, moved across to the ashtray and deposited the Havana that had long since gone out.

'Now where was I when I was so rudely interrupted?' he said with a faint smile on his face. 'Ah yes, I was talking about Jack and his assistant.' The smile lasted only seconds before a puzzled frown creased his forehead and he started talking in riddles again.

'The whole thing didn't add up,' he said. 'At least not until I visited Boston and saw an eighty-two year old statue and heard a tale about how a bottle–opener can open more than bottles! The statue alerted me to the lies, half-truths and fabrications, which I'll come to shortly; the bottle-opener illusion gave me the answer I desperately needed. Two answers come to that; how the murderer entered this room via the fireplace and…' he pointed an accusing finger at the woman in black, '…why Laura decided to take a bath!'

Laura was about to get to her feet again when the library door was thrown open.

George stepped into the room. He was breathing heavily as if he'd been running hard and the shotgun he carried was pointing straight at Giles!

Chapter 20
EVIL UNMASKED

The calming voice of Giles was in sharp contrast to the dread emanating from the others in the room. 'You can put the gun down, George! I think we have everything under control!'

Giles walked towards the old retainer and laid a hand on his shoulder. 'Is there a problem?' he asked gently. George shook his head slowly. 'So everything is ready, old friend?' George nodded as the Prof gently took the gun away from him.

'We're now ready to tell the whole story so I suggest you all sit down.'

Giles looked at Freddie and made a slight movement of his head that was enough to suggest he assist the groom to an empty chair. That done he broke open the shotgun, removed two cartridges, and laid the gun on the oak floor in front of the poster of Chung Ling Soo. He looked at the poster as he straightened up.

'I did mention the warning Harry Kellar gave to Houdini about not trying the bullet-catching trick. To my knowledge Houdini never did try, yet I fear that Jack really did intend to ignore that warning. You see, after Chung Ling Soo's tragic death, rumours even started that he had been murdered or had committed suicide. Nothing was ever proven. It was classed as an accident! Regrettably, on the night of Isabella's birthday fourteen years ago, Jack Ramsden kept...his appointment with fear!'

There was a noisy clatter from below the library floor that caused everyone to jump. It seemed to come from the depths of the cellar where the stage props were stored.

'Good lord, what on earth was that?' Isabella begged with a trembling lip.

'Nothing to be alarmed about, I assure you. Probably a bit of tidying up, I think.' Giles, hoping his words of reassurance would be accepted without question, decided to press on.

'Let me go back to when Jack returned from America,' he said. 'In the hotel he'd visited he had been a witness to the disappearance of an individual, in front of an audience of magicians, from a room that was locked and had no windows. This illusion was the brainchild of a dealer in conjuring apparatus. It seems he discovered, attached to a wall, a cabinet above a washbasin complete with bottle-opener that when pulled, came away from the wall to reveal an airshaft, extending the full height of the hotel. With his imagination working overtime, and with plans already in the pipeline to have renovations to the chimney and fireplace of the library, he decided that the necessary trappings for a similar illusion be created in his own home.' Giles looked at the sea of faces staring at him in the darkening gloom of the library.

'Builders were brought in, the chimney was modified, and a hand-operated pulley system installed thus creating a sort of dumb-waiter used in some large hotels. The top had been bricked over when the safe was built in to the fireplace and although the door of the safe could be opened and closed from inside this room, using the correct combination, the safe itself could also be released from its housing using a device operated from behind so that, when opened, it revealed a small hiding place just like the priest-hole in bygone days.'

At this point The Prof paused and thought he could detect, on some faces, a realisation as to where his story was leading.

'Some important alterations had to be completed; the bathroom, that is directly above this room and has a wall backing on to the chimney, required an opening giving access to the chimney and the small platform connected to the pulley and, when this was done, a large cabinet complete with the essential release mechanism was fitted to cover the opening in the chimney wall; he then had all the necessary elements in place for his pièce de résistance – the bottle-opener illusion he'd witnessed in that Boston hotel. One final component was added which enabled the cabinet to be closed and securely locked from inside the chimney shaft thus preventing anyone, other than the person authorised, to enter the dumb-waiter. I have gone over the cabinet in the bathroom with a fine toothcomb and found all as I've just described.'

The Prof took a deep breath, his probing eyes searching for the slightest sign of serious concern from the others in the room. His worry that at least two in the gathering were sitting like dormant volcanoes waiting to erupt would soon become reality.

'It was always intended that the assistant would enter the chimney and use the dumb-waiter as I have indicated, gain access to the library, and act in liaison with the magician for the purpose of the Jekyll and Hyde illusion. Attempted murder was the last thing on the mind of Jack Ramsden – yet *murder* is what happened!'

The murmur emanating from the previously hushed audience was instantly dwarfed by a torrent of words bursting from the lips of Isabella Ramsden.

'I can hardly believe what I'm hearing,' she shrieked. 'Are you seriously suggesting that someone entered this library from the upstairs bathroom, shot my husband, and returned to the bathroom?'

'Yes I am!'

'But that means…the answer to your question!'

'Yes, Isabella…the answer to the question that puzzled me for so long! Why should Laura decide to take a bath when she was supposed to be the magician's assistant?'

Laura had to be restrained again as Giles expanded on his theory.

'It all boiled down to the probability that Jack's assistant would go to the bathroom before the illusion was to take place; she had, after all, made it abundantly clear that she was going to take a bath, even telling Edgar to warn his fiancée Sally not to use the main bathroom but to use the alternate bathroom instead for washing her hair. She intended to go upstairs and lock the bathroom door, put on her black cloak and hood, similar to the outfit Laura is still wearing, climb into the dumb-waiter via the wall cabinet then close and lock the cabinet from inside the chimney shaft. The space was small and narrow and only a person slender and flexible enough to manipulate her body into confined spaces, as a magician's assistant is usually required to do, could have managed successfully.'

Giles moved to the ash tray, picked up the cigar and thrust it between his lips before laying it down once more. Clearing his throat he stared at Laura.

'By operating the silent rope pulley with her hands the dumb waiter would transport her to the bottom of the shaft behind the safe where she could manually free the safe from its anchorage and enter this room, close the safe and hide behind the large Japanese screen. What happened next would be pure conjecture without a statement from the actual murderer… and I'm not entirely sure I have any chance of getting that!'

Moving across to the ashtray the Prof picked up his cigar and relit it.

'What I'm about to say is pure surmise but I firmly believe the actions of the magician's assistant to have been something like…let's see? The figure in black would move to the gun supported on the stand that would've been roughly there.' He pointed to the area in front of the Chung Ling Soo poster where the shotgun now lay. 'This action by the assistant must have been contrary to the original plan for, according to her testimony,' he checked his notes again, 'Mrs. Ramsden heard her husband say "Leave that alone!" He was probably referring to the gun but it wasn't easy to identify sounds coming from the library and Jack's actual words may have been misheard. To whatever he said there was no reply – nothing that was audible at any rate.'

Giles glanced at his notes once more.

'The next thing Isabella heard was "put your mask on!" which I assume was a direction to his assistant to cover her hood with something similar to the one used earlier in the illusion we watched.'

He checked his notebook again.

'Jack's last words before the shot was heard were "no, no…don't touch that…it might be…" suggesting that his assistant was not following the script and demanding she put the rifle down in case it was loaded. Whether the gun was already loaded or not we may never know, but the figure in the cloak and hood must have removed the rifle from the stand taken aim and fired before returning the rifle to its original position on the stand. We now know the gun had been modified and the recoil was less but the actions I have just described are my own account of what may have happened. Perhaps the assailant then moved to be with Jack after he fell to the floor.'

The Prof took a puff of the cigar, removed it from his mouth, smiled and nodded at the burning object in his hand.

'Mrs. Ramsden says she heard a dull thump and, after a short silence, Jack's voice saying something like "good God, what have you done, Hyde?" followed by "We must keep the secret, so go now!" But why, I asked myself, did Jack not call out for help at that moment?'

The Prof drew on his cigar blew smoke out and watched it rise in the air.

'I'll tell you why, he said, '…it was because he believed he was talking to a person who was *in on the trick*! And that corroborated Edgar's view that he thought the other person *was a friend*! As it seems it was not unusual for strange unexplainable things to occur prior to birthday performances it was several seconds for the two persons outside the door to react, enough time for the assistant who had some of Jack's blood on her gloved hand to reach the safe. In closing the safe she left traces of blood on it but, by the time Mrs. Ramsden and Edgar got the library door unlocked and entered the room, the assassin was well on her way back to the bathroom where she removed the hood and gown and hid it until it could be put amongst the props elsewhere.'

Giles, who was beginning to warm to his task of lecturing his small but captive audience, puffed at his cigar several times blowing smoke into the air in an almost pensive manner.

'When Mrs. Ramsden finally entered the room after a great deal of prompting from her youngest son she…'

At this point Giles hesitated, screwed up his eyes, and lines appeared on his forehead as if he was trying to recall the sequence of events that puzzled him. '…She saw Jack lying on the floor over there,' he pointed towards the illusion box on wheels, 'by the bookcases. He was holding his chest and there was blood on his hands. We know that Edgar said he would get the girls and dashed upstairs presumably to alert Laura and Sally in the two bathrooms. From here on in I accepted everything I was told without reservation. That is until my trip to the States. As I mentioned earlier two incidents opened my eyes to a possible solution to the problem. I have already explained how the illusion in the Statler Hotel provided clues about the concealed entry. It was now the turn of the statue in the grounds of Harvard University to prod my brain and cause me to question the statements of those present at the scene of the crime. Lies, half-truths and fabrications – many of them made unwittingly!'

He took another puff of the cigar creating ghostly smoke that punctuated the deathly atmosphere inside the library.

'Let's consider what Mrs Ramsden told me when I asked her to describe what occurred that fateful evening. Remember it was fourteen years since the shooting and memories can play tricks. She told me she was the first person at Jack's side after he was shot.'

'I was! I was definitely the first one there!'

The Prof ignored the lady's protest.

'Not true!' he said, his words reverberating around the room. 'I'm inclined to think that the first person to go to Jack's side after the shot was fired – *was the murderer herself*! Haven't I suggested that was how his blood was transferred to the safe? You couldn't possibly be the first to reach him – *unless you were the murderer*!'

The old lady looked subdued and the expression on her face conveyed to Giles that her error had not been intentional.

'Do not fret, dear Isabella!' he said. 'Your words were genuine and understandable and made in good faith. Nevertheless you were mistaken. What you said was a lie!'

The words boomed out with apparent relish.

'Jack's last words were spoken in a whisper. You quote him as saying "I didn't mean it to end like this" and I took that to infer that he thought the whole thing was a disastrous mistake – a mistake that could be rectified at some future stage.'

Mrs. Ramsden was nodding in agreement.

He looked at his notes again before speaking.

'Prior to that he asked, in a whisper, and an almost inaudible whisper at that, "did you see Dr. Hyde?"'

'That is correct!'

'By your own testimony this was a strange question. Jack was hardly likely to get Jekyll and Hyde mixed up so I checked to see if the name of Hyde had been used in any previously heard utterance. You see it is perfectly possible for someone who has just been shot to be confused and delirious and say things that weren't meant. When you heard the shot you thought you heard Jack shout "good God what have you done, Hyde? We must keep the secret…so go now!" Giles cleared his throat before continuing.

'When I wrote that down I must admit that I wasn't sure whether to write "hide" meaning disappear or Hyde as in the man's name. It was conceivable that he would use the name of the character being played by his assistant and yet it could easily have meant he was telling her to disappear especially when he used the phrase "*we must keep the secret…so go now!*" The confusion arose with his question "Did you see Dr. Hyde?" The Prof looked across to Isabella who had a puzzled expression on her face.

'If Jack did say that he might have been repeating the previous error in his confused state by using the name of Hyde. That statue in the grounds of Harvard urged me to be aware of more untruths. Was it just possible, when Jack said "good God what have you done, Hyde", that he might have paused slightly between "done" and "Hyde" and actually said "what have you done? Hide, we must keep the secret – so go now!" You see how everything changes. If that were so since he knew his daughter had just fired the gun might the final question to his wife have been "*did you see daughter hide?*" He might have been unaware of the seriousness of his injury and thought they would live to fight another day if his daughter could retrace her steps and get back to the bathroom undiscovered. He could pretend it was all an accident. He never got that chance. There we have it. Maybe he didn't ask, "Did you see Dr. Hyde?" Another lie, perhaps?'

'You mentioned the statue of three lies but you never did tell us why it was called that. I think you should come clean, Giles. Or is this just another of your cheap tricks?'

'I'm so sorry Victor,' Giles addressed the eldest son who had made the remarks. 'I should have given the facts about this statue or, as Freddie would put it, the inside information. Let me mark your card!' He winked at Freddie who smiled back.

'The bronze statue that was presented to the University was supposed to be of the founder John Harvard but since there was no known portrait of the man a student was used as a model. That was lie number one! Harvard College was not founded by John Harvard but named after him. Lie number two! Finally the College was not founded in 1838 as stated but two years earlier. Lie number three!'

'Thank you Giles. You have offered us two possible lies regarding events that took place fourteen years ago. Are there others or have you run out of plausible excuses?'

'No Victor, there's more to come. All that I've said falls neatly into place if we assume that the person in the black cloak and hood was Laura. If however that person was an impostor, someone that Jack thought was Laura…but wasn't, other factors come to the fore. This brings me to the crux of my argument. There were many questions still to be answered. What possible motive could Laura have for wanting to murder her father? If Laura was not the person in the library with Jack that night…who was? It had to be someone that could easily have been mistaken for Laura. Is that possible? Well, yes it is! Haven't you seen it with your own eyes in this same room during the illusion performed by Laura dressed in the cloak that she is still wearing? Without knowing how the act was done it doesn't take a great stretch of imagination to conclude that a substitution took place at some stage in the proceedings since Laura is still in this room and yet someone, dressed in similar garb that we genuinely believed was Laura, actually left this room and has never returned.'

The ripple of acknowledgement, as understanding began to dawn on his audience, broke the eerie silence.

'So you see we could be fooled by two persons dressed alike and with the same kind of figure as long as the faces were concealed and no words spoken! Is it possible that Jack could have been equally deceived? I say to you – *Yes!*'

The word thundered and reverberated around the room once more.

'I am convinced that is exactly what happened! So who had a motive strong enough to commit murder? Who, apart from Laura, would have the expertise and know-how to operate the bathroom cabinet, the dumb-waiter and the safe? Who would have the ability to contort his or her body to negotiate the small lift? Only Jack and his daughter knew of the plan and method to effect entry via the chimney…unless one of them confided in someone else! Which one? Laura would be unlikely to do that unless she required an accomplice…but why the need for an accomplice, who would have to be an exact double, when she was already capable of performing everything herself? That left only one person – Jack himself! Did he tell someone else how he was going to bring off the illusion?'

Giles paused briefly and took another puff of the cigar.

'Of course he did! Looking back at the list of motives produced by my criminologist friend in America I noted his comment against Revenge – a powerful motive for murder! So which of my suspects would murder in order to exact revenge? Why, the person to whom Jack told every single detail of his planned illusion! The person Jack coached and instructed before he was forced to change his plan and rely on his daughter…the only logical person who was Laura's double when dressed in black cloak and hood and had the same ability to be his assistant as she was!' his voice rose to a crescendo. *'The assistant he dismissed!'*

The hubbub of dissent that followed was intermingled with a cry of 'Not possible!' from Isabella Ramsden. 'Didn't I tell you?' she exclaimed. 'Weren't you listening? After their almighty row I told you Jack said his assistant had gone for good. We never saw her again!'

'I believe that's exactly what you told me for I have those very words written in the notebook.' The Prof spoke with quiet innuendo. 'One more untruth to add to our list I think, Mrs. Ramsden, though I concede that was what you genuinely thought?'

'I don't understand! How could that be possible?'

'I asked myself that same question, Isabella, and here's the answer I came up with. We know that Jack brought his assistant to this house on several occasions between the time he arrived back from America, had the library and bathroom renovated, and the day he dismissed her sometime in September. We also know that the assistant always remained in some form of disguise and never stayed for meals, which meant that nobody in the house except Jack knew of her identity. This may have been another one of those lies! Suppose, by some quirk of fate, another co-incidence perhaps, Edgar and the assistant bumped into each other and started meeting regularly both inside and outside the house but without the others knowing? I have no doubt their original plan was to become engaged but not announce it to the remainder of the family until Halloween, the evening of Isabella's birthday.'

The Prof started pacing the floor.

'This was thrown into chaos when Jack dismissed his assistant after their almighty row, as Isabella described it. Supposing Edgar's fiancée decided to go through with the announcement and hatched a plan to play a trick on the magician without mentioning the possibility of the trick ending in murder. Would Edgar have gone ahead with such a plan? I asked myself that and came to the conclusion that the one reason he might not would be that he was the youngest member of the family and might have a very strong allegiance with his father and be reluctant to be a party to anything that could cause embarrassment.'

The Prof looked around at the sceptical faces and tried to coax his cigar into some sort of life again.

'Edgar had puzzled me for some time! I couldn't put my finger on it but something nagged at the bottom of my mind. Something to do with his fear of the dark! His fear of the dark was matched by his horror of fire. No, Edgar would never have condescended to be a party to such a prank except for an assurance of it being harmless fun. Unless...!'

He looked across at Isabella Ramsden. She was watching him with apprehension in her eyes.

'Perhaps you will confirm my suspicions, Isabella after I have finished my explanations!'

The nod of her head plus the understanding that emanated from the elderly lady's misty eyes was all that Giles required to continue expounding his theory.

'Something I couldn't quite get out of my head was what had brought me here in the first place? It was the letter from Laura with the riddle. The riddle was supposedly by the psychoanalyst Sigmund Freud. Was it coincidence, I asked myself, that the riddle was the writing of a man who believed that childhood events have a powerful psychological influence throughout life? Was Laura aware that this particular riddle might direct my thoughts in a certain direction or had she already a suspicion of a specific member of the family without any plausible explanation? This set me thinking. It wasn't difficult to assume that Edgar's phobias stemmed from childhood but try as I might I couldn't imagine what had been so scary for him. That is until I recalled staying here at the Hall one night in March 1941.'

'It was the thirteenth and we were down at the lodge playing Monopoly with Doreen and George. Those were the days of the blackout and it was just about time to return to Maskelyne Hall when the faint sound of the air raid sirens could be heard coming from Lockerbie. We could barely hear them but I remembered the look in Edgar's eyes; it was the same look of fear he showed in the lounge one evening at Halloween when a log fell out of the fire causing a shower of sparks; it was also the same look I'd seen at dinner the night the lights went out and Conrad struck a match.'

The Prof studied the expressions on the faces of Isabella, Doreen and George.

'It also was evident when we discussed flak and barrage balloons. I knew I'd seen it before but couldn't remember where! Then it came to me! It was the night the German bombers flew over Lockerbie on their way to Clydebank. George, who was an air raid warden at the time, had to react to every "yellow message" that we, as kids, used to think was hilarious. He had to go on duty and Doreen was left to take us back here. We thought it all a bit of adventurous fun; all of us that is except Edgar who was crying in a kind of hysterical fashion. Doreen was running on tiptoes and telling everyone to be quiet as we headed back to the Hall. We could hear the uneven drone of the aircraft engines overhead and Doreen kept warning us to lower our voices to a whisper to avoid being heard by the enemy airmen. By the time we reached safety Edgar was inconsolable and it has taken me all this time to understand why.'

The nod from Isabella was received by Giles with quiet satisfaction and he returned her movement with a similar nod.

'You see,' he continued, 'if my theory about Edgar and Jack's assistant was to have some meaning I had to know if there was anything in Edgar's past that would have convinced him to support her in a prank against the family. I decided there was no harm in doing some research; that's why I checked official records. I have no doubt that you'll confirm what I learned, Isabella?'

The matriarch of Maskelyne Hall clasped her hands in her lap and looked straight at Giles. There was a tear in her eye.

'I knew you'd learn the truth sooner or later. There seemed no point in making it known at the time, that would've made it more difficult for Edgar to adjust, and the rest of the family accepted the arrangement as natural.'

There was a shuffling in the quietness of the library as everyone waited for her to continue.

'Jack's brother and his wife died in the blitz on London in 1940. Edgar, who was their only child, survived so it was logical for him to join us and grow up as a member of my family. It was fairly easy to explain that he'd been away to boarding school and nothing was ever questioned.'

'Thank you, Mrs Ramsden, for being so helpful. It confirms everything I found out. It was good to hear it from your own lips even though official records are difficult to dispute. It was the one piece in the jigsaw that encouraged me to believe that Edgar might be an accomplice to a prank, a prank at the expense of his uncle and not against his father. After all it was only to be a practical joke. He would introduce the ex assistant to his family as Sally, his fiancée, on the day of the birthday party before the illusion and then to the magician after it, when they could laugh at the whole affair. At any rate that was the plan.'

'Come off it Giles, you may be correct in one or two of your assumptions, but you can't expect us to swallow your story that Sally was Jack's assistant! That's what you're saying, isn't it? Come on, pull the other one!'

'Victor is quite right,' Conrad said, getting to his feet, 'It's a bit far fetched even by your standards. I mean if Sally and Edgar choose to refute your allegations you really won't have a leg to stand on. It's your word against theirs! You're dreaming again!'

'I suppose, in a way, you are perfectly correct. Since the only other person who could testify that Sally *was* Jack's assistant was Jack himself, but now he's dead, that would leave those two suspects as my only chance for a confessional corroboration. I accept that, Conrad; as you say it is my word against theirs! If you'll sit down again perhaps I can convince you all.'

Victor lit a cigarette sat back in his seat and crossed his legs.

'I challenge you,' he said, 'to produce both Edgar and Sally right now as if you were the master magician and ask them to tell you exactly who they are. I can't wait to see the look on your face when they tell you that it's a cock and bull story you've concocted!'

'Have you hidden them away so as you can play the great detective?' Mabel enquired. 'Is that why George had the shotgun when he came in?' she said in a tone that suggested she was now seeing the significance of everything. 'You've deliberately prevented them from listening to your accusations because you know they would deny all you've said!'

'I'm sorry to spoil your fun, Mabel, but neither Edgar nor Sally is able to confirm or deny my suspicions…!'

Victor got to his feet in outrage.

'We'll soon see about that,' he stormed. 'I'm going looking for them this very moment!'

'Sit down at once, Victor. You're going nowhere!'

The Prof's words were delivered like a stern schoolmaster.

'*Edgar is dead* – he was murdered this afternoon. The noise you heard coming from the cellar was the police removing his body and I assure you he won't be making any statements to them!'

'Murdered, you say?' exclaimed Mrs. Doreen Gardner, at the same time putting an arm round Isabella Ramsden who had slumped in her chair.

'Yes! No doubt about it! He asked me to meet him in the cellar earlier this afternoon, as he wanted to tell me something. The note he left for me suggested he knew who the murderer was. I'm sure he wished to get the whole sordid business off his chest. Someone had tampered with the fuse and it was dark in the cellar when I arrived; I almost fell over him. I'm positive he was going to tell me what I already knew but had no real proof…when he was silenced!'

'There you are then, Giles,' exclaimed a triumphant Conrad, 'you've just shot yourself in the foot. Sally would never kill her own husband! She would never…'

The knocks on the library door stopped Conrad from completing what he was saying. The knocks were repeated and the door opened on silent hinges. A senior police officer entered and removed his hat, crossed to Giles and had a whispered conversation with him. Giles nodded his head in quiet understanding of the news he was hearing. His face was grave and he looked decidedly older. The police officer turned, left the room and closed the door.

Giles went over to the ashtray and stubbed out his cigar before turning to the assembled group.

'I think we should all retire to the lounge,' he said, 'where we can be a little more comfortable. I'll complete my findings to you there. Meanwhile I am sorry to be the bearer of further bad news…*Sally is dead*!'

Chapter 21
THE HANGING JUDGEMENT

And naked to the hangman's noose
The morning clocks will ring
A neck God made for other use
Than strangling in a string.

A.E. Housman

George brought the smouldering embers of the log fire to life as the rest of the household gathered in the lounge. The rosy glow of firelight was starting to warm the ashen faces around him as the Prof prepared to deliver his final pronouncements.

'Don't you think you owe us an explanation?' Victor demanded belligerently. 'Two more deaths, you say, in mysterious circumstances and you haven't had the decency to give us an idea of what has been going on. You have made accusations against two members of this family who apparently cannot now defend themselves. If Edgar and Sally are dead as you say they are, and I'm not sure whether to believe you or not, don't you understand that your trumped up case has just died with them?'

'Oh they're dead all right and, contrary to what you've just said, their deaths prove my case and I'll explain why I think so and let you be judge and jury.'

The stoical housekeeper was comforting Isabella who was sobbing quietly; Laura was standing beside Victor looking pale and frightened, her older brother, with jutting jaw, stood legs apart and arms folded ready to assert his authority; Mabel knelt in front of the fire with hands clasped, shivering ever so slightly, whilst Conrad stood with one hand on her shoulder. Freddie had wandered over to the windows and looked out on a dark foreboding sky.

'Your explanation had better be good!' Victor said in a threatening manner. 'Otherwise you may become the subject of a full scale investigation!'

The Prof cleared his throat several times and scanned the assembled group.

'You may or may not have noticed,' he began, ' that when we were all gathered here earlier this afternoon, before asking Laura and Sally to leave us and make final preparations for their illusion, I asked Laura to do something for me. I asked her to tell Sally, when they were alone together, that I knew what she was doing in the cellar this afternoon, that I knew she wasn't in the smaller bathroom washing her hair on the night Jack was shot fourteen years ago and that I now knew who the murderer was!'

He looked across to Laura.

'Did you speak to Sally, Laura?'

'Yes I did!'

'Did she say anything?'

'No! She just stared at me in a strange way. There was a faraway look in her eyes, as if she was going away and had difficulty saying...goodbye.'

'She was saying goodbye, but in her own way. She knew the game was up and had two choices. You see I arranged that particular illusion because I knew that at some stage Sally had to substitute for Laura in order for Laura to enter the empty caravan then reappear after Sally had left the room. When she left the room she could either have returned as soon as the show was over and challenged me to prove my allegations or she could try and make a getaway. I was banking that she would try and make a run for it and the noise Mabel heard was, as she rightly thought, a car. It was Sally leaving in Edgar's car and I had already warned George to be prepared for such an emergency. The "yellow message" I gave him was the same as I gave to the local police.'

The Prof paused to allow what he had just said to sink in.

'They manned a barricade at the entrance gate and that was also the reason dear old George carried his shotgun, though the police did not care too much for that action.'

Giles looked across at a chastened groom – his smile and nod saying a silent "thank you" before his expression changed to one of doom.

'Sad to say,' he continued, 'Sally did not stop at the tractor blocking her only way of escape. Instead she swerved, crashed through the fencing and, because of her speed, failed to turn on to the road, but careered across and down the embankment on the other side. Her car rolled over several times before hitting a tree and, although she was still conscious when the police and George reached her, she apparently died shortly afterwards. That was the news the police officer brought me in the library. She was still wearing the black robe when she died!'

'Tell me, George, did she say anything before...?' Isabella Ramsden's quavering question choked in her throat.

'Yes, Mrs. Ramsden!' George replied, his voice quiet but ominous. 'She said *"Edgar had to die you know...and all those years ago I thought I'd committed the perfect murder until Giles...!"* then she closed her eyes.'

Mabel looked up from her place by the fire, her eyes showing bewilderment.

'I still don't understand!' she cried. 'Where was Sally if she wasn't in the other bathroom washing her hair when poor Jack was shot? If she entered the library the way you've described she had to get in through the main bathroom and we know that's impossible 'cause Laura was already there...sorry, Laura, I didn't mean to suggest...!'

At that point Mabel started biting her lip.

'I'm just so confused I don't know what I'm saying!'

'Oh but you do, Mabel!' The Prof's gently spoken words brought a fleeting smile to her face. 'All along I was just as confused until I saw how it could be done! Then it all fell into place!'

Giles paused for a moment then crossed over to Laura, took hold of her hands and looked earnestly into her eyes.

'I want answers to several questions,' he said, 'and much depends on what you say! No more lies, you understand!'

She nodded in agreement.

'On the night your father died did you go to the main bathroom intending to enter the library via the dumb-waiter?'

'Yes!'

'What stopped you assisting your father in his Jekyll and Hyde illusion?'

'I couldn't get into the chimney! The bathroom cabinet wouldn't budge…it was jammed!'

'So what did you do then?'

'I wasn't sure what to do. You see it had never happened during rehearsals and I wondered if Daddy had fixed things that way and altered his plans.'

'So what did you do, Laura? Answer me truthfully!'

'I took a bath!'

'Exactly! As simple as that!' Giles let go of her hands and smacked both of his together in one loud clap that startled Mabel into a half scream.

'Exactly!' he repeated. 'But why did you not tell me this when you brought me back to Maskelyne Hall? It might have saved a lot of trouble!'

'You wouldn't have believed me! You'd have been convinced I was lying …you'd have believed I was the murderer! I couldn't prove that I didn't, after all, carry out the prearranged plan of entry to the library and it would've seemed I was the only person who had the opportunity. All the others had to do was deny everything!'

'Quite possibly!' Giles stroked his chin and sighed audibly.

'So you couldn't open the dumb waiter! Do you now know why?'

'No!'

'For the simple reason that someone was already inside the chimney and had locked it from inside. That someone was Sally, Jack's previous assistant, who knew all about the planned route for the illusion.'

'You still haven't explained how she could get into the dumb-waiter ahead of Laura without being noticed and, more importantly, how she could return to the other bathroom while Laura was still taking a bath?' It was Conrad's turn to pose the question.

'Let's not get ahead of ourselves.' Giles replied. 'Why don't we start at the beginning and I'll take you step by step right through to the…' He cleared his throat then gestured to Victor, Laura and George to sit down. Freddie came away from the windows and took a seat close to where Giles was standing.

'Unfortunately we'll never know exactly what Jack and his assistant were rowing about before he sent her packing, but Isabella said something that puzzled me when describing the "almighty row" she'd overheard. It didn't register at the time, I grant you that, but later when I examined possible motives it started to make sense. You see, Isabella said it sounded like...*she was threatening – blackmail*! Whatever it was – it was serious stuff! Since we are now aware that Sally was Jack's assistant and had been having a serious relationship with Edgar for some time, but with no intention of being introduced as such until after the birthday illusion, I wondered if she might have been testing the water by asking the magician to introduce her to his unmarried son with the possibility that, in time, she could become a future daughter-in-law? That would've been like a red rag to a bull as far as Jack was concerned and he would have told her so in no uncertain terms. His reaction would certainly throw a spanner in the works and might have sparked a chain reaction where she conceivably threatened to inform his wife about certain unconfirmed allegations regarding his conduct with his assistant – blackmail of the worst kind that could destroy his reputation! All surmise and conjecture, I'm afraid, as none of the prime characters are in a position to enlighten us!'

The Prof looked pensive as he dug his hands deep into his trouser pockets.

'When Jack booted her out of his house he assumed she was not only out of his system, but out of his life as well. He would never have believed he had already created the blueprint for his own death! When Sally formulated the plan with Edgar to play a prank on Jack, who was his uncle and not his father, remember, it was on the understanding that it was only to be a jocular exercise in teaching him a lesson. I'm sure that Sally had other ideas right from the start. She was a conniving temptress who was planning murder but was perfectly happy to let her fiancé believe otherwise. After all Edgar was a rather naive seventeen years old and was probably easily dominated by this beautiful femme fatale in his life who was several years his senior.'

Freddie looked over at Giles and both men nodded in silent approval before the explanation continued.

'On the day of Mrs. Ramsden's birthday Sally accompanied Edgar to Maskelyne Hall and, for the first time, was introduced to all members of the family except Jack. Having been Jack's assistant she was well aware that he would be totally engrossed in his preparations for his spectacular illusion and would rarely leave the library except for emergencies such as calls of nature. She'd become quite adept at concealing herself in this large house because of previous visits as the magician's assistant and now she didn't have to hide her identity except from her previous employer.'

Giles shuffled his feet as he positioned himself in front of his audience before expanding his theory.

'When the time approached for everyone to congregate at the library for Jack's briefing and the inspection of the room, to ensure that, apart from the magician, the library was empty, she stayed out of sight at the back, well away from the gaze of Jack Ramsden, without creating anything abnormal as Jack was not expecting anyone to be with Edgar.'

'Before final preparations were complete Sally made it clear in the presence of Laura that she intended to wash her hair. That was when Laura warned Edgar to tell his fiancée not to use the larger of the two bathrooms, her reason being that she wished the main bathroom kept free so that she could gain access to the dumb-waiter and play her part in the illusion.'

All eyes were on Giles as the gathering awaited the remainder of his explanation.

'When Sally went upstairs she most likely went into the smaller bathroom, turned on the shower then came out and shut the door. She then had to cross to the main bathroom, quickly put on her cloak and hood that she'd probably have had hidden on her person or somewhere in the first bathroom, unlock the cabinet from the wall, climb into the chimney then close and lock the cabinet behind her. She had practised that routine many times before being dismissed.'

'But wouldn't the whole plan have been ruined if Laura had reached the bathroom before...?' Mabel's interruption trailed to a whisper.

'Yes, that's true,' said Giles 'but downstairs Edgar opted to remain with Isabella outside the library door, which was then locked.

He probably was fully prepared to delay Laura to allow time for Sally to conceal herself in the shaft'.

'On her way to the larger bathroom Laura noticed that the door to the other bathroom was shut and she could hear the shower running. Believing all was well she went into the room with access to the chimney, locked the door, put on her cloak and hood which was probably hidden in the cabinet then tried to move the cabinet away from the wall only to find it wouldn't budge. Puzzled and bemused she eventually had to accept the inevitable and abandon the idea of assisting her father. To ensure future legitimacy of her intentions and avoid any suggestion that going to the main bathroom had an ulterior motive she decided to take a bath.'

It was now Conrad's turn to intervene. 'Wouldn't Laura have heard the gun being fired?' he asked.

'It would almost be impossible for her not to hear the rifle shot but as the annual spectaculars at Halloween invariably were accompanied by strange sounds she probably treated the noise as not entirely unexpected.'

Giles cleared his throat before continuing.

'When Isabella finally opened the library door and saw her husband on the floor Edgar dashed upstairs as had been agreed between himself and Sally. You see he had to enter the smaller bathroom and turn off the shower, bang on the door and shout his warning, leave the door open as if Sally had just left and gone downstairs, then dash to where Laura was, hammer on her door and announce there had been an accident. By doing so he knew that Laura would rush from the room and allow Sally, who was still inside the chimney, to unlock the cabinet from inside, climb out, remove her cloak and hood and hide them in the other bathroom, cover her head in a towel then go downstairs and join the others, at the same time keeping in the background and well covered, just in case Jack would see and recognize her.'

Giles took a deep breath.

'In her evidence to me Isabella said she overheard Sally ask Edgar "if he was dead?" I should have had some suspicion then as most people might have asked what's happened and not...! Anyway when Laura left the bathroom, wrapped in a robe, she noticed the other bathroom door was open and there was no sound from the shower.

267

She presumed Sally had already gone downstairs little knowing that she was still behind her. In all the confusion at the library there was not much chance of Laura figuring out that she ended up downstairs before Sally did and so Jack died believing his daughter had accidentally shot him and was never, at any time, aware that his previous assistant had substituted herself aided and abetted by his young nephew and, as it turned out, had carried out a revengeful assassination! I have no doubt that since the murder Sally has always seemed to be a stabilising influence on young Edgar. Yet all the time she was the opposite! She used Edgar and, because of their mutual plan, always had a strong hold over him – right to the end!'

You could hear a pin drop in the comparative silence except for the subdued crackle of logs in the fire. Nobody spoke until Laura rose and came over to Giles.

'Can I get you something to drink?' she asked. 'I feel we could all do with a little something; it's been quite a marathon! What about you Mr. Oldsworth?'

'No, nothing for me, but thanks all the same. I have a long drive ahead of me tonight. And please call me Freddie. I'm beginning to feel part of the family.'

'Yes I'm afraid we have to go shortly. Freddie wants to have a day or two at home with his family. And talking about family…I'm so sorry about…you know! As your dad said…*I didn't mean it to end like this!*'

Giles could see the look of disappointment that suddenly clouded Laura's face and he desperately wanted to take her in his arms and stay a bit longer.

'Look Giles I'm so sorry for being such a bloody fool and doubting your veracity since you returned to the Hall. I hope you'll forgive me!' Victor came across and held out his hand. 'There's still something I'm not quite clear about. Perhaps you can explain.'

'I'll try.'

'When father was shot he was only wounded – fatally as it turned out – but what if he had survived? Surely Sally would've been exposed when they eventually met?'

'I doubt it! If your father had recovered I believe Sally would just have broken off the engagement and disappeared…that is why she was so anxious to know if he was dead. Edgar would've been left with

268

egg on his face, would probably have shut up and retained his silence for eternity.'

'I see, well once again let me say how sorry I am. I could've ruined everything!'

'There were times I wanted to shake you warmly by the throat, but I accept your apologies and knowing you of old this comes as rather a surprise. Coming from you an apology isn't the easiest gesture to make but life's too short and I for one would dearly love to be counted as a close friend of the family. Like old times!'

As he spoke he found himself looking straight into the eyes of Laura who was now handing him a glass of whisky. She was half smiling with a wistful look and as he took the glass there was a definite moment when he felt she was reluctant to take her hand away.

'Two questions I'd like to ask you, Giles?' Conrad said. 'Seeing as we're tying up the loose ends, when you were apparently attacked in the cellar do you now think that was something to do with Edgar and Sally?'

'I think it was probably Sally for although Edgar had been inextricably involved from the day the supposed jest was planned I very much doubt if he had the stomach for murder. Remember they had only arrived before the incident in the cellar and had just been told about my being here and the probable reason for my visit and it presented an opportunity to end any awkward investigation. You must consider that even after Jack died Sally probably convinced him that it had after all been a horrid accident. Edgar was stuck with that until he reached the end of his tether and decided to spill the beans; a decision that cost him his own life!'

'And what about the séance?'

'I think they were trying to frighten Laura who was in a confused state after her riding accident...you know, it almost worked!'

'Do you also think it was Sally who tampered with the stirrup leathers on the saddle you were supposed to use but which resulted in Laura's accident?'

Giles thought for a moment before answering. He raised his glass and looked across to Laura who was administering drinks to the others.

'Unquestionably!' he said. 'At the start of the ride I thought I detected someone using binoculars at an upstairs window but I couldn't be sure who it was. I can't even be sure whether it was Laura or I who was meant to fall. Either way a fatality could have been well worthwhile, as Laura's death would have prevented me from finding out the truth about her sojourn to the bathroom on the night of Jack's demise and I shudder to think how this would have turned out if…!'

He never finished the sentence.

Isabella, who had seemingly recovered her composure, broke into his suggestion of morbidity.

'Look here, Giles, you mustn't leave us without something in your stomach and I'm sure cook will conjure up some appetising leftovers!'

'I will indeed,' Doreen Gardner replied, 'there's enough of everything to go round and I'll set about getting things ready right now.'

'That's settled then.' The matriarch of Maskelyne Hall almost shouted with relief 'Now I won't take no for an answer!'

'As you wish, Isabella!

A light buffet supper later Giles and Freddie went upstairs to pack their belongings just as two senior police officers arrived and confirmed that Giles would be required at a Fatal Accident Inquiry regarding the deaths of Edgar and Sally. Giles left a contact address with the police and prepared to leave. He loathed goodbyes and was determined to avoid prolonging events.

When he finally managed his farewells to the family Freddie had already brought the red *Spitfire* round to the front of the Hall and George was helping him to load the bags.

Giles went forward and put his arms round the likeable retainer before turning to look back at the house. Laura was standing at the top of the steps backlit by the light spilling out from the hallway. She came down the steps as he approached.

'When will you come back and see us, Giles?' The appeal in her voice was a warm contrast to the chill night air.

'Are you going to send me another conundrum or can I take that as an invitation?'

'Of course silly, you'll always be welcome here. You know that. You don't need an invitation but please don't leave it quite so long next time!'

'I promise!'

'Look, I intend riding *Samson* at the point-to-point in April; will you come and bring us both luck?'

'I'd love to do that! On one condition mind...you promise not to fall off. I've too many bad memories of another girl of mine in similar circumstances!'

'Cross my heart!'

Then she was in his arms. He kissed her long and passionately on the lips and the fresh smell of her hair was something he'd not forget in a long time.

Freddie drove towards the lodge and the main gate and, at the turn of the driveway, Giles looked back at the house. Laura was silhouetted in the doorway with an arm raised.

He waved back and vowed...that in the spring...

NOTES FOR CURIOUS MINDS

1. The "Good Taste" incident in Chapter 2 happened in the author's household exactly as described. The author's mother, Isabella by name, who was born on the 31'st October, made the uncanny prediction that was met with disbelief.

2. The strange co-incidence of the girls' names in sequence in Chapter 14 happened in the life of the author with the only change being the substitution of the name Linda, for that of the author's fiancée, Sheila, for the purpose of the story.

QUOTATIONS

"The Mourning Bride" by William Congreve (1697)

"Haunted Houses" by Henry Wadsworth Longfellow (1858)

"A Dream within a Dream" by Edgar Allan Poe (1827)

"They Can't Take That Away From Me" Song by George Gershwin

"Reveille,A Shropshire Lad" by Alfred Edward Housman

"Silver Blaze" (The Memoirs of Sherlock Holmes) by Sir Arthur Conan Doyle (1894)